Little Red Rider

Audie Cockings

"Audie Cocking's compelling debut novel, *Little Red Rider*, is a superb meditation on the themes of grief, the redemptive power of love, and finding meaning after great loss."

- Jill Allen, Clarion Reviews

ISBN: 0615798306
ISBN 13: 9780615798301
Library of Congress Control Number: 2014902713
Little Red Rider, Hampstead, MD

Little Red Rider

By Audie Cockings

Table of Contents

~

Part I

1	Introduction	1
2	The Longest Day	3
3	Alone	6
4	Prudie	9
5	Creamy Cheese and Army Rangers	14
6	Doggie Shrink and the Twelve-Incher	16
7	Spring, Fried Pickles and Tatas	27
8	Hitler in Hell	29
9	Year Two, Dreams, and Psychobabble	36
10	Forty-Three	40
11	The Wookie and the Outer Buddha	46
12	Back in the Saddle (of a Springer)	65
13	One-Star Dork	75
14	East Africa	84
15	Crap Trap	100

Part II

1	A Very Brave Lime Bikini	115
2	Blondie and the Pacer	122
3	Bald Churchgoers and Mr. Moo	130
4	The Brass and the Doggy Stuffer	139

5	Note To Self, Keep Mouth Shut	169
6	Jimmy Deans and Buttered Nipples	194
7	Brown and a Hunky Seal	216
8	Homeless Hit Man	240
9	Between a Rock and a Hard Chest	273
10	Jack	320
11	Big Boots	328
12	Reproof	333
13	In Stitches	334
14	Prognosis	342

Little Red Rider, Part I

1
Introduction

〜

I suppose you could call me a late bloomer. At the tender age of forty-two, I went from unremarkable to seemingly pleasant-looking, rather abruptly. It's funny how losing twenty pounds and adding some red hair dye can change one's prospects. Would John notice me now? He's the one man I have always loved. I never felt less than beautiful with him. He left me twenty-four months ago. He's spiritual now, in every sense of the word. But, I lie awake at night, awaiting possible reverie. Eager to feel his consoling arms hold me while I sleep. I haven't seen him with my eyes, but I know he's there, watching over me, just as I'd requested. Until now, I wasn't aware that the Maker would put our deceased loved ones on loan to us for comfort.

It was nearly spring when John was killed. Our son was in Georgia, finishing Ranger School. James was planted in my belly three months before our wedding day. We had every intention of waiting, but I pleaded, rather convincingly, and John finally threw in the towel. I was burning for him. Just a tiny little taste produced a bulls-eye on our first horizontal excursion. James emulated his father. Mirrors him unerringly.

Now a reluctant widow, my former life as a spoiled, moneyed housewife is hard to recall. The fiercely protected wife and mother of two burly men. She, the domestic, self-consumed churchgoer with rounded edges and a naïve worldview. I never imagined that mouse of a woman doing anything of consequence. I was content in my small box. Never intending to matter. But, it seems there was a reason to be left here without John—to change courses and protect a few innocents with my latent little talent.

I have very vivid dreams. Dreams that affect the security of our nation and our forces abroad, including James. I think these premonitions come from John, or even higher up in the celestial food chain. I shared these dreams with John's best friend, Allen, a general at the Pentagon. Soon after, the anonymous threats to me began. Allen insists that there's been no breech on his end. But, somehow, Petrov, a Russian nuclear arms dealer (and frequent character in my dreams) got wind of my bent. The intelligence I provided Allen botched plans for a jihadist attack on Old Jerusalem. That attack would have made Petrov millions, as he was to supply the fireworks.

After all of the threatening letters and packages and my home being vandalized, I'm convinced that Petrov's got a mole at the Pentagon. Allen says he and his two top guys are the only ones who know about me. But, it's all just been a bit too coincidental. I suppose it doesn't matter now, anyway.

As I lie here, bleeding and broken beside a familiar highway, John's voice summons me. His deep tenor, calming me, making me still. "I'm here, wife...Everyone is waiting for you..."

2

The Longest Day

~

Our neighbor and his wife, both cops, showed up at our home after I hadn't heard from John for several hours. He was out on his Harley, taking advantage of an unseasonably warm day in March.

I hated it when he was out by himself on that bike. I couldn't relax until I heard him turn the corner and head up the hill to the house. But this particular night, I didn't hear the roar of the engine as John accelerated up that hill to our home. Because he didn't make the corner.

It was getting dark. He never stayed out late without calling. When my neighbors pulled up in their police cruiser, I immediately knew what had happened. Their grim faces were all the confirmation I needed that John wasn't coming home.

Is this what shock feels like? I couldn't drive to the hospital by myself. I went in the back of the police cruiser. Thank God they offered; otherwise I would still be standing, as still as a rock, at the door, listening to the horrific details. How could that truck driver have been driving so carelessly? I said a quick prayer for the unlikely chance that John's shattered body could somehow be salvaged.

I pleaded with God in silence, "Please let me keep him, just awhile longer. I know I've been difficult and selfish with him from the beginning, but I need him, and you don't. You can have anyone you want up there. Please let me keep my John."

I called James. He was in the field. I left a message at the barracks for him to please call home, that his dad was in a serious accident.

John always said that wearing a helmet wouldn't help because his insides would be mangled before his head was split open. After he hit that poor groundhog last year, I was sure that he wouldn't have any more close calls, at least for a while. So much for my estimating skills. He always pictured himself going down in a blaze of glory. I could see him wrecking his car after hitting warp speed, scaling the North Face, or even getting hit while taking down a gunman at a mall. I knew he'd succumb to death some day, but not like this, not when he was so young. Not while we were still youthful enough to enjoy each other.

They dropped me off at Johns Hopkins Hospital. I ran to the reception desk and quickly checked in. A volunteer took me up to where John was.

I tried not to gasp. That couldn't be him lying there, red and swollen. He was minutes from dying. Seeing him so defeated was excruciating. I wish he would have been taken quickly, painlessly, so that he wasn't suffering, struggling. I couldn't be angry at him for leaving me alone. His hurting that much was unbearable. I searched for a place to touch him, a square inch of skin without wounds. His waist was unmarred. An indentation where his belt had been, but no blood.

My fingertips floated over the soft matted curls that had kept me warm at night since I was nineteen. If only it had been cold today. He would have had his leathers on, not just the T-shirt from mountaineering school and a pair of worn jeans. I don't even know where he was riding all day.

My tears soaked the bandages covering his neck. The nurse said he could hear me. I whispered, ever gently, in his ear, "John, honey, if I could somehow know you're still with me, then I'll be OK. You can go on ahead of me." A jolt of fear struck me, and I lost my breath. I was lying. I wanted to die with him.

My words, now a quiet whimper, were nearly inaudible over the sound of the heart monitor. I forced out my last love note. One he would hear. "I haven't been without you since I was sixteen...You're my life. No woman's loved a man the way that I love you. I don't know why you chose me. It never made sense, John. You could have had anyone. I understand if you need to go...But, if you have any fight in you left... please stay...I love you." The monitor protested John's slowing heartbeat. He was leaving me.

We had talked so many times of leaving this life together. We had hoped to. The thought of separation never entered the equation.

The plans we made for the coming warmer months flooded my mind. For July, I had rented the beloved coastal Maine cottage where we'd spent our tenth anniversary. Then we planned a road trip to his folks' place in Michigan for their fiftieth. We'd go fly-fishing in Virginia in September, and, in October, have a low-country meal in Savannah, where John was stationed early on in our journey together.

I lay next to him in his bed. I needed to hold him, even if it pained us both. Maybe if I clung to him tight enough, he'd take me with him. I was fixed on his face, hoping to see his soft, gray eyes open one last time.

His lungs labored two last efforts, an unsettling sound. He opened his eyes. I tried to catch his gaze, but he couldn't see me. My love looked to his Maker in obedience. He hushed John's broken, earthly body and took the spirit of my beloved home.

3

Alone

⁓

"Mom, I just got your message. Is he gonna pull through this?" James asked, his deep, tender voice shaking.

"No, sweetie. Come when you've finished the course. I'll book a flight for you. Check your e-mail when you get back. I love you, son." I kept the call short. I didn't want to cry. James would have come home immediately. I needed to be strong for him, so he could stay focused.

I didn't want James to miss the last two days of Ranger School. He was one of the few to make it on the first try. Three months of cold, wet, pain. James is just like John. Rugged, an off sense of humor, and an unmatched loyalty to all things right. John had planned to take James shopping for a bike, then ride out to Mt. Rushmore together, next year.

Things are a mess in this world. But that didn't seem to hinder James's desire to follow in his dad's footsteps. I will travel to Fort Benning, Georgia, after the funeral, to see James graduate, without his father.

I know it was wrong to play Eve with John that night, three months before our nuptials. But if I hadn't, would James have come to us later? We were never able to conceive again, despite my well-managed attempts. I sometimes thought God was punishing me for following my own timetable instead of his. I suppose He feels my lack of trust now. But I don't know what else He could possibly expect from me after taking John.

My husband of twenty-four years was laid to rest at Arlington National Cemetery. It was an overcast day and about fifty degrees. We had just celebrated John's forty-fourth birthday a week ago, on the first day of spring. It took all of my concentration just to keep from breaking down. I was going through the motions, as I thought I should. I don't remember much else about his burial, just my blank stare, a forced smile, and gripping the hand of my son for comfort.

The following morning, James and I drove to Georgia together for Ranger School graduation. Tears flowed as I watched James get pinned and don a black beret for the first time. I saw John in our son. The same build, face, and eyes. The same smile and humility. I was proud but less than enthusiastic. The person I love most in this world, the only physical tie to the husband I lost, was headed to the Middle East. I drove home after the ceremony. I wanted James to enjoy the festivities without worrying about me. He and his buddies had much to celebrate. Completing Ranger School is something that few accomplish or even attempt.

It was finally over. I was thankful for the calm of my home. No more comments. No more hugs. No more tears from folks who barely knew John. I was glad to have everyone gone, except for James, whom I would miss the most. It was finally quiet. Absolute silence. I could let myself go. It came all at once. I had no control. My body was mourning its mate, its constant companion, its source of warmth, safety, passion, and comfort. I was cold and empty.

I don't remember falling asleep. Too emotionally spent. I curled up in John's big leather man-chair and pulled his favorite gray wool blanket up over my shoulders. My eyes were exhausted. My mouth hurt from faking that monotonous smile for nearly four days.

It was five in the afternoon, the time John and I would have a cup of coffee together almost every evening. I couldn't bear to make coffee for one, let alone sit with my solitary cup. I'd rather just lie in his chair and curl up with his blanket. It wasn't long before I felt a tingling sensation in my limbs. They were going to sleep. The stillness crept into my torso and then up my neck.

In my dream, I was in our bed, weeping. John must know how badly I'm hurting. He was behind me, holding me, brushing back the knotted hair washed in tears.

I woke up the next morning at eleven. Eighteen hours of sleep. My arm hairs were standing on end. He had been with me the whole time. Easing me into the loneliness. A night without fear, without hopelessness. I knew then that John would continue to be my calm, my safe place, even after his physical presence had ceased. He provided an easiness while I slumbered and dreamed of us. Almost two months would pass with him here every night, with the sensation of his body holding mine, consoling me.

James calls when he can. It's good that he was busy. Shortly after returning to Georgia, my son, the freshly minted Army Ranger, got his orders. He would be deployed to the Middle East. I'm not sure what good he could possibly do there, but I don't discuss my politics with him. He's a patriot, and I respect his decision to follow government orders, even if it pains me to know that I could lose him, too.

4

Prudie

~

"Honey, you home? Sweetheart, Prudie, are you there?" Mom's voice has a rather unintentional patronizing tone to it. I don't know what in the world got into my mother the day she named me Prudence. My dad wanted to name me Elizabeth, which would have better lent itself to nicknames. There isn't much one can do with Prudence. My friends know to call me Pea, but for some reason, my mom insists on Prudie, a nickname I abhor.

It's been eight weeks since I've seen anyone. I don't care because I've been asleep whenever possible. Benadryl and red wine may or may not have assisted with the near-comatose state I've been residing in. Everyone around here knows to leave me alone. I'm rather specific when anyone stops by or calls to check on me. Besides, I have Tarzan, our geriatric Grand Mastiff, to keep me company. He is the only soul on this planet who may miss John as much as I do.

My folks can't seem to stay away any longer. I'd like to see them. But, I just don't feel like being psychoanalyzed right now. My stage of grief is my business. I want to be sad by myself. Besides, I haven't been by myself entirely. John is here; I can feel him when I sleep. And I don't want him to go. I unwillingly opened the door to my mother's horrified face.

"Oh my God, honey! Have you eaten anything since the funeral?" asked Mom, with an overly dramatic, shocked look on her face.

"No. My appetite seems to have gotten lost," I snapped.

"Prudie, you look awful! Why didn't you call and have us come sooner?"

I looked at Dad. His face was more sympathetic, less judgmental. Dad gave me a hug and squeeze. It's funny how he used to be the talkative one, and now Mom has taken over for him.

"Thanks, Mom. I know I look awful. What exactly am I supposed to look like?" I asked, as I cocked my head.

"How much have you lost?" queried Mom, looking me up and down, brow furrowed.

"Mom, I don't know. I'm not camped out on the scale all day." Mom hates it when I'm thinner than she. She's supposed to be the skinny one and gets irritated otherwise.

"Prudence, you know this hurts me more than you can imagine. I loved John the way I love your brother," she insisted.

"Yeah, Mom, I'm sorry I didn't take into consideration how difficult this all must be for you..." I held back the rest of what I wanted to blurt out. Like the fact that everything on God's green earth somehow revolves around my mother. I know she loved John. Maybe even as much as Teddy.

My little brother, Teddy, forty, is someone I *would* like to see. He and I are so similar. He wasn't able to make the funeral. He was hammering out an airline merger in Hong Kong.

"Teddy's coming to see me as soon as he can get his old job back," I stated. I miss him. He's tired of Asia and asked to be transferred back to the Atlanta office for a while.

"Does he plan on seeing us right away, too?" Mom asked, defensively.

"I'm not sure, Mom, why don't you ask him?" Heaven forbid Teddy comes to see me first.

"So, honey, can we help you get dressed and take you out for a nice dinner?"

"Mom, I'm not really ready to go out yet. I don't feel like being around people. I keep bursting into tears out of nowhere. I just want to stay home. How about we stay in and have a glass of wine?"

"Fine, honey, but you shouldn't be drinking if you don't eat anything."

"I'm not downing a fifth, Mom. I'm just having a glass of wine."

"Whatever, dear. Whatever you want to do is fine. We just want to see you smile, if possible, before we leave, please."

"I'll try my best to smile, if you promise to stop looking at me like that. I know what you are thinking. Can we just eat now?"

"Deal. We stopped by Whole Foods and picked up some fig jam, Mt. Tam cheese, and crusty bread, all your favorites!"

"Perfect. I'll go get some wine in the cellar."

After dinner, Mom washed dishes in the kitchen. Dad and I just sat on the couch. I felt his hurt for me, too, even though he doesn't say much, which I appreciate. I'm a lot like him. Mellowing in my old age. Finding myself in the quiet.

Eight weeks, and everyone thinks I should be in a peachy mood, getting out, enjoying friends, or whatever widows are supposed to do. Two months is such a short time compared to the almost twenty-six years since I met John. I wish people would just stop calling if they don't really want to know that I feel like shit. I think they call because they feel guilty if they don't. Everyone thinks I've lost it. I have, and I don't care. I'm starting to think that reclusively is a perfectly reasonable way to exist.

"So, Sweet Pea, when will James be able to come home again?" Dad asked.

"Six months. I know he's anxious to get back and check on me. Dad, I know I look like hell. I'm just not that stoked about getting out of my PJs each morning. I'm not going anywhere. Staying in my jammies equals a lot less laundry, which is an upside, I suppose."

"Pea, you won't always feel this way. God has a plan for all of us, regardless of how it might present itself. For some reason, He took John, and I know you're angry with Him. John was only forty-four. But, honey, maybe you should ask Him to show you what's next."

"I'm not ready for what's next. God's plan sucks as far as I'm concerned. It's not something I'm keen on this week after all of the *fun* I've been subjected to...Besides, I don't want another future...I just want to sit on the couch all day and miss John. I don't know why everyone seems to have a problem with that!"

"OK, Pea. You'll know when. You're still young, honey. Your life is not over, even if you feel like the senior citizen that I am."

"Funny, Dad. You just hiked across the Swiss Alps. Medicare would cancel your coverage if they knew you had the body of a thirty-five-year-old man."

"Perhaps. Let's not tell them. And don't tell your mom, either. And for the record, I was in Switzerland scoping out banks in case Obama gets elected again...The mountains were just a little side trip," Dad said, winking.

"Right. Roger that." I giggled for the first time since the morning John died.

Dad liked John for many reasons. But, the one thing that they clicked on immediately was that they had both been stationed on the Demilitarized Zone (DMZ) in South Korea for a time. They could use their army acronyms and talk trash.

John was easy, comfortable, and down-to-earth, despite his big brains. Even after he left the army to be a businessman, he still stayed pretty grounded. He never looked down on anyone or anything. He read his Bible every morning before he started work, and he prayed whenever he felt compelled, which was often.

We had a light dinner. I was relieved when Dad pressed Mom to go home. I wasn't up for much more chitchat. I downed another two glasses of wine, put my hair up, slipped into the tub to wash off then slipped on John's favorite white cotton eyelet nightie. It had been hanging on the chair for eight weeks, waiting for John to get home from his bike ride. Finally, I was alone in our bed, waiting to feel his fingertips write on my back. John writes me love letters while I sleep. I don't care if it's real or not. I'm content to know that he misses me, too, even if it's a dream.

5

Creamy Cheese and Army Rangers

~

Several months passed, very slowly. It's been more than half a year since I last saw my John alive. He's visiting less while I sleep, but James was home last week, and John was certainly here for that, in spirit. At twenty-three, my son resembles his big, beautiful father.

James and I watched John Wayne movies while he was home. *She Wore a Yellow Ribbon* is my favorite. Of course, James likes *Bridge Too Far* because there's a lot of shooting and, of course, the Eighty-second Airborne in it.

Three years ago, John, James, and I traveled to Normandy to celebrate the sixtieth anniversary of the D-Day invasion (I was just there for the antique copper pots and creamy cheese). The boys specifically wanted to tour the Eighty-second Airborne Museum in St. Mere Eglise. There's still an American paratrooper figure hanging from the church turret in the town square. That life-size suspended soldier is a tribute to the liberators of that tiny town in France during Operation Overlord.

James and John were in history buff heaven that entire week. The weather was brisk, but sunny, for March. The Norman French were so gracious. John told our hosts that he was in the same Ranger battalion that had scaled the high cliffs of Pointe du Hoc with the German batteries firing at them from above, sixty years prior. The barbed wire at the top of the cliffs and bullet holes in the stone buildings nearby still remain. I imagined all of those young men, fighting to live, scared and uncertain, as they moved forward, many to their deaths and a handful to glory.

In my dream last night, John was holding my hand and cheering me on as our James was born. Just an hour prior, we had ordered pizza to be delivered to the maternity ward and made out one last time before I went from zero to eight centimeters in one hour.

My inexperienced young nurse told the doctor on call that I wouldn't be ready until the morning. Maybe she should have checked me before calling. The pain was unbearable and the epidural an hour late and a dollar short. It hurt so much that I couldn't get the words out. Then my John, with his masterful comic relief, said, "Now remember, dear, this is harder for me than it is for you." I wanted to clock him, but at least he made me laugh.

John was so stingy with that baby. He actually accused me of monopolizing James at the hospital. Yesterday, I'd found a picture of James sleeping on John's furry chest only hours after he was born, which explains why I had that dream.

The following week was unremarkable, primarily because I didn't have any dreams of us. It's been a week since I felt John near me while I sleep. I can't tell anyone. It seems that he's already been forgotten by most of our casual acquaintances. I don't expect people to keep a lit candle in the window for him each night, but it seems too soon for people to be saying that I should be happy that he is with the Lord. Why in God's name would that make me happy? What an asinine thing to say.

6

Doggie Shrink and the Twelve-Incher

~

I guess I need to leave the house. The Graul's grocery store a mile from here has delivered the fresh food I've needed. I've been ordering everything else online. I've lost about twenty pounds, none of which were deliberate. Nonetheless, I need to buy a pair of jeans because my old ones are huge. I look like a stick in a bag.

Being thin at my age, after becoming a mom, looks so different than a thin woman of, say, twenty-five. My skin is not so elastic anymore, and my belly area has not receded with the rest of my body. I look like a widow, and I am tired of looking like a widow. So, I called to make a hair appointment.

Tiny answered the phone, "Mrs. Brandt, I'm so glad you called! I just had someone cancel for this afternoon. I was thinking about you and James the other day and wondering how you two are doing...You can fill me in when you get here." Great. I was hoping for an appointment next week or later, but I guess my hair is getting help today. Also sounds like I will be engaged in conversation, which is just more interaction that I was trying to avoid. Tiny goes to my church and has probably noticed my absence.

Tiny is James's age. They went to high school together, youth group at church, and even a homecoming dance. She was a track and field athlete. She got her nickname from being the only female high jumper at the high school. She's not actually tiny; she's nearly six feet. It's kind of a joke that stuck. She's just about as long and lean as they come. Anyhow, she's going to do my hair. I hope she has some ideas because I want to look like I care a little.

When I arrived at the salon, Tiny was waiting with a warm, kind smile. She hurried over and gave me a hug. "Mrs. Brandt, it's so good to see you! You're my last client today, so we've got all afternoon. Would you like a glass of wine or some mineral water?"

"Do you have any red?" I asked, all of a sudden happy to be there.

"Basignani winery brought over a bottle of Lorenzino for us to try out on our customers. It's their good stuff!"

"Then yes, please."

"Head on over to my station. It's still in the same spot, the corner with the window. I'll hang your coat and purse in the closet. Do you want to get your cell out first?"

"No. I'm not expecting any calls today, Tiny." Calls are fewer and fewer the longer I hide out at the homestead. Tiny returned with my glass. I swished the deep garnet wine around in the glass then took a little taste. It had nice legs, a ripe raspberry nose, medium body, and a pink peppercorn finish. "It's perfect. Thank you, Tiny."

She put a smock on me then gently raked her lengthy fingers through my tangled, mousy, dishwater-blond hair. She fluffed it up at the roots then watched it promptly fall flat to my crown again. Next, she sectioned off my mane to inspect the new hair growth.

Tiny is too sweet to say so, but I know that I look terrible. I've aged ten years since John died. And I'm a little self-conscious about how I've let myself go.

"Tiny, I've gotten a few grays since I saw you last. It seems that my hair is just as fatigued as I am these days."

She smiled compassionately. "Mrs. Brandt, I think you look great. But, if you're really tired, and your hair is more limp than usual, then it might be your diet. You could pick up some prenatal vitamins for a cheap hair and skin boost. And, those prenatals have extra goodies for tired gals, like iron and vitamin D. My Towson State track coach used to stockpile those in her office for us. But, boy, did my mom flip out when she found a bottle in my gym bag! She wasn't keen on the idea of her coed daughter popping pregnancy vitamins!"

"I imagine I would have done the same thing! But, I doubt you ever gave your mom much to worry about in that area, Tiny."

"That's for sure! I've never had a serious boyfriend. I keep thinking that some great guy is out there looking for me, but he certainly *is not* in Parkton! I suppose I could go downtown, but I would rather stay home on the weekends. I'm on my feet all week. Standing at a bar and dancing are the last things in the world I want to do with an evening off. I'd rather curl up with a good book. At some point I may get proactive about finding my dream guy, but I want to get my own place first. I still share a room with one of my four sisters, at my folks' house. I've been staying there to save money. I've almost got my down payment ready and will start house hunting this spring, I think. So, finding my dream guy will have to wait—at least until I have some privacy. Besides, who'd want to date a twenty-three-year-old who still lives with her parents? Embarrassing!"

"Tiny, what did you study at Towson State?"

"I was studying physical therapy. But I didn't finish. I was only there for three semesters. My shin splints got really bad, and I had to stop running. To make a long story short, I lost my track scholarship."

"Oh, honey, I'm sorry."

"I was relieved, to tell you the truth. I always wanted to do something creative, and all that health-science stuff was snooze-worthy. I ended up in downtown DC for six months at the Aveda Institute and graduated at the top of my class. Hair and skin is what I should have been doing all along. But I'm glad I got to try the four-year thing. To see what university life was like."

"I didn't finish school, either. I was a Terp. I guess I went to College Park because John was a year ahead of me and already there. He studied business. I was studying art. I wanted to be a curator. But then James came along, and we decided I would stay home. John had a commitment to the army, so we had to move before I would have finished anyhow. I never regretted staying home with my boy. Especially now that he's all I've got."

Tiny looked sad for me, like she wanted to cry. Instead, she took a deep breath and quickly returned to the task at hand—my bad hair. She smiled while casually examining my split ends. "So, Mrs. Brandt, are we doing the usual today? Or, can I talk you into a little something new? Perhaps some color?" she suggested with a glimmer in her eye.

"I guess the usual would be fine, but I want to keep it longer than I used to," I said unenthusiastically.

"It feels a little too heavy. It could definitely use some movement. If you want to keep the length, then we should add some longish layers. And, I'll soften it up around your face with some wispy bangs. But, Mrs. Brandt, I can't help those grays without a little color. We just got a new line in. It's an oil-based color that conditions. It covers gray quite nicely and leaves lots of shine…"

"Color? You mean a color like mine, darkish blond?"

"Well, actually, I have a box of red back there that would be perfect on you. It's a warm red, with blue undertones…"

"Blue?" I asked, scared.

"The color would be a blue-red versus an orangey-red. More like an auburn, less like a carrot. Or, better yet, we could go with a really deep copper."

"Geez, Tiny, I've always been a blonde. I haven't dyed my hair since high school. My buddy, Jenny, and I bleached our hair. Mine ended up a brassy yellow. It was terrible. Of course, Jenny's turned out perfect—a buttery blonde. Can you make me a buttery blonde?"

"I'm kinda thinking red, Mrs. Brandt. With your really fair complexion, a blond that light might be too harsh. It would wash out your skin. But red would do the opposite. You'd look fresh, not tired. Besides, I've never known a tired redhead. I think that energy's all in the hair!" I was unconvinced. As much as I disliked the look of me, a drastic change seemed too much to commit to. Tiny added, "I think you'll like it. And I bet James will, too!"

"Tiny, he's deployed. He may not even be back for Christmas," I said in a depressed tone.

"Then let's surprise him! I'll bet he'd love to see you brighten up with a sassy new 'do! I'll take a photo when we're done and post it on my Facebook page, then send him an email invite to see it. Does he get to check his email often?"

"Not really. I send him notes almost every day, but I know he's busy. He calls me every Saturday morning at seven. We have coffee together and catch up for an hour, sometimes two. He likes to check up on me. But, Tiny, I'm not ready for red. Can I think about it?"

"How about we do the usual today, then do red when I have an opening, probably in two weeks or so? If you change your mind, you can always cancel your appointment. But for now, let's get your hair washed then do a deep conditioner. While your hair's getting silky, I'm giving you a facial, my treat!"

Tiny took me over to the shampoo bowl, and I reclined. She rinsed my head with warm water, then put a gingery-grapefruit-smelling shampoo in and began to massage my scalp. The smell was intoxicating, so delicious. And being touched felt so good. I hadn't been given attention in so many months. After a good rinse, she worked in a deep conditioner before wrapping my hair with a steaming-hot towel.

Then she began to remove my scant makeup with a towelette. "Close your eyes. This is the good part!" she said excitedly.

The fresh, calming herbal scent flooded my sinuses while the ice-cold cream filled my pores, instantly soothing my skin. "What are you putting on my face?" I asked curiously.

"A whole-milk Greek yogurt, fresh mint, lemon, honey, aloe, and cucumber mask. It's my new secret weapon. I make a fresh batch in the blender each morning and then refrigerate it. All the girls use it now. The clients love it! It completely detoxes your face. Heavenly, right? If you come in again for the red, we'll do this again!" exclaimed Tiny.

Getting red hair seems more probable now—especially if that means more green goop for my rutty complexion. She let the mask linger on my face for ten minutes, and then wiped it off with a warm, damp rag. She rinsed the conditioner from my hair then took me back to her station.

Tiny gave me a wink then rolled over a large tray full of dainty tubes. "This stuff is actually good for your skin, very nourishing," she said while dabbing potential foundation colors along my jawline. She applied a little of the plant-based cream makeup on my skin for color, some mineral setting powder, then a little bronze highlighter on my cheeks. She finished with some deep-brown mascara that made my eyes pop, and a nude lip glaze. "Natural is a good look for you, Mrs. Brandt, but even natural gals need a little help sometimes," she said while handing me a mirror.

I couldn't believe what I saw. My skin was pinked and glowing like a girl on her wedding night! Tiny was happy with my reaction. She didn't stop smiling for the remainder of my appointment. She combed out my hair, snipped in some layers, and then gave me bangs and a great blow-out. I was thrilled with my new glowing skin, but alas, the gray was peeking out from my roots, so I made another appointment—knowing full well that I would not be canceling.

I left the salon feeling decent for the first time since John died. And, I guess I needed the company. Tiny was fun to talk to. She didn't ask too many questions, *and* she had an entirely new look in mind for me. But, first, I needed to take another baby step. After getting help with my hair on Saturday, I attended church for the first time since losing John. Seeing some familiar faces was nice. Folks made an effort to say hello, and Pastor Jim and his wife asked me to get some dinner with them after the service. It was nice to have somewhere to go besides home.

* * *

Its been almost nine months now, and I'm not as angry at God. I told Him that I am willing to accept His removal of John from my life, if He will find something useful for me to do with my time. I miss taking care of my boys. James won't be home for several months, and I need something to do besides take care of Tarzan.

Tarzan, my geriatric Grand Mastiff, is on a mechanical diet and has severe arthritis. I suppose he will be joining John shortly, and if he poops on the floor again, even sooner. I am tempted to put the stinking dog in Depends, but they don't actually make his size. If he were a small dog, a few Jimmy Dean sausages to clean up wouldn't be a big deal. However, his load resembles that of an elephant. It doesn't quite fit in the standard pooper-scooper. That said, if Tarzan dies, I don't know what I'll do. I bought him for John as a tenth anniversary gift. That dog loved John. He just hasn't been the same. Would it be so bad to take him to a doggie shrink and get some antidepressants...then medicate myself?

Anyhow, church was fine. Of course, the sermon was about God's Plan, and how He has a plan for each of us. I am starting to wonder if He has a plan for me or if my plan was interrupted by a sleepy truck driver named Toby.

About a month ago, I opened John's daily Bible study book and decided to finish the year for him. I've been reading through the book of Matthew this week. A verse has been stuck in my brain like a ticker across my forehead. It's about loving your enemies and blessing those who persecute you. And, although my lawyer has been pushing for a lawsuit, I've felt my conscience telling me not to sue the trucking company for John's death. The fact is, I won't be able to move forward with my life without forgiving that driver named Toby.

I know he did not intentionally kill John. I was at the sentencing. He was so apologetic, remorseful. His wife and two teenage daughters were there, crying, as he was sentenced to one year in prison for vehicular manslaughter. They would suffer one year, then be reunited. But, I was on the other side of the isle. The side that would not be together again, not ever.

Toby sent me a letter from prison, asking me to please forgive him. Explaining that he didn't realize how tired he was, and that he was unfamiliar with the winding road that we lived on. Those two simple truths caused John an immeasurable amount of pain and left our family shattered in every sense. But, a lawsuit would not bring John back, it would just put a trucking company out of business, and it's fifteen other employees out of work. My life is, if nothing else, comfortable. I want for nothing but my John. And, I'm tired of being angry. I thought about how my anger had been alienating me. From my family, friends, and myself, a woman I actually liked before all of this started.

I do have one regular companion of sorts, aside from my loneliness. My housekeeper, Ada, still comes every Monday. She never asks if I want her to come, she just shows up, always five minutes early, as she has for eight years. She knows that I need her. If she hadn't been with me, the house would have probably fallen apart by now. Her visits give me something to look forward to.

Ada's from Albania. She grew up under a communist regime there and has become quite the little capitalist since getting her green card. I've never seen anyone with a greater distain for laziness. Ada supports her family through housekeeping, and sells handmade jewelry on the side. She's also in her third year of an accounting degree. To top it off, she's a great cook. She's given me an education on Feta cheese and even taught me how to make bread yeast from grapes. She's been a good friend through all of this. One of the few not pushing me towards a new life that I don't want to be in. I haven't had anyone else in the house because I don't know what to do. I have John's things, still where he left them. I am not ready to put them away, give them away, or otherwise. Maybe in the spring the task won't seem so daunting.

I got a note from John's old army pal, JD, this week. He recently learned of John's passing. He's been away doing something secretive, from what I gathered. John always envied this particular buddy, despite the fact that he had been injured on many occasions, nearly mortally wounded in one instance, and still managed to get back home to rack up a few more medals. His personal life, however, was a little messy. He was on his third wife already, and I wouldn't exactly call him discreet. He wasn't apologizing to anyone for cheating on the first or second wife. I don't understand it, but he seems happy with the third one. JD's note said that he's headed stateside next month and wanted to give me some pictures of John and me from Ranger School graduation, circa 1992.

It's January now. I spent Christmas by myself. My parents were furious with me for having no desire to celebrate. I love our God and appreciate his Christmas gift to us in Christ, but I am not prepared to celebrate without John or James here with me. Mom's just gonna have to deal with the fact that I am not the type to pretend I'm happy when I'm not.

How does one contact a dead person without going to a hokey fortune-teller? I decided to write John a note and leave it on his desk...

My Dearest John,

Are you still here? It's January. It's cold out now. I'm sleeping better, but my dreams of you are less frequent. Are you leaving me? Do you have other things that you need to do where you are? Like a job, or something? I miss you. It's been almost a year. Actually, in nine weeks the anniversary will be here, and I am starting to lose myself again. Where are you when I sleep now? I'm not ready for you to leave yet. Please help me dream about you tonight. Can God just give you a few more passes? Please ask him. I love you.
—Wife

He did come. In my sleep tonight, he was fishing for trout in the creek behind our home. There's a fire in the stone fireplace in the kitchen. James (fifteen) just put himself to bed. I peeked in on him, already snoring, and then headed downstairs to the wine cellar. Tonight we will drink a 1995 Profile that's been sitting awhile, since our first trip to Napa. I think we spent eighty dollars on that bottle of red wine. Almost twice as much as the hotel we stayed in without hot water. That trip was one of my favorites. We walked into St. Helena each morning for fresh pastries at the bakery and figs at a nearby fruit stand. It was an inexpensive trip, considering we got the plane tickets free for signing up for a credit card that we cut up two months later.

I heard the back door shut behind John. He'd caught a twelve-inch rainbow trout in the creek. John cleaned and gutted the fish in the laundry sink. I fired up the range and tossed some herbs and clarified butter into a shallow fry pan. Then I felt John's chin on my shoulder and heard his soft, suggestive voice in my ear: "James is asleep. Whatever shall we do, my bride?" My body tingled as I slept and dreamed of John and me finally christening the kitchen island.

The twelve-inch trout was a little tepid by the time we ate it. It was, by far, the only cold fish in the kitchen...

7

Spring, Fried Pickles and Tatas

~

I called Mom this morning to come up to the house. Dreams of John seem so far and few between now, so there's no point in trying to sleep all day just so I can possibly spend time with him. Mom was gracious and kept from asking too many questions during her visit. I appreciate it, knowing how hard it is for her not to meddle.

We went out to lunch, and she helped me go through a few boxes of sympathy cards. Reading the cards should have been more comforting, but I found myself being jealous of memories other folks had of John. For instance, I had no idea John liked fried pickles from the Minnesota State Fair. And, I didn't remember him running a marathon. Lastly, during a brief break in our relationship, all of about two weeks, he was being pursued by a girl who made *Playboy's* college coeds issue that year. Why did that make me feel insecure? It was almost twenty-seven years ago! The fact that anyone would mention that in a sympathy card just goes to show that common sense is not so common.

I have to admit, Mom's company made me feel good. Besides the boxes of cards, she and I did some shopping for warm weather clothes. Anthropologie was having a sale, and since their clothes fit my new, trimmer body, I bought some stuff, most notably a dress. I have absolutely no reason for buying a dress, but I did. It made me feel pretty—quite an accomplishment for a piece of fabric and a zipper.

My dad has been in Atlanta, working on a few house projects there before Teddy gets home for good. It seems Teddy's renters will not be getting their deposit back. The house was nearly trashed while he was in Asia. So, I asked Mom to stay a few more days. I need her more than I'd like to admit. She and Dad have been so patient with my pushing them away this past year. It's just that I prefer to cry alone. I don't want anyone to feel sorry for me. I need to figure this out by myself.

The anniversary is right around the corner. I've been getting so many calls, messages mostly. I have the answering machine on all the time now. I am not up for chitchat, so I just listen to the messages, then send e-mails responding to the ones that I can remember.

8

Hitler in Hell

~

It's Saturday morning. I haven't turned the news on in two weeks or more. I had no idea how bad things have gotten. I didn't renew John's *Wall Street Journal* subscription, so I don't get the headlines via e-mail each morning. James is in the Middle East. I don't want to know what is happening there. I guess a responsible citizen and loving mother would just turn the news on and watch, even if it scares her to pieces. But, I am a bit of a sissy.

All the unrest last year has boiled over into the biggest mess of this young century. There's a mass exodus of Christians from Israel trying to enter Lebanon, to escape the threat of attack from Iran. Lebanon is being less than hospitable to the refugees. There is a leader calling for the surrounding countries to take in their Arab brothers, even if they are predominantly non-Muslim Catholics and Copts. This leader, Abram Barishmel, seems to be a bright man, educated here in the United States, a PhD in economics from Stanford.

I can barely sleep each night, even without the news. Knowing that James is out there is eating away at me. I wish John were here to calm me down. He was so proud of James. John could have easily calmed my nerves about James's career choice.

The weather forecast is calling for seventy degrees and sun today—something positive to be thankful for. I called my buddy Ellie, to see if she's around. She and her husband live in Annapolis. I thought maybe some lunch in the harbor would be nice. It's pretty warm out considering spring isn't even technically here yet. I guess I could wear that dress I bought when I was out with Mom. My hair looks OK, and Mom dragged me to Sephora for a makeover (ick!) that actually was a good thing. I guess, at forty-two, it's OK to finally break down and buy some undereye concealer. I feel like I've aged ten years since John left me, but maybe being thinner has taken a few years off, too. I'll see what Ellie thinks.

Annapolis has always been my favorite town. Lots of people walking around, the salty smell of harbor, and cadets strutting around as proud as peacocks in their dress whites. There are children tossing cracker crumbs to the pigeons and ducks, and folks boating in every direction.

* * *

"Hey, chicky! Boy, have I missed you!" Ellie said as she put her eager arms out to hug me.

"Geez, Ellie, I've missed you, too." I gave her a big, long squeeze. She's really the only friend from high school that I still keep in touch with. An easy friend. Rarely has a negative thing to say and sees the best in everyone.

She and I have been close for over twenty years. Our boys are about the same age. Ellie's a career woman and has always been so driven. She's the head events planner at the Kennedy Center. She and her hubby also own a chain of upscale men's barbershops in Annapolis. Ellie looks so stinkin' great. The woman doesn't age. It's uncanny.

We were sitting outside McGarvey's Tavern having some mussels, a crab cake, and an Arnold Palmer. I would have preferred a stiff drink, to relax a bit, but I have the ride home to consider. Anyhow, it's fun watching people walk by. I haven't noticed or been noticed in such a long time. I guess at some point that might change, but not now. I'd just like some company, maybe an old friend, to have dinner with like this from time to time. Nothing else.

"I think he likes your dress, Pea," Ellie whispered as she gestured for me to look toward a man entering the City Dock coffee shop next door. He caught me looking back, and I quickly looked away.

I whispered, "Ellie, don't be ridiculous. He's too old for either of us."

"I'll bet he's about fifty-five, which is not exactly archaic, Pea," she chided.

"Geez. I guess not. I haven't so much as looked at a man in...ever. I guess I forget that I'm well into my forties...probably too old for a fifty-five-year-old man, anyhow! Don't they go for something younger when they are that age and single? Look at Larry King, or Imus, or Donald Trump, or Billy Joel."

Ellie agreed. "The only mature entertainer with any sense is Bruce Springsteen. He's got the same honey as he did twenty years ago, and they're adorable. Those young girls leave their aging husbands as soon as they start wearing diapers. Who'd wanna grow old alone?"

"I don't, Ellie, but I probably will."

"You don't know that. I think, when you are ready, you may be surprised at your prospects."

Yuck, I thought to myself. Just the thought of another man was nauseating.

"Look! He's just come out of the coffee shop and is looking at you again. You could crack a smile. He's not asking for your hand!"

"Stop, Ellie," I ordered.

"OK, I'll stop. I'm sorry." She uses her hands a lot to talk. Must be that Italian thing.

"Don't apologize. I'm sorry. I guess I could loosen up a bit."

"Yes, you could." She smirked.

"Got it, Ellie. Point taken." I don't want to be uptight. It's just that everyone under the sun thinks I should be interested in another man now, and I'm not. Not even close. Not at all. Besides, no one could know me like John and love me anyway. The thought of even letting someone else look at me is weird. Maybe the guy in the coffee shop *was* looking, but it made me uncomfortable. All I could think about was my need to see John tonight. And he did come.

It was his senior prom. I was sixteen, in a peach-colored dress with puffy sleeves. And my hair! Nothing held those big bangs up like that sticky Aqua Net hair spray in the silver can.

John had that awful army haircut even back then. ROTC had really gotten into him. He'd never been so happy. He'd bark orders at the underclassmen in his unit with such confidence. He had his black uniform on. Not as good as his dress blues or his camo, which was my favorite. After we got married, he'd often come home from the field to find me in his camo T-shirt and nothing else! Ha!

If it were possible to have three left feet, John did. He wasn't much of a dancer, but he made up for that in other areas. Prom was the night of our first kiss, which was pretty awkward. I had absolutely no idea what I was doing. I wasn't sure which way to cock my head, and I kept bumping into his nose. He was trying not to chuckle at my lack of experience. I don't know how many girls he'd kissed, but I imagined a lot. After he coached me a bit, kissing him quickly became my favorite after-school activity...I remembered being behind the foreign language building with John, for hours on end, learning how to smooch.

I woke up the next morning with a goofy smile on my face. I wondered if there was anyone who kissed the way he did, so intently, so perfectly. I slipped into my Bogs and took Tarzan out to the creek to splash around.

Later that morning, there was a message on my machine. "Prudence, hey, it's JD. I'm back for a while. Got stationed at the Pentagon for a year. I have those photos from Ranger School graduation. I want to confirm your address before I put them in the mail. Gimme a ring. Thanks! Bye."

I put some coffee on then returned the call, "Hi JD, it's Prudence."

"Hey, Prudence, thanks for calling me back. I'm sorry I couldn't make it to the funeral. I was out of the country for a while. I didn't find out about you losing John until months after and didn't have your number with me then."

"How'd you get this number?"

"That's classified, ma'am."

"Ha! You are such a dork, JD. You tough guys just love having all kinds of juicy secrets at your fingertips! Did you find my number there at work?"

"Yeah. The Pentagon has access to every number there is. I could dial up Hitler in hell if I wanted to! But since I've got you on my screen, are you still at 314 Shiloh, 21104?

"Yes. That's it."

"I have your photos here in my office, and now your address. Will have the admin put 'em in the mail today. Hey, uh, Allen Gravenstein's here, too. He has some hotshot office upstairs. Are you guys still tight?"

"No. He wasn't at the funeral. I haven't talked to him since before John died. I guess Allen is busy or whatever. Anyhow, I appreciate your help with the pictures. John's mom had a few from that day, but she's doesn't know where they are."

"You're welcome. I'm sorry again for not making the funeral. Take care of yourself, and let me know if you need anything."

"OK, I will. Good-bye."

The photos came two days later. They were beautiful. Luckily, JD's first wife, Janine, took the pictures because she was the one with the good eye. JD took pictures like John did. Terrible.

Most of the photos were of John and James. James was still a toddler, maybe three or four. We lived off of John's modest salary while he took courses and finished up college. Would have been nice if I was working, too, but John and I decided I would stay home with James. We knew deployments would be in our future and wanted at least one parent to be home fulltime.

John looked so thin in these pictures. And, he never told me how he got that black eye. I guess he could keep a secret or two. I looked so young. My hair was thick, and my arms looked great from carrying around my little prince all day. I don't think I ever put James down.

I sat up in bed until 3:00 a.m., looking at photos, trying not to think about what I'd seen on the news. More UN troops were killed on the Syrian border today while trying to keep the peace. Many of the Palestinians are trying to get out of Israel now. I think they know something is coming. I can't help but think that they are right. It seems that our troops are so overwhelmed in Iraq and elsewhere that they have lost all control of Afghanistan. It makes me sick. All of those men and women may have died for nothing. It seems like a mess.

John didn't come tonight, not that he could have, since I didn't actually fall asleep. Tarzan jumped up onto the bed and scared the crap out of me at 4:00 a.m., and I just couldn't relax enough to get to sleep after that.

9

Year Two, Dreams, and Psychobabble

~

Finally, a call from my son. It was in the middle of the night, but I was awake anyhow. No dreams the past week or so. I wish John would get his priorities straight and send me some good dreams about us. I wonder what he's doing or if he misses me. Do deceased people in heaven miss their loved ones, or are they too happy to be with God to be sad? I can't imagine there is any sadness there, but it makes me feel better to imagine he might feel my absence. Today was the anniversary of John's death.

"Mom, can you hear me? Sorry the line is a little fuzzy. I only have a few minutes before we are leaving here," he shouted, over the static.

"Where are you, sweetie?" I could barely hear his voice with all the background noise.

"Uh, I can't really say, Mom. But I'm fine, and I miss you. I miss Dad, too. If I weren't so busy here, then I'd call more, so please don't be worried, OK?"

"OK. Thank you for remembering to call today, honey. It was a rough day. It doesn't seem like a year has passed. I don't feel like I've gotten anywhere."

"Mom, I'm sorry I'm not there. I really wanna be."

"I know, my boy. I'll be fine. Just anxious for tomorrow to get here. For some reason, the date has just been hard to get out of my head. I guess it's been like any other day, really, just, I dunno. Hard. I miss you, doll. Did I tell that that I saw Tiny? She did my hair. I'm going back next week. What do you think I'd look like as a redhead?"

"A redhead? Should this worry me?" he asked, concerned.

"No, honey. I think I just need some new scenery, starting with me."

"Gotta go, Mom. Love you."

"You, too. Good-bye, son." I wonder where he is. If he's safe.

I need to stop watching the news. It's upsetting, and I don't need any more images that I can't escape. Before James called, I was thinking about how John looked when he died. Like he'd just bolted from a foxhole into a field of spraying bullets. He had blood all over him, even after they tried to clean him up. His skin was red from the asphalt. His arms, face, neck, everything. At least I heard from my boy, and he's in one piece. The call eased my mind, and I started to drift off to sleep.

My dreams were vivid but scattered. I saw the last moments I spent with John in the hospital. Then bits and pieces of the news I had watched. Israel was gearing up for something. Iran has been threatening a nuclear attack for over a year now. Would they really do that, or is that unstable president of theirs just trying to frighten everyone else in the world?

Then I saw that peaceful Middle Eastern leader in my dream, Abram Barishmel. His mother was Jewish, and his father was Egyptian—very interesting family lines. Just goes to show that understanding comes from reaching out of the box that you were born into. The Living God is bigger than our labels anyhow. It must pain Him to see so many fighting on differing sides, all claiming His favor. It will be interesting to see how He deals with those who have taken lives in His name.

Thousands of protestors from Egypt, Syria, Yemen, and now Iran, who had been marching for a more democratic type of government, are being victimized. Barishmel has been supporting them via the media. He seems to be truly concerned for their safety as they push for more citizen control of their governments.

This Barishmel is handsome and has an honest voice. He's been gentle and peaceful, even in his criticisms. He's become quite popular with moderate Muslims and even some Jews who would welcome any Middle Eastern leader with some Hebrew roots. His popularity is spreading. Many in that part of the world are pushing for him to try to unify the Middle East in a fashion that resembles the European Union.

There is no excuse for anyone in the oil-rich Middle East to be ignorant or poverty-stricken considering the valuable resources they own. You can only keep the poor uneducated and hungry for so long. At some point, I hope they will realize that their leaders are to blame and will fight to be lifted up out of the seventh century. Maybe a moderate leader and a centralized form of government for the region could help with that.

The next morning, Ellie called me for some help designing a new interior for their boat. They lived on that boat in the marina for almost two years before moving into a townhome. She wants to rent the boat out, but it needs some updating. It's very *Miami Vice*. At one point, I thought about asking her to rent it for a few months, just to simplify my life a little and get away from this house, where the memory of John's death is still an open wound.

This house really is too big for just me. I may as well live in an English manor. John got a sizable inheritance from his aunt Betty, who never married. Because of her generosity we were able to afford the house in the first place. But John's not making a killing in stocks each month now, and without him bringing home the bacon, the six grand a month expenses for this house are taking every bit of my income to pay for. The house will be paid off in seven years, but it's a shame no one is using it much. This house deserves to have some life in it.

Ellie spotted a row house for sale in the historic district of Annapolis. She thinks it would suit me. I could walk everywhere and maybe meet some new friends. I've given Ada notice that I'm considering a move. We both cried when I told her. I wish that I could take her with me, but I won't need a housekeeper for a little row house. I'll be sure to see her when I'm in Reisterstown for church on Saturdays. I have so few close friends now, and I'm not willing to part with her.

I hate to admit that I was so attached to John, that I let many of my friendships go. I just didn't feel like there was any other person I'd rather spend my time with, so I didn't. Besides, we moved around so much when John was in the army that I kind of got used to disengaging, protecting myself from attachment to people other than John. I'm sure there is some psychobabble to explain me, but I'm not interested in any of that. I'm not changing at forty-two. I suppose when I turn forty-three next week, I could reconsider.

10

Forty-Three

~

The phone rang. It was Mom calling to wish me a happy birthday, of all things.

"Happy birthday to you, happy birthday to you, happy birthday, dear PRUDIEEEEE, happy birthday to YOU!"

"Hi, Mom and Dad. I am happy to report that your singing this year is just as bad if not worse than last year. Do you *try* to be that off-key, or does it just happen naturally? You guys sound like two teenage boys with a hormone imbalance."

"Don't be grouchy on your birthday, dear. It's bad luck."

"Sorry, Mom, habit. And by the way, it seems I am bad luck."

"Sweetie, don't be silly. John's accident had nothing to do with you. It was not your fault. Now stop this nonsense, and unlock your front door. Daddy and I are outside."

"You're here?"

"Yes, dear. Please don't be upset. We miss you. We ran into Ellie's mom at Safeway, and she mentioned you were thinking about a house in Annapolis. This was news to us. Good news, of course, because you'd be closer, and you wouldn't have to spend all your money on maintaining this house...Not to mention, there are lots of single men in Annapolis! All those uniforms and clean-cut officers!"

"Mom, I'm into tough guys. Actually, I'm still very much into John. He was going to get my name tattooed on the back of his shoulder for my birthday this year. It took me twenty years to talk him into it, and he up and died before paying up."

"Sweetheart, that aside, I think you've lived a very blessed life. Besides, why would you want John to go and hurt himself like that? Tattoos are for convicts and masochistic perverts."

"Masochistic perverts? Geez. That's quite a blanket statement, Mom. Oh, and please forgive my momentary relapse into self-pity. I know I should be thrilled to be forty-three and alone. Even James couldn't be here. I feel like wallowing, so please deal with it. Dad, could you please say something?"

"Sure, Pea. I'm starving. Let's go eat something. And happy birthday. I brought you a box of Godiva. Get some clothes on. We're going out. Oh, and Teddy wants you to call him. He's scheduled to arrive from Jakarta in the morning."

We went to a Turkish restaurant downtown. They have my favorite soup. Some kind of dumplings in a tomato broth. The staff there put a candle on my baklava and sang to me. "Happy Birthday" sounds pretty funny in Turkish. Mom and Dad dropped me off at home after dinner. There was a thoughtful e-mail from James and a message from him on my answering machine wishing me a happy birthday. I listened to his message over and over. His voice sounds so much like John's.

Around seven the next morning, my doorbell rang. It was Teddy! I gave him a serious squeeze and tried not to cry. I hadn't seen him since before John died.

"Hey, sis! Sorry I showed up so early. I just got into BWI an hour ago and thought I'd come right over. I wanted to surprise you on your birthday but couldn't get an earlier flight." I took his hat off and found him void of follicles. I gave him a puzzled look and started to giggle. Teddy smirked, "Don't say it! I already know!"

"Geez, Teddy, it seems that you accidentally left your hair in Jakarta!"

"Well, aren't you funny? Mom made it seem like you've become an anorexic recluse. I am glad to see that you still have your humor to keep you company."

"Ouch, Teddy. That's rather harsh, no?" I said, grimacing.

"Sorry, but the hair thing is getting to me. I am tired of vendors chasing me down trying to sell me the Asian equivalent to Rogaine."

"What is the Asian equivalent to Rogaine?"

"I dunno, something about monkeys and elephants, snake venom, and whatever else. You can't imagine the smell of some of that stuff! Anyhow, I missed you, and I'm so sorry I missed the funeral. Work's been so intense. I couldn't take a week off and come home. There was nobody else that could run the Asian hub and spearhead the merger. I've been working nonstop for sixteen months!"

"Thanks, Teddy...But honestly, I was such a mess. A wreck. I wouldn't want you to see me like that. I just wanted to be alone."

"Dad said he thought you've handled yourself very well, and he's proud of you."

"He told you to say that to me, right?"

"Yeah, and he's a little embarrassed of Mom's constant hounding. He said she's already trying to get you to date some fat, bald guy from their church."

"Yep, as if someone else will just make it all go away. Maybe now that you're home, she'll focus on your lack of a mate."

"I'd rather her pester you. Oh, and she said you were thinking of moving to Annapolis. Are you?"

"I was thinking about it. I'd really like less house to keep up. The yard and gardens here are ridiculous. It's a full-time thing. I'm feeling a little isolated." We went into the kitchen, and I started some breakfast.

"Well, you look amazing. It's not likely you're gonna be isolated in Annapolis with all of those sailors around. John may actually come back from the dead if he hears you went navy on him."

"I'd never do that! He would come back from the grave just to give me a spankin', which might be a little weird if he's not alive, but whatever, I'll take whatever John I can get."

"That's gross, sis," Teddy said as he raised an eyebrow and took a sip of coffee.

"Ugh! Don't be such a deviant. That's not what I meant. Really, Teddy, you are off—and not by just a little. Besides, John's not gross, dead or alive. I'll take what I can get."

"Hey, where's King Kong? Is he still alive?"

"It's Tarzan, smartass, and yes, but barely. Actually, I'll put him in the basement since he doesn't like you, either."

We spent most of the morning and afternoon sitting on the couch and catching up. It was so nice to see my little brother. He seemed to be able to wrap his head around the loss I feel, having gone through his former wife's infidelity. He's the only one so far who hasn't hinted that just because I've managed to hit the one-year mark without John, I might find someone else. He gets it, or at least has the wisdom to know that I'll never heal, at least, not entirely.

Later, we went to Annapolis for some seafood. I also wanted to drive by a few homes that were for sale and get Teddy's opinion. He's got a good eye for real estate, and I had some questions for him about renting versus buying.

I've missed my brother enormously. I enjoy his intelligent humor. He tries to be positive about things in general, so his company was a nice diversion. Mom called about twenty-five times and asked when he'd be coming down, so he finally left to go see her and Dad.

I can't believe summer is here. Today, I put in what may be my last veggie garden. I'm thinking more and more about moving. Next week, Ellie's going to meet me in Annapolis to see a couple more houses that I might be interested in. She's got a better idea of what things should cost. If only house hunting *for one* was less depressing.

* * *

My dreams are getting less restful and more bizarre. Last night, I dreamed about tens of thousands of Middle Eastern protestors dressed in long brown cloaks, like an army of monks. I asked them why they were standing in Red Square. They simultaneously started into a creepy, ghoulish laugh. That was it. I was happy to wake. I have no idea what that was supposed to mean or who they were laughing at. Weird.

This morning, I turned on the news and saw that Gaddafi is sending out forces to snatch men and boys to kill or force to join his legions. This is very reminiscent of the atrocities on the Ivory Coast in the mid- to late 1990s. Our forces, along with the British and French, are trying to help the Libyan rebels, but it looks as if the fight cannot be won from the air.

It also seems that anti-Christian violence has escalated in Pakistan. A female Christian reporter was raped during a protest, and a cemetery has been bulldozed, exposing the remains of many deceased brothers and sisters. Of course, this story was on The Drudge Report, not the TV. The local television stations would never post such stories; they are too consumed with sports and the weather to actually have any respectable news.

I'm spending most of my days worrying about James now. But, I hope that my mind isn't so preoccupied with current events that I don't see John in the twilight. I'm hoping by chance, or by grace, that I will still see glimpses of him or feel his touch while I sleep.

11

The Wookie and the Outer Buddha

~

We are well into summer now. It is getting hot, as it always seems to be toward the end of May. I can hear the neighbors' young children getting on and off the big yellow taxi each day. I remember my James sprinting from the bus to the house and asking me how many more days until school was out.

Our summers were spent on the Chesapeake, where my folks have a modest cottage. It is a place of family, where I can catch up with my aunts, uncles, and cousins, and their kids. That beach has the best driftwood. Sometimes entire trees wash up after a storm, their soft gray bones exposed, literally sanded down under the current for many years before being released to the shore again. That is the beach where my parents courted. John and I had a few memories of our own there. James learned to swim, fish, and crab in the Chesapeake.

Today I got a message from Allen, who I thought was John's best friend until the accident. Allen's a single guy, in awe of himself most of the time. It seems he's still in the army, at the Pentagon, up the stairs from JD. Allen and John were like brothers from the start. Complimentary opposites.

I remember the first time I met Allen. We had him over for dinner. He was John's executive officer (XO) at the time. John went to pick him up at the metro station nearby. Allen walked into our house, looked at me, and seemed a bit stunned. He made a few too many comments about John marrying *way* out of his league. Of course, that was when I was much younger.

He was trying to be funny, but after getting to know Allen, I realized his flirting wasn't really a compliment. It seems he had many, many casual acquaintances over the years. And by acquaintances, I don't mean acquaintances. He'd always brag about his female toys and exploits. I always thought he must be empty inside.

I'm not going to call him back. I can't imagine what he could want to talk to me for. I called him numerous times and e-mailed him right after John's death. He never bothered to acknowledge my correspondence, which I will never understand.

Ellie called and wanted some company. We headed over to St. Michael's for a change. I met her at her place, and we drove over to a crab shack with a huge deck, right on the bay. We didn't need to go any farther than her backyard to get crabs, but I think she wanted to take a ride.

"Pea, how is James?" she asked.

"I don't know exactly. I assume he's fine. Not sure where he is or what he's doing, but when he calls, he sounds pretty good. He's coming home for two weeks around Christmas, hopefully."

"Cool. Luca's finally graduating from school on June 1. Did you get my invite?

"I'll be there for sure," I said enthusiastically.

"He's hoping to get a job with my brother's engineering firm in New Jersey. I'll miss meeting him for dinner and going up to Baltimore to visit. He's really enjoyed Hopkins, but I can't wait to be rid of those tuition bills. They are really killing us. I wish he'd studied premed so that he'd at least be making more money out of the starting gate."

"Yes, but he'd also be racking up four more years of tuition in the meantime..."

"I guess. He's not cut out to be a doctor anyhow. He likes to play too much," she said and winked.

"How is Grace? Are they still exclusive?"

"Yes, she's fine. A little more driven than Luca. She's decided to get her law degree, out at USC. Luca's not happy about that, but she got a scholarship. I can't see them managing to stay together with all that distance, new job for him, and intense studying for her. I guess they'll figure it out. Is James seeing anyone?"

"I think he's going to see Tiny. I mentioned I saw her for a hairdo awhile back, and he seemed interested in catching up with her. She was so awkward in high school. It's tough being so tall and athletic, when all the other girls are so petite and shapely. Tiny's really come into herself, though, and has that killer sense of humor to boot! I think he'll find that she's quite something. The fact that she goes to my church doesn't hurt, either. I'm just going to keep my mouth shut and see what he says when he sees her."

Our waiter finally made an appearance, saying, "Hello, ladies! I'm Justin, and I'll be your server. Are you two having crabs today?"

Ellie and I ate crabs for two hours—enough crab to serve as an appetizer to someone from the Midwest. I tried to explain the fine art of picking crabs to my mother-in-law once. You eat before you pick crabs because the point of picking crabs is to socialize, drink beer, etc. Blue crabs are small compared to their deep-sea crustaceous cousins. If one intends to fill him- or herself on blue crabs, one may as well plan on starving.

The rest of the week went well, except the fact that I haven't had restful sleep since Teddy came to visit. Of course, last night was no exception. I'm starting to wonder if any of this is supposed to mean something or if I really have lost my mind.

John was in my dream, surrounded by three men in white robes, beautiful men who towered over him. They had their hands on John's head. Their eyes were fixed on a woman in the corner of the room. She was speechless, afraid, and crying. John put his hand out to her, and she slowly moved toward him and the three in white robes.

I'm hoping that the next time John visits my dreams, he'll leave the three dudes and the crying chick at home. I don't understand what that dream is supposed to mean, if anything.

Allen called again and left a message. He wants to come see how I'm doing. I know this is ridiculous, but I wouldn't be surprised if that guy was moving in on his dead buddy's wife. To say the guy lacks discretion would be an understatement. He said he'd be here in an hour. He didn't even give me a chance to object.

He pulled up in his SUV with some loud, ridiculous 1980s hair-band music on the radio.

"Hey, Pea! Great to see you. You look good but thinner than I remember."

Is he serious? He was John's best friend and didn't even acknowledge John's death. It's been over a year. I'll hold my tongue since John loved him so much. Why he's so interested in how I'm doing *now* is beyond me.

"Allen, nice to see you, too." I managed to fake a smile. He gave me a big squeeze that felt surprisingly authentic.

"Geez, the house looks great. I haven't been up here in two years. How are you holding up with all of this to take care of?"

"Taking care of this behemoth house is a full-time job. Time is passing, and things are better, but nothing really relieves me but seeing James. I'm not aching as much as a year ago, but I still miss John enormously."

"Are you lonely most of the time? I mean, do you have any friends who you see regularly?"

"Do you mean the kind of 'friends' you have?"

"I'm not really seeing anyone anymore, not the way I used to. I'm feeling more and more like settling down, but I think I've missed the boat. There aren't many nice gals out there looking for a guy like me, flawed, injured. I've got arthritis in my knees, and my thigh bothers me when I run. My way of life has changed quite a bit. I'm feeling a need for a little peace in my life."

"There is peace, Allen, but not where you've been looking..."

"Come on, Prudence, you know I'm not into that spiritual stuff."

"It's not about spiritual. It's about being realistic...that we are not accidental beings or simple matter floating about the universe."

"I'll agree with that. But, that's about as far as I'd go. The science just isn't there."

"It's called faith. It's like gravity. Look, there's no chance we're gonna tackle this subject tonight. Are you hungry?"

"Are you cookin'?" His face lit up.

"That's the rumor," I said nonchalantly.

"Then, yes, ma'am."

Allen hasn't been over for dinner in ages. He used to be over all the time when John was alive. Allen would hang around the kitchen while I cooked or would toss James around in the living room and play Matchbox cars with him. Then he and John would sit out back, drink scotch, and smoke cigars until the wee hours. I wonder if the person he seemed to be ever existed, the lavish guest and loyal friend to John. I guess Allen moves on rather quickly.

But, Allen's visit was a good excuse to make a nice dinner. The fact is, I haven't cooked for a while, and I miss it. I used to make really stellar meals. My family used to rave about my cooking, although I think they exaggerated quite a bit.

It was nice out. Allen and I sat out on the porch. He told me stories about himself and John when they were in the Eighty-second Airborne together. It was nice to hear John's name from someone else. Good to know that I wasn't the only one with splendid memories of him. I found myself feeling less lonely with Allen's company. But, it was getting late. I told him it was time to go. I was hoping for a date with my literal dream man.

That night, my dream was familiar. The three tall men in white robes formed a triangle. And the woman in the corner, she was walking toward the three, with John in the center of the triangle. Her face was blurred. She'd stopped crying. She was praying, "He's made me feel alive again, and I thank you for his company. Please send him a worthy sparring partner as well." But what does that have to do with John? And the three? She had something in her hand. It was a photo, but I couldn't make it out.

That's it. I can't sleep, and I'm no longer looking forward to sleeping each night. I guess I've had a grace period of happy, togetherness dreams, and now I'm on to the heavy stuff. John knows that I have difficulty with nightmares. Maybe I need to pray for a clear head and peaceful thoughts. I'll do that right now...and hopefully go back to sleep. It's 3:00 a.m., too early to get up yet...

I prayed silently to myself, "Dear Lord, my celestial Father, Maker of all, You hold the blueprint of the universe in Your perfect hands. All of creation is at Your will. Lord, my life is a small and insignificant second in your plan for eternity. But, I know that I matter to you. I know that You love me...I'm trying...to need You again. Please forgive my doubt. I know you must have a plan for my life...You know my heart is full of pain and indifference to You. But, You made me. Only you know how I miss my John. Please heal my heart. Cleanse the negative thoughts that leave me frightened and feeling so alone. Fill the loss of John with the joy of knowing You and Your Son, the One You sent to advocate for me, for all. And, God, please keep my son safe, Lord. Protect him. He is all I have. Please give me a purpose. Give me Your purpose."

I finally broke down. It had been fourteen months since I'd prayed with a sincere servant's heart. I had been angry for too long. My heart is tired of hurting. Being mad at God just takes too much energy, too much effort. I've belonged to Him my entire life. He knew I'd return. He was as patient with me and my anger as the father of the prodigal son. I am the prodigal son.

I took everything He gave me and just expected my charmed life to go on until further notice. What I didn't see was that I had more joy and happiness in my years with John than most people have in their entire lives. I was being stingy, ungrateful, and unappreciative of God's generosity.

I suppose He is teaching me humility. How to hurt, how to lose, and how to go on and find another life that is worth living, to be thankful for the memories of John but to know that John is with Him now. If I could just convince myself that John doesn't belong to me anymore. My eyes are red and my cheeks stained with tears. I need to let go. I can't control everything. Finally, I felt myself drifting off around 5:00 a.m. In peace.

I woke up two hours later to the phone ringing off the hook. It was James. "Mom, I'm in Germany, on my way home! I wanted to surprise you. I hope you don't have plans for dinner tonight!" God is, indeed, good. I could hardly keep from crying. It was so nice to hear James's voice.

"Shall we go out, or do you want to eat at home, son?"

"I want spaghetti and meatballs, the ones you used to make, and make a lot. I'm a little bit bigger than when I left, and I eat a ton more." I know the meatballs he's referring to: when he was three, he went through a meatball period when that's all he wanted to eat, except for ketchup.

"Point taken. You look like the Hulk, huh?"

"Uh, yeah, almost, give or take an inch or two. There isn't much to do where we are but patrol and lift, so I take advantage. And I can't wait to have some sweet rolls and Diet Coke! Can we go to Koko's and get a crab cake for dessert?"

"Whatever you want, honey. I can't wait to see you! Are you flying into Andrews?

"Yep, we'll be there at seven tonight, your time. I've already called ahead and got you a pass to the airstrip, number four. Gotta go, Mama. See you soon."

"I love you, son. See you tonight!"

I did my happy dance and shouted out loud, "My son will be here in twelve hours!" Then the phone rang again. Ugh, it was Allen. I let the machine pick up.

"Hey, Prudence. Just wanted to leave you a message. Thanks for dinner last week. Meant to call before now and tell you how much I enjoyed it but had a trip outta nowhere and just got back. Lots going on, as you know. Anyhow, thanks! Next time you get lonely for some undeserving company to cook for, gimme a ring."

I would prefer not to call Allen back, but, I probably will. I wish spending time with him was not so comforting.

I ran around trying to pick up the house a bit before leaving to pick James up at Andrews AFB. I started the sweet rolls and baked some cookies. My son has a sweet tooth like I do, not that salty stuff that John liked to munch on. I downed a pot of coffee so that I could stay up late with him. I figured his internal clock would be off, about seven hours ahead, and I didn't want to miss anything.

He arrived at seven on the nose.

"JAMES! Honey, I'm so happy you are safe! And HOME! Give your old mama a hug!"

"Are you an 'old mama' now? Since when? You look great, Ma. I like the red hair. Did Tiny do that? I'll have to thank her. You look ten years younger! And you have a little color. Thank God you are finally getting out of the house. I was worried."

"No need, Lieutenant Brandt. Mama is well and somewhat emotionally intact. I just missed you. My God, how many hours a day do you work on your muscles, son? You're an absolute beast!"

"Mom, speaking of being a beast, I am so stinkin' hungry. Can we eat? Starving. Literally, my big ones are eating my little ones."

"Your great-grandma Flo used to say that."

"I know. And, boy, could she fry up a pork chop. So hungry!"

There is nothing in the world like having your grown child visit and enjoying his company, as an adult. Our boy has such wonderful manners and his daddy's humor and looks. What a treasure he is.

"Hey, Ma, can I borrow the car tomorrow? I was gonna have Tiny shave my head and that pesky hair that's started up my back and outta my shirt collar. When the heck did that start? I'm looking like a bald Wookie!"

"You got the Chewbacca gene from Daddy. He started getting hairy around twenty. So...Tiny, huh? You two are officially talking now?" James looked bashful all of a sudden.

"Tiny found me on Facebook. She wanted me to see your new hair. We've been joking back and forth since then. She mentioned that she's seen you at church. I was glad to hear that you're finally getting back. Helps you stay centered. We don't have much right now by means of spiritual guidance in the field. Shortage of priests and pastors, I guess. They don't send those guys where we go...too dangerous..."

"James, I don't want to hear about any dangerous anything, please. As far as I'm concerned, you're baking cupcakes and playing on the beach all day, every day."

"Playing on the beach is close..." James said then winked.

"No more info, please, James. I can hardly sleep, honey. My imagination is outta whack. Seriously. Anyhow, I've been going to services on Saturdays. It's a lot less crowded, and I can always sit in the same spot. I think I'm getting OCD, at forty-three. We can go tomorrow, if you want, before you head over to your 'hair' appointment. There are plenty of folks that would love to see you. The girls will go nuts. We don't have fellas like you come very often, if ever. You look like He-Man, minus the breastplate."

James ate his weight, 225 pounds, in spaghetti and meatballs. We slept in the next morning, James ate some more, then we headed off to church that afternoon.

"Hey, Ma, do you know that guy?" James whispered, as he scanned the pew across the aisle.

"Shhh, James. Quiet, honey."

"That guy is looking at you. Is he a friend of yours? That pepper-head over there."

"Pepper-head? Is that what graying folks are referred to as these days?"

"No, his is just more peppery than usual. At least he has hair, more than me, anyhow."

"James, the baby in front of us has more hair, and possibly better manners, than you do. Shush!"

"Mom, the guy has been fixed on you since we sat down. Maybe I need to flash him the 'stink look.' He's obviously not bothered by me. A little brazen, don't you think. dude?" said James, looking at the "pepper-head."

This was very strange. My twenty-four-year-old son was defending my honor. Ha! In church of all places! Quite amusing. The service was finally over, and James rolled his eyes as the "pepper-head" made a bee-line to where we were sitting.

"Hi, Prudence. I'm Ed. I was in your small group a few years back. I'm sorry to stare, but I haven't seen you in years and almost didn't recognize you...Oh, and forgive me, I was so sorry to hear of John's passing. I haven't been to church for quite a while, and I just heard. I'm so sorry."

"Yes, I remember now. Your wife is Sherri, right?"

"Actually, Sherri and I divorced a year ago. She just wasn't into it anymore. She had breast cancer a few years back, and I thought I was going to lose her. I told her that when she recovered, we could do all the things she always wanted, like travel, and move someplace warm, that I'd be right there with her, but I don't think that's what she wanted. She just wanted to start over...completely...Without me."

"Geez. A new lease on life gone awry, huh?"

"You could say that. Anyway, is this James, who we've been praying for?"

"Yes, this is he, my hulky son, back from only God knows where. He and your daughter were in the same youth group, I think. How is she? I don't recall her name."

"Charlotte, she's an aspiring artist. She lives in Charlotte, of all places. Anyhow, she's married to a great guy, and they love it down there. She's been studying oil painting under a guy named Keysar. I guess she's like his apprentice."

"That's great, Ed. It's good to see you. The son and I have a brunch date. Crab cakes Benedict. We're starved, so we'd better go." James and I headed out to the car.

"Geez, Mom, why didn't you just go ahead and ask him to join us? He was beaming at you!"

"Easy. You're straddling the line, son. If I only get you for five days, then I'm not willing to share you. Besides, it's kind of creepy that my son thinks I need to ask a guy out. Ick. Your dad would kick your hairy Wookie butt! Besides, Ed's too nice. I miss your papa. Unless he comes back from the dead to ask me out, I won't be having a date anytime soon. This old lady just isn't there yet."

"It seems her suitors are lining up, waiting for a change of heart. Besides, I don't think Dad would want you to be alone. I know you miss him, but it's been long enough. Would you mind having a companion or something? Are you even thinking about it?"

"Nope. Your papa's still my man. The relationship is just a bit one-sided at this point. Next topic, please. Lunch, perhaps?" James put his arm around my shoulder and gave me a big squeeze, just like his papa used to.

Those five days were truly the best I've had in over a year. Being with my son made me feel complete again. As much as I think about John, I found myself thinking less about him when James was with me. It was almost as if James was John, and I was able to catch up with them both that week. I wasn't sad for a second, and my disturbing dreams were put on hold. Nothing would steal my joy. My boys were so alike. I would see and hear them both, in one, until James went off to report to his new station.

I got a letter shortly after James left. It was from the woman who owns the home that my grandmother grew up in. The house is in Adisham, England. I wrote her over a year ago, asking if she knew anything about the family that had lived in the home during WWI and WWII.

I opened the envelope to find a very brief letter:

Dear Madam:

I have received your letter regarding your interest in your grandmother's childhood home in Adisham. I will certainly be in touch if we are able to gather the information you requested.

Regards,
Regina Fairfax Jones-Wilkinson, Primary Historian, Kent Trust Foundation

I loved Winnie, my British grandmother. She gave my dad his boisterous laugh and his love of tea. Few folks relish a good cup of tea the way Dad does. I remember being a young girl sipping tea, sitting in the living room in the evenings with my mom and dad, while we all pored over our respective books. I don't remember Teddy being with us much...

Teddy, a stinker even back then, was always out making trouble with his best buddy, Moff. Moff was short for something, but I hadn't been privy to exactly what Moff was short for. The two of them would find a way to irritate someone in our small town almost daily. One evening, a neighbor came over, in tears, claiming that Teddy and Moff had stolen the Buddha statue from his front yard. It seems that the remains of his mother were in the Buddha. Teddy and Moff didn't own up to liberating the Buddha, but it certainly got them both in a heap of trouble, despite the fact that their guilt was never actually confirmed. The Buddha magically resurfaced in the neighbor's yard about a week later.

Anyhow, I'm thinking about going to Britain to see where my people are from. My mother's family is from County Cork, Ireland, and I know more about them than my dad's side of the gene pool. His mom, Winnie, was really something. She had a sad life, except for her children, all of whom still emulate her.

Teddy said he'd go with me. He just wants to skip London, as he's been there enough to have seen the good stuff (is that possible?). I was hoping to go the markets, so maybe I'll hang around the city an extra day or two when Teddy goes home. John dearly loved Indian food, and I feel I need to eat some for him, too, in London.

I slept soundly tonight, all but the last five seconds before I woke...I saw John and the three glowing men comforting the woman from the corner. Then she was glowing like the three. Then my eyes opened.

I woke up, and it was eight in the morning. I turned on the TV.

If I were a betting woman, I would say that my dreams are getting stranger the more I watch the news. On BBC, there's a clip from yesterday. Abram Barishmel has addressed the nations of the Middle East, and they are in agreement regarding the importance of a sort of United Nations of the Middle East. That's not what they are calling it, but all Muslim nations are allowed to join if they are willing to pay the dues and work bilaterally against the violence there, so that the West will stay out of the region. Seems to make sense.

There are too many types of folks in the Middle East to generalize. But, it's hard not to think that the whole area is a mess after watching the news each day. Just this week, the president of Yemen is fleeing for his life and the Egyptians are putting Mubarak on trial for murder. That seems like a lot of deposed leaders in a short period of time.

Almost all of North Africa is without leaders who are accepted across the board. Things are no doubt tense in that region. Thank God my buddy, Janie, is arriving from Minnesota today. I need some company and a distraction from all the doom and gloom.

Janie pulled up in her minivan an hour later. "Janie! You're early! How is that possible?"

"Hey, Prudie Pie. I've gotta pee. That drive was a bit much for the bladder of a mother of three! I held it all the way from Pittsburgh!!"

"That can't be healthy. How long was the drive?"

"Twenty-two hours...but I stopped at some cool places along the way. And traffic was light around Chicago. This might be the only week in history that Gary, Indiana, was free of giant orange cones."

"I'm glad you agreed to stay at least two weeks. Twenty-two hours in the car is no joke."

"Yep. A bit of a trek. But I'm happy to trade in cool Minnesota for a little heat. It hasn't even gotten to eighty degrees this summer! The boys are all taking summer classes at school, so they'll be busy enough to stay out of trouble. Jim is set to get back from Afghanistan in six weeks, so I thought a little trip would help pass the time."

"Janie, I needed some company. I'm so glad I was able to twist your arm. James just left a few days ago. He reported to his new post at Hunter Army Airfield in Savannah. He's pretty stoked. He loves those southern girls, although I suspect he has a pen pal back here now. He went 'out for coffee' until 2:00 a.m. with a nice girl from my church that we've known for years. I'm hoping they were just talking and lost track of time..."

"Prudie, that's a little naïve, wouldn't you say? Two o'clock in the morning? Sounds like more than just a good talk to me..."

"No, not this girl. She's different. Besides, I know my boy. When he got home, I was up sewing, and he came in to say goodnight. There was not an ounce of guilt on his precious face. Entirely innocent. Besides, his dimples peek out when he's being sneaky or trying to hide something from me. What about your boys? Are they seeing anyone? Oh, geez, sorry, Janie. You haven't even gotten your bags out of the car yet. And I have some goodies for you. The garden's in full bloom. How about a coffee or something cold?"

"Beer's good. Maybe something I can put a lime in?"

"Splendid idea. Do you mind if I have iced coffee?"

"Nope, knock yourself out, you rebel, you!" she chided.

"You know John was the beer lover. I'll pour a cold one for Tarzan in memory of John. Tarzan loves beer. I'm more of a caffeine junkie."

"Whatever. I'm starving, Prudie. What'd you make me? Some weird flesh-free cuisine that only you would go to the trouble to prepare for a vegetarian friend?

"Yes, but only for my weirdest, most troublesome veggie friend!"

We had a great dinner outside on the deck. Eggplant stuffed with some fancy grains and Gruyere cheese, spicy baby greens with shaved French radishes in a quick clementine vinaigrette, and a minerally Riesling from Austria. I hadn't seen Janie since John's funeral, and I had missed her enormously.

Janie and Jim have three boys. The oldest changed his major twice, so he and his two younger brothers will all be at the same University of Minnesota graduation ceremony next spring. Pretty funny. At least all of that time Jim spends away in the army paid for college for his kids. Not exactly what I'd call a bargain, but he likes being Colonel Jim Kaminski, so it seems to work out fine for all parties involved.

Janie and I stayed up late every night, and slept in, just like two college girls on semester break. She'd never been to New England, so after she recovered from her drive, we spent a few days searching out potential tag sales, and then headed up the East Coast. We took John's fancy car and sped up 95 like our arses were on fire.

We stopped first in the Hamptons, then went up to Rhode Island, then onto the granite beaches of Down East Maine, where John and I celebrated our tenth anniversary.

It didn't seem that long ago that he and I were there together, in a converted 1850s boathouse. We watched the lobster boats come in and out of Southwest Harbor and did some hiking. John never appealed to me quite the way he did that trip. It must have been the salt air. He and I couldn't get enough of each other. It was just a glimpse of the happiness that would follow the next fourteen years. We were so in love.

Janie fell asleep watching *Army Wives* on TV.

As I drifted off that night, I could hear John's soft, confident voice.

"Wife, shall we find a little wine shop and celebrate our vows? How about some chocolate...I know how much you like some good chocolate after..."

"Dearest, what makes you think I want to have chocolate with you tonight? I'm tired. Give me one reason to have chocolate with you instead of some delicious sleep. I mean, aren't you tired? If this continues, I'm afraid you'll throw your back out, soldier!"

"Not funny, wife. However, you may remedy that potential problem...I could...let you 'drive.'" He chuckled as he tucked his hands in the back of my jeans.

"I'd rather sleep," I insisted, obviously lying since I couldn't keep a straight face.

"No, you wouldn't," he teased as his hands made their way up the back of my shirt.

"Fine...But, I'm too tired to 'drive,'" I whispered, looking up at him with doe eyes. He smiled and leaned in to kiss me.

"Just close your eyes. Wife...you are...so beautiful..."

John was always eager for my funny finish face to show up after he started working on me. I think he liked the challenge. By the time we'd been married twenty years, it had become so easy. Either way, I don't remember ever being too tired for John's attentions. His soft gray eyes would smile at me, and I'd just fall into him. The next morning, I woke with pink cheeks, with good reason. Janie asked if I felt OK. I suppose I did...

Janie and I went home a couple days later. We'd planned on going to Prince Edward Island, but it was starting to get chilly out. Fall was making her debut early in Maine, so the ferries to Canada were closed due to cold, choppy waters. Late August was nicer in Maryland, anyhow, so we packed up the car and headed south, down 95.

12

Back in the Saddle (of a Springer)

~

When we got back, I packed up an enormous care package and gifts for James. I was hoping to celebrate his twenty-fourth birthday with him, but he's too busy at work this week for company. And Janie had to go. She would have stayed longer but insisted that if she didn't get home and pay bills, that her home would be foreclosed on.

The following Thursday, I got a phone call from James. He was back from the field and wanted some company.

"Hey, Mom, I have the weekend off. Why don't you come down to Savannah?"

"Uh, well, Janie left last week, and I still haven't changed the sheets, paid bills, or gotten the garden ready for the cold weather, and Tarzan's been sleeping so much lately, I think I'm gonna lose him."

"Mom, it's a weekend, not a month. Ask Carrie to take care of the dog for a night. Stop acting like an old lady and get your bony, redheaded self down here to see me. I told all my buddies about your cooking, so they've already put together some dinner requests. Come on!"

"OK. Sorry. You're right. I have your address right here. I'll use your dad's airlines miles that are sitting around collecting dust."

"Great. See you tomorrow?"

"Yes, son, see you tomorrow. I'll e-mail the flight info."

It'd been about six weeks since I'd seen James, not long considering we'd only see him on holidays before John died. James is tender for such a tough guy. I don't know for sure, but I think he spends more time at his barracks catching up on his reading than looking for easy targets at the bar. I arrived the next afternoon, and James took me back to his garden apartment on base.

"Mom, this is Hammer, Fritz, and Duff."

"I would probably remember your given names better. Any chance you care to share?" I looked them all over then smiled.

"Yes, ma'am, I'm Chuck, this is Christian, and this is Dennis. Springer, I mean, James, said that you might wanna eat in tonight?"

"James, you wanna tell your mother what 'Springer' means?"

"Uh, Mom, I bought a bike after Dad died last year."

"A Springer?"

"Yeah. I'm sorry. I didn't want to tell you. I knew you might be upset because of what happened to Dad. I know this sounds wacky, but I feel like Dad is with me when I ride...And, Mom, I'm really careful. I wear a skid lid and everything. I hope you can understand." He was so nervous and apologetic. But I wasn't angry.

"I know your papa wanted to get you a bike so the two of you could ride together. I think he'd be happy for you, honey. I'm not mad. You were right about not telling me a year ago. I may have sent you up to be with your father! Son, you haven't been in the army long enough to be buried next to your dad at Arlington. If you die on that motorcycle, I'll have you charred and scatter your ashes at the naval academy. Remember that!"

"Mom, I'd rather be dead than have any part of me at the naval academy. And enough of the morbid. You want to go for a ride, Mom? My buddies have bikes, too. It's a great way to see Savannah!"

"You want your old mama on the back of your bike? That's kind of lame."

"These three dorks are gonna have their girlfriends come, too. We'll be like a posse. It's perfectly safe riding in a motorcade!"

"I haven't been on a bike in two years, sweetie. I'd love to."

My hair was blowing in the wind. My arms were tight around our son, whose resemblance to John is uncanny and getting more so each time I see him. I can understand why this makes him feel close to John. I feel close to him, too. It brought back memories of our early years. I closed my eyes and started to daydream...

John and I rode all over the place on our 1984 Shovelhead. We couldn't afford a new bike, so we bought an old green bike from a Vietnam vet who rode the thing so much, he had no idea how many miles were on the engine. The odometer stopped working years before we bought it. We took it out for the weekend sometimes when my folks would offer to babysit James. We felt so free...until it overheated, and we had to stop and cool it down. We didn't care. Often, we needed to cool down, too.

We hit every diner from Richmond to Charleston and back. I liked the nondescript mom-and-pop places with full parking lots, but John preferred Waffle House, so we took turns. In between stops, we'd yell back and forth over the roar of the exhaust pipe. I'd kiss his ears, and he'd reach back with his right hand and rub my calf or touch my face.

"Wife, are you comfy?" John shouted over the exhaust.

"No. But I don't care. I feel like a badass, and I don't think a badass would care if she was comfy or not," I yelled back, while giving him a squeeze.

"You're a badass, babe! My badass with a great ass!"

"John, you're an awful liar! When are you getting my tattoo?"

"Pea, you know that getting someone else's name stamped on your body jinxes the whole thing. I'm not getting one, specifically to save our marriage."

I smacked the back of his Kevlar helmet. "You're a chickenshit, John!"

"I'm a little chicken, but you're the little shit! Ha ha. Love you, wife. Hang on! I'm gonna pass this guy!" I felt like a queen on that back of that tattered bike with my freckled arms around my man's svelte waist.

James rides just like his father. So easy, confident. Our little motorcade followed the canal along the river, passing the paddleboats, the bars, and the fountain. The antique stores sparked my interest, but maybe for another time. At that moment, I was with my boys again, no worries, wanting for nothing, suspended in joy.

That night, I made a serious meal for James's friends and their ladies. We ate outside under the bright moon. Late September must be the best time for good weather in Savannah. It was 65 degrees out. Just cool enough to build a fire outside. After dinner, we sat by the fire, and I got to know James's new brothers.

These young men will be tied to my son for the remainder of their careers. They will trust each other with their lives while they protect ours. I would pray for them, too, each night. I felt so honored to spend the evening with them.

It was late. James was passed out on the couch, and his buddies and respective ladies went their separate ways. I don't know why I couldn't sleep. Just too happy, I guess...I turned on Food Network for some gastronomic entertainment.

The next morning, James got up around 10:00 a.m. It was Sunday morning, and I had a burning desire to go to church. I had so much to thank Him for.

"Hey, Ma, did you get any sleep? You look kind of tired." James shuffled into the kitchen in Homer Simpson boxers and a "Hard Rock Charlie" T-shirt. He rubbed his eyes and poured himself a cup of coffee.

"Good morning, sweetie," I said, giving him a hug. "I'm not awake yet. I was dreaming about eating and woke myself up at 4:00 a.m. You know me, my imagination never goes to sleep. I made some coffee then couldn't find any cream. Did you start drinking your coffee black?"

"Mom, the guys would think I'm a puss if I didn't. Besides, I have to drink it black because there are no dairy cows where we go." He winked. "The stuff they give us tasted like motor oil anyhow. Cream wouldn't help that..."

My face sank. I knew he had been deployed to Iraq, but didn't want any specifics. James must have seen the worry on my face and changed the subject. "Hey, you wanna go to church on base this morning or to that cute old church downtown you spotted?"

"You pick. What's your brand these days?"

"Haven't paid much attention to affiliations the past couple years. I figure we're all on the same team as long as they call the Lord the chief. Besides, you get what you get, out in the field. We'll take any pastor or padre they send us. They all seem to be good at helping you keep focused on the prize, the Big Guy!"

"I wish I had been that wise when I was your age. Your dad and I would have had a lot fewer arguments." I was so proud of James. Very mature for his age, at least around me.

We went to church, a Baptist church—big surprise. We were, after all, in the South. The sermon was fiery and convicting. It was not surprising that the preacher was covered in sweat by the end of the hour. Anyone delivering a message of such consequence should not take it lightly.

I read an excerpt from Ephesians yesterday morning in John's Bible study book. It was about the apostle Paul leaving the Ephesian church for the last time. He was headed back to Jerusalem. His followers cried a great deal as he departed. I wondered if being called to God makes one emotional. I used to cry while I prayed for John when he was deployed. I felt God's comfort on me as I poured my heart out to Him. But, after John died, I didn't feel God's comfort. Perhaps it's because I didn't ask for it. I was too angry and proud. But, my apathy has left me, and I again feel at home in His Word.

The following afternoon, I reluctantly headed back home. I opened the front door to the detestable quiet. Tarzan was lying under John's desk, as always. The dog hasn't barked or really made any noise at all since John died. Carrie must have taken him out to play a bit, because his toys are in the front yard.

Evening set in, and I watched the news, just to see what I had missed over the weekend. Of course, not much has changed—lots of unrest, lots of people demanding a more democratic government, lots of leaders being overthrown by angry rebels.

I drifted off to sleep, watching the trial of Mubarak...Pretty soon, I was seeing John. He was talking to me in my dream. His voice was angelic. He said the Middle East would soon rise up behind one solitary leader, peacefully uniting the Arab nations, but that peace will only last forty-two months.

I woke unsettled by the fact that John was speaking directly to me in this dream. It was different than just seeing random things. The dream, coming directly from him, made me wonder about the future— not my future, but the future of all. What was the significance of the forty-two months? Three and a half years of peace seems improbable with all that's going on in the world now.

Could I have imagined John speaking to me? I'm starting to think that these dreams are a manifestation of my fears, for James, of being alone, of unending wars and people dying. Fear for the innocent civilians of the world, caught in the crossfire of today's political scene.

I wondered if fear was keeping me from moving forward, from doing something meaningful. Maybe Dad's right, and I need to find my purpose. Why am I still here when I should have been on that bike with John? God knows I have my health, resources, and the time to do something, but what?"

I needed some direction. I was stuck in my small, dark box, too scared to look out. I decided to contact a fearless woman, someone

I knew from Bible study class many years ago when we lived in the Midwest.

Her name is Ginger. She lost her husband when she was about fifty-five, only months before retiring. Her husband had booked a safari in East Africa as a retirement gift for her before he died. When the time came to go, she took Nora, a family friend, in her husband's place. While in Kenya, they spent some time in the city. Ginger was just sickened by the vast number of street children who've been orphaned by AIDS. Two years later, the Fatherless Mission was born. They have two orphanages now and a reputation for healthy, well-educated children. The government doctors are always impressed when they go to the village and check on the kids there. They are the lucky ones, plucked from destitution and happy to be alive.

I sent Ginger an e-mail and asked if I could visit her in Kenya. I mentioned my recent widowhood and knew she'd understand me better than anyone.

I also called Teddy to see if he had any ideas about getting a cheap ticket to Nairobi. Namely, I asked him to get me one with his miles and status. He said he has half a million frequent flyer miles, which means if I went on a slow day, I could even sit up front. Teddy was happy to get me a ticket. He'd been to Kenya on business and even suggested a safari outfitter if I wanted to do a safari.

I heard from Ginger two days later. She said I could come visit, but I'd have to stay at least two weeks because the three-hour car ride to and from the Nairobi airport is dangerous. Westerners are often stopped and prompted to pay to pass. It's like a toll road, just less organized. No one technically owns or maintains the roads, and there are often guns involved.

Teddy got my ticket this week. Dad wants to go with me. He's always up for an adventure. We can scoot outta here in a month or so. That will

give Mom time to warm up to the idea of Dad and me in an impover-
ished nation. She's a worrier, and I suppose there are safer places than
the Kenyan bush to visit.

* * *

Things moved rather quickly in the weeks following. Everything, that
is, except my nights. My dreams became all the more vivid as the political scene heated up on the news and on the Internet.

A helicopter carrying a team of Navy SEALs was shot down and
all perished. James called me shortly after that happened to assure
me that it was nothing more than a lucky shot by an enemy insurgent
with a rocket launcher. He says they couldn't have known whom
they were picking off, but I find that unlikely. My son spends plenty
of time on Helos. I tried not to think about it anymore, but my heart
was breaking for the wives and mothers of those men. The bodies of
beloved husbands and sons shattered at the hands of those who call
us infidels.

The only good news, if that's what it's to be called, is that the rebels
in Libya have turned a corner and are now closing in on Gaddafi. Of
course, Israel and the Palestinians therein are once again at a standoff.
And later this week, many in the UN are planning to vote to make an
official Palestinian state, with East Jerusalem as the capital.

I don't know what that will mean to the Old City of Jerusalem, if
anything. I hope that the people there will stay tolerant of each other, if
nothing else but to keep the tourists at ease so they can sell their wares.
As segregated as the religious groups are there, they are certainly in
agreement on the significance of that tiny piece of shared real estate.

Israel seems to be preparing for what seems inevitable. They will
fight for the land they were officially given after WWII, and the slivers
of land they've carved out since then.

I wonder sometimes what would happen if our country was invaded from all sides. Would our leader lead? Or would we, average citizens, be at liberty to defend our own? I vividly remember the movie *Red Dawn*, the eighties' flick from the end of the Cold War era. Whether it was propaganda or not, it made me think, even as a teen. Would average folks be called upon to take up our own weapons and fight for the freedoms gifted by our forefathers? After all, isn't that what the Constitution so clearly imparts on us as citizens? I can only hope that never comes to pass.

One feels helpless in these uncertain times. How is one to know who is right and who is wrong, when that changes with the political scene each election year? I wonder if we are all but pets to the people we put into power. I exhaust myself just thinking about it. Moot point, all around.

13

One-Star Dork

~

I got a message from John's buddy Allen this morning. He's going to be near Baltimore and asked if he could come by and "check" on me. What that means exactly, I don't know. I certainly do not need "checking" on, not by him. Besides, tonight, Dad and I are headed for Kenya. Hurrah! I don't have time to entertain some unscrupulous, fair-weather friend.

The impending trip to Kenya has been catalyst for action. I finally decided to sell the house that John and I built together. It was a really heartbreaking decision, but I just can't keep it up by myself. The sheer size of the house makes me feel even more lonely than I thought possible. I'm here night after night, by myself, except for Tarzan, who is so depressed I can hardly stand being around him. And I scare myself silly most nights while dreaming. I haven't had a pleasant dream about John since Savannah.

With Ellie's help, I've zeroed in on a row house in Annapolis. I put in an offer, and it's been accepted (after three rounds of counteroffers and a dispute over what appeared to be built-ins). Anyhow, I'm closing on it when I get back. I didn't look at a lot of homes; I just wasn't up for it. This one was just the right size, two bedrooms. It has a sunny kitchen and a small garden. It was also well within my price range, which, I guess, made me go ahead and bite.

The phone rang. Caller ID says it's Allen. Great. I picked up. "Hello, Allen."

"Hey, Pea! Wanted to come by and see if you need anything?"

"You can hop on the tractor and mow the lawn," I suggested sarcastically. "Look, Allen, I've got a ton to do today. It's not a good time."

"Have you had lunch? I was hoping to have a decent meal. I've been working late, eating crap all week...I'm going to die of cafeteria food intake."

"Kitchen's closed, Allen. I'm going out of town tonight."

"After we eat, I'll drop you at the airport."

"Allen, this is all very cute, but, no, thank you."

"We could eat out. What's that place you and John used to go for crab cakes? I'd love a crab cake."

"Really, Allen, I've got a hundred things to do. I don't have time for a leisurely lunch."

"I'm coming anyway. I'll be there around one. I'd really like to see you."

"What, I don't have a choice?" I protested.

"Look. I need to relax, and it sounds like you *really* need to relax."

"I need nothing of the sort, Allen!"

"Come on, Pea, I'm not trying to hustle you here. I like spending time with you. You don't put up with my shit, and that's refreshing. Just lunch, OK?"

"Fine, but you are going to have to help out today. Seriously, I have a ton to do."

"Gladly. See you soon." And he hung up.

As irritated as I was, Allen *could* actually be useful to me today. I need help with the yard. I need to pack. He's been all over the world, especially Africa. He can answer questions I didn't remember to ask Ginger, like how to behave, what to wear, personal hygiene, etc. I do need a ride to the airport. Dad offered, but it is two hours out of the way, and he's got Mom to deal with. We'll be gone for three weeks, and Mom is hyperventilating already. She's called here five times in three hours. I'm considering turning my ringer off. Somebody needs to get that poor woman a paper bag.

I have all my real estate paperwork done and gave power of attorney to my accountant while I'm out of the country, in case of emergency (i.e. ransom following kidnapping, hospitalization in a foreign country, etc.). All that's left to do is to get the house in order and mail a key to Pierson, who built the house and also happens to have a real estate agent's license. I'm hoping he'll be able to find someone to love the house the way that we did. Tall order, considering the economy, but the quality of the home will definitely stand out. I'm not in a hurry to sell anyhow.

Allen beeped his horn to let me know he was outside. Good thing, since he was early, and I was in the basement. I came up the stairs in some dirty overalls and my hair in a ponytail.

"So, let's get some lunch, then you can put me to work," he said, grinning.

"Honestly, Allen, don't you have anything else to do today? Are all of your 'friends' busy or something?" He knows what I mean.

"Ha. You're funny. I told you I'm done with all that. And I'm done explaining myself to you. I've changed a bit. I don't really get a kick out of that life anymore."

"You mean, it's not cute when an unnamed forty-eight-year-old man is at a bar trying to picking up twentysomethings?"

"Hey, I don't date anyone younger than my sister..."

"And how old is she?"

"Thirty-two."

"So she was born when you had a driver's license?"

"Yep. Mom had me pretty young, then married my sister's dad ten years later."

"Enough about your fraternizing with children...I guess I am hungry. But just to be clear, this is not a date." My face was slightly annoyed and definitely serious.

"Pea, don't be offended, but you're a little uptight to appeal to me," he chided.

"Then I'm assuming you're here out of guilt?" I suggested.

"Look, I just want some seafood...Baltimore is the city of the eternal crab cake. You live near Baltimore. You were married to my buddy. Just checking in on you. Don't read into it. You won't find anything there on this end. If spending time with me makes you uncomfortable, then perhaps you're the one who's got ideas in her head." Ugh. His smile was definitely flirting. Yuck.

I headed over to John's car. "Whatever, Allen. Get in. I'll drive."

I guess I should feel lucky to have any kind of company today, instead of being by myself, which is generally the case.

We got to Koko's around two, and the parking lot was full of devoted addicts. The place is tiny, maybe fifteen tables, and Saturdays are always crowded, so we sat at the bar.

Allen asked about my trip. I shouldn't have told him where I was going. His response was as follows: "Why the hell would you go to Kenya on vacation? Are you looking to get kidnapped?"

"Very funny, Allen. I'm going to see a friend. I'll be gone for a few weeks. I've registered with the state department, so I'm sure we'll be fine."

I was having a hard time figuring out why he seemed so angry with me then realized I was reading into his behavior too much. He's about as deep as a puddle. He's probably just feeling like he should keep me out of trouble since John's not here to do it—some sort of latent protective feelings for a buddy's widow that he ignored for a year.

"Who's 'we'?" His eyebrows were furrowed and his eyes a bit squinty.

"Me and my dad. He's going with me. I'm not a big fan of solo travel, especially to a place that's so remote." Not like it's any of his business. I'm sure he could read the irritation starting in on my face, but I may have been overestimating his perceptiveness.

"Where are you going, *exactly*?" He sounded like my father when I went through a brief period of wanting to join the Peace Corps at fifteen.

"A little village about three hours' drive from Nairobi...And I'm really looking forward to this, so don't ruin it for me, please." I knew full well that he was going to ruin this for me. I should have just told him that I'm going to Canada.

"Does James know where you are going?"

"Yes, thank you very much. He had some doubts, but it's not like he never goes anywhere without a little unrest." I felt like he crossed the line. James is my son, not my husband, for cryin' out loud. I don't need to ask permission from him. If Allen doesn't butt out of my life, at this instant, I'm going to light him up so fast...Of all the...irresponsible...telling me what's safe...the guy probably has ten kids around the globe that he doesn't even know about.

"That's James's job, Pea. You know, John wouldn't like this at all. It's a bad idea. You and your ninety-year-old father traveling to a village in East Africa. Do they even have water there? What are you going to be eating? Did you ever consider they may be having you for dinner? There's a famine going on in half the countries on the African continent."

"OK, Allen, now you're just plain irritating me. My dad is not ninety. As a matter of fact, he acts a lot younger than you, less your ridiculous exploits. He's not the one chock-full of shrapnel or arthritis. You're the one who insisted on lunch today. Butt out before I spit in your beer!"

"Ouch. Nice one, Pea. Real diplomatic. Look, I'm proud of my scars. At least I don't wear them on my sleeve. But, you seem to have some wacked agenda here that I'm apparently too slow to follow. This is a stupid way to put yourself in danger. It's not just about you, Prudence. Who do you think they call in to get silly girls like you who go off to unstable countries and get swiped? Not rent-a-cops. It'll be some twenty-year-old sergeant from Texas with a wife and two kids at home worried sick about him."

"Allen, I'm going, and I'd like for you to drop it now, please. I've heard enough of your unfounded concerns. You're an inch short of a kill-joy!"

"All right. I'm done ranting. It's just that I've been there, Pea. Life is cheap." Couldn't he see that I was seething?

"So, Allen, are you mowing today or moving the stuff from the attic to the garage or will you be changing the batteries in the smoke detectors or dusting or..."

"Real work? Fine, then you're buying lunch," he said, with a curdled look.

"Deal." Not that I would have let him buy me lunch anyhow.

"Can I make a minor suggestion, please?" He wasn't actually asking my permission with that tone.

"If you do, I will launch into why you are forty-eight, alone, and miserable."

"Currently, I am not alone or miserable, smartass. Just cover your hair and leave the makeup at home. Look as awful as you possibly can. No perfume, no nail polish, no fancy shoes, and no jewelry! Wear long baggy pants and long-sleeved shirts. Just please take my advice so that I can sleep at night. And do not smile at men, especially if you are alone; they'll take it the wrong way! By the way, red hair is not exactly a great way to blend in with the locals. What the hell is going on with you?"

"Anything else, before I leave you here?"

"No."

"Good. Food's here, and you've frightened me enough already." I was excited about leaving until ten minutes ago. And he's calling me uptight! He's an absolute fun-sponge!

We finished our lunch and headed back to the house. Allen moved all the stuff I needed and even did a little dusting, but poorly. I imagine he's never dusted before. His sneezing was more bacteria than I care for in my home.

"My dad called and will be meeting me at BWI in an hour. I appreciate your help today. Really, thank you."

"I'll drop you off. It's on the way back to DC anyhow, so don't argue."

"Wasn't going to."

"Yeah, right. Not likely."

Allen dropped me off at the departure area, where Dad was waiting for me. Dad looked confused when I got out of Allen's truck and waved him off.

"Pea, who was that?" Dad asked slowly, seemingly stunned.

"John's friend Allen. He helped me get some stuff done at the house today. He feels guilty for missing John's funeral and not calling for a year, so I thought I'd abuse his guilt a little since I needed some help. He's not as bad as he used to be but highly irritating nonetheless."

"I didn't ask if you were dating him, dear. I was just wondering how you know a one-star general."

"I don't. He's a colonel, I think."

"No, Sweet Pea, he's got a star on his truck. I know what that means."

"That means that he's got something to do with the mess in the Middle East. Figures. He's so dense. It's a wonder things aren't more disastrous. He's a dork, Dad. A one-star dork."

"Well, are you ready for this trip? I couldn't be more excited. Your mother had me up my life insurance to two million. I'm not sure what she's got planned if I die, but it sounds posh."

"Yes, it does. Let's get a cup of Dunkin' Donuts coffee and toast to our impending demise!"

We got through security rather quickly, probably because we had nothing but one carry-on each. We learned to travel light from Teddy. And, thanks to Teddy, we got upgraded to first class. Thank God, because after spending the day with Allen, I needed a drink (or two). They have good wine in first class. And it's free.

14
East Africa
~

The hefty dose of Benadryl began to wear off about fifteen hours later. Apparently, I needed the sleep. Or, more likely, I should have followed the directions on the dosage chart.

Light slowly trickled into the first-class cabin. I saw it through my eyelids then slowly opened my eyes and the window shade simultaneously. The light was a vibrant pink with orange undertones. This was my first sunrise on a plane.

The flight attendant saw me stir and asked if I would like some coffee. She was stunning, with the most clear, creamy, tawny-brown skin I have ever seen. I sensed my stare was embarrassing, so I quickly asked for a regular coffee with lots of cream and two Splenda packets. She smiled and fetched the coffee along with a hot towel for my face and hands, and freshly baked pastries. I could get used to this.

I peered out the window as the plane took a turn. I could see the sunrise over the line of the horizon: the watercolor sky, the wind leaving brush marks across the curve of the earth. A reassuring gift. A reminder that He makes all things beautiful.

I decided to give myself a much-needed pep talk, which went something like this:

This trip will show me more of what I need to get my life started. I will be all right by myself. I will no longer pity myself, this pathetic widow. I will embrace her unwanted freedom. She and I will finally be civil to each other. I have twenty-one days to see what true tragedy is. I will experience life through the eyes of the poorest of the poor, children who have lost absolutely everything, only to find happiness through the efforts of an old white woman who cared enough to give her last years to them. No more excuses. I can do this.

Dad was still asleep. I was glad to have a morsel of silence before the rest of the cabin began to wake and the staff started breakfast. I knew change would come quickly now. When I return home, I will close on my row house, in Annapolis, and pare down my belongings. I can't keep everything I want to, but letting go will be part of my healing. But, first things first.

We arrived to a warm greeting and warmer weather. Ginger and her friend, Charles, a young Kenyan man, who was also the pastor in the village, were waiting past customs. It was easy to spot Ginger, an attractive, petite, white-haired woman. She didn't get to Nairobi often, as the car ride was treacherous and expensive. Soldiers at the "toll roads" always stop cars with white folks (and money) inside. Ginger wanted to get some school supplies, medicines, and personal items for the new children who were lucky enough to join them. I asked what else the children could use. Ginger suggested some soccer balls, since the kids rarely have access to them in the village. The children were currently using a ball of discarded paper covered with tape. Dad and I spotted a little shop in the market with soccer balls of all colors and lots of jerseys. We bought two of each color and ended up with ten balls and twenty jerseys. It was expensive, but five hundred dollars to entertain thirty-three children seemed like good deal to me.

We were hoping to arrive at the village three hours later. We were stopped twice by "soldiers" who guard the roads; for whom they guard is not exactly clear. It was rather odd having two older white folks and a middle-aged woman in a van with a Kenyan man driving into the brush. I guess we stood out quite a bit and looked promising to looters.

Charles had come along to translate for Ginger and to help us with our belongings. He also hoped to deter any parties looking for an easy target. The first stop was easy enough, though it rattled Dad and me a bit.

The largest of the five men stopped the car when we got off the major thoroughfare and started into the country. They all had guns. God only knows where they got them. The man asked Charles who we were and where we were going. Charles smiled widely and said, "Friends, these are good people visiting our orphanage to give gifts to the children there. They would be happy to pay for your assistance in getting there quickly. They have had a long plane ride from America. These are good people, brother."

The large man looked at his comrades, then smiled at us while peering through the windows, looking at our baggage and bags of balls. "I have three sons; would you spare a ball for them to play soccer? We also require a toll to pass. We keep the roads free from dangerous men."

Charles looked up at the man and then looked at Dad and me, asking if we had brought cash for the tolls. I handed him a fifty-dollar bill and Charles handed it to the large man. The large man smiled at us, saying, "Yes, I can see that these are good people," and motioned us to pass through the barricade. I wondered if these men shared their bounties with local officials who allowed such things. Fifty dollars is twenty-five times the daily income of those fortunate enough to have a job in Kenya.

The second stop made me think of Allen. His warnings became very real to me. About forty miles later, a less-friendly group of young men, several looking no more than fourteen years of age, stopped our van. It was dusk by now, and there was no one around to see us being taken out of the vehicle and patted down. They took all the cash from Dad's wallet and asked Charles for my pearl earrings. No smiles. No niceties. No chitchat.

I quickly took off my earrings. The apparent leader then put his hand out for the pearls. I should have remembered not to wear jewelry. That was stupid. Allen said no embellishments. They searched our van, opened all our bags, and took a couple soccer balls and four jerseys for themselves. Had I known soccer balls were such popular booty for land pirates, I would have bought more for the trip. At this rate, we only had six balls left for the kids and sixteen jerseys.

Two of the teen soldiers examined us closely, in a line, about ten feet from the van. The other five rifled through our things. Dad and I were holding hands at this point. We were both trying to keep calm. Ginger and Charles looked indifferent. This was an exercise they were very familiar with. The smallest of the armed teens found my makeup bag and took my lipstick, toothpaste, hair products, and a blue box of Tampons. I doubt that kid has any idea what tampons are for, but if he does, I imagine he will be gifting them to his mother and sisters later that night or selling them to locals. It seems that toiletries were not widely available in the bush.

After some deliberation, they told Charles that we were free to go but that it would not be wise for us to tell anyone what had happened there. Charles smiled and agreed, then thanked them for their kindness. I was hoping to avoid such kindness for the remainder of the trip.

Finally, we began to see the flicker of lights over the village. The children saw our headlights coming toward them and knew it was the wealthy Americans, who would, of course, be bringing them gifts. I felt bad for not having more for them, but Ginger assured me that those children are the most gracious hosts we would ever encounter and the balls and jerseys would be greatly used and appreciated.

Fifty or more little ones were running alongside the van. They were orphans and village children, brown and beautiful, smiling and chanting something very welcoming. I couldn't hold back my tears. That moment was worth the trip in itself. I felt as if I were the luckiest woman on the continent. All of those children, with absolutely nothing of consequence, were so happy to meet me.

Guilt overwhelmed me. It was so selfish to think that my life was anything but year after year of blessings. I had everything in the world compared to these little ones. As the tears streamed down my face, I prayed to the Most High, my Heavenly Father, for this experience and for His faithfulness to me, despite my undeservedness.

For the first time in a little over a year, I felt gracious, thankful for my lot. I would find my joy again, permanent joy, not just shards of memories that I needed to sleep to feel. I wonder if John could see me here, feeling full and thankful for my life, even in my loss of him. I have to think that this idea may have come from John.

DAY ONE, IN THE VILLAGE

"Miss Prudent, Miss Prudent, wake up!" There were six little brown eyes staring at me from the other side of the mosquito net. Creamy, chocolate-pudding complexions, deep and glowing. "We eat now, Miss Prudent. Please come now!" They all had very short hair, kept that length, I suppose, for hygienic purposes. With thirty-three kids to care for, custom hairdos are probably hard to come by around here.

But, that didn't keep the little girls from wanting to braid *my* hair. They were fascinated with the color. They had never seen a fiery red-head (I didn't have the heart to tell them that I had been a mousy blonde just a few months prior). Besides, I was feeling bold for going to Africa on a whim. I felt like a redhead, which is almost as good as being one, in my estimation.

Breakfast is a big production around here, not because of an elaborate four courses but because of the sheer energy it takes to feed so many children at once. The orphanage is set up like a dormitory. The kitchen is an outdoor room made of cement blocks, a door opening, and a window (i.e., big hole in the wall) for ventilation.

The dining area is made up of five long, plain wooden tables made in the village. Each table seats eight children. Overhead, a large tarp keeps them shaded or dry, if it happens to ever—God willing—rain. The plates and forks are carved of wood by locals. The beverage is clean water. Goat milk is expensive, and soda is a luxury that few can afford. Ditto for coffee. Ginger said anytime they want to hold a village meeting, all they have to do is start a rumor that coffee will be served. It's so ironic that much of the coffee in the world comes from Africa, yet few Africans villagers can afford the exquisite, acidic buzz.

The village was blessed with a new well that provided the only clean water in a five-mile radius. Ginger's church, Providence, had donated the well and also the van that we arrived in. The children here have it much better than their countrymen, women, and children living in the Nairobi slums facing the real possibility of death, starvation, disease, and abuse on a daily basis.

The cool morning was short-lived. A little one named Mary sat and braided my hair for almost two hours. It was nice to have it off my neck. It was only ten o'clock, and I was sweating already. I'd hoped to see my perfect braids, but mirrors are scarce. No need for vanity here. Ironic, since all of the children are so beautiful and have no idea how much they are.

There is one female child here in particular who would be quite a head turner stateside. Some talent scout would see her high cheekbones, flawless skin, and unusual, almond-shaped, transparent brown-green eyes, and sweep her up into a life of photo shoots and commercials, makeup and manicures. I wonder if a life at the orphanage might be better. At least here the children can be children.

I was cleaning up the dishes after breakfast when a stout woman with a caramel freckled face and dimples sashayed into the kitchen. She had an orange bandanna on her head and some brightly colored tribal fabric wrapped around her curvy body like a bandage dress. She took one look at me, and I knew I looked ridiculous.

As she began to tie an apron on, she snickered, "Sweetheart, aren't you hot in that getup? Don't worry about with the men in this village. They're all lookin' for work, not a honey. It's gonna be hot today. You may wanna peel off a layer or two." She picked up a towel and began to dry the wooden tableware that I had just rinsed off, humming the theme song to *Deliverance*.

I felt like an idiot, like one of those pre–civil rights old white women who for some reason think that black men are always looking for trouble. I don't think that at all. I just don't want to bring any more attention to myself, and I don't know all the ins and outs of the male/ female caste system here. I finally got up the courage to respond to her spot-on estimation.

"Yeah, I probably overdid it packing all of these long sleeves and pants. I just didn't know what to expect. I'm probably a little paranoid after the shakedown we got on the way here. I thought they were going to light us up, right there, and leave our bodies to scavengers!"

"No need to wear a tent. You ain't in Ali Baba, honey," she said with a wide grin on her face. I smiled. She was just teasing me. I was relieved.

"I'm Pea. I'm here with my dad. Have you met him yet? He's the balding seventy-something with the physique of a marathoner."

"He's your papa? That man could make a mosquito feel fat! Where's your momma, dear? Is she still living?"

"Yes, but she wasn't invited. I just wanted to spend some time with my dad. Besides, he's very physical and practical. He loves manual labor. The man is an absolute machine. He'll be able to help out much more than my mom would have. She's not into heat or dust or labor. Dad's built for speed. She's built for comfort. We'll be here two weeks and on safari for about a week. Are you a permanent fixture around here? You sound southern to me, maybe...Alabama?"

"No, baby, I'm Nora, from Mississippi. The kids all call me Nana. You can call me Nana, too. I'm an old friend of Ginger's. Ginger's husband, Herb, was like a big brother to me. My mama was his wet nurse and practically raised him. People did that in the South back then. Anyhow, when Herb married Ginger, they moved to Jackson. Herb stayed in touch with mama. He left her some money in his will. Enough cheese to put my son through medical school at Howard University. He's a doctor in Atlanta now, and his wife is too. I'm a mostly retired nurse. I spend a month helping Ginger out here, every year. She and I are old friends now, although, she is a good ten years older than I am! I'm turning sixty this year. Can you believe that? I don't think I look a day over 45!"

Nana took a breath and continued, "I love it here. It's kind of nice to be around so much brown. Growing up in the South when I did was tough. Saw a lot a stuff that I can't bring myself to repeat. Being here feels like family. My ancestors were from East Africa." Her smile was infectious, but her life had been difficult. I wondered where her son's father was.

"Is your son's father in your life now?" I asked curiously.

"No honey, that man can rot in hell for all I care, and he may well be! I haven't talked to him since my son was two. We were married. My mom warned me not to get involved with him. But that man was so good lookin'! Like a movie star! He could smooth talk the skin off a peanut!" Nana was giggling. He must have been something because her cheeks were pink just talking about him. Nana shook her head and rolled her eyes. "I tried my best to stay with him, but he was in the sack with every loose brown Sally in town. It was humiliating. I took my baby boy and moved in with mama. She watched my son in the evenings so I could go to nursing school after work. I finished in three years, and got a job at the local hospital. There weren't many black R.N.s back then but I worked hard and the patients loved me. I was managing the whole geriatric unit by the time I was forty. Later, when my son was in high school, the bus would drop him off at the hospital after school. He'd sit behind the desk and look at charts with me. He learned a lot about medicine that way and decided to be a doctor. I hope he'll come here with me someday. He could do a lot of good here. There are plenty of street kids out there in the slums. The ones we take in here at the orphanage don't have anybody. They would have died if Ginger didn't find them." Nana sighed, "So, what's your story, Sweet Pea?"

"Hmmm. Well, I'm here for a reality check, I suppose. My dear husband was killed last year in an accident, and I've been feeling sorry for myself ever since. My dad suggested I find God's plan for my life, so here I am, quickly getting focused on what's real and the fact that I'm a very spoiled woman who is entirely self-centered. I'm here to work on that."

"Sounds like you made some progress. Didn't you just get here last night?" Nana asked, while fanning her face with her hands.

"Yes. This trip is working better than I could have imagined. Would you believe I've been sitting around my enormous house for a year, being angry, sulking, instead of praising God for what I do have, like my son, my folks, my brother, and my friends? I can't believe what a pill I've been!"

Nana laughed. She probably knows lots of stuck-up, gilded white women just like me.

In came a stampede of little bare feet to lighten up our rather heavy conversation.

"Miss Prudent, Miss Prudent! My chance to braid your hair! Then we play soccer!" The three little sets of eyes from this morning were watching Nana and me discuss a whole lot for two women who have known each other for a total of twenty minutes. Nana just says what she thinks, and, at this point in my life, frankness is just about my favorite trait.

* * *

"OWWW! Please don't pull so hard, ladies!...My hair comes out easily!"

A little one named Agnes patted me on the head, laughing, while trying to console me, "Sorry, Miss Prudent, your hair too soft! Hard to braid! We get you ready for church!"

The strange thing is that pain incites laughter around here, and the kids found my low tolerance for pain rather funny.

After some braids, we went to church in the village, then played a very, very long (think World Cup) game of soccer. I was beat. We had a light dinner with the kids then I needed sleep. The time difference hit me hard. Next thing I knew, the sun was up and the eyes on me again. It was time for breakfast, but I wasn't hungry. I pulled the blanket over my head and went back to sleep.

Sleeping here is easier than I thought it would be. No phones ringing. No TV. Just some great white noise. The hum of those large industrial lights outside the girls' dorm was like a lullaby. I was just happy to have slept soundly, even if I wasted eighteen hours.

DAY TWO, KENYA, EAST AFRICA

I spent the morning cleaning up with Nana. She is someone I could get attached to very quickly, a wise woman with a real knack for revealing the obvious to a knucklehead like me.

Here, things are simple. The way they do things makes sense considering the climate and what's available at any given time, which is never much. The kids here take baths in metal tubs we'd use to keep beer cold back home. And the water from the well is too precious for baths. It's used for cooking first. So the water for baths is a little murky. And after bath time, the used water (used by quite a few, actually) goes on the crops. Water does not get dumped out here. And, brushing teeth does not involve water, ever. I got my head bit off this morning for doing just that. Oops.

Very few people own cars and trucks. Ginger has one of only four vehicles in the area. Vehicles are expensive, and gas is hard to get and pricey, so driving is a luxury. If only we could conserve gas the way they do here. But, I guess if there were any industry and folks here had good jobs and needed to get to work, then vehicles would be more accessible and common. However, since there are no jobs, and the infrastructure is seriously corrupt, change may never come.

There is no idleness here to speak of. The kids here have chores. They help plant the food and maintain it throughout the season. They also clean their dorms on the same day each week. The only children to get off the hook are the oldest, who are studying for the university exam. They spend the week at the private high school nearby. Because of the focus on education here, they are brighter than average and are used to intense study. Ginger was excited to introduce me to them.

"Prudence, I want you to meet the children who hope to attend university in the spring. There are three. Two boys and a girl." She smiled at me as if there was something for us to discuss. And there was. She mentioned when I booked the trip that there was a need that I may be able to help with. A new need, something that didn't seem possible until recently.

We started across the small orphanage campus into the main building. The three were at a table, waiting to meet me. Ginger and I sat down with them. They wanted me to know what they intended on studying. One by one, they told their stories, with such impressive English language skills and vocabulary.

Ginger began to explain her fortunate problem, "These three took the university exam last month, and all passed, with very high scores, which has created a bit of an issue. With all of the mouths to feed, medical, and the building projects to house new orphans, we haven't any savings to send these precious ones on to higher education. University here is much more reasonable than in the United States. A student can have a high level of instruction, meals, a place to live, and books, for about six hundred dollars a year. The three of these kids could attend a good university in the city nearby for eighteen hundred, total, per year. Please prayerfully consider helping them do this. They have worked so hard."

I could see my purpose in this trip unfolding. I would fall hard for these three, and their future would depend on my generosity. Of course, as soon as I looked at them, I had already decided to pay for their education. A little over a hundred a month was not enough to make a noticeable dent in my income, now that I'm downsizing. I will be selling most of our furniture and probably John's fancy car, which will net about forty-five thousand, even used. I was planning on buying a knockabout car anyhow, since I won't have parking at my new place in Annapolis. A parking space would have added about eighty grand to the cost of a row house in Annapolis, and the whole purpose of being there is to walk everywhere, so selling John's fancy car is more of a necessity than anything. That car is a cream puff. It would never put up with parallel parking, rain, snow, or dings. It was made for a cushy garage, not city living. Getting rid of it could educate quite a few eager minds.

So, after these three graduate, I suspect there will be more hungry minds to follow. I hope to send them as well. I have lots of ideas now. Perhaps I could talk to my accountant about setting up a nonprofit. I don't know if I have enough money to do this, but I know that Dad will pitch in after being here. We can create a scholarship fund. Then I could also then make contributions to John's favorite organizations, Wounded Warriors, Catholic Outreach International, and the Archdiocese of the Armed Forces. This would make John very happy.

Maybe John's life insurance policy will serve a greater purpose. I can live off our retirement, and really put the life insurance money to excellent use. I have a few expenditures that I can do without, and after moving, I won't have that mortgage each month. And I'll cancel John's wine club membership, which is $1800 a year. I have 180 bottles in the basement, which should last me at least until I join John in Glory.

I'll learn to be thrifty. Only buy what I must have, on sale. I did some bookkeeping when James was in school and could easily manage a small nonprofit if Teddy will set up everything on my computer. I'll need help with investing the money so that it can go further. Maybe friends and family will make donations in John's memory. Maybe Ginger's entire lot can go to college!

I can't believe I've been here less than forty-eight hours and have had such breakthroughs. I feel like a new woman. A new, strong, focused, driven woman. I always wondered if I could do something on my own. I never really pursued anything because we were moving every few years. And, I guess I used James as an excuse for the fact that I never did finish college after getting pregnant. I just relied on John for everything. What a burden I must have been to him! I will make him proud of me. Maybe I should finish college. Come to think of it, I never really finished anything. John was always the chronic overachiever. I was happy just to wear his rank around. Lots of officers' wives did it. Back then, it was just the norm.

I hadn't seen Dad since breakfast, so I took a walk around the village until I spotted the glare off of his bald head. He was repairing a roof, a rusted piece of scrap metal. No Rust-Oleum in Kenya, I guess. It would be such a blessing to leave this village in better shape than when we arrived. I started to hand Dad tools. Too bad nobody has a blowtorch around here. That would certainly make the repairing of metal roofs a more feasible task.

Building materials are scarce in these remote villages. People use what they can find, mostly materials that others have discarded. I wonder if Charles will take us to a nearby town to buy some supplies. I still have my cash, quite a bit, and I can't think of what else we might use it for, except for tips and things on the safari next week. I was planning to pay cash for the whole thing, but I think I can charge it. I'll pay for Dad, too, since he lost his shorts on the "toll road."

Charles agreed. This would be fun. He borrowed a little homemade trailer to pull behind the van that we will fill up and bring back with building materials. This will be the first purchase for John's nonprofit.

DAY THREE, KENYA

I got a telegram today. It was from Allen.

P - You in one piece? Have e-mail there? Shoot James and myself a note pls.
- Allen

I wrote a return note and sent it back with the messenger, a kid about ten years old, who brought the message by foot—from where, I don't know. I gave him a few dollars, and asked him to take this back and send:

A - You are very nosey. Could not be better. No e-mail. Power outage. Tell James I love him and will call when I can.
- P

I have to say that it is nice to have someone concerned about me, actually two people, I guess. I'll have to debrief them both when I get back. I'm sure I can guilt Allen into supporting my new legacy for John. Maybe he could pass the info around to their old army buddies, and they'll give, too.

Nana and I are spending every morning together. She and I clean up breakfast, then do laundry, which seems to take hours. Things get dirty here so quickly. Each child has three sets of clothes: one for play, one for school, one for church. When it's warm, they all wear flip-flops, even to school. Flip-flops last quite a long time considering the minimal cost. I wish I had some myself. My leather sandals aren't faring well.

Dad and Charles are really putting a dent in the villager's Harry Homeowner projects. I still have about eight hundred bucks in cash left. And with the going rate of three dollars per day for a laborer, we had plenty of money to hire locals to help with these projects. They were delighted at the chance to earn some money. They work so hard. Dad and Charles made four more trips for supplies this week.

NOT SURE WHAT DAY IT IS, KENYA

Time has started to go by rather quickly. I've been able to spend about three hours each afternoon helping the younger students do their homework and another hour or so showing them how to knit. This is fun.

The kids had no need for the thick woolen socks I was making, so we started knitting soakers (woolen undies) for the babies in the village. They don't have diapers, and wool is very absorbent and inexpensive, so the soakers were accepted with great enthusiasm. We managed to knit about fifteen pairs of soakers, some off-white, some brown, some purple, and the rest light orange, all dyed with root veggies. One size fits all, since the babies here are tiny compared to the standard seven-to-ten-pounders in the United States.

I discussed my nonprofit idea with Ginger. She spent quite a bit of time with me going over the basics of starting a nonprofit. It seems very doable. She's excited and pleased to have inspired such an endeavor. The details were all that needed attention at this point. Ginger said that it only took her a month to get all the paperwork taken care of on the US side. This included all the tax info, exemption numbers, bank account, and a financial plan to put her capital to work, earning interest to add to the capital.

There will be absolutely no overhead in John's nonprofit. But what should I call it? I was lying in bed that night sans mosquito net, staring at the bottom of the bunk above. I need some ideas...Hmmm...The John Brandt Foundation...The John and James Brandt Foundation...JJL Foundation...Two Js Foundation...The No Longer A Psychotic Widow Foundation...Finally Got My Head Out of The Toilet Foundation...I Haven't Had a Nightmare in Three Weeks Foundation! Maybe I could ask James what he thinks. He's got to have something a little more creative than what I can generate here. I think I need some sleep...foundation...

15

Crap Trap

~

DAY ONE, TANZANIA

Dad and I left for a five-day safari, next door in Tanzania. We decided to go ahead and see another country, since we are already here in Africa. Like Kenya, Tanzania is full of warm, curious folks.

Our little motorcade of four Americans, two Canadians, and a British couple made its way out of one beautiful (but desolate) land into another, called Northern Tanzania, home of the Serengeti. From there, we took a prop plane to Lobo airstrip to meet our new guides and their vehicles.

I have heard of the striking sunset skies on the Serengeti. There aren't names for such lavish colors. We entered the camp early that evening, in antique Land Rovers. I could see the yurt huts waiting for us, and the corresponding smell of dinner. I haven't had food with flavor in nearly two weeks. Food at the orphanage is strictly for nutritional value. Flavor is secondary. But tonight, I smell bread and some kind of meat, and I see the fruit and rice dishes. The Pavlovian response was immediate. I was salivating by the bucketful.

Dad was excited, too. He has lost some weight already, and Mom will not be happy about that. She likes it when he's a little heavier. When he's a twig, it makes Mom's soft body appear chubby.

The pool was an oasis in the red earth. The sleeping quarters (high-end yurts) surround the pool. Beyond the pool is a veranda that juts out over the side of the hill, with miles of views. The yurts are set up for couples, but Dad and I each have our own. The bathing area is communal. I can't wait to submerge myself in water. It's been awhile since I completely washed off. I can't imagine I smell much like a girl now. John used to say that after being in Ranger School, stink is only relative. Once everybody smelled bad, nobody noticed. But, I think our little motorcade is well on our way to being highly offensive.

That night, I sat up until after midnight on the veranda. I looked out at the never-ending night sky full of lights, stars brighter than I'd ever seen. As one star shot out across the sky, I wished for the company of my John. The dark is cold here. I imagined his fuzzy chest on my back. I haven't felt really warm at night since he left me.

DAY TWO, NORTHERN SERENGETI, TANZANIA

The painted sunrise gave way to heat and dust. I could hear the clanking of pots and bottles of water as the men prepared our day's supplies. We would spend the first part of the day in a caravan and the later part on foot. October is a good month to see the wildebeests migrate en masse near the Mara River. If we're lucky, we may get to walk alongside some elephants today or go for an evening drive to quietly watch a cheetah settling into sleep.

Nothing could have prepared me for the excitement of this morning. We started with a huge breakfast spread. All were readying cameras and lenses. We looked like a bunch of tourists dressed up like Dr. Livingston.

The Canadians looked the coolest, but the Brits were the most relaxed. I'm sure they were not on their first safari. Then there's an American couple, empty nesters who don't like each other much. Lastly, there was Dad and me. Dad is always up for anything. But I must have looked a little nervous. I am not a fan of animals that can consume me in two bites. Not sure why I'm here. I don't even like going to the zoo.

There are no windows on the Land Rovers. The sides are entirely open, less a bar or two. At any time, a lion or tiger or confused wildebeest could mistake Dad or me for a fast-food drive-through. Do all large animals see colors? Maybe red hair really isn't a good idea for me. Hopefully the wildebeest and the bull are not related. I'll wear a hat.

I ate too much. I kept putting food in my mouth to try to relax my slight bout of paranoia. The food was just too good to pass up after all that rice and corn at the orphanage. I suddenly had to pee or something...which made me wonder about the bathroom accommodations during the outing today. Perhaps I should have left that extra plate of fruit alone and limited my coffee intake.

The coffee was just too good to stop. Seriously, I think the beans were picked last week, dried, then roasted this morning. I would have traveled to Tanzania exclusively for the coffee. But my bladder was already giving me notice that four cups of coffee was overdoing it. Crap. I mean Pee. Cramp! Ugh. Why does coffee have to be a diuretic?

I camped out in the bathroom for the next half hour until Isabel, the female half of the British couple, knocked on the door of the froufrou outhouse (essentially a bathhouse complete with copper fixtures, rain showerheads, and, thank the good Lord, toilets that flush!).

"Dearest, are you all right in there? It's near time to go. Take a Pepto, and you'll be brilliant by lunchtime!" Isabel sounds like an older Mary Poppins.

"I'll be out in a minute, Isabel. I think I ate too much fruit last night at dinner." Which was a serious understatement. I think I ate two or more pounds of fruit...and I have no idea what fruits they were—perhaps the African equivalent to prunes.

"Darling, your papa said you've been eating orphans' rations for two weeks. Why ever would you do such a thing, dearest? It's no wonder your poor tummy is a mess. Can I fetch you some cold water? What can I do to help?" Isabel asked in an empathetic tone.

"Just freshening up here. Will be out in a sec." Or an hour. If she'd just give me some privacy, I could finish what I've started here without an audience. At forty-three, I still can't stand anyone hearing my gassy outbursts. When I was a kid and trying to go to the bathroom at school, I'd always get stage fright when someone else was in the other bathroom stalls. I couldn't go; I just froze up. I'd end up bending all the way over and grabbing my toes, trying to hurry the stuff up so that I could get back to class without anyone noticing my twenty-minute bathroom break.

When I was a really little tot, I'd avoid the toilet room altogether and pee myself as soon as the school bus dropped me off in the afternoon. My mom could have killed me. I did that almost every afternoon. I just couldn't make it down the street to the house. I had to go. Right then and there. That yearlong habit was enough to justify my mom's short fuse with me for the rest of my entire life.

Finally (thank you, God!), I joined the others who were waiting (impatiently) in the vehicles. We sped off into the brush, literally. There are no speed limits here, only bumps and gullies that dot the makeshift path for trucks. My camera and extra batteries were ready for action. I put my hair in a floppy hat that I got for free at San Diego Padres game years ago and an olive-green safari-style shirt that I got at the Gap before the trip. Teddy suggested a shirt from Orvis, but my Gap shirt was under ten bucks, and I don't need padded leather shoulders, as I am not using a rifle for hunting. I'm just being a tourist.

Everyone wore khakis and hiking books. I brought the hikers that I'd taken to Normandy with John and James. We went for the sixtieth anniversary of the D-Day invasion. I wonder where the live bullet John found on Omaha Beach ever went? God love the French. At the airport, they searched my bag and left the bullet in there, along with the stash of Cuban cigars that John purchased in Paris.

Anyhow, the morning was off to a great start. The guide in our Land Rover Defender scanned the beautiful orange, brown, gray, and yellow desert with his binoculars. Moments later, he signaled the driver. He had spotted a group of over five hundred wildebeests getting a drink in the river about half a mile ahead on our left. We prepared the cameras and braced ourselves as the vehicles bounced about en route to the mammals straight ahead. They heard our approach, then started to run, a little scattered, alongside us. It was the most thrilling experience. The drumming of heavy hooves on the ground! These majestic animals were only a few feet from the vehicle! Thank God for memory cards. I think we each snapped more than twenty photos. We couldn't believe our luck!

We followed alongside the wildebeests for nearly a mile before the river became wider and too deep for us to cross. The animals slowed and began to cross the river to the opposite bank. Perhaps they were convinced that we were not out to hunt them. Not like it mattered. There were plenty of hungry cats nearby watching, too, waiting for a calf to stray from its mother. What did they think of us? What a funny animal we must have seemed, with cameras flashing and wheels spinning, goofy hats, and varying shades of hair and skin.

We were able to observe an elephant pride later before heading over to lunch in a nearby Massai village. The villagers had many things to sell to us or to use for trading. What a friendly bunch of natives, curious and full of questions, yet steeped in their own traditions, without concern over our influence. We must have looked silly to them, too. Our group of Westerners was obviously wealthy enough to travel to Africa, yet instead of adorning ourselves in saturated color and beaded splendor, we wore baggy clothes the color of dirt and no jewelry.

The tribesmen and women looked beautiful in their traditional dress, brightly colored togas with intricate patterns. The men and women had short, neatly kept hair. They were average height and lean, with deep shale skin and nearly black eyes. Their teeth were white and beautiful. Makes me wonder how Europeans ended up with all the yellow snaggletooth chompers. I guess modernity has its drawbacks.

After lunch and entertainment by the local Massai folks, we headed back to the camp. We were all anxious to clean up before our white-tablecloth dinner and champagne. After dinner, Dad and I found ourselves sitting on a nearby boulder to watch the orange balloon in the sky settle into a purple river of clouds.

I didn't feel tired, just anxious for privacy, hoping for the twilight arms of my beloved. I can't see him. But, while I dream of him, my arm hairs stand on end, like his presence was obvious to my spirit, the part of me that would forever be part of him, even though the physicality of our love is over. I climbed into bed. The next thing I knew, the sun was rising. No John.

The next morning was better. I took it easy on the fruit and steered clear of any fibrous fodder. We took a long hike, with escort from our new tribal friends, who would protect us from any animal who may mistake us for luncheon meat later. We returned for more coffee and to spend some time in the beautiful pool made of the natural surrounding rocks. This place was like no other. Each yurt, the bathhouse, and even the pool were hidden from plain sight, as if they had sprouted between boulders. The camp was built into a large hill. Animals can't see the camp from below, so they nose around the base of the hill, most of the day and night, trying to figure out where the strange-smelling human animals were hiding.

Around lunchtime, I fell asleep by the pool for an hour. Thank God for sunscreen. Otherwise, I would have been barbecued. It's hot today (again). Julius, the head safari guide, who speaks quite good English, suggested we take a side trip to the beach tomorrow to cool off a little. There is a very long stretch of secluded beach that he says is quite beautiful. There are no hotels or homes there, just dunes. He also suggested Zanzibar for shopping, but I feel uneasy in large crowds, especially in places where I stick out like a sore thumb.

Most everyone retired to their quarters to lay under the fans then resurfaced for afternoon tea. Tea was very formal, with lots of small finger foods, but no cucumber sandwiches or scones. I actually have no idea what I was eating. But, it was sweet and delicious, and I ate too much of it.

By the time evening rolled around, I found myself outside waiting for the sunset. I was almost two hours early but wasn't in a hurry. I sat on a boulder the size of Rhode Island and watched giraffes nuzzle each other's necks. It was interesting to see them actually hug each other with their necks, but I suppose humans can hug each other with their bodies, too. I guess we just got lucky that way. I suppose we have quite a few options that common mammals don't because of their bodies' designs. Yet one more thing to thank Him for—variety! I giggled as I pictured John and myself intertwined in ways that would make me blush, even now.

When dinner came, we were all still stuffed from the "tea." However, once the platters of meats and breads, local specialties, and bottles of South African wine started to make their way to the table, everyone gave in and just started eating. You just feel guilty for not being hungry since nearly 60 percent of the people on this continent are severely malnourished.

Tonight, we all dined together by the pool at a tabletop made of a single slab of stone on large wooden trestles. Isabel and Henry were discussing the most exciting animal appearances they've seen, and of course, the running with the wildebeests, which will remain in our memories as the most exhilarating experience of the safari to date.

Henry spent time in Africa, primarily Northern Africa, with his father, as a young lad. His father was a commander in the British army during the Anglo-Egyptian War (1951-1952) and later served as an advisor to the British government on North African affairs and politics.

As a young boy, Henry was smitten with this continent. He had lost his mother to polio when he was just six. So, he traveled with his father and his tutor quite extensively in Africa. He met Isabel many years later at King's College, both studying international politics. They've been together ever since. This trip has them seeing various parts of Africa, with no plans to return to Dover until Christmas.

Henry and Isabel are in their early seventies. They gaze at each other with such affection. They are always touching each other, on the hand, the face, the arm, the waist. I imagined John and I would have been like that in twenty-five years, had we the chance.

The Canadians, Jen and Gavin, are both quite tall and thin. They are both about fifty and have three children, all college-age or older. They are on safari to celebrate their twenty-fifth anniversary. They hope to meet some locals and really get a taste of East Africa. They get along like best friends. I haven't seen so much as a cross word between them the past few days. John would have liked them. I could see us taking a trip up to Toronto to visit them, if they would have been fortunate enough to meet John. They are very liberal, but Gavin has a reticent interest in guns, which he's not yet indulged. Gavin has never actually held a gun. John would have loved to have helped him with that. I can just see John taking Gavin to Duffy's Gun Shop then the shooting range. I'm not sure if they have that kind of thing in Canada. Gavin said that firearms are not readily available there.

There is one other couple here, Americans. They prefer to dine alone for dinner each night. They aren't terribly pleasant to be around. There is something to be said about dinner by candlelight overlooking the desert. Very romantic. But, I suspect they are not taking advantage of the moonlight, or the flicker of the candles, or the delicious South African wine. From what Isabel tells me (she seems to be in the know around here), the couple, Lane and Junior (that's really his first name), don't seem to be on speaking terms.

How funny to vacation with someone you dislike so much. Isabel said Lane and Junior's kids surprised them with the safari trip for Lane's sixtieth birthday, not realizing that they were going to announce their plans to divorce the following week, following mediation with their joint attorney. Too bad. I can't imagine being a grouchy prude under these conditions. There isn't much else to do in the afternoon but lie by the pool or indulge in some "Sky Rockets in Flight"...I know what I'd be doing if my dreamy John were here...However, I need to stop thinking about all of that stuff, since I am, alas, alone, at my peak.

DAY THREE, THE BEACH, NORTHERN TANZANIA

Dad and I went on a short trip this morning to spot some lions nearby devouring a bloodied mound of fly-covered flesh. Whatever it was, it had longish legs, maybe a zebra or young wildebeest? Definitely not a giraffe. We returned around lunchtime. Julius suggested we head for the beach, so we took our lunches to go and headed out with the two amiable couples. Lane and Junior apparently had no intention of seeing each other in a swimsuit. Another guide took Lane to a nearby village to purchase a handmade rug, and Junior stayed at the camp to read *Barron's* and sulk.

We made it to the beach by midafternoon. I think they must have filmed a few movies here. This particular beach seems familiar although grander than any American beach I've seen. The dunes are even higher than those on Lake Michigan—three or more stories high. There were no tourists, no hotels, no cheesy knickknack shops, and no saltwater taffy. This place is simply the ocean at its finest, free of debris and human hands. I wonder if this is where they filmed the last scene in *The Constant Gardener.*

The vast waters are a sapphire blue, and there are sharks in these warm waters, according to Julius. He says that he doesn't go out past his knees and suggested we follow suit.

I just can't imagine, after seeing all of this coastal water, why anyone hasn't started a filtration system to make the seawater fit to drink. With all of the waterborne illness here in Africa and thousands of people dying from bacteria-ridden water each week, why aren't there giant tubes running from the coasts, inland, carrying clean water?

So few people here have their own wells. Generally, communities share one, but it is often miles away, and the water must be carried back somehow. Water is, unfortunately, heavy, and therefore, people can only carry so much. No one here has a water tanker. If anyone really cared about what is going on in this part of the world, then water would travel like oil, under the ground, in clean pipelines, into community wells that could be treated, if needed. Why isn't anyone doing this yet?

Africa is so beautiful and frustrating. I wish our government would stop sending condoms that no one uses and start building water pipelines so that people can have healthy water here. I know there must be ways to make seawater drinkable. If I only had a microbiology degree and some clout! Being a nobody is a definite disadvantage at times.

We returned much later than expected. Dinner had been waiting for us for almost two hours. However, we ate it anyway and were happy to have full bellies. All of us had sunburns, except for Dad. He looked more like a flounder, white on the front and dark on the back. Must have something to do with bushy chest hair.

We have only two days left before getting on that fleahopper and heading back to Kenya. Although I loved the animals, the untouched earth, and the skies here, I was missing the children and Nana. I missed our morning talks over kitchen duty. I've had enough small talk with the others in our camp, and Dad is, I think, tired of hearing about me missing John. He's ready to move on. I wish I were, too.

DAY FOUR, TANZANIA

Today we had access to a telephone for the first time. I called the only number I had for James. I have no idea where he is. For all I know, he could have been on the other side of a sand dune at the beach. However, I have a feeling that he might be in Libya. We are there, fighting alongside the French, the British, and the rebels, against Gaddafi. I can't imagine why James would be there, as he does not speak Arabic. I imagine he has other talents that I would prefer not to know about. I dialed a long, strange number. Two minutes and five beeping sounds later, I heard a gruff voice answer. Oops. I asked the gruff voice for James Brandt then waited while someone went and found him.

"JAMES! Honey, I didn't think this number would work. And please tell your XO that I'm sorry for calling the emergency line. I didn't know I was calling him. He sounded a little irked." There was static on the line, and I could hear people in the background.

"No worries, Mom. I've been thinking about you and hoping you are safe and having a great time with Grandpa. Allen was here for a short time to brief us on some stuff. He mentioned he saw you before you left. What's up with that?"

"Nothing. Seriously. I asked him to help me pack up a few things, and he wanted a crab cake, so we grabbed one at Koko's and then he dropped me at the airport."

"Sounds like a date, Mom." I could see him grinning as he teased me.

"Yuck. No way. I'm not ready to date, and even if I was, I certainly wouldn't date someone that has been so *free* with himself, if you know what I mean."

"Uh, yeah. Got it. Thought so. Just had to clarify. Mom, you can start going out, you know. It's been long enough. Think about it, OK? Who's the dude from church that was drooling all over you? Maybe you should call him or something."

"Or something? What, like, *text* him? I can't even figure out how to program your number in my phone. Really, I need some help."

"Uh, Mom, I gotta go, we're heading out soon. I love you."

"You too, baby. Good-bye." Then more static. Who knows when I'll hear that precious voice again? He doesn't have leave again until Christmas. It was nice to talk to him, but now I'm wondering where he is and where he and his guys are "heading out" to. Is it dangerous where he is going? I think I'll go get Dad so we can sit down and pray together for James. I will also need to pray for some peace in my head, as I am now worried about yet another something I can't control.

Over dinner that night, I told the Brits and Canadians about my idea for a scholarship fund for the children at the orphanage. They all seemed very excited and wanted to know how to help. I think they will be the first to get e-mails about the foundation. Maybe they will want to participate or even visit the orphanage themselves sometime. It's a wonderful opportunity to send abandoned children on to white-collar jobs. These former orphans will be healers, or economists, or pastors, or humanitarian workers—whatever they feel led to do. There is no limit to the impact those kids could have on their country as educated professionals from the most humble of upbringings. God will use them for great things; I just know it.

We took an evening ride into the desert for a few more animal sightings and to say good-bye to the Massai tribe that had been so hospitable and patient with us. Gavin and Jen, Isabel and Henry, Dad and I decided to take our dinner on the road that night and share our meal with the tribe. Also, Henry had great luck hunting that afternoon and wanted to give to the local tribe the eight guinea fowl he shot. The tribe was very pleased.

We arrived back at camp in time for a nightcap, dessert, and a starlight swim in the pool. Dad had a couple drinks and was feeling quite jovial. I think he was laughing hard enough to scare away any hungry lions.

He and Henry were talking about the army, swapping stories about interesting characters they had met while overseas, namely the females. It seems that my dad had quite a few friends "in the profession" while stationed near Seoul, Korea. Henry had similar acquaintances after college, while serving in Asia in the British army.

Isabel was aware of these friends. She said that Henry is a natural-born rescuer and had it in his mind that he could help these young girls straighten out and live respectable lives. He and Isabel would invite them to dinner, to church, and do whatever else they could. Henry and Isabel married young and never had their own children. They tried to be parents to the young prostitutes who had so few choices and needed to feed themselves. I suspect they tried to take them in and reform them, only to have them return to selling themselves, for lack of better options.

Isabel said with a tender look, "It's easy to judge them on the surface. But if you dig deeper, the lack of education and lack of love for themselves made the profession seem like a reasonable, temporary way to support themselves. What it became was neither reasonable nor temporary. As their fresh faces looked away while enduring the humiliation, time after time, their bright eyes gave way to blank stares, tolerant at best, worn at the very least. Poverty is indeed a thief of youth, especially for these girls, with no future." We were all feeling less like laughing now. Reality is certainly sobering.

Everyone trickled back to his or her sleeping quarters, including Dad. I decided to spend some quiet time on the large rock I'd gotten attached to. There wasn't much going on by way of animal activity. However, up in the sky, I could have sworn I saw stars that were larger and brighter than the others, perhaps dwarf planets, lighting up our solar system or another universe completely, made by the same hands that I hope to see some day.

The next morning was spent packing up and heading back to Kenya. We all said our good-byes and exchanged e-mail addresses. I am hoping to see more of Henry and Isabel. I suspect that they will come see me in Annapolis in the coming year. The Canadians, Gavin and Jen, were also on my list of folks to keep in touch with. I need more laidback people in my life, and they love southern Virginia, so maybe they'll stop in and see me on their way down from Toronto. We boarded our tiny respective planes and headed into the blinding sky.

Back in Kenya, Dad and I settled back into our routine. I was so happy to see Nana! I nearly knocked her over when I hugged her. The children enjoyed the gifts we brought them from the safari. We were able to stop in a decent-size town on the way back and stockpile candy and flip-flops. I brought home a very large zebra rug for myself, some carved horn utensils for Ellie, and for Teddy a really nice handmade leather bag. After all, he did provide the airline tickets. Dad got Mom a few things, including some Massai jewelry and some handwoven textiles.

I spent the last few days of the trip playing with the children. I would miss them, but my purpose had now been made clear. I wanted to get home and start my foundation for John. I finally had a very long list of things to do and direction—something to benefit others who were as lost as I was.

Our flight back from Kenya was, thankfully, uneventful. I slept the whole way home, except for two hours to watch a cheesy movie.

Little Red Rider, Part II

1

A Very Brave Lime Bikini

~

Dear John—

In case I am incoherent when you get in tonight, I want you to know that it never ceases to amaze me that I get to be the one you come home to. Does that make sense? It's 11:30 p.m., and I'm almost asleep already. I probably sound like an idiot. Will you tell me in the morning if I do? I didn't mean to write this much. Sorry about that. You are probably too tired to even register what I am trying to tell you here. Maybe tomorrow morning, over coffee, we can discuss my infatuation with your behind after twenty years together? That is quite an accomplishment. How is it that your butt looks exactly the same as it did when you were twenty-three? It's god's gift to me...you and that beautiful hiney. It is hard to keep up with you, my darling, but I will continue to try. I wish my bottom had the same effect on you. I guess I can be content with the fact that you like my hair. I am keeping it long for you, Caveman. I love you. Kiss my back tonight when you get home (also, please write a note on my back with your fingertips).

Love —Wife

He kept my note. I do sound like an idiot, but he must have thought it was cute, or funny, or something, if he kept it in his special cigar box. There are a few other things from me there, too, that I haven't seen in years. One is a picture of James, four years old, with John's motorcycle helmet on. You can't see much of his face, as it is lost in the helmet, but James is smiling ear to ear. I remember that afternoon well. A wide grin commandeered my face as I pulled out the last photo. It was me in a bikini just strong enough to withstand, my new feminine fleshiness.

I was pregnant with James, at the beach, in a neon-lime bikini. The large, torpedo-shaped belly and other curves had gotten out of hand during the pregnancy. My boobs looked great! But they didn't last (despite John's pleading with them). Now my tiny cha-chas just droop. They resemble a 1970s-era National Geographic photograph of some village woman who nursed a quiver full.

John's hands were all over that bikini. And, the afternoon sun over my exposed skin felt amazing. There were two older ladies at the beach who made comments about how things used to be done—modestly—during pregnancy, but I didn't care. I was only nineteen and not about to wear a tent to the beach. We were proud of our baby, whom we would be meeting in less than three weeks...

I put the cigar box aside so that I could hand deliver it to my new residence, my row house in Annapolis. Not sure if I'll show the box to James or not.

Pierson, my builder and now realtor, took three couples through our home while I was in Africa. He said that one of the couples is relocating, but only for two years, before they return to their permanent residence in Connecticut. They asked if I would consider renting out the house. I think I would. I'm not positive, but if they are willing to pay the mortgage and taxes for two years, then I guess that would take a lot of pressure off, for now.

The best thing about renting out the big house versus selling it is that I have lots more time to decide what I want to keep, and I have a place for the stuff I can't decide on. Luckily, the couple doesn't mind my décor and asked if they could use the furnishings, too. It seems they found renters of their own who want to use the furniture in their Connecticut home. I guess things can work out for the best on rare occasions. Perhaps the housing market will improve in two years and I can revisit selling the house. I wasn't ready to let go of it anyhow.

James is coming home in December. Only five weeks away! Hopefully the move will keep me busy so I don't miss him or worry as much. He's anxious to hear about Africa. I think he probably knows more about Africa than I do, as he's hinted that he's been there...Like I said, baking cookies.

Allen called twice and left messages that he wants to help me move, if I need his help. Do I? Not sure if I want his help. I don't think I want him hanging around the house for a weekend. He may get the wrong idea; after all, he is a facetious light-wit.

I'm probably reading into this, but from what John used to tell me, Allen's particularly interested in any girl who's not interested in him. It seems that having women swooning over him leaves him rather bored. I would definitely fit into the "not interested" category. I hope that doesn't put me on his hit list.

I've placed an online ad for John's fancy car. Now that people (men) are calling about it, I want to keep it. Go figure. My only conciliation is that the proceeds will be serving in God's work for the very poor who deserve an education. I haven't had an offer yet, but there aren't many of these cars for sale for the price I am asking. It won't be long before someone stops by with a cashier's check and a pricey fountain pen to sign the title.

I have to admit that I am having a little bit of fun purchasing furniture for my new digs. The only concern I have is that Tarzan is starting to lose control of his bladder, and I'm hoping he doesn't pee on my new stuff. He will enjoy the tiny four-hundred-square-foot fenced yard—just enough of a postage stamp to allow him a quiet, private place to sunbathe, pee, and otherwise. He'll get in and out without using stairs, which are tough on his joints. His eyes are very cloudy, and his hearing isn't good. Sound like I'm taking care of an elderly person...I suppose I am. Tarzan thinks he's a person, so why upset him by telling him otherwise?

I've been car shopping. I've narrowed it down to a used hatchback. Gas is nearly four dollars a gallon, and any kind of savings is good. I wanted to get a Volvo hatchback, but I couldn't find a used one under twenty thousand dollars, and they don't get good gas mileage anyhow. I'm planning on walking to the grocer and planting a small, boxed garden off the patio for herbs and kitchen staples.

The only thing I'll be taking from my yard here in Baltimore is the French Fig (Violet de Negron) that I purchased when James was born. I've had it in an enormous pot for all of these years. I'll take it over to the new residence in Dad's pickup. In September, I will pop open a fabulous bottle of red and eat crusty bread, artisan cheese, and fresh figs from my very own beautiful tree to celebrate our son's twenty-fifth birthday... hopefully with him present.

My dreams are starting to return again, now that I've been back home. Last night around midnight, in my dream, I saw the jihadist leaders of the Middle East meeting secretly in Iran to plot Israel's last fight. Then my mind flashed to another meeting. Abram Barishmel was holding a peace summit in East Jerusalem. It was being televised live by Al-Jazeera.

My mind was racing. A commotion in the crowd. Horrified faces in the audience. The sound of a single shot. Then silence, as the placid leader of peace, both Jewish and Muslim by birth, fell to the ground. Then my eyes opened, as if the story were over. I can't understand how my mind, which detests violence with such gravity, could fabricate such things.

I woke up precisely at 5:55 a.m. By now, I shouldn't be shocked by my own imagination. I wish it would just let me sleep peacefully. It was still dark out when I got up. I sipped coffee while Tarzan inhaled his blended doggie mush.

I spent the entire next week emptying dressers and cleaning out my closets so that my renters would have space for their stuff. I pared down the kitchen to the basics; it's not likely the renters will need my spaetzle maker or pasta machine. Do I even need it? I'll call the Habitat for Humanity store and have them come haul away all the stuff I don't use and never opened. I have six new windows, two doors, tiles, stone, and wood flooring that we never used to finish the attic. Maybe someone can use it.

I took my basic wardrobe over to the new house—just enough to get by for now—a few pairs of jeans, long-sleeved Ts, two sweaters, a jacket, and boots. I have a box of socks and underpants, makeup, a brush, and some toiletries. I can't bear to let strangers sleep in the bed John and I shared. Movers are bringing it over with John's man chair and our artwork that is precious to me.

I bought most of my "new" furniture on eBay and Craigslist. I prefer an eclectic décor. I plan to strip and paint all the wood with milk paint. I'll make some throw pillows for the couch and chair. This new home is less than a sixth the size of the Baltimore home. I hope to pare down almost everything and just keep the stuff I can't part with.

The row house is in pretty good shape. It has great character: heart pine floors under the dated carpet, original moldings, and some fancy woodwork. But, the kitchen hasn't been redone since the 1960s. The former owner just didn't eat at home enough to care, so he gave me a kitchen allowance of five thousand dollars with the purchase. That's a small amount compared to what we spent on the Baltimore house kitchen, but I don't need an industrial range, oversized fridge, or warming drawer. I don't plan on entertain much, and I'm only cooking for one now, if at all. I think I could get by with a toaster oven, a blender (for the doggie food), and a microwave. Frozen meals for one, here I come...

My zebra rug looks great on the floor. It's the only thing I brought back from my trip besides some great photos, which I had processed in black and white. I've picked up some vintage frames of all sizes at the Goodwill and painted them in a creamy cottage white. In the living room will be a couch and one chair, John's chair. I will use Grandpa Brandt's cedar trunk for a coffee table. The primitive desk my Irish great-grandpa made will go in the corner. I'll sew a slipcover for the couch this weekend—flax, perhaps? And the room will be complete.

The kitchen is cozy (read: small). I've decided to take all the cabinets out of the kitchen and replace them with open shelving, which will be cheap and have an airy feel. I found some appliances on Craigslist from a kitchen store going out of business. They are standard sizes, so I'm sure I can make them work. I may have Pierson send Alfredo over for a few days to install the shelves and new appliances. I'll paint the wall behind the shelves in chalkboard paint for a café feel.

The dining table was the first large purchase John and I made after he was promoted to captain. It's going to stay at the big house. At eight feet long, it just won't fit in the kitchen here. I need a smaller table that will also function as a kitchen island and allow seating. I have a church pew that I bought when we lived in Minnesota, which will seat four. Maybe I can use that for seating at the kitchen island, when I find one.

The master bedroom is very small as well. Our king bed will fit, barely, with one small nightstand on my side. No need for two nightstands anyhow. There will be just enough room to put my rocker, the one where I nursed our child, in the far corner.

The smaller bedroom is nothing of consequence, but I can at least make it feel cozy. I'll get a queen bed for James and some new bedding then change out the light fixture for something softer. The upstairs bathroom is in fair condition, nothing special, except for an original claw-foot tub. There's a powder room off the kitchen, and that's it for bathrooms. I won't miss cleaning five bathrooms at all, especially that ridiculous urinal John *had* to have in his man-cave bathroom.

This poor little row house seems to have an identity crisis. Modern lighting, sixties' cabinetry, seventies' carpet, and eighties' country colors (dusty-pink and light-blue duck wallpaper?) on the walls. Ugh. Lots of work to do. With all of my free time, I should have it looking uniformly soothing in a month or so.

2

Blondie and the Pacer

~

James won't be stateside for Thanksgiving. Thank God I have Mom and Dad to spend holidays with. I'm wishing that I were in my old home, with a fire going in the kitchen fireplace, John outside smoking the turkey, and James and I making his favorite sweet potato pie. Mom, Dad, and Teddy joined us almost every year for that.

I need to make some new memories to subsist on, so I'm staying at Mom and Dad's for turkey day. Although I'm officially residing in Annapolis now, my little house is being remodeled. My little kitchen is ripped out, so I can't really entertain. Besides, it's been years since I slept in my old room. It hasn't changed since I was thirteen. Mom has all my high school artwork, in the original frames, adorning the walls. She saved boxes of notes and letters from friends. I read a few for a chuckle. There were also photos of old classmates and myself with ridiculous seventies' hair then, later (and worse), eighties' hair.

At one point, I tried bleach. Blondie was really in then. I wanted to look like Debbie Harry. My girlfriend, Jenny, and I bought a couple boxes of hair dye. I must have left mine on too long. My hair was the color of urine—not what I was shooting for. I was sixteen. That very same week Jenny introduced me to John in the school parking lot.

Late this evening, following dinner, I fell asleep (read: turkey-induced coma) in my childhood bed, remembering my first impression of John...

"Hey, nice car," said the deep, chiding voice behind me. No need to turn around and see who it is. He's either too sarcastic or too stupid to acknowledge. It's not like I don't know my vehicle is hideous. I was hoping my dad would get me a really cool used Camaro, but he opted for a 1976 burnt-orange AMC Pacer. It takes fifteen minutes to get to sixty miles per hour. Perfectly reasonable, according to Dad.

Luckily, I had an out. I heard my good buddy, Jenny, shouting my name across the parking lot. She hurried over to my car. We'd planned to sneak over to White Castle for lunch. The sophomores and seniors had the same lunch period, so there was always a mass exodus from school between eleven and noon.

I finally turned around to see who was trashing my car, when Jenny smiled and said, "John Brandt, have you met Pea Sullivan?" I gave Jenny a cold look. She added, "John and I have CCD [Catholic doctrine classes] together." Leave it to Jenny to introduce me to the stodgiest guy in our school. She's too sweet to even notice his arrogance.

"Uh, yeah, nice to meet you, John. And don't bash my car. At least it runs...and it has panoramic windows...That's why my dad got it for me. He says I won't be able to hit anyone in my blind spot because there isn't one."

"Makes sense. I mean, if you're a bad driver, panoramic windows could be useful..." He looked down at the scowl on my face then quickly retracted his statement. "Hey, I was just kidding. You know a joke?" he said, with a serious look on his face.

"Yeah, well, people generally smile when they are kidding. Perhaps you could use a bran muffin?" I figured he'd have a bland sense of humor. He seemed too harsh to laugh anyhow.

"Are you calling me uptight?" He cracked a smile then promptly returned to his poker face.

"Yes, and I can't imagine I'm the first one to do that," I said, with my head cocked to one side as I looked up at him. He must be the tallest guy who's not on the basketball team. I started to see something I liked in his face, when he opened his mouth again.

"So, uh, who did your hair? Is it supposed to be that color? I mean, it's cool and everything, but I hear bleach kills off brain cells," he said, chuckling.

"Luckily, I have plenty to spare. And don't concern yourself with my brain cells. I can see here that speaking with you has the same effect as bleach. Are you always so complimentary to females you just met, or do you unintentionally scare them off?"

"Scare them off? No, actually, quite the opposite."

"And *your* hair? In the likely case that you're ill informed, the war in Vietnam is over with. Why are you so anxious to be in the army at seventeen?"

"I'm eighteen. In ROTC. You don't like my crew cut?"

"No," I said, stiffly.

"That's funny. Most girls think it's tuff." He seemed taken aback.

"Where are these 'most girls'? I'm sure I've never heard anyone mention your hair in the girls' locker room."

"Who said they go to our school?" he countered, smirking.

"Oh, right. Sorry. I'm sure all your hair groupies are in college already. Hey, I hear *An Officer and A Gentleman* just came out on Betamax. Maybe you should ask Santa to buy you a copy, since you think you're in the army."

"That movie's about the navy. Not even in the same hemisphere. But, have you seen *A Bridge Too Far*?"

"No. Is it new?" I asked, uninterested.

"No, but it's a classic. Wanna come over Friday night and watch it?"

"You can't be serious," I huffed. But he was. It was then I realized what I liked on his face. I'd never seen gray eyes like his before. I started thinking about sitting on a couch, with all six foot three inches of him. His face was really nice once I got past the hair...He looked so much older than the popular guys at school (with the punk-rock hair). I started wondering if he'd kiss me after the movie. He interrupted my daydream by clearing his throat. Then he gave me the only ultimatum that he ever stuck to...

"Prudence Sullivan, I'm only gonna ask you out once. This is your first and last chance!" he stated, in an arrogant, nearly provoking tone.

"What?" I was offended by his overconfidence and lack of tact. "That sounds an awful lot like a threat, John Brandt!" I spat, annoyed.

He chuckled at the dour look on my face, then leaned down and whispered, in a true voice that made me feel a peculiar kind of nervous. "I just don't want you to miss out on the rest of your life, that's all," he said, with a quirky, beautiful smile. His eyes lit up, and his lips were suddenly soft and pouty. He was beautiful, and I was curious, even if he did have a stupid haircut.

I was happy to wake up the next morning with thoughts of that first afternoon with John in my head. I couldn't stop smiling. We had something. I knew it, right away, and so did he.

John later confessed that he'd asked Jenny to introduce us. That whole parking lot scenario was a setup. I was glad he waited to smile at me until later. I couldn't have been sassy while staring into that smile. I wouldn't have had the words. Even now, I don't know what he saw in me.

* * *

The next morning, I headed home to Annapolis, with Tarzan in the backseat. I put a fire on and made some tea, then spent the entire afternoon thinking about John.

It's cold out now. We haven't had snow yet, but the almanacs are predicting a very cold and wet winter this year. I think I'll be stuck inside my little village here quite a bit. Luckily, Ellie and her hubby live within walking distance. The local grocer is close, as are more than a few coffee shops and an unending number of cafes. I'll have plenty of snowy walks in my Bogs, maybe even meet a few neighbors.

The foundation is coming along. I have almost everything done, even the name: The John Brandt Foundation. James agreed that I should keep it simple. John's old buddies have all been very generous in donating and helping me get the word out. I'll be able to gift quite a bit, nearly $15,000, to John's favorite charities this Christmas. I'll also continue with my monthly contributions to his church. Father Rick set up a fund in John's name to assist military families in the parish who are hurting. And, of course, the orphanage will be able to send my three students to university in the spring.

John's car sold a few days before I permanently moved into my new digs. I cried after the guy drove off with John's car, but it just didn't make sense to keep that car. It doesn't suit my lifestyle anymore; it's too bourgeois. My little hatchback is easy to park, and I don't care if it gets dings, which is inevitable in a college/tourist town such as Annapolis. It is a bright yellowish-green color, so it can't get much uglier. All I need now is a bunch of obnoxious stickers, and it will look like a coed's car. Ellie says it looks like a go-cart. I'd say it's more like the offspring of a rollerskate and a big booger.

* * *

I was still pretty blissed out by the recent dream of when I first met John. Hoping to see him again, I went to sleep in his chair. It was so easy to do. I sipped tea and looked through some paperwork for the foundation. Soon after, I found my tired eyes drifting off into a place that scared me, but I couldn't seem to wake myself up.

The Israeli border was surrounded on all sides by Iranian and Syrian troops. The army of Israeli soldiers, all trained citizens, were armed and standing arm's length from each other, making a human fence. There were nearly two million men and women who would stand and fight for the land that was granted them after WWII, as well as the scant land won in the Six Day and the Arab-Israeli Wars. This ancient acreage, promised to Moses, would be the land where Abraham's children would fight each other to the death, each side asking God for His mercy and favor.

The Israelis stood with the tenacity of the Maccabees. All was silent until the Hebrew soldiers laid down their machine guns in unison, and each pulled an ancient shofar from his or her respective rucksack. As if led by the Almighty Himself, the troops began to sound the instruments to indicate the start of a war. The same distinct, deafening sounds that Joshua used to crumble the walls of Jericho.

The jihadist Muslim forces across the border stood in shock, disbelief, at what they were hearing. If the instruments hadn't been ordering such thunderous sounds, then they would have laughed at the thought of being disarmed by hollowed-out rams' horns.

After forty seconds of continuous booming from the Israeli army, it was instantaneously silent. The trumpets were laid down as all eyes greeted a large cloud descending from the heavens. On the cloud was King David, playing the harp of his youth. A beguiling melody, restful and soothing. The armies on both sides stood down. King David addressed them with the authority of the heavens in his voice.

"Sons and daughters of the Most High. A message from the Lord, maker of heaven and earth, author of life..." His voice became sorrowful, soft and disappointed, but at the same time uncompromising.

"You continue to destroy creations that are not yours to destroy. You worship Me in arrogance, not in devotion. You kill in My name. You lust in your hearts and envy the ruthless. I have sent the Cornerstone, yet you build your lives on fruitless, loveless thoughts and works. He who was sent to redeem was rejected and humiliated at your whim. You've testified against the Living Sacrifice. Even those called Christians have sought war to add riches to their purses. The end is near. Grace will be relinquished from this earth. The 144,000 will testify. Seek redemption, or follow the Dark One to damnation. Choose your side, but do not call on My name but for redemption, for even your very young are guilty."

King David again began to play his harp. The eyes of his audience became heavy, and every soldier, from both sides, fell into a deep sleep. For three days, they slept. When they awoke, they were confused, unaware of why they stood armed and prepared for war.

Not one remembered what he or she had witnessed. But all were overwhelmed with humbleness, feelings of insignificance. Both sides retreated. They returned to their countries, to their homes, and each began a new journey of hope and love. Their families and neighbors witnessed the changes in their hearts, and all repented. Peace spread through the lands for a period of three and a half years.

As I woke, I felt surprisingly calm. The Maker does know what is going on in the world. He is in command, even when situational control seems impossible to achieve. Of course our world leaders are impotent peacemakers. They are like me, sinners, who fall short by the simple fact that they are human. I hope that my dreams are finished now. Perhaps this was the end.

I slipped into my winter gear and took Tarzan for a walk to the coffee shop.

3

Bald Churchgoers and Mr. Moo

~

Nana's been emailing me. She plans to come up for a visit in April. Then Isabel and Henry may be crossing the pond in May to visit an old university friend in Boston. Isabel would like to stay here with me while Henry's off socializing. A splendid plan. I certainly enjoy her company.

I'm still attending my old church in Reisterstown. It's about forty-five minutes away, but I'm too attached to old friends there to go anywhere else. At some point, I'll start looking for a church in Annapolis. But for now, I am not interested in any more changes.

Ed, or "Pepperhead" as James refers to him, finally talked me into letting him call regarding a possible lunch after church sometime. His voice was so anxious.

"So, Prudence, where do you want to have lunch? You mentioned you like the Oregon Grill, I think? Shall we just head over there after the late service on Sunday? Should I pick you up for church?" His excitement frightened me. This was a bad idea. However, James won't stop bugging me, so I thought I'd try.

"Um, no, Ed, I live in Annapolis now. Why don't we just meet after church for brunch?" I was worried that if he picked me up, he'd also sit with me in church, and then the rumors would circulate, and then I would need to switch churches, which, like I said, is not part of the plan at this point.

"OK. Well, are you sure? I mean, I don't mind. I mean, it's no problem picking you up." I was wishing I hadn't agreed to this already. I'm feeling like this is more than a casual after-church lunch. I hope he isn't already emotionally invested, although I suspect that ship's already sailed.

Lunch was fine. Food was good, and Ed was very sweet. He didn't talk too much about his ex-wife, although his eyes were sad when he did mention her name. He's a really attractive guy. He could probably have anyone he wanted, within his age range. He talked about dating a little. He and I agreed that starting over with a new person seems almost too daunting a task.

I think because I knew him before his divorce, he felt I would understand him better than some random woman, which is true. But, he seems to want to settle down again, real soon, which is why that would be our first and last date.

There just wasn't anything there for me. I know in my heart that John is my true love. Getting involved, on any level, with anyone else just wouldn't be fair. No one can equal my John. Even thinking of Ed that way was a tad bit nauseating. I wish I would have known I'd feel that way before accepting his lunch invitation.

As if I couldn't be less interested in talking to a man than I was after my date with Ed, Allen had called and left a message on my machine saying he was coming over for dinner. Hmmm. He figured I had no plans for dinner, a fair, but nonetheless insulting, estimation. I guess it is my own fault for hanging on to my dinosaur answering machine instead of just getting instant voicemail. If I were into modern technology, I would have gotten the message right away in time to intercept his visit. Why did I give him my new address?

* * *

As if his stupid truck is all that, Allen took one look at my green hatchback and laughed. What a jerk. "Not exactly the AMG, huh?" he mocked. The irony. He didn't seem to understand why I would want to downgrade to middle class.

"I don't need a car that's froufrou, Allen. Besides, I have no garage. And even if it's paid for, the tires need replacing often, which is $1,500 a set. The thing got lousy gas mileage, and it sucked in the snow. It needed constant attention. It's just not for me anymore...Although, it was really hard to watch it drive away."

"I'm just teasing you, Pea. You don't have to get your panties all in a bunch every time I open my mouth." He had a flirtatious smirk on his face, and I wanted to slap it. He really irritates me.

"John, I know you're trying to be funny, but if you ever use a sentence that includes my undergarments again, it will be your last. I'm not in the mood to feed a wiseass. Besides, I had lunch date with a friend today after church, and I'm not hungry, so you are very fortunate that you are not at McDonald's right now, eating alone."

"Uh, I'm not John, Pea. And you had a lunch date, huh? Was it a lunch or a date? Glad you're rejoining the land of the living, despite the fact that you are calling random men your husband's name."

"I wouldn't consider you random, and that will certainly be the last time I accidentally call you John. You're not in the same league, character-wise, as he's in."

"You mean, was in. Who knows where he is…or *if* he is, now?"

"Whatever, Allen. I do happen to know where he is and where to find him when my number's up!"

"So…next subject…About your date today, why are you in such a sour mood? What, was the guy a jerk?" He seemed a little protective now.

"No, nice guy. Just a little too anxious. Makes me nervous. Seems like everyone under the sun is trying to set me up. To make things worse, these guys are looking for a wife! Mom won't leave me alone. She has every single, fat, bald churchgoer in five counties on her speed dial! Can you believe she's even given out my phone number? To men who are strangers to me? I don't care if they all go to church. That doesn't make them perfect…I mean, they still could be nuts or, worse, perverts. I have no intention of ever being bonded to another man again."

"Nuts? Perverts? Pea, you're starting to sound like a paranoid recluse." He gave me a piteous look, then continued to insult me. "Why do you think you're never going to need anyone, ever, *for anything*, again? You're not an eighty-five-year-old woman, not even close. If you don't want any attention from guys, then gain a hundred pounds and grow a beard. Long, wavy, fire-red hair is not exactly a deterrent either. Maybe you should shave it off or something."

I don't understand why everything out of Allen's mouth sounds like a lecture. I am pathetic. I know this. I am stuck on a dead guy who hasn't even bothered to visit me in my dreams in weeks. I'll change the subject…Allen really likes to talk about himself…"So, Allen, why don't you tell me what's going on with you. I know thirty years is coming up. Are you going to retire this time?"

"I dunno. I'll probably make two stars soon. Seems like the only thing I'm good at. I'm not really looking forward to retiring, although there are plenty of young Turks waiting to take my place. I guess I'll retire when I decide that I have nothing good to offer anymore. I mean, considering my age, and the fact that I'm single, I'm a lot more willing to take the crap trips that the other guys don't want to. That gives me an advantage, I guess. I mean, I still believe in what we are doing, so, I guess since that's the case, I'll stick with it. I have to tell you though, Pea, it's a mess. I would love to help fix some stuff before I bow out. Everything's just come to a head."

"I know you don't believe in anything spiritual, but have you thought that maybe this is it? Maybe a serious change is coming, something that we have no control over? Something that governments have been trying to avoid but can't anymore? Like, the will of something greater, Someone greater?"

"What, like Armageddon? For Christ's sake, Pea, you sound like a freakin' televangelist!"

"'For Christ's sake?' That's interesting that you say that considering you think the guy's a fraud."

I wanted to tell him about my dreams. I need to tell someone. He already thinks I'm a delusional, pathetic wreck, which may be mostly true. But I can't argue the fact that there is a God, and there are things that humans simply cannot account for...

"Allen, I've been having strange dreams since John died. Frightening, strange dreams. I'm going to sound like a nut, but you already think that, so...A couple nights ago, I had a dream that some Middle East leaders, primarily radical Islamists, were secretly meeting in Iran to discuss the demise of Israel. They were planning to invade Israel from all sides. Syria was in on it, too. Thousands of jihadist troops lined the Israeli border. And Israel knew they were coming. They armed every willing adult in the country and lined their own border with a fence made of citizens and professional soldiers. There was a standoff. No one moved. The two sides could see each other..."

Allen looked at me with an intensely concerned face. I was worrying him, but I decided to keep talking anyhow.

"But two weeks ago, I had a dream that was even weirder...Abram Barishmel was assassinated after organizing a peace summit of sorts in Jerusalem. It happened on live TV, in my dream. After that, there was no hope for peace...Even those who had been peaceful were full of anger after the assassination. It was a mess!"

"Pea, since when are you interested in the Middle East?"

I should have kept my mouth shut. But it was too late for that. "What happens in the Middle East concerns average people of all walks. The occurrence of such events would change everything and everyone, involved or otherwise. You know James is over there! I can barely sleep at night! How can I not worry? And the fact that nobody seems to know what to do to help the situation makes it all the more terrifying and probable! Besides, I said it was a dream. I'm not trying to prophesy, for heaven's sake!"

Allen thinks I'm a lunatic...and I didn't even get to the part with King David and the harp....the Cornerstone...the dark one...and the end. I wish he would at least laugh it off as the wild imagination of an under-sexed, sleep-deprived, intellectually feeble widow who lies awake at night thinking of all the ways her son could be in danger.

He continued to look me straight in the eyes, mouth gaping from whatever it is that I said that offended him. Finally, he said something. "Pea, have you been on some blogs or something with people talking about stuff like this? I don't understand why you would dream something so politically charged and so ridiculous. I thought you avoided such things."

His eyes looked softer now. But, his reaction to my dream really caught me off guard. He was looking at me like I'm a sad little idiot, a simpleton who has nothing to do but fret over the news. He continued to speak, "Besides, what goes on over there is too complex to explain over dinner. I've been living it for twenty-eight years. Even I have a hard time with the way things work, or don't work, over there. What else are you afraid of? You may as well spill it."

"Well, I am concerned about this Abram Barishmel. Who is he, and what is his purpose in all that's going on? Is he trustworthy, and where do his loyalties lie? Why do I keep thinking he is some sort of anointed one, someone to fix the mess...I mean, he's really the only peaceful person who gets any airtime over there."

"Pea, honestly, I think you watch too much TV. The guy's a politician. He's like any high-profile media darling over here. Just so happens that the centrist media in the Middle East is in love with the guy. But, considering his opponents, he seems genuinely decent. I've met the guy. He really is a beacon for peace over there." Allen seems to have calmed down. I guess I won't tell him that I think John is somehow playing a part in all of this, maybe trying to tell me something.

Allen stayed late. We sat on my back patio with the space heater on and talked about our ideas regarding the purpose of life and all that. It troubled me when he began to share some of the gruesome things he has seen and how that's affected his ideas regarding end-of-life stuff. He sees God as a possibility but a distant one. He doesn't see the tough but loving father figure that I subscribe to.

My dreams are comical to him. Now, instead of uptight, he just thinks me ridiculous, which is more entertaining, I suppose. He seems so harsh and careless, but I suppose his line of work is easier to deal with if you only answer to yourself versus a higher power, a belief system, or whatever...especially since our political climate and military allies and foes seem to change every few years. If you have no convictions either way, I guess doing your job is easier to stomach.

After he left, I sat outside and stared at the dome on the top of the naval academy chapel. That view may be the sole reason I decided on this place. I think the chapel calms me. It's not as ornate as a basilica or a European cathedral, but more subdued, more controlled, and, therefore, more to my liking. I finished off a glass of wine and went into the living room to lie down in John's chair and wrap up in his gray blanket.

It was very late when I finally drifted off to sleep. It was the first time in my new place that I dreamed of John. Maybe it was because I was missing him so much. Allen's company always makes me think of John, even more than I normally do...And the lunch with Ed just solidified the fact that my heart belongs to John, always.

Tonight, John and I were giving James his first haircut. He sat on John's lap in our tiny bathroom. I think that army base apartment was a total of six hundred square feet. We made the dining area into a nursery and ate at the coffee table. Anyhow, I was not happy about cutting his baby hair, but John was tired of people thinking James was a girl, which was silly since James was only two. Most kids are androgynous-looking at that age anyhow.

John had been threatening to take James to the barber on base, who only knows the one army haircut (high and tight). So, I gave James a bath in the kitchen sink then wrapped him in a fluffy brown towel. John had his favorite striped zebra toy on hand to distract James while I combed his hair out and started snipping. It went pretty well. I kept a locket of hair and put it in his baby box, which I still have. After the haircut, we all fell asleep in bed together while John read aloud *Mr. Brown Can Moo, Can You?* The three of us were fast asleep midbook.

John woke up around midnight and put James in his crib, then came back to bed. I opened my eyes to find John shimmying out of his boxers and reciting the book he had read to James—with his own naughty twist: "Oh, all the wonderful things Mr. Brown *can do to you*! You'll soon be making sounds like AHHH and OOOO!"

I can't remember laughing that hard, ever. The dance he did with that splendid ass while molesting the words of Dr. Seuss was enough to send me into hysterics. He figured out early on that laughter was the key to my chastity belt.

4

The Brass and the Doggy Stuffer

~

T-minus twelve days until Christmas. James will spend Christmas in my new Annapolis row house. I got out the Christmas bins from the basement and started adorning the house (in excess). I can't bear to have James here without a sick amount of holiday decorations. He and I are still a family, even without John. Maybe having the house dooded up will make me feel better—more festive, less lonely.

Before John died, Christmas Eve was the same each year: perfect. We'd get up early, each open one gift, go to Mass, then pile in the Yukon and head to the Boy Scouts' Christmas tree lot and hunt for that perfect towering blue spruce. Then we'd come home, and I'd start the chili. James and John would decorate the tree, while I got all the sides and fixings ready. We'd invite all our friends over, eat chili, and watch football. Then around midnight, we'd gather around the Christmas tree and sing carols. For the grand finale, James would wrap Tarzan in lights then plug him in. We'd sing "Oh Canine Bomb" to the melody of "O Tannenbaum." The dog wasn't a fan of that particular tradition— especially if a few beers had everyone singing it over and over and over...

This year, Mom and Dad helped me get a little Christmas tree. There's not room in this little house for a tree that could hold even half of the ornaments I've collected over the years, so I trashed the "Made in China" ornaments and kept the special ones.

I have the "Our First Christmas" ornament John's folks gave us when we got married and the "First Christmas" baby ornament they bought us when James was born. Wooden ornaments we bought in Maine on our tenth-anniversary trip were placed alongside handmade embellishments that James made in Sunday school. Then there were the ornaments that I made each year for John out of felted wool...

Two years ago, I made John a wool ornament with two fuzzy pink ass cheeks on it—an anatomically correct, smaller version of John's buns. His folks were out that year visiting, and they didn't get it, but John did. He knew I kept him around mostly for his super-fine ham. Living without a daily dose of his backside has become increasingly difficult.

Ellie came over for a pre-Christmas dinner on December 20. First, we caught up over French press coffee in my kitchen. She told me about the fun events she'd recently planned, and her two-week family vacation to Malta. When she asked what I'd been up to, I was a little embarrassed, because the foundation aside, I don't have much to do. She suggested I promote my sewing to some local shops, and start volunteering to meet some locals. Ellie mentioned that her friend, George, a gallery owner, needed more hands around the holidays. I agreed to go by and see him.

After coffee Ellie and I started eating (and drinking). John had been an amateur wine collector, and I had two bottles of Leviathan ready (finally!). We popped open those bottles with great tenacity, then went from zero to funny in fifteen minutes. Like two old cackling hens. Apparently, we were laughing at nothing in particular, with great enthusiasm.

The best part about having a girlfriend within walking distance is the amount of stellar wine one can consume without having to drive home. If I weren't a recent widow, I might think I have an alcohol problem. However, it is one of the few things I do to indulge myself now. I'll revisit the issue next year, if I'm sober enough to do so.

Ellie stayed until almost 2:00 a.m. I barely got myself to bed without passing out on the floor. I'm not sure if I was lit up or just tired. Either way, I didn't care, and it felt good to be so ready to sleep, instead of just lying there. I could have slept for fourteen hours if there weren't a wet, cold nose on my foot.

Tarzan and I continue to have our morning walks. They're getting earlier and earlier, as his bladder can't make it much past 6:00 a.m., which is perfect, because the City Dock coffee shop opens at that time. After several months of regular attendance, I am considered a regular. It's nice to see the same faces each morning. I'm beginning to know a few neighbors.

Per Ellie's prompting, I took some of my sewing creations around to potential vendors. I was thrilled when a children's boutique owner showed interest in my wool soakers. She thinks they'll appeal to those eschewing disposable diapers for environmental purposes. I plan to take samples in when I complete a little collection of sorts. And, I've been toying with some antique French fabrics that I got on eBay, too, for warmer-weather children's duds.

Ed asked me out again. I told him that I'm just not ready for dating yet and wasn't sure if it would ever happen for me again, because I didn't really want it to. He found that odd but, nonetheless, was understanding and bowed out gracefully.

On December 22, I got a very odd call from Allen around lunchtime. He was on his cell phone, in Old Town Alexandria, down the street from the Pentagon, where he works.

"Pea, are you at home?" he asked quietly.

"Yes, as usual. Are you calling to make fun of the fact that I have nothing of consequence to do each day?" I accused.

"No, it's the middle of the day, during the workweek. I usually save my teasing for the weekends. Look, this is not a social call. I was wondering if you had told anyone else about your wacky dreams."

"No, just you. You already think I'm some wacky Jesus freak, so I figured why not give you the whole megillah?"

"Pea, I'm serious. There's something going on right now that sounds a lot like what you told me last week when I was over. I did think it was nuts. But, apparently, you weren't off by much. Barishmel was assassinated a few hours ago. It happened during a live broadcast from East Jerusalem. Look, I don't know what's going on, but just keep your mouth shut about all that stuff, OK? People might think you know something."

"WHAT PEOPLE? Is this a joke? It's not funny. You're scaring me, Allen!"

"Look, Pea, just don't say anything about your 'premonitions' to anyone. There's plenty of brass in Annapolis, and I just don't want anyone to hear you say anything about this, OK?"

"All right. I'm sorry. I mean, I didn't think anything of telling you. I shouldn't have said anything. I wish I hadn't now."

"That's not what I mean. I'm glad you told me. It's just that, I wonder if you don't have a gift or something ridiculous like that. Can I come by after work tomorrow so we can talk about this?"

"No. James is arriving tomorrow at Andrews AFB. I don't want him to think something is going on, with me and you or otherwise. This is too weird."

"Pea, just let me know when I can stop by, OK?"

"OK. Bye," I said in a hushed tone. I was already feeling uneasy.

I don't know how I am supposed to sleep tonight knowing that Allen thinks I know something. Do I? I'm frightening myself just wondering what will come next in my dreams. I wish I could shut my brain off and just sleep like a normal person. I will need some Benadryl tonight, for sure. All of this could be coincidental. After all, people get assassinated all the time in the Middle East, especially people who are popular and somewhat modern.

The phone rang at 4:00 a.m. It was James. "Mom, can you hear me? The line's a little fuzzy."

"James, honey, did you get in early?" I asked, groggy but excited.

"No. I wish. I'm really sorry, Mom. My leave got canceled. Turn the news on, and you'll see why. They just want to have us available in case this turns into something. I'll come home as soon as I can. I love you. Gotta go."

"I love you, sweetie! Please be safe. I'll make Christmas dinner whenever you are able to get here. We'll celebrate, and I'll let you smoke one of Daddy's cigars." The line cut off before I got all my words out. I don't want to be alone this week. My folks left yesterday for Teddy's house. I might go, too, now that James won't be here.

I couldn't get back to sleep, so I packed a bag for myself and one for Tarzan. Christmas is in less than two days, and I'm feeling pretty down now without either of my boys here. Teddy has room for me, but all the flights are booked, so I decided to drive. It's ten hours, but I'm a mess over James. It's not like I can sleep anyhow. I hope Booger can make the trip.

* * *

I pulled into Teddy's driveway in Morningside around midnight. I let myself in and slept on the couch with Tarzan at my feet.

It was raining on Christmas Eve and didn't let up until 3:00 p.m. on Christmas. I tried to be in a good mood, but the past week was gnawing away at my sanity, and I needed to tell someone.

I called Allen while everyone was watching the football game. He didn't answer, so I left a message, "Allen, it's Pea. James didn't come home. I'm sure you know that. I don't want any specifics but can you find out if he's OK? Also, your call made me really freaked out. I'm coming home the day after tomorrow if you want to drop by. I'll cook. My nerves are just...Well, I'm kind of a mess. I'm sorry to bother you on Christmas. Oh, that reminds me, Merry Christmas. OK. Bye."

Christmas was a blur. Opening gifts without my child present just plain sucked. Mom was trying too hard to make me relax and be happy, and it was irritating me. She said that I was ruining the Christmas spirit. I tried to explain to her that I felt Christmas is not all about fun and happy. Christmas, at its innermost core, is about a godly young woman who knows her newborn son will be sacrificed for the sins of others. I'm not a Catholic, but quite honestly, the older I get, the more I get why Mary is so esteemed in the Catholic Church. She was selflessly obedient, so that others could live. Strangers, sinners, all of us, could come to God someday and ask His forgiveness and truly be forgiven. I am not such a woman. I have no desire to have my son die in place of another, not anyone, and especially not someone who would call my James an infidel.

Teddy was really my saving grace. He has no problem with silence. He was just happy to have company, even if I was less fun than a root canal. He understands loss—not permanent loss like mine, but close enough. Enough that his silent understanding was a gift in itself.

Dad didn't say much, either, but he did try to intercede on Mom's behalf, which made him suspect. He just wants Mom to be happy. She hasn't had her kids to herself for a Christmas holiday in I don't know how long. Teddy's been in Asia for years, and I was always fussing over my boys, so Mom didn't really get to be the center of attention, as she'd prefer. I guess this year won't be any different.

We went to a bistro in Virginia Highlands for dinner. Despite my lack of appetite, I managed to thoroughly enjoy a well-executed plate of venison tenderloin, chestnut mousse, and pickled beets. Delicious. Teddy and I shared a jammy bottle of zinfandel from Outpost, which was worth the trip in itself. By the time dessert arrived, I was ready for bed, feeling a bit like a pickled beet myself.

I left early the next morning and drove straight through, only stopping once for gas, twice to pee, and three times for Starbucks. I got home around eleven, exhausted from driving but not tired enough to sleep. My mind just wouldn't shut down. I took some Benadryl and curled up in John's chair.

John was there with me. I could feel his presence. He was holding me. His arms were around me, and he was whispering in my ear: "Wife, you need to let go of things you can't control. I'll watch over James. Stop worrying about the world. Rest, and heal. It hurts me that you are still suffering by yourself. Please. Live. I'll still be here."

My eyes opened. It was 5:00 a.m. Tarzan had barely recovered from the car ride. Poor dog could barely walk after sitting so long. His joints must be killing him. He wasn't up for a walk this morning, so I went to get a coffee by myself.

I'm a wreck but relieved to be home. Allen called. He'll be coming by later. I picked up a pound of artisan coffee beans for him in Atlanta at the restaurant. I figured he doesn't get many Christmas gifts. I don't remember Allen mentioning any family. John said it was a sore spot, so I never asked. Allen always spent the holidays with us when he could.

* * *

It's December 27, surprisingly sunny, and unusually warm, almost 55 degrees. I swept the leaves off the patio and put the cushions on the chaise longue and chairs. I started some bread and soup and picked up some cheese at Whole Foods. I'm not sure how long Allen's planning on staying.

He arrived early, as usual. Parking was pretty easy as so many folks on my block are out of town for Christmas. The house smelled like yeasty bread. I made a soup that John used to really like: chicken, veggies, a little Southwest spice, cilantro, and fresh lime juice. Allen isn't picky. I have a feeling he's eaten nearly everything. Allen was in a jovial mood and, as usual, ate enough for four adults. I don't know why he isn't heavier. The cheese alone was enough to give me a gut bomb. He ate half the loaf of bread and a trough full of soup. He patted his belly and smiled.

"Pea, that was 'soup-r,'" he said, while stuffing a brownie in his mouth.

"Allen, you have the worst sense of humor I have ever encountered," I said, while picking up his plate and taking it to the sink.

"You don't find me clever?" he asked, half teasing.

"Does it matter what I think? You're going to amuse yourself regardless, so I'll just sit here and listen to you entertain yourself, OK?"

"You're the one who talks to your dead husband and predicted some major news this week. I'd say that you're a bit odd yourself to be criticizing my behavior, hmmm?"

I sat down next to him and nibbled on a piece of bread. "I was wondering when you'd bring that up. I can't sleep. I've been wondering what's going on, you know, the aftermath of the assassination. Can you tell me anything, or do you know about the same as the media does? Should I be worried? I mean, more than I am already?" I looked at him intently, trying to read his face, but he wasn't giving me anything.

His face softened. "Let's see, OK? If you're gonna have clairvoyant dreams, then shouldn't I be looking to you for intel?"

"I'm sure it was a coinkydink. Nothing, right?"

"Nothing. Maybe. Maybe not," he said nonchalantly. He spoke as if trying to keep me from worry, knowing full well that I should be worried. That worried me. "How about some of this coffee, Pea?" he asked, changing the subject.

He popped open the coffee I bought him, just to try it out. It went really well with the Peruvian chocolate brownies I made and, of course, some really great vanilla ice cream. I could barely move from eating all of that. Of course, Allen ate all that bread, soup, cheese, then three brownies and a pint of Haagen-Dazs. That guy has a bottomless pit for a gut. Allen leaned over and gave Tarzan a belly rub.

"You're lookin' tired old boy," he said tenderly. Then Allen got up and gave me a squeeze, "Thanks for lunch, Pea. Really, it was superb. And don't worry so much, OK? I'll be in touch." He grabbed another brownie and headed for the door.

I spent the next few days trying to find a reputable financial planner for the foundation. Mom and Dad offered to come up and spend New Year's Eve with me, but I'd rather be by myself. I have brunch plans with Ellie, and that will be all the company I need for a while.

Allen left me a message that James is well. He had better be, as I was on Drudge.com, and it seems the Afghan president the United States put into power recently said that he would support Pakistan over the United States if ever needed. Forget the fact that he said he hopes that would never happen. Why would anyone say something like that if there weren't a reason to?

Gaddafi was killed this week, too, and the first law their interim president repealed was a law regarding polygamy. Apparently, polygamy is a rightly Islamic practice. Of course, I'm assuming this does not mean that the women there can have more than one husband. It seems the seventh century is descending on the world, and no one seems to care...I want my boy back home. Now.

Ellie is one of my oldest buddies, and being with her is easy. She's very tolerant of my rants, especially today when I was upset with James being somewhere, protecting someone who wouldn't hesitate to turn on him, given the opportunity. It's all sickening to me. Ellie listened and commiserated with me.

No one can fix anything. Things only seem to get more complex. More disastrous. The only way I can cope is through prayer. Prayer for peace. Prayer for the safety of innocents. Prayer for understanding.

After brunch, Ellie and I headed over to The Gatz (as in the Great Gatsby) in St. Michael's. They were having an after-Christmas sale. I found an absolutely perfect kitchen island/table. It's an antique. French oak, weathered to a soothing gray. A bit of a splurge, but I paid up, and it was delivered two days later. I suppose it is my "happy New Year's" gift to myself.

* * *

I finally got some good news from Kenya this week. The orphanage received my check and paid the tuition for the spring semester. Each of the three students sent me a letter to thank me, along with photos of them together, driving the payment to the university office. It seems their mail service is not very dependable, and the kids were excited to see the dorms and the university cafeteria. I will pray for God to grant me the kind of gratitude that those three have. I can't wait to get another letter from them.

I was personally invited to a fundraiser for Wounded Warriors about a month ago, after making a large donation. The event is tonight. I'm a little nervous, since John won't be with me. The last WW event we went to was in Annapolis, at a crab house. It was casual and fun, but there weren't any young, single girls, which is what young guys like to look at and talk to. They were very gracious, but imagine coming home from Iraq, missing a foot or a limb or two, and having a dinner out with a room full of former vets (now businessmen) and their middle-aged wives. What a hoot.

Anyhow, I thought about taking my dad for company, since he is still fluent in army acronyms, but then decided against it. I need to start getting out more and doing things by myself without hyperventilating. This is for John anyhow. The fundraiser is specifically for voice-activated computers and equipment for guys who have lost limbs. John would have been very happy to get these guys the tools needed to reacclimate to civilian life.

Ellie planned the event. It's at the Kennedy Center. She's lent me something to wear, for which I'm grateful. That one dress I bought last year is getting tired. Besides, it's too cold for a spring dress. I had Tiny dye my hair red again. I wanted to forgo the continuous expense of red hair, but now if I let it go too long, it becomes a brassy pink color. Only Cyndi Lauper could pull off that look.

I drove over to Arlington National Cemetery early in the afternoon to see John's grave first. I needed his strength tonight, going out by myself for the first time. I was looking a little puffy and red-faced when

I arrived at the Kennedy Center. I hadn't planned on crying that much. Ellie said I could change and put more makeup on in the catering area. That worked out fine.

I was so nervous. My armpits had the less-than-fresh, warm, clammy, wet, musky smell of a marathoner. Great. Good thing I'd brought a tub of baby wipes and more deodorant. At least my hair looked pretty good. Bright and fiery. Both of my grandmothers were natural redheads. That should count for something.

I took a deep breath, tried not to trip, and entered the ballroom to find my table. I wondered where they would put me, since I only needed one chair rather than the conventional two. I was hoping that there were others like me, non-society types who just liked to participate in such a great organization.

The tables began to fill as the event got started. Lots of brass filed in, mostly looking around to see who was looking at them. Some had wives; others did not. I imagine all of the officers and enlisted guys and gals here had at least one buddy wounded or killed in action since 9/11, when the War on Terror officially began.

I wonder how much good the death and maiming of our young ones has done to secure our freedoms, our safety. It seems impossible to find a way of measuring such an unquantifiable thing. It should be easy. Either we are safer, or we are not. For some reason, this simple question cannot be answered simply.

A friendly woman sat beside me and started up a conversation. Her name was Maggie O'Connor. She's married to Lee, who retired from the navy last year. I assume he was in the special operations area of the navy since he's huge and has so many medals for a guy of only forty-two years. They have four kids, all in school, two boys and two girls. If I were only so lucky. If I had four kids, maybe I'd stop obsessing over James—but probably not.

Maggie seemed so much younger than me. She's thirty-six, but my forty-three seems old in comparison. She still has the look of a young mother, freshness about her. Her husband, Lee, seems much older. His eyes are astute, aware.

I was happy to have someone to talk to. Maggie and Lee introduced me to the rest of the table, since they all knew each other. Maggie and the other wives made sure that I didn't spend much time alone. There was one other widow there at our table of twelve, Helen, who lost her husband in Vietnam. She never remarried, even though at the time, she was only twenty-three and had no children with her fallen love.

Helen was considerably younger than her husband. He was a family friend who was almost thirty when he proposed to the twenty-one-year-old Helen, at a barbecue in Birmingham. Helen never desired the company of another man after he was killed. I respected her for that. Of course, there is a big difference between twenty-three and forty-two, and had I been twenty-three when John was killed, I may have considered some new company over widowhood. Even in her seventies, Helen's quite a stunner. I suppose family money had something to do with it, although Southern women do seem to age better than we Yankee females do.

Everyone enjoyed the guest speaker a great deal. He was able to offer a firsthand account of what it's like to be on the ground, in a foreign country, and leaving part of your body behind when it came down to it. He was brave and had such dignity and pride. He didn't want our pity. He wanted us to understand that having the support he needed through Wounded Warriors when he returned to recover at Walter Reed two years ago made all the difference in continuing with his life— not his life as a disabled person but his life as a differently abled person, proud of his service to our country.

As he was speaking, I was thinking of all the mess, the protestors, the deaths, and the threats of Iran. Despite the turmoil, I felt a sense of relief. At least the troops who are coming home broken are having their needs met. I thought of Helen, losing her husband in Vietnam. I wondered how many of her husband's brothers in arms came back to protestors, negative media attention, and ignorance.

Toward the end of the evening, I noticed Maggie across the room gesturing in my direction. She was talking to a tall man with a shaved head and dress whites on. Of course, he was far from being the only shaved head in the ballroom that night. His height, however, made him stand out a bit. Maggie was pointing over toward me, and I felt nervous all of a sudden.

I was hoping to escape any introductions, to make it through the evening without a setup. If Maggie's tall friend hadn't reminded me of John, I would have run the other way. Besides, Maggie insisted, and I didn't want to be rude, so I casually made my way over to meet him. He, unfortunately, got better looking the closer I got.

I was embarrassed. He looked a little amused at my discomfort but was a gentleman and tried not to chuckle as my cheeks began to take on the hue of my crown.

Maggie said that we had lots in common. But, I wasn't really comfortable talking to a man I didn't know at all. She had given him the paraphrased version of the story of my adult life, so I was already at a conversational disadvantage.

"Prudence, I'm Jack Houchins. Maggie's husband and I have been buddies since I was his XO. She was telling me that you like to ride. Do you have a bike?" His voice was deep and serious. My nerves were further exposed when Maggie made things worse by excusing herself to dance with Lee. I tried to collect myself and come up with some (painful) mindless chitchat...difficult for someone who had just visited her dead husband's grave and who dreams about terrorists, assassinations, and the like.

"Uh, hi, Jack. Maggie and I have been buddies for all of two hours. It seems she was listening to me blab about my last trip to see my son, James. He has a bike. A Springer. His dad and I used to ride our Shovelhead that was probably older than you are."

"I doubt that. I'm closing in on forty-eight. I don't know that there are bikes my age that are still around. Maybe in a museum. Those older models had a habit of overheating. Even my '85 is too temperamental to take far these days. I mostly leave her at home and take out her younger sister, a '99 Night Train." He finally smiled. Nice teeth...

But, I was suddenly feeling sorry for his older, overheating bike.

"Aren't you worried about hurting her feelings? I mean, just because she's a little temperamental, does that render her useless?"

He chuckled then clarified, "No, not at all. She's actually OK with me taking her little sis out as long as she still has command of the garage, and I keep her really clean. She's my arm candy. Doesn't like to get dirty or wet. So I take her out on sunny days, she gets looked at, feels pretty, then I take her home, wipe her down, and buff her body, so she's shiny again. She and I have an understanding."

"Oh, I see. You have a gal you spoil and a gal you seriously ride?" I asked with a furrowed brow.

"You make it sounds so vulgar," he countered, laughing.

"Isn't it? I mean, why don't you just get rid of them both and get something that is pleasant looking but functional—you know, pretty *and* practical?" I suggested.

"Is there such a bike?" he queried.

"Not sure. I'm not an expert on bikes. I just know that no old gal likes to play second fiddle to a young, spry one, even if she seems satisfied with just being pretty. Perhaps you're overestimating her contentment. She could secretly wish that her younger sister gets caught in a hailstorm, for instance."

"You think? Should I talk to her about that?" Jack was looking intently at me, trying to figure me out or guess my age, since I'm championing his old bike with such resolve. He spoke, "Of course, it's not likely you'd know what an 'old gal' would feel like anyhow. You can't be much older than Mags."

"Yeah. I'm forty-three. Not even close to Maggie's age. She seems so young to me."

"She told me you lost your husband last year. That would make anyone feel fatigued. But, you don't look that way. In your forties, huh? Really, really hard to believe. And I'm not trying to butter you up or anything," he added. Yeah, right. Jack was the best-looking guy in the room, and not by a little.

He seemed a little too smooth, too much charm. Maybe that's the navy versus the army. They seem to be a little better at compliments, not as brash as John's old buddies, who seemed to like ribbing and teasing a girl if they liked her. But I wonder if those florid navy compliments really mean anything. Hard to tell.

Anyhow, Jack was fun to talk to. He smiled a lot and seemed very interested in monopolizing my attention. We ended up having a glass of wine on the roof of the Kennedy Center, and he told me about himself.

His marriage was less than ideal. He was away a lot, and his wife was anxious to have children. By the time they went to see what was holding up the baby-making process, they learned that he wasn't able to father a child without help. I couldn't believe he'd admitted that to me, a near stranger. Maybe it was the alcohol talking, but he seemed sincere and a little relieved to tell someone about his infertility "issues." Anyhow, his wife was like many women, myself included. I wanted children or, I should say, more children, after James. I was desperate. I can understand a woman's need to breed.

I felt sorry for Jack. His wife ended up leaving. She wanted to have a child. Jack said that, in hindsight, he would have just done whatever she wanted to make her happy. I suspect he initially felt defensive, less manly, when he learned that his swimmers aren't exactly Olympic material. The fact that his wife quickly remarried and is currently pregnant with her second child couldn't be easy for him to take, either. He was very matter of fact about the whole thing, but he seemed far from being unaffected.

He asked to call me, but I froze up and declined (out of guilt). Maggie has my address and number, so I guess if he really wanted to contact me, he can. I live in Annapolis, for heaven's sake. I'm sure it wouldn't be hard for a naval officer to find someone there. But, I shouldn't have talked to him for so long. I felt terrible, like I was looking for something, when I'm not. I shouldn't have spent so much time with him, even though I was having fun for a change.

When I finally got home, around 3:00 a.m., I tried not to think about the event. That was quite a party. I was happy to have met some of the wounded warriors in person and be around some military folks. I feel at home in their presence. I miss spending time with John's old buddies and their wives.

It seems like after John retired, it became difficult to see them. They were still moving around, traveling in and out of the country, or deployed. I think John regretted retiring after twenty years. I pressured him to do it. I hated being without him every third year for deployments. I knew he didn't want to get out, but he never made it an issue. He just put in his papers and started looking for his next gig.

For years, John had been reading every business journal and book he could get his hands on. He studied the emerging Internet industry and had been investing whatever we could afford. Later on, he followed the energy crisis in California and dumped every tech and commodities stock we had while they were high. Around 2003, when everyone else was mourning the onset of the bear market, John had his first six-digit annual income, just from trading. But, the brotherhood to which he belonged was something he'd never have in the civilian world. He loved being a soldier more than anything. He loved it more than anything but me.

* * *

It was cold in the house tonight. I turned the heat up and put another cover on the bed. I took my makeup off, brushed the wine off my teeth, put on flannel pj's, and slipped into bed. The forecast was calling for flurries.

In my dreams, there was a king. I assume a Saudi king, as he had the head covering of Arabian royalty. He was in a hospital bed and had a heart monitor on and a drip going. There were guards outside of his door.

Then I saw a man outside of his home in DC, getting into his car with diplomat tags. It was early morning. He was being approached by a jogger wearing sunglasses and a hat. As the jogger passed by, the man slumped over and fell out of the open door of his large, black car. No one saw what happened—no one but me.

Again, I saw the Saudi king. His fair-skinned nurse was speaking English with a heavy Brooklyn accent. His heart monitor flat lined and she pushed the button for help. A team with an AED came in and jumped him, but there was no response. He was dead.

The next morning, I opened my eyes at 10:00 a.m. and realized that Tarzan had not woken me up to go outside and pee. I looked down and saw him by the end of the bed, curled up on the blanket I had thrown off in the night. He looked so peaceful.

Tears began to well up in my eyes. I lay down with him on the floor, put my arms around him, and began to sob. It was just too much for me to take. Tarzan was almost fifteen. He had waited for me to get home before he let go and went to sleep.

It was too late for me to call in sick. I had the 11:00 a.m. to 5:00 p.m. shift today at the gallery, which meant that I had one hour to get myself out of hysterics, clean up, and look presentable. My problem is that Tarzan is dead, in my room, and I can't pick up a 130-pound dog by myself. What was I supposed to do with him? They don't take dogs at Arlington Cemetery, which is where he'd want to be buried, with John.

I didn't know what to do, so I called Allen.

He picked up on the first ring. "Good morning, Pea. You want some company? I'm hungry!"

"Allen, I know it's Saturday, and early, but I need help." I tried to stop crying long enough for Allen to understand what I was telling him.

"Pea, are you OK? You sound awful."

"Tarzan didn't wake up this morning...He's on my bedroom floor... and...130 pounds. I don't know what to do...I can't bury him here, and people are living in the other house now...I'm sorry to bother you. I don't know what I was thinking to call you...I just...well, you know how much that dog means to me...and I bought him for John for our tenth anniversary. I think...I'm having a relapse...and I have to work at the gallery today. Is it safe to leave Tarzan in the house all day?"

"Uh, Pea, I don't think he'll go anywhere while you're at work."

"Are you trying to be funny, Allen? I mean, how long 'til he's starts to decompose or smell?"

"Unless you recently gave him a bath, he already stinks." He paused after hearing me sniff again on the other end of the line. "I'm sorry, Pea. I'm not being nice. What do you want to do with Tarzan? I think you can call the vet and ask who comes to take, uh, 'expired' animals away."

"I can't just let them take him away and not know where they are putting him. I mean, what if he ends up in soup, somewhere in North Korea? John used to tell me that the famine there is so bad that the bark has been eaten off the trees, and there are absolutely no birds in the air. All eaten!"

"Pea, if you were starving you'd eat whatever you could get too...It's called survival..."

Allen, you are absolutely no help at all! And you're mean! I hope it's you getting mangled in my dreams tonight instead of all those Middle Eastern guys I know nothing about."

"You had more dreams? About anyone in particular?" he inquired.

"I don't want or need your jokes today, Allen!"

"Pea, I'm sorry. Really. When do you get off today? I'll come over and help you with the dog."

"Five. Fine. Thank you." I hung up.

Being at the gallery helped me cheer up a little. Artsy people always have interesting ideas for creative problem solving.

George, the manager of the shop, told me about his aunt Trudy, who had her standard poodle stuffed after he died. George said that as long as you keep the dog cold and get the corpse to a "dog stuffer" quickly, then they can stuff and pose the dog however you like. I liked this idea. Maybe a stuffed Tarzan in my front window will work as a theft deterrent. And, he will still be able to keep me company. I just can't live without him, especially now that I won't have to pulverize his meals in my blender or clean up his giant elephant poop from my tiny backyard.

Allen was driving around looking for a parking spot when I flagged him down. Saturdays in Annapolis are always crowded, even when it's cold and snowing. There is nothing more peaceful than moored boats in the harbor, snow gently falling on their bows. Peaceful, that is, unless your mind is preoccupied with a 130-pound dead dog on the floor of your bedroom.

We decided to grab some dinner. I was starving, and I didn't want to go home to see Tarzan dead yet. Besides, I wanted to run my ideas for Tarzan by Allen and get his opinion. We went to the little Café Normandy on Main Street and had a one-pot French dinner, including beef, potatoes, carrots, and some wonderful clear broth that the crusty bread sopped up quite well. About three glasses of wine and ten macaroons later, I told Allen about George's idea for stuffing Tarzan.

"Allen, at the gallery, I googled 'taxidermies' and found one that would pick up my precious Tarzan and transport him to Pennsylvania to stuff him. I could pick him up in about one month. It would cost me about $2,500 to have his skin and fur preserved, but his eyes won't look the same." As soon as I finished my sentence, I knew Allen's opinion regarding my bright idea.

"Geez, Pea, why don't you just have his head mounted and save yourself two grand?" he huffed.

"Allen, I don't want to decapitate my dog!" I snapped.

"So you'd have him gutted, stuffed with sawdust, and sewn back together, so that he can stand on the couch by the window and keep the bad guys away? That makes about as much sense as cremating the dog and putting his ashes in a bookend!"

"People do that, you know," I insisted. As a matter of fact, that was something I was considering as a backup plan if I decided against the taxidermy idea. I chewed on my lower lip a bit and started to look for the waitress so I could get a coffee or some pistachio gelato.

"Some people treat animals better than they treat people, Pea. It just doesn't make sense to spend $2,500 to stuff your dog when you are trying to save all of Kenya's orphans! How about throwing your money away somewhere else, perhaps for things that are still living?"

"You're a little self-righteous this evening, I see, Allen." Our server poured our coffee. I took a sip and glared across the table.

Allen softened his voice, trying to be sympathetic, "Pea, you're not a ridiculous person. You are a reasonable person. Tarzan is a dog. It's not like he's Trigger or some Hollywood icon that was stuffed and is sitting in a museum somewhere in California. It's silly. I just didn't take you for the silly type."

He was disappointed in me. John would think this is a stupid idea, too, and I know it. Maybe that's why I called Allen. At least he's honest with me, which I appreciate, even if he's mean about it.

I leaned in and whispered, "Fine. Then will you help me bury him in my backyard tonight?"

"Is that allowed? You live in the historic district of one of the most stringent towns on the East Coast!" he quietly argued.

"I don't care. Besides, no one else will know. Please, Allen?" I mouthed.

"Pea, I could get arrested for digging a giant hole and burying what resembles a dead bear in your snooty neighborhood! I could lose my security clearance!" Allen's face got a funny look all of a sudden. He was trying to be serious, but we were plotting like two gangsters. I remembered Allen likes to gamble, and my proposition was essentially a challenge to not get caught doing something very illegal. I sweetened the deal. Allen can't say no to good scotch.

"Please. I promise you won't get caught...and I'll throw in a bottle of Oban."

He finally agreed. "Deal."

We shook on it. I love a small victory. But, I was going to have to get Allen pretty liquored up for this. The hole needs to be six feet deep and wide enough to fit grandpa's cedar trunk, which I'm using for a coffin.

"Allen, we'll need to stop by the florist and get some lavender to put in the box with Tarzan..."

"Pea, we are not having a funeral! We're doing something illegal! No flowers! Period. And you're paying for dinner since I'll probably throw my back out tonight."

The eighty-something woman having dinner alone at the table next to us heard Allen say he'll throw his back out tonight, then looked at me, then Allen, then me again, and started to crack a very mischievous smile. My face turned red with embarrassment. Allen finally caught on and started to chuckle. I held my napkin to my mouth and whispered,

"I think she'd like for you to throw your back out at her place tonight!" then I started to giggle. Allen suddenly had a very unamused look on his unshaven face.

"You owe me, Pea. Seriously," he smirked.

"I know. Let's go!"

There is something inherently thrilling about doing something naughty. I hope my neighbor doesn't call the cops. I only have a neighbor on one side (let's just call him Mr. Roper). He's never home, so maybe we'll get away with our little burial ceremony (not funeral) for Tarzan.

We got back to my house around 9:00 p.m. I went next door to see if Mr. Roper was home. No one answered. Coast is clear. Luckily, it was cold enough to snow but not cold enough to stick or freeze the ground, so the ground was a bit waterlogged from all the moisture. It's much easier to dig wet ground than frozen ground...not that I will be the one digging.

Allen was much stronger than I thought. And quiet. I didn't even hear him grunt once. Must be all that secret stuff he did and never talks about. He had the hole dug in about two hours, but he was exhausted. We used the blanket that Tarzan fell asleep on to wrap his cold, still body, then gently placed his curled-up corpse in the large cedar trunk (formerly known as my coffee table). Tarzan would be comfy and would still be near me. No gut removal, no glass eyes, and no ride in the back of a truck to Pennsylvania. This was perfect.

After putting the trunk in the ground, we replaced the dirt and put a tarp over it. Tomorrow, I will go to the plant nursery and get some hardy shrubs to plant over Tarzan, so Mr. Roper doesn't think something's up. He's on the historical (read: hysterical) society board for the neighborhood and wouldn't hesitate to bring my little charade up at the next meeting...or call the police and whoever else is called for such an infraction.

Allen was tired and dirty when he came in the back door. I handed him a glass of scotch, a towel, and a gift I'd bought for James for Christmas that was never opened. Allen looked at me strangely as I handed him the meticulously wrapped gift.

"It's pajamas," I said. He nodded and headed up the stairs to the bathroom to shower. "You can sleep in James's room!" I shouted up the stairs.

"Do not wake me, Pea. That's an order!" he shouted back from the steps. I didn't argue. He was spent. And I was thankful for his efforts.

The next morning, I had Allen's clothes clean and dry when he woke up. I suggested we go get a cup of coffee and breakfast. I felt a little weird having male company overnight...that is, until Allen, the one-star dork, shuffled into the kitchen wearing flannel Santa-pig pajamas. I wish I had a Polaroid.

We went to Chick and Ruth's diner down the street. It's probably the only diner in town where you can get a great meal, say the pledge of allegiance in unison with other patrons, and get a room upstairs, if needed. Allen was interested in hearing about my latest dreams.

"Allen, I'm not sure you want to hear this one...It's all over the place. A Saudi king dies at a New York hospital, and a diplomat is taken out by a jogger in DC while getting into his car in the morning."

He looked at me as if I'd just flicked a booger at him. "Pea, what kind of sleeping pills are you taking? Because I want some. Geez, did John know how weird you are?"

"Yes, John was fully aware of my degree of weirdness. He liked to call me quirky. I think it sounds better than weird, even if 'quirky' is a little mild. Allen, would you please put some food in your mouth and stop looking at me like that?"

"Sorry, Pea. I'm just trying to figure out whether you're some kind of Jean Dixon or if you need to be committed for observation. At least you're not violent. That would be a problem."

"For who? Nobody cares what I think. A forty-three-year-old widow who suspects the government of awful, sneaky stuff and sees high-profile Middle Eastern people getting whacked in her dreams. I know that I'm weird, but really, Allen, there is *plenty* to worry about! And you know darn well that our government makes a mess of nearly everything!"

"*Sometimes*, but never intentionally. Sneaky things are sometimes necessary for our national security, Pea."

"Oh, sorry, Allen, I forgot you're one of them. I'll be sure to keep my opinion of your commander and colleagues to myself." Allen's had too much of the punch to think straight.

"Pea, you should come down to my office for lunch sometime…I'm sure you'd change your mind. I work with some stellar folks."

"Not likely. You know what I think about guys like you?"

"You're gonna tell me, I gather?" he said, sinking back into his chair and looking irritated.

"Well, just that once you've been out of the infantry, you get the 'army lobotomy' and start to think that pushing papers and trading info with whomever for whatever reason is what it's all about. You make war via e-mail and memos, by politicking and opening your mouths a whole lot but not actually saying anything of consequence." I took a breath then continued. He was already pissed off, so it wouldn't make any difference if I just got it all out at once. "The upper echelon of officers is no different than politicians. As a matter of fact, the army has gotten so PC that no one's allowed an opinion about anything. Young soldiers are getting court-martialed over stuff that they were told to do by people like you. It's just too confusing. Who really knows who or what we are fighting against? I mean, that changes from week to week, right? Even the Afghan president who *you* helped put into power says he'll side with Pakistan over us if it ever comes down to it. And, forgive me, but Pakistan is supposed to be an ally, yet Bin Laden was hiding there, in some big house, *for six years*, and nobody seemed to care until a SEAL team took him out. Now the Pakistanis are burning our flag, photos of our secretary of state and president—all because there's one less psychotic terrorist in the world!"

Allen took a deep breath and crossed his arms and sarcastically said, "WOW. That's an interesting synopsis. You have some considerable ideas here, but you just don't know enough about this stuff to really see it clearly, Pea."

"Well, if I, being an ordinary citizen of above-average intelligence, can't seem to understand it...I mean, if it's that complex a problem that the average American can't wrap her head around it, then is it something to throw billions at each year? Is it right or wrong? Or should I say, who's right and who's wrong, because I am getting really irritated watching the news each morning and not being about to tell myself exactly why my only child is risking his life for a cause that no one seems to get. Are we hated so deeply that our allies are not even allies? They want our aid, our dollars, our weapons, then they use them against us ten years later?"

"Pea, we are friendly with most countries. The region you are talking about is just a mess right now."

"When was it not a mess?"

"Good question. Eat your breakfast, and calm down. Please. Knock it off."

I don't know why I let myself talk to him about stuff he thinks I am too silly to understand. It's not like I can deprogram him. He's been in so long that he's probably in favor of those cameras that Homeland Security is putting in intersections now and drones! What is the purpose of those, if not to encroach on our liberties? And the signs over the highways saying to report any suspicious activity—who are we reporting suspicious things to? And what behavior is suspicious?

John used to say that those highway signs reminded him of the government propaganda he saw in East Germany, before the wall came down in 1991. It seems that protecting the privacy of the average citizen no longer applies here since 9/11. I decided to let it go and try to swallow my breakfast despite the fact that I was just an angry mama bear inside. James is an intelligent adult. It's not like I didn't know what my son was getting into. Things just seemed to make more sense twenty years ago.

John had one tour in the Gulf War then things were pretty quiet until we were about to invade Haiti in the early nineties. Jimmy Carter stepped in with some last-minute negotiations, and the planes en route to Haiti with the Eighty-second aboard turned around and came home. John was on one of those first planes and would have surely died, jumping into the middle of Port Au Prince at night, trying to secure a safe place for the rest to land.

Jimmy Carter is probably my least favorite recent president. It used to be that past presidents refrained from critiquing their predecessors. I remember the inflation, gas crisis, and hostage crisis. Carter was less popular than he remembers. He seems like a very decent human being, but I prefer a president with a big sack. That aside, I will always be grateful to him for helping save John. Diplomacy *can* be effective... with the Eighty-second Airborne already in the air ready to take care of business.

I looked up, and Allen was still sitting there, steaming, with a clean plate in front of him. I had barely touched my food. I need to establish time limits on my inner monologue. I was about to consider Haiti's current government when our waiter interrupted my thoughts with the check. "Whenever you're ready. No rush," he said. I was too worried about James to eat. I handed him a twenty, and a highly irked Allen and I headed back to my place.

I thanked Allen immensely for helping me with Tarzan and apologized for my rant at breakfast. I know his job is important. He must know things that make it easier for him to understand current political situations here and abroad. Allen put his newly acquired scotch in his truck and sped off without so much as a good-bye.

I headed over to the plant nursery. There's little to choose from this time of year. I don't want a pine tree or a holly. So, I ordered some bricks for making a small retaining wall. I'll build a raised bed and plant a fruit tree there in the spring, on top of my wonder pooch.

I e-mailed James about Tarzan. He'll be heartbroken. He loved that dog almost as much as John did. James was only ten when we got him. I got a reply back soon after e-mailing.

Mom,

So sorry about Tarzan. I can't believe it. I was looking forward to seeing him when I get home, which may be in a month or so. Did you have Christmas with your folks and Teddy in Atlanta? I miss you, and don't worry. Not much going on here.

Love you, J

Mr. Roper stopped in to see what I was planting in the backyard. I told a fib. I said that I had ordered a specimen fig tree that was arriving in late March, and I wanted to dig up the ground and get the soil pH and nitrogen levels prepared for the fig's arrival.

Roper has quite a green thumb. His garden is featured on the Historic Gardens of Annapolis tour each June. I thought if I threw in some botany buzzwords like "pH" and "nitrogen levels" that he'd stop asking about the large mound of dirt in my backyard. As soon as I mentioned the imaginary specimen fig tree, his eyes lit up. So I promised him a ripe fig tart in September (another fib—damn!). That's all it took for him to never bring it up again.

As soon as I shut the door, I went online to find a specimen fig, mostly to ease my conscience about fibbing (twice) to Roper about the dirt mound. If I put in a fig, will it still be a fib?

5

Note To Self, Keep Mouth Shut
~

It was nearly a month after Tarzan died that I turned the TV on and saw that the Saudi king had just died in a New York hospital. Very creepy. I didn't even know who the guy was or that he was sick. It seems he'd been fighting a disease for some time, and his heart gave out. This made me wonder if my dream was a prediction or just a premonition of something that was already going to happen.

I was pulling some weeds in the yard when Allen called. "Pea, do you remember telling me about your last dream?"

"Uh, yes, I think. I don't remember mentioning it, but I could have, I guess."

"Did you see who died earlier today in a New York hospital, just like you said?"

"Yes. I did. I guess it was bound to happen since he was very ill."

"Did you know that he was ill when you had that dream, Pea?"

"No. Why are you asking me this?"

"Last week, an Iranian tried to take out a diplomat in the early morning. He was getting into his car and headed for the Saudi embassy. He was shot and nearly died. What would you say to that?"

"Well. I would say that I'm sure things like that almost happen all the time."

"The Iranian was dressed as a jogger, and it happened outside the diplomat's DC home."

"I hear that jogging is great first thing in the morning. Although, after having James, my bladder didn't allow for such activities. I prefer gardening, walking, swimming, or biking...."

"Pea, look. This isn't funny. There are two people here at the Pentagon that I talked to about your...well, I'm not sure what to call it. Maybe a gift? If it's possible to know things that might happen that are crucial to our national security, then it would be a huge help to all of us, especially someone like James, who bears the brunt of the backlash after events like this."

"I see." And then I was silent. And angry.

"Pea, are you there?"

"So...You told two others. Just out of curiosity, are they listening right now?"

"No."

"Allen, is this call being recorded?" I asked, in a snotty tone.

"Pea, don't be silly. They just want to ask you a few questions."

"Are 'they' the same people who OK the traffic cameras to look for anything 'suspicious'? Are you going to rat me out because of some coincidence? Geez, Allen!"

"Come on, you know looking into stuff like this is part of my job. I collect interesting information and move bodies around to protect our interests here at home," he said, patiently.

He was being calmer than normal. I was convinced that someone could hear us talking. It's not like there aren't hundreds of people listening for cryptic verbiage to pass along to someone who would care. It's not like anything I told Allen was cryptic at all. I should have been more careful.

"Allen, I'm not a government stooge. I'm sorry to learn that you are!" I said very coldly then hung up.

I don't think I've been so angry since John died. I had felt like Allen was kind of an irritating but playful and protective big brother of sorts. I thought that maybe he was in my life to offer a frank opinion when I needed one and company when I was missing John the most. To say that I feel betrayed is not severe enough a statement. I will never tell him anything again. Using James to get me to cooperate was just too low, even for him, a guy who has been so happy to scrape the bottom of the ethics barrel for years on end.

I've gotten too paranoid for my own good. I was a much more tolerable person to be around before my dreams started getting weird. I know I shouldn't have told anyone. I must sound like an anarchist lunatic to a Pentagon eavesdropper.

Now I wonder if I should tell James about any of this. It's probably better not to. He would worry and probably wonder if Allen isn't somewhat right about helping the nation with my warped dreams.

* * *

James called, and he'll be home the first week in February. I couldn't be more excited. I've been feeling a little isolated lately. I haven't been to church in two weeks, and I haven't talked to Allen either. I'm wondering if I flew off the handle a bit. Doesn't matter anyhow. The fact is that I don't feel like I can trust him anymore. And, at this point in my life, I don't really want to invest myself in someone I don't trust, even if that particular person buried my beloved Tarzan, before turning me in to the Pentagon's Psychic Friends Network.

Teddy came up to see me. He has a few buddies in DC and wanted to catch up with them, and me, of course. I ended up having him invite all of them here so he can see them all at once, have a meal, and relax. I know most of them anyhow.

We had a great visit, albeit short. He's still single, and so am I. It was nice to be around someone who isn't in a mad dash to coupledom, or worse, a married couple in a state of perpetual bliss. He and I did some shopping at the mall and saw some art galleries. There was a 10k run this weekend in Annapolis, and Teddy decided to participate at the last minute. He can do that, as he is built like Dad. Exercise and exertion are, for them, mutually exclusive.

James e-mailed and suggested that we go shopping for a new dog when he's here in February. I like that idea. I did feel less lonely before poor Tarzan croaked. I think I may be dealing with a mild bout of depression over losing the big shitter. He was my best friend, my coffee buddy, my walking partner, and my watchdog. You can't just go out and get a replacement for a dog like that, but we'll try.

James will be here in February, and I'll have a visit from Nana in late March, then Henry and Isabel may visit in May. It's Thursday night. Perhaps I should be at happy hour somewhere celebrating the (almost) end of the workweek. Unfortunately, just as when James was a baby, my days are all the same.

I have been trying to keep busy. I've sewn more one-of-a-kind children's clothes. I think I've got enough samples to show to the boutique owner down the street. I'm going to volunteer at the gallery more, too, as I have gotten somewhat attached to George. He makes me laugh.

The next morning, around ten o'clock, the doorbell rang. I had a towel on my head and was in some baggy jeans and John's Fort Bragg hockey team T-shirt. I thought it was the postman. As soon as I cracked the door, I cringed. It was Jack, from the Wounded Warriors fundraiser last month.

"Uh, Jack, hi. Were you just in the neighborhood, or are you a Jehovah's Witness?"

"Yes to the first, no to the second. Catholic. Uh, I'm sorry. I was out with Mags and Lee last night. You said I couldn't have your number, so I asked Mags if she had your address. I was going to send you a note and tell you how much fun I had with you at the event, but then I needed to leave unexpectedly for two weeks. So...I had your note and was over at the Harley shop three miles from here. I decided to try to hand deliver my note instead of mailing it since I was nearby. Do people do that kind of thing anymore?"

"Hand-delivered notes? No...but they should." I smiled. How nice to have company. I looked a mess, but it didn't seem to bother him. He looked a little nervous but not *entirely* revolted by my towel head and less-than-fresh face. Thank God I at least had clothes on and not that ratty robe that I usually wear around the house.

"Come in, Jack. I just made a fresh pot....Just gimme a few minutes to clean up here..." I failed to mention that I was up late last night thinking about things that are out of my control and wondering if maybe I should go meet those goons at the Pentagon.

"Prudence, if this is a bad time, maybe we could get some dinner this weekend?" He must think I'm pretty lazy—no makeup and a towel on my head at 10:00 a.m. But, I didn't want him to leave.

"Or you can have some coffee while I finish up, and we can get some lunch in an hour? Are you off today?"

"Yeah. They give us time to decompress after we have unexpected work overseas."

"Oh. I get it. Super-secret stuff, huh?" I handed him a mug of coffee and smiled. "I'll be quick!" I said, then hurried up the stairs. When I made it to the top, I let loose a mile-wide smile. I was so happy he ignored my "no" that night and contacted me anyway. I had been hoping he would. I quickly dried my hair, got some makeup on, and brushed my teeth (again).

We headed out for a walk so I could run a few errands. Jack mentioned he needed a haircut, which is ridiculous since he had it shaved so close already, but whatever. I took him to Ellie's husband's barbershop on Maryland Avenue. Jack got a razor shave with hot foam and left with a shiny new melon. I found myself wondering what he looked like with hair...He doesn't appear to be balding, but it's hard to tell.

I needed to drop off those samples at the children's boutique for the owner's opinion. I left Jack outside for a few minutes and went in to meet with her. She seemed to like the rustic style of my children's linen gowns and was going to put together an order. I was over the moon, especially since I had someone to celebrate with.

"So, Jack, I'd like to say that I'm usually engaged in some kind of intellectually stimulating project by 10:00 a.m. each morning, but the fact is, my dog died, and he was my alarm clock. We'd take a walk at six every morning and get a coffee. I miss that. I've been staying up late and sleeping in a lot since he died."

"I'm sorry you lost your buddy. Was he sick or just up in years?"

"Just old, I think. I got him for John...a tenth anniversary gift. I think that dog was just one more thing I wasn't ready to lose. But he lasted much longer than his breed usually does. I miss his wet nose waking me each morning. I guess I'm gonna need to get an alarm clock..."

"Or...You could just use your cell phone?", he suggested.

"I don't have or want one...I still use a landline and an answering machine."

Jack looked back at me, smiled and chuckled, "You're right. Maybe an alarm clock would be better for you. I wish I needed one. I have an awful habit of getting up at five each morning. It's from years of military life. I usually hit the gym early, eat breakfast, and then head to work at the Pentagon."

"Oh, you work there too?"

"Yeah. Do you have other acquaintances there?"

"Just some old buddies of John's. Most of his friends are still in the army, stationed at the Pentagon. They check in on me sometimes."

"Anyone I might know?" he queried.

"Yes. Probably too well, so let's just pretend you don't, OK?"

"Whatever you say. You hungry yet?" he asked, patting his svelte stomach.

"Yeah. I was about to sit down and eat breakfast when a big, bald fella knocked on my door this morning," I said, smiling.

"Well, in that case, let's eat something. I ate breakfast at six, so I'm pretty famished."

"What sounds good, Jack? We've got about forty restaurants in a quarter-mile radius."

"I'm not particular. I just want to eat something that had parents. I'm not into froufrou unless I've already eaten something ahead of time."

"OK, I'll pick then. I want a BLT. I know a place."

I took him around the block once then headed back to my house. He smiled when we arrived at my front door. "Are you a good cook?" he asked enthusiastically.

"I have heard that once or twice. Besides, I need more coffee."

I made BLTs on my homemade bread, with extra-thick bacon from the butcher down the street. We had some soup that I made yesterday and more bread and cheese. I had half an apple-berry pie in the fridge that we finished off, then we had more coffee. It was fun to have company again. Especially really handsome company. I tried not to look at him too much.

Jack seemed a little surprised when I told him it was time to go around 2:00 p.m. I made the suggestion because I didn't want him to think that I had nothing else to do today or to know how utterly boring my days are compared to his secretive meetings in foreign languages and frequent traveling. He must have lots to do if he's been away for two weeks, anyhow.

He startled me with a big bear hug out of nowhere. I just turned around, and there he was, picking me up in the process. I didn't know what to do and couldn't move. I was as stiff as a day-old dead fish. He found it funny, how nervous I was while being hugged by him. If he had any idea how nervous, he would have squeezed even harder, just to get a reaction out of me. Jack's more playful than his serious façade would suggest. My face was more than a little red. He put me down and said, "I'm considering your idea about getting rid of my two bikes and just having one, since they are both getting somewhat neglected. What do you think about a Lowrider?"

"Uh, well, if they have a lower center of gravity, then maybe they're easier to ride?"

"Yep. Can I get your number from Mags?"

"Yeah." I said casually, with a smile peeking out of the left side of my mouth. I was trying to be cool, but cool isn't my forte. He said a quick good-bye then was out the door.

I spent the rest of the afternoon picking weeds and putting seeds in for the spring. It would only be a few weeks until I had microgreens for my salad each night. I couldn't wait. I was sick of buying everything from the store and paying too much for stuff that even a starved rabbit wouldn't eat.

I went into the basement for the first time in several weeks. It was cold, of course, since the basement has a two-hundred-year-old stone foundation. I was thinking about trying to make my own cheese in the spring, maybe putting a little cheese cave and wine cellar in to keep all John's wine. I thought about getting a nice wine cooler, but one that holds 150 to 250 bottles starts around six thousand dollars—too much. So, I thought I'd see what I could do to the basement to make it wine friendly. I guess I could also keep root veggies down there, too, and maybe my flower bulbs that can't be overwintered.

I was trying not to think about Jack. Trying hard not to think of how nice a warm hug from a man felt. Allen used to hug me when he left our house, but they felt like hugs from Teddy. Jack's hug nearly squeezed the breath out of me. He's big but a little leaner than John was. I hope he didn't find my kind-of squishy body repelling. I am in my forties after all. I'm thin, and my belly looks fine in a pair of jeans and a T-shirt, but if I hadn't been the only single woman under sixty at the Kennedy Center, I doubt Jack would have paid me any attention.

I finished up the backyard and started to sketch a new design for the basement. The temperature in the basement close to the stone floor is perfect for aging cheese—between 50 and 55 degrees—and I can store the wine closer to the basement ceiling, which registers around 62 degrees. I spent the evening surfing the Internet for books on artisan cheese making and building wine storage.

It was midnight before I was tired. Our little block is so quiet. So is the house. With no dog to keep me company, I'm starting to realize just how lonely I am, especially after having such a fun morning with Jack. I decided to make some tea and curl up in John's chair. I was missing John's company, the easiness of it, the fact that he was always with me at night in the quiet. As I started to doze off, I heard John's voice in my head, "Don't be afraid, wife..."

I settled into sleep. There were so many things going on at once. I saw rockets coming from Gaza into the Old City of Jerusalem. I saw a face, a jihadist, ordering an attack on the Jews in the Old City. Another man asked him a question. He answered, "Any Muslims killed in the Old City will be martyrs...It is not our will, but Allah's."

His face was distinct. He had a long, poker-straight beard, unusual, high-end eyeglasses, and thick, unruly eyebrows. I heard screaming and sirens. The Western Wall fell to pieces. There were worshippers in the rubble, the men on the left side, and the women on the right, crushed by the ancient stone, their bodies burned by exploding rockets. The children were in their schools as the buildings were crushed. Mothers and fathers, searching heaps of shattered concrete, were crying over small, silent bodies.

In the background were the sounds of the afternoon prayers being chanted in Arabic, from the turrets outside of the Old City. Mobs of angry Jewish men began to form and head into the Muslim quarter to vandalize the Dome of the Rock mosque, the third-holiest site in Islam.

From outside the city came teams of Israeli commandos, trying to determine the extent of the damage while keeping chaos from spreading, but it was too late. The Muslims inside the Old City thought that they were being purged, and they armed themselves. Mobs of Jews headed toward the mosque to take the holy place in return for the destruction of the Western Wall. They marched past me. I was there in the crowd of weeping mothers, holding a baby photo of James, for he was among the children in the rubble. My head was covered with John's blanket and my eyes drowning in salty tears.

It was eight in the morning when I woke, still sobbing. I couldn't keep this dream to myself. I had seen the face of the man who gave the orders. As improbable as it was that I could help anyone with anything remotely important, I picked up my phone and dialed Allen.

My voice was nearly inaudible. "Allen, it's me. I'll come in. The dream I had last night, it was...very...explicit."

"Pea, are you crying? Are you OK?"

"Yes, just shaken. I'm a bit of a mess," I mumbled in a cracked voice.

"I'll send a car for you. Can you be ready in an hour in front of the coffee shop on Maryland Ave?" Allen's voice was gentle, reassuring.

"Yes."

"OK, don't worry. This will be painless, Pea, really. I wouldn't ask you to talk if I didn't think you might have something. I didn't even tell them your name yet. I gave you a secret code name. Want to hear it?"

"Allen, I'm not in the mood to joke."

"I think you'll like it..." I could just see him smiling, obviously pleased with himself.

"You're gonna tell me either way, aren't you?"

"You're Red Rider! Pretty clever, huh? Because of your hair color... and, you like to ride Harleys. You get it?"

"Yes. I get it. You're a dork, Allen." I started to smile. He is pretty funny when he tries so desperately to be clever.

"Yep. Funny huh? Anyhow, the guy picking you up won't know your name or where you live, but he's a good guy. Used to drive President Bush around. His name in Mac. Please don't be scared."

"Unmarked cars and drivers and code names? Allen, is all of this necessary?"

"Just taking precautions, Pea. No worries, OK?"

"All right. One hour. I'm a mess, so don't expect much."

"Worse than when we buried Tarzan?"

"Yes."

"Calm down, OK? I'll see you soon." And he hung up.

It was hard getting rid of the red eyes and blotchy patches on my face from crying so hard. I took a hot shower to calm down and relax. I was so tense. The muscles in my neck were tired with worry, and if I weren't going in to see some super-secret agents, I would have had a couple stiff drinks first.

I managed to get my hair out of the shower cap, mostly dry, and touched up the limp parts with the curling iron. What to wear? The temperature was only in the thirties this morning. I put my jeans, boots, a blouse, sweater, down jacket, and wool gloves on. I slopped some cream on my face and light makeup. I thought that if I tried to look casual, then I would feel more relaxed...Besides, I had nothing businesslike to wear anyhow. The twenty pounds I lost after John died made all of my slacks look very untidy, and I didn't have any reason to buy new ones, I guess, until today.

I grabbed my purse and dialed Dad to tell him that I was having lunch with a friend in Old Town. I asked for him and Mom to come by for dinner tonight. I was being paranoid, but I wanted to have someone looking for me, just in case I ended up in some Jack Bower-like situation, hauled off to some secret basement room at the National Security Agency, a room that even my uncle, who works there, wouldn't know about.

The black sedan with dark windows pulled up. A tall, thick man in his sixties got out and looked at me. He asked if I was Red Rider. I said yes and asked if his name might be Mac. He smiled and said, "They usually send me out to get fat, ugly guys, not cute redheads! Do you want to get a coffee to go? General Gravenstein is expecting you in forty-five minutes."

"Yeah, I'll get one, and yours, too. Do you take cream and sugar?"

"No, just black, Miss. Thanks."

"Right, of course."

Mac sped down Route 50 like Roscoe P. Coltrane in hot pursuit. Rush hour was a nonissue for us, as we were trucking along at ninety miles per hour in the HOV lane, with the lights on and cars pulling over to get out of our way.

We made it to the Pentagon, at rush hour, in less than twenty-five minutes—a new record, I think. We entered the security gates on the east wing of the building then Mac took me inside, through the x-ray machines and metal detectors and past soldiers with machine guns who patted me down and searched my bag. I was sweating bullets.

We headed to an elevator and went up to the third floor. Allen was waiting in the hall. He had on a perfectly pressed uniform and his work face. He actually looked handsome. I had no idea he had so many medals. There was barely room on his uniform for his nameplate. I was feeling small next to Allen, for the very first time.

Allen could see that I was nervous, so he dismissed Mac, took me to his office, and asked his secretary, Jean, not to disturb us until his appointment arrived. He shut the door behind us then showed me to the small, cigar-colored leather couch across from his desk. There were two other chairs there, I suspect, for our company. Allen finally turned his smile on to relax me. He apologized for the formalities but insisted that people are on edge in the building, and not following protocol makes them even more so.

Jean brought in the coffee service then quietly stepped out again.

Allen sat down next to me. "Pea, this is all kind of new to us, too. I mean, we don't stumble across people like you too often, and when we do, they are rarely so accurate. What made you decide to call me this morning?"

"Well, late last night, I was falling asleep, and I heard John's voice in my head telling me not to be afraid." He looked at me sympathetically then nodded for me to continue. "I started into a deep sleep, then saw so many disturbing things...Rockets from Gaza, the Old City being destroyed, shattered bodies under the rubble of the Western Wall, the mobs, the crying mothers, dead children, commandos storming the Old City, utter chaos. It was just too much. But I saw a face, someone giving the orders, a jihadist with distinct facial features..." I went into as much detail as I could recall. The look of fascination on Allen's face was impossible to miss.

Jean peeked in to announce the two intelligence guys. Allen sensed my anxiety and took my hand. "Pea, they don't know your name, but I've known the tall guy five years or more. He's been through a lot, like me. The other guy's my 'heavy.' He handles my security and a few other things. Don't tell them anything about yourself, just what you dreamt of. All they know is that your husband was a good friend of mine."

I was feeling guilty for thinking that Allen was trying to exploit me. "Allen, I'm sorry I flew off the handle last time you called. I'm just very private, and I don't like any of this. I'll try to be helpful, but I'm really uncomfortable telling anyone what's going on in my head. I feel like it's John. Or, somehow related to John. I'm not sure what all of it is supposed to mean or why it's me who's seeing these horrible things."

"Pea, all kidding aside, you and John had something remarkable. It's obvious that you miss him, and no one would think you're nuts for that. The way he felt about you...Well, I've just never seen anything like it. I'm glad you called this morning. And I'll try not to tease you about your dreams anymore, OK?" Just as Allen finished his sentence, there was a quiet knock at the door. Two men stepped inside, one in a crisp white uniform (and lots of medals) and another who could pass for a mean, hairy tree trunk. Allen started the introductions.

"Pea, this is..."

Holy crap.

"Jack?" I asked, confused. Jack was the crisp white uniform.

"Pea, you know Jack?" Allen shot a chilly look at Jack, who seemed just as surprised to see me here.

"You're Red Rider?" Jack asked me with a cautious look. His eyes were less warm than I'd seen them. Maybe he was thinking that I'd met him on purpose to get information from him. This was too awkward for words. If Jack's face hadn't looked quite so stupefied, then I would have been angry. It was obvious that he didn't know that it was me Allen had discovered as a possible informant—or whatever you'd call someone like me.

"And this is Joe. He knows the region we'll be discussing quite well. He'll be able to find out if anything you've dreamt about is in the works or not." Allen gestured to the solemn, unkempt man next to Jack.

Joe wasn't tall (or clean-cut) like Allen or Jack. Joe had very thick shoulders, rather disheveled civilian clothing, a beard, and kind of oily, tangly, chin-length hair. Very intense. Who knows what the guy really does. He didn't show an ounce of emotion during the hour I spent rehashing last night's dream. Neither did Jack. The only one who gave me decent facial feedback here was Allen. He knows how private I am and how uncomfortable it was being here, talking to these guys.

Allen pulled up some head shots of jihadists who could have been the face giving orders in my dream. Surprisingly, there was one photo that stood out—a man who looked younger than the man I saw, but Allen said that the photo was dated and that the guy's been off the radar for a while. Jack and Joe sat and listened as I finished telling them about when my dreams started getting violent. I tried to remember as much as I could, but it's been nearly a year since this all started.

The three of them kept looking at each other, silently communicating with their eyes. I stopped talking and asked for some water. Jack and Allen both got up at the same time to grab some from the tray. Allen glanced at him, and Jack sat down, obviously outranked at this particular juncture. I took a sip, then looked at the three faces and said quietly, "Please pardon my frankness, but if telling you these things isn't much help, then I'd rather keep it to myself. It's frightening enough just knowing that some of my dreams may have happened...But, all of this...being here...having my thoughts dissected...is really unnerving."

Allen responded, "I think what you've told us here, this morning, will be very helpful. It's very important that you do not discuss this meeting or your dreams with anyone else. Seriously, there are people who would like to know such premonitions. Don't tell your family, friends, or whomever. These are very sensitive subjects. And don't watch the news. If anything, we don't want your dreams to be influenced from the outside. They'll be less reliable."

"Gladly. The news makes me crazy paranoid anyhow." I was feeling relieved that they were finally ready to wrap up. The only thing that would have made the past two hours worse would have been a dark room with a bright light shining in my face or maybe some live wires and a spray bottle.

"Jack, Joe, you two want to add anything before I send her home?" Allen asked.

"Thank you for coming in today," Jack said, with a vacant look. He and Joe left and shut the door quietly behind them.

Allen immediately looked at me with a smirk, "Pea, how do you know Jack?" Geez. As if my life wasn't already some cheesy satire for Allen to critique at will.

"I met him at a Wounded Warriors fundraiser at the Kennedy Center last month. He's good buddies with a couple that were seated at my table, Maggie and Lee O'Connor. Do you know them?"

"I've met Lee once or twice. Did he retire?"

"He did. Maggie introduced me to Jack. Neither of us had a date. We ended up talking a bit. I had to go to the event. My buddy, Ellie, planned the whole thing, and I was invited personally after the donation I made from John's foundation. It was a fun night until Tarzan died. He was waiting up for me then fell asleep next to my bed. I called you shortly after..."

"Pea, don't get me wrong, Jack's a decent guy...I just didn't know that you guys were familiar." His face was different now, soft.

"Well, we weren't, not really, anyhow, until a few days ago, when he showed up at my door, and we spent much of the day together." Allen was no longer smiling.

I realized that I was giving him too much information. I hadn't talked to him in a month. He must feel a little stupid for not knowing about my time with Jack. He seemed, if possible, a tiny bit jealous or protective or something. It was an expression I hadn't seen on him before. I couldn't believe he was letting his poker face waver. Maybe he was hurt.

I changed the subject. "Allen, do you want to get lunch? I'm a little hungry, and I was wondering how I'm going to get home."

"Let me finish up some paperwork here, and then I'll take you home myself. Can you wait an hour or so to eat, or are you starved?" Allen had his work face (and voice) on again.

"I can wait. Besides, Mac's driving scared me. I'd rather you take me home."

"Fine. But, I need to take care of a few things first. I'll have Jean get you a cup of tea, or would you like some fresh coffee?"

"You're going to talk about me to Jack and Joe, aren't you?" He didn't answer. He instead looked as if he were gently scolding me.

"Coffee or tea, Pea?"

"Is the coffee any good?"

"No."

"Then tea, please," I whimpered.

"Don't touch anything. I'll see if Jean has any magazines you can flip through."

"Yes, sir." I said with a furrowed brow then smiled. He didn't smile back. He had work to do.

I don't know when Jean has time to read magazines, but she had tons of them stashed under her desk—maybe for Allen's "friends" when they come by to pay him an afternoon(er) visit.

Jean is matronly, not at all what I expected. I imagined he would have some buxom bombshell in a tight-fitting blouse and pencil skirt with a slit up the back. Jean seems more along the lines of a mother figure. I can't imagine much getting past her. I guess she hears and sees a lot. I'm not pretty enough or cool enough to be someone of consequence. Maybe that's why she was so sweet to me. She knows that I'm not some floozy stopping in to service Allen over lunch.

Two hours later, Allen returned. He apologized for taking so long, but he's not the type to rush work. I imagine I gave them a lot to chew on today.

It was almost 2:00 p.m., and I was famished. I suggested we grab something in the cafeteria to go. But he kept looking at his watch, so I let him off the hook. "Allen, have Mac take me home. I know you're busy. I was kidding about his driving. Besides, I like feeling like a diplomat."

"Would that be OK? I wanted to take you myself, but I think I need to stay here and work late tonight. I'm sorry. It's just that what you said this morning seems to have tied together a few leads. I'll be away for a bit. I'll call you when I get back." His focus was strictly on work now.

"Has what I said put anyone in danger?" I asked quietly.

"No one you should feel sorry for, Pea."

"Just bad guys?" I didn't expect an answer.

"Always just bad guys. Go home; relax if you can. Try not to worry. I'll be in touch." It would be weeks before I heard from him again.

As Mac drove me home, I thought about what would happen to the jihadist that I had identified. I couldn't bring myself to chitchat, although I suspect Mac had some funny stories to tell. Driving the president around has to be the most interesting job there is. To know everything, to be trusted that way, must be very gratifying for someone in the Secret Service.

He dropped me off around 4:30 p.m. Allen must have told him not to put the lights on and speed through traffic as he had this morning, which I greatly appreciated. I didn't need to be any more tense than I was already.

I checked the answering machine. Dad called. He and Mom would be over at seven to join me for dinner. I had just enough time to hit the market for a couple big steaks, some salad stuff, and a few éclairs from the French bakery. I threw a bistro dinner together with some seared beef, a big Bordeaux, rosemary pan-fried potatoes, crusty bread, and greens dressed with my homemade red wine vinegar and some fruity olive oil. They arrived a little late, around eight. As we gathered in the kitchen, I poured the wine and asked my folks about their recent travels.

Mom and Dad had just returned from a Munich trip, taken on a whim. I think Teddy floated the idea to Mom first. Dad, of course, was thrilled to go just about anywhere at a moment's notice. He gets a natural high just from getting on a plane. He should have been an airman.

Mom went into detail about the Eagle's Nest, where the third Reich and Nazi command were. The stories told on those tours were hard for Mom to stomach. Their tour guide, an Austrian, mentioned that many of the Nazis who initially fled after the war returned many years later with extravagant riches from looting their prey. Mom thinks she spotted a few old Nazis in Munich. They were hard to miss—tall, proud, and unabashedly wealthy older men.

We were eating dinner when there was a knock at the door. I just about jumped out of my seat. Dad looked at me like I was crazy. I think I am. Nine o'clock seems a little late for casual company. I answered the door and was surprised to find Jack standing there. He didn't smile. He looked detached. I slid out the front, took his arm, and headed down the street a bit to speak with him privately, before Mom got nosy and stuck her head out to peek.

"Jack...You must have lots of questions for me, huh?" I couldn't read his face in the dark.

"Prudence..."

"Just call me Pea. Everyone else does. I think you know enough about me now to use my nickname. Of course, you can call me Red Rider if you're here on official business."

He cracked a smile. "Actually, I'm gonna be working a lot. Out of town. My calls will be monitored, so..."

"So, are you disappointed that I'm not as boring as you may have thought, or perhaps you think me psychotic?"

"Tell you the truth, I was definitely surprised to see that you're the woman with the dreams. But, I'd say that makes you interesting, not psychotic." Jack paused for a moment. He looked down, took a deep breath, and continued in a less confident tone, "I noticed that Allen had your hand...And...well, I'm here to ask if there's anything I should be aware of before I come by to see you again."

"Did Allen say something to you?"

"No. Not specifically."

"Then...Are you asking if there's something between Allen and me?"

"Yes," he said with a staid look.

"I'm not sure what to say. Allen's helped me a great deal this year. I've had a hard time. I'm sure the fact that I dream about my dead husband all the time and hear him talking to me when I'm passed out asleep doesn't make me much of a realist. But I can tell Allen things and expect an honest response."

"Geez, Pea. I don't think you're crazy for dreaming about John. I still miss my wife sometimes. But, I'd be willing to give it a shot with someone else at some point."

"Jack, I'm not at the *some point* yet," I muttered.

"I figured that, and I get it, I do. But, I guess what I'm asking is, if you *were* willing...I mean, if I was to pursue you, would I be competing with a dead guy or my current boss?"

"Uh, Jack..." I wasn't used to such bluntness. Or maybe it was the fact that no one's asked me out in twenty-five years. At least, no one I was drawn to. I could feel my cheeks getting red.

He slowly moved his hand out to touch my face. But, I instinctively stepped back and looked away. He slid his hands in his pockets. Seeing the terrified look on my face, Jack smiled and softened his voice.

"Pea, Allen's a good guy, a stellar guy, even if he is in the army. But, he outranks me. There could be a problem if you two have something and I unknowingly try and horn in. I'm just trying to get my bearings here, before I toss my hat in the ring." I was nervous and started to fidget with my hair. Jack just stood there, calmly. He was used to speaking his mind, I guess. I tried to be succinct, too, but a bunch of garbled—but honest—nonsense made its way out of my mouth.

"Uh. Well, nothing has ever happened between Allen and me. I feel safe with him, but more in a big brother sort of way. I don't know if he feels anything more for me or not. I highly doubt it. Spending time with him makes me miss John less. He knew me before I was a wreck, understands the extent of my loss. He loved John. They were like brothers. He must feel somehow responsible for me, or something. I don't understand it completely. I've never actually tried to analyze what we are..."

"You mean like you are now?" he teased.

"I guess. I think he still sees me as his buddy's wife, and I'm most comfortable with that definition."

Jack was unconvinced. "Allen doesn't look at you like you're a buddy's wife," he stated, lifting his eyebrows. "Well, I guess you've answered my question. Can I see you when I get back?"

I was hoping to spend a little more time with him, before he went wherever. "Jack, stay for dinner. My folks are here. We were just discussing the rich former Nazis posing in Munich with their stolen loot."

"Pea, don't you ever talk about simple stuff?"

"I'd like to, but nobody's letting me today."

"Ah. Yes. Maybe I could lighten up the conversation a bit?"

"Please!" I pleaded. "My folks have no idea what happened this morning, and quite honestly, I need to calm down. Maybe you could turn on some of that navy charm with my mom. She's easy. If you give her one compliment, she'll be yours forever!"

"My kind of gal," he said, winking.

"Is that so?" I smirked.

"Yep. But I need a drink or two, to digest all of this. It's been a long day. I generally try to steer clear of women who possess supernatural powers," he chuckled.

"Real funny, Jack." I tried to look serious, but my lips curled up, and I was unwillingly smiling. I seem to find myself having fun with Jack, even when I try really hard not to. And, he knows that I still love John. How perfect that he misses his wife, too, sometimes.

We walked back. It was cold out, and I was shivering in my thin sweater. He opened the door for me with one hand and held the small of my back with the other, gently nudging me inside to face my mother... with a new male friend at my side...How silly of me to think the Spanish Inquisition was over for today.

6

Jimmy Deans and Buttered Nipples

~

"Mom! You look great! I'm starved. When are we eating?"

"We have to get to the car first, and then home. It's nice to see that you're exactly the same—always hungry. I was worried! You've been gone so long, and I know things are ugly in the Middle East..."

"Who said I was in the Middle East?"

"Well, I asked Allen if you've been in the Middle East, and he didn't deny it, so..."

"Mom, you know Allen isn't gonna tell you anything. Besides, I thought you disowned him for skipping Dad's funeral."

"Well, I'm tolerating him now. He's turned out to be a good friend, I think. You can't repeat this, but he dug the hole that Tarzan's buried in behind the house."

"How'd you get him to do that?"

"I traded his services for a bottle of scotch."

"I wish I would have known that bribing a general was that easy. You think he's got a thing for you?"

"I don't think so. I think he feels like he needs to keep tabs on me. You know, keep me out of trouble. He gave me a hard time about my Africa trip."

"Speaking of which, why didn't you put the pictures on the web so I could see them?"

"James, honey, you know I don't know how to do all that stuff."

"Time to learn, Mom. I'll just put that on the list of stuff we need to do this week."

"I only get you for a week?"

"Mom, I'm really sorry. I actually have about two weeks, but I need to take care of some stuff, before I head out again...like seeing Tiny a little bit."

"Tiny? Have you two been keeping in touch?"

"Actually, a little bit more than keeping in touch. She came out to Germany a couple months ago when I had a long weekend off. And we've been writing pretty much nonstop for six months now."

"I don't understand why you didn't mention this before! I've seen her for two hairdos since then. Boy, am I out of the loop on that one!" I was hurt, and he could see that. I tried not to pout too much; after all, my son is a man in his midtwenties. He can have a girlfriend or whatever she is without getting the OK from me first. I guess I encouraged it, so I should be happy.

"Mom, I wanted to make sure there was something there, I mean, long term, before filling you in. I know you like her, and I didn't want you to get upset if we dated and things didn't work out. And that's not the case, so I need to tell you...I think she's *the one*. It doesn't make sense, especially with me being away so much and never knowing when I'll be home. But, I'd like to take her somewhere next week, just the two of us...and...ask her to be my wife..."

"Whoa! What? I can't believe you kept this from me!" I took a minute to let it all sink in. I was feeling abandoned, again, even though his dad didn't actually choose to leave me. I knew James would someday marry. Just hearing him say it, out loud, hit home. He's not mine anymore. It was quiet for a minute, until I realized I was being a baby.

I tried to smile and took his arm in mine. "I'm sorry, son. I'd love to help with whatever you need. Were you hoping to make this a sooner or later event?"

"Well, I don't have much time. I was hoping to have something small, next time I have leave. But, she may have other ideas. We'll need to figure that out."

James was a little irked when I pointed out Booger in the parking lot. "Holy shit! Mom! Are you serious? This your car? Where's the AMG?"

I guess I'd forgotten to tell him that I bought a snot-green go-cart. It seems we both had a few surprises to share tonight.

We headed back to my little place in Annapolis. James hadn't seen it yet. I knew he'd rather have stayed at the big house in Baltimore, but this is my life now, and I needed to pare it down. Not having to care for that house, or the grounds, has made my life a whole lot easier. Besides, the renters are paying the mortgage, and I won't have to make any decisions on that house for a while still.

I wish that the lights and Christmas decorations were still up in the historic district, but it's nearly March. Spring is almost here. And the two-year anniversary of John's death is coming up. I feel like I've grown a lot this year, but I still see him, feel him, and hear him, just rather seldom now.

We pulled onto my street. James seemed excited. Apart from all the midshipmen, James always liked this town. It has a charm that escapes very few.

"There it is...the yellow one on the end, with the Christmas lights still up."

"Really cute! It suits you, Mom. You always had simpler taste than Dad. He was definitely the peacock in the family. Where's all our stuff?"

"Mostly still in the other house. Now that you may have your own home, with Tiny, I'll have some things for you two to start your own home with, if you like."

"Does that include Dad's chair?" James asked excitedly.

"That's a negative, Lieutenant Brandt. Chair's mine. Period."

"OK, just thought I'd ask. I remember falling asleep on Dad's lap in that chair."

"Answer's no. You can have it when I'm dead and not a sec sooner!"

"How about Great-Grandpa's cedar trunk?"

"That's a no, too. Tarzan is in it, and there's gonna be a fig tree growing on top of it in a week or two."

"You put Tarzan in Grandpa's cedar trunk??? Ma, you know how much I liked that thing! I wanted to give it to my son!"

"What son?"

"The one I'll have someday."

"Are you sure there's no other reason you're in such a hurry to get married?"

"Mom, I'd be lying if I said I wasn't anxious. I just want to do things in the right order. And, if it's not really soon, the order may indeed get fuzzy."

"Point taken. Please don't elaborate. It's weird enough that I have a hair appointment next month and I'll have to pretend that we didn't just have this conversation."

James ducked as he fumbled out of the passenger's seat. "How do you lock this thing up? Is there something I missed here?"

"It's manual, and the windows are, too. Not exactly luxury, but I don't care if it gets dinged up, which it already has since moving here. The college students can't park worth a lick. Seriously, I think they are trying to hit me."

"A few dings might actually improve this car. Or, better yet, maybe it'll roll into the harbor some night while you're in bed, sleeping..."

"Very funny. At least I have a car! How's your bike in the rain, son? You'd better be nice, or I'll take your Christmas presents back..."

The evening went faster than I wanted it to. I imagine my time with him will always seem short now. James will soon be a husband. I'm already agonizing over that, and she hasn't even said yes yet. I'm feeling more alone already.

The next morning, James got up early. The time difference didn't allow him much shut-eye, but it didn't seem to matter. We went to the diner up the street for some breakfast and coffee.

"Sweetie?" I asked, while fiddling with my mug.

"Yeah? Mom, you look nervous. What's up?"

"Do you want my ring for Tiny?" I asked quietly, as the server poured more coffee.

"That one?" he asked, looking at my left hand, "Really? It's beautiful. But, are you ready to part with it?"

"Yes, this one. I'd like to keep it here, but it's been almost two years. I should probably stop wearing it on my ring finger anyhow. If you don't think Tiny would like it, then I won't be hurt, I promise. It's your call. I had Daddy's band soldered to mine after he died. I don't really need the diamond ring, as long as our bands are together."

"In that case, can I have the chair, too?"

"No. And stop asking about the chair!"

"OK, sorry. Thought I'd give it one more try."

"James! You're rotten!" I said, trying to be mad. He shrugged, stuffed a whole biscuit in his mouth, and smiled, crumbs falling all over his fitted Charlie Company T-shirt.

I reached down and pulled a small, navy blue leather box from my purse and put it on the table. That box had been living in the middle top drawer of my dresser since John proposed. "Here's the box, sweetie. I think Daddy would be OK with me handing it over to you now, since you picked such a stellar mate. I remember the two of us picking it out at an antiques shop by his folks' house. It's not exactly Tiffany's, so if Tiny wants to upgrade in a few years, then I want it back!"

"Fair enough." He was beaming. I can't believe my little boy will soon have a wife. She'll be his everything, just as it should be.

We stopped by the small jeweler in the harbor to have the diamond ring cleaned, then walked back to the house. I was feeling a little down. I sat and stared at my now-unremarkable left hand. James caught on to my sadness and tried to cheer me up. He immediately got on the Internet to look for dog breeders in the area who had puppies ready to go. I didn't think I was ready to love another dog, but now that James is leaving me, a puppy doesn't seem like such a bad idea.

"Mom, you need a little buddy! It's too quiet here! There's a Weimaraner breeder over in Easton."

"Those gray dogs in the funny photos?"

"Yeah, they've got a girl and a boy. Here, look!" I leaned over his shoulder and looked at the screen. I've never seen a puppy with bedroom eyes before...like a little, goofy, gray, Paul Newman...

"So beautiful. But I think I like ugly, slobbery dogs better. They seem to have better personalities. Do you see anything else that looks promising?

"Nope. I think this is the dog for you, Mom. It says here that Weims don't shed, and they think they're human. They get separation anxiety when their owners are away too long."

"Perfect. A psychotic dog. Just like me. And no dog hair to pick up? Let's go!"

I suspect most people who buy a thousand-dollar dog drive a finer car. Weims are a tad aristocratic but still very playful and love to be outside. Good, because I need a walking partner for the mornings. James and I headed over to the Eastern Shore and, forty minutes later, pulled into a very long driveway. We could hear the kenneled dogs howling as we rolled up to the house. Perhaps the dogs were laughing at Booger. I rang the doorbell. A friendly woman about my age with a soft ponytail and clear sun-kissed skin answered the door wearing a white button-up shirt and overalls.

"Hi, I'm Sally. Go ahead around to the side yard," she said, pointing us toward the noisy, nosy dogs. "Four other people have called today, but we only the have two available. The male is $1000, and the bitch is $1200. They're weaned, dewclaws removed, and tails docked. The male was the runt of the litter, but since he's been on puppy food, he's about average size for ten weeks. This is him. His name is Calvin. He's a sweet little guy. Would you be training the dog to hunt? Weims are bird dogs, you know."

"No, not for hunting. Just a pet. I just lost my buddy, a Grand Mastiff, about a month ago. I'm at home most of the day, and I have a little back-yard that he could play in. I walk every morning, so he'd get adequate exercise. We go down to our cottage in St. Mary's a lot, when it's not too cold, so he could chase birds and swim there."

Sally looked me up and down then got an eyeful of James. She was probably looking for owners with pure bloodlines like her dogs...

"You're interested in the male, then? My dogs have very distinguished ancestry. I don't allow them to be bred. He'll need to be neutered by the end of this month. You'd have to sign some paperwork regarding that," Sally said in a stern voice.

"Yes, boys just seem easier...And neutering sounds like a good idea. I have no desire to be a grandma anytime soon. DID YOU HEAR THAT,

SON?" I shouted over to James. He was chasing Calvin in the grass. James rolled his eyes and saluted me.

"OK, well, you can spend a few minutes with Calvin out here. Just ring the doorbell when you are leaving. If you decide to take him, I only take cash, and you'll need a crate. I have those for purchase. I'll be in the house."

Calvin and I took to each other rather quickly. He seemed shy and gentle, until he bit my big toe. He had a crooked kind of smile, and his right ear flopped over backward. He was the softest puppy I'd ever touched. Bluest eyes I'd ever seen. I sat on the ground to see what he'd do, and he climbed right up on my lap and turned over for me to rub his belly. I think he chose me to be his new mommy.

After paying for Calvin (and getting his ridiculous amount of stuff in the car), signing papers, etc., we left Sally's house with our new family member. James drove so that I could keep Calvin on my lap. He cried a little when we pulled away from the house, but then cheered up when I rolled the window down a little bit. He stuck his nose out and sneezed as the cool wind blew up his little pink nostrils. Then he stuck his entire head out, and his ears began to flap wildly, as if he would take flight. He pulled his head back in the car and shivered, then licked me square on the mouth. He somehow knew I needed a smooch and someone to take care of.

When we got home, I set up Calvin's room in the laundry area. He had already peed on the floor twice before I put the puppy mats down. James opened the back door, and Calvin ran for the small patch of grass. He sniffed around the kidney-shaped mound of dirt and looked a little concerned. Did he smell Tarzan in there? Calvin started digging in the mound. I'd need to get that retaining wall up, today, before Calvin got to the bottom of our little covert operation. The bricks were on the patio on skids. James could help me put them in.

After lunch, we went over to the gallery and the children's boutique. I wanted James to see that I wasn't completely antisocial, and I did have a few things on the calendar each week. He got a haircut and shave at the barbershop. Then it started to rain, so we headed to the mall.

James needed new sunglasses. His were scratched up from wearing them constantly, so I bought him a nice pair that he picked out. I wanted to get James something else anyhow, since Allen was the new owner of the Santa-piggy pajamas I had gotten for James for Christmas.

We grabbed a coffee then headed back to the house. I called my folks. They wanted to have a belated Christmas dinner party, so we invited them up the next night. James called John's folks, too, and caught up. They're well into their eighties now and no longer travel, which is sad to me. James looks so much like John now. John's mother would cry if she saw him. John was her rock, as well as mine.

The next day, my folks showed up after fetching Teddy at the airport so he could eat with us. And James invited Tiny so we could all spend some time with her. It was perfect. We had Maryland stuffed ham, mashed potatoes and gravy, crab-stuffed mushrooms, homemade bread, roasted root veggies, corn pudding, three bottles of wine, and two pies. I haven't been that happy in three years, since my last Christmas with John. After dinner, we drank coffee and played Balderdash until 1:00 a.m.

Everyone stayed over. It's a good thing my new couch pulls out. Mom and Dad stayed in James's bed, Tiny and James in mine (after James promised me he is not having relations with Tiny), Teddy on the pullout, and I curled up in John's chair, just where I wanted to be.

As soon as I drifted off, I could feel the damp salt air on my cheeks and smell the briny seaweed underfoot. John and I were in Maine, on the beach at Acadia. He was standing behind me, his burly arms surrounding my shoulders. It was cold, and the wind was blowing my hair into his face. He whispered in my ear, the things he loves most about me...

"You smell like the ocean. You are such a wonderful mother to our son. You put up with me when I'm grouchy and give my pink parts lots of attention. You tolerate my business travel, my need to run, and my weird habit of circling the house when I'm on the phone. You make me cookies at 10:00 p.m. if I'm craving them and put up with me climbing glaciers to feel young. You indulge my passion for fast things. You supported me and held down the fort while I was deployed so many times...And you're kind to my parents. And you sew, and cook, and tell me when I'm being an idiot. Wife, you make me feel sexy...And let me smoke cigars...And you like my whiskey kisses. Babe, you are so beautiful...But you're shivering again...Mmmmmm, do you need some warming up?"

"John, did you come up with all of that just now, or did you have a list prepared?" I smiled, still having a hard time believing that he was all mine. My nose and cheeks were cold. I turned around to face him and snuggled into his chest, his arms still around me. He was wearing a tattered gray flannel shirt that I'd bought him, the very same mourning-dove gray as his eyes. His shirt smelled of cinder, of the charred birch driftwood in the fireplace up the hill at the cottage we rented every year on our anniversary.

I looked up at him with wide eyes and ran my fingers through his soft chestnut hair. "John, if you can come up with five more reasons that you love me, then I may be open to you warming me up...If not, then I'd prefer to have some lunch," I said, teasing.

"Sorry, wife, my mind turned that corner—now I have to go down that road...Shall I carry you back to the cottage?"

"John, you had *dessert* before breakfast! Wouldn't you rather go get a sandwich?"

"Hmmm. A sandwich? Sounds good. *How about a lobster roll, wife? I know where you can get a great one, free of charge! I know just how you like them!* Ha ha!" That man always had his wiener on his mind, front and center.

He laughed at my unamused face. "John, you are the most self-centered man on the planet! I can't believe I put up with you. You're a pig!"

"I am a pig. And you love my ham, so just stop pretending that you don't. Ha ha!"

"UGH! I'm going to eat! You can join me or not!"

"Yes, but first, my bride, we shall retire to the cottage..." He let out a booming laugh as he scooped me up and carried me back to the cottage.

It's not like I could tell John no. I loved playing hard to get just as much as he loved to chase me. We couldn't even put a dent in the need we had for each other. The kind of playful interface that started in a parking lot over my Pacer got us through numerous arguments and too many deployments. The kind that would have me missing him until I someday join him.

I woke up to a piercing cry from the laundry room that scared the crap out of me. It was 4:00 a.m., and poor Calvin was afraid. He must have been dreaming of his momma, while I was dreaming of John. I took him out the back door to pee, then brought him in and put him on my lap in John's chair. He sighed and rolled over onto his back. I have never seen a puppy sleep on his back before. He does think he's a human.

Everyone filed into the kitchen for coffee an hour later. I had some muffins in the oven, and Calvin was licking the floor where I'd spilled a little milk. We moved to the heated patio for a breakfast of blueberry muffins, bacon, and scrambled eggs with fresh basil and parm.

Mom and Dad dropped Teddy at the airport around eleven, and James took Tiny home around noon.

It was quiet again. I should have done some laundry, but instead, I turned the space heater on outside and sat on the new double chaise I'd bought myself for Christmas. Calvin ran around in circles for a few minutes then examined the mound of dirt again. James promised to help me with the wall this evening. I was anxious to have the retaining wall up before Calvin unearthed Tarzan.

James got home after dinner. We managed to put the wall up in a few hours. Calvin was very unhappy about that but forgave me when I offered him some leftovers from last night's dinner. James and I went to the French bakery for some late dessert and coffee then hit the rack.

All that contentment was nearly exhausting. I replayed the last evening in my mind, over and over, feeling full and blessed with such a family—my James, my folks, Teddy, Tiny, and my little Calvin. Who knew I needed him so much? I suppose there's a good reason that James was in such a hurry for me to get a new dog. He had plans for a new companion of his own.

James asked if he could have two buddies up to visit, since he wanted to hang around the house and not travel this week. These were the same buddies that we went with for a moonlit ride along the canal in late September. They took a hop up the following night from Hunter Army Airfield.

Tiny came down again to join us for dinner, so she could meet the guys. They would be her friends, too, as would their soon-to-be wives. I suppose getting engaged is contagious. She and James sat very close and held hands as Christian and Dennis each told us about their engagements and upcoming nuptials. Tiny listened, quite smitten with the idea herself.

The way she looked at James was borderline worship. She was so taken with him. He seemed the calm and collected of the two but was very attentive to her, grabbing a pair of his socks (hopefully clean) when her feet got cold and keeping her glass full. They shared a pint of ice cream. It was weird seeing my son share a spoon with a girl. This was all very strange to me. I'd never seen James pay attention to *any* woman before now.

James's buddies had never been to Annapolis and were hoping to (playfully) harass some midshipmen. I live within walking distance of several pubs, so the four of them went out after dinner.

John and I had spent some time at those nightspots. I had my twenty-first birthday party in Annapolis. James was a year old then, and my folks babysat. We met all of our friends within a sixty-mile radius at Griffins for drinks and a little dancing. My friend Rich and his band were playing live music that night, and we couldn't have had a better time. John kept buying me these shots called "buttered nipples" as a joke because I was always putting cocoa butter on my boobs while I was nursing James. My poor tatas have never been the same... The cocoa butter, unfortunately, did not keep the sags at bay as I had hoped.

It was quiet again in the house, just me and my little Calvin, in John's chair, sipping jasmine tea and listening to Sara Brightman. Calvin started to howl when she hit the high notes on "Time to Say Good-bye." It was hysterical! Such personality for a creature of only ten weeks.

Two days until James leaves to get engaged. I must be sleeping so peacefully because he's here. He's a wise soul for his age. Politically, he's neutral, but he has opinions on what we should be doing and where. I suppose his firsthand view of the world, through his job and travels, have given him a well-rounded opinion on our foreign policy and aid, as well as the differences between the countries that all seem the same to me.

They got home very late from the pub. I wasn't quite asleep yet. A dream was starting, but I didn't have time to really see what it was about before the dog barked when the front door shut. I heard Tiny come up the stairs and the couch unfolding downstairs. After her light went off, I went down to say good-bye to Christian and Dennis. They were heading back to Hunter early in the morning. James was in the kitchen, eating pie, by himself. I spoke quietly.

"Hi, sweetie. Did you have a nice time?"

"Yeah, too much. Tiny had to carry us all back here." He winked.

"Do you think her family has any idea what's going on between you two?"

"No, but her mom is very anxious to get her married off. Typical of a mother of five girls, I think. She's got two sisters in high school and the twins in eighth grade. Tiny was looking to buy a little house in Parkton, by the salon. Then things started to get serious with us. I think she's waiting to see what I'm gonna do first, which is good, since she'd have to move down to Georgia, where I'm stationed."

I tried to sound casual, "Oh, I was somehow imagining you coming back up here..."

"Mom, I'm a lifer. I don't have any desire to do anything besides what I'm doing. I don't think I'll retire after twenty years, but we'll see...I have eighteen years to figure that one out."

I wanted to offer him an alternative vocation. One where he'd be safe. "I could turn your dad's foundation into a full-time job for you, pay you a salary and everything to manage it. All your dad's old buddies have been sending checks in since the second anniversary is coming up. Are you sure you want to be in danger with a wife at home, maybe children?"

"Tiny knows how I feel and is very supportive."

"She's never been through a deployment, honey." She doesn't know what it's like.

"OK, I know where you're headed with this, Mom. I know you'd rather me be here, but I love my job. I feel like I'm doing something significant. I mean, it's not like I'm a millionaire...That's just not in the cards for me, Mom. I'm not the business guy that Dad was. I didn't get the investment gene," James said firmly.

"Honey, Daddy and I were happy with nothing and happy with lots. Really, it wouldn't have made any difference. The important thing is that you find someone you can have nothing with and be crazy about each other."

"That's my plan for us...She doesn't have extravagant taste. We like to sit and talk or read together. She's got a quiet kind of intelligence. It catches me off guard sometimes. And she's witty, the way that you were with Dad, you know, letting him know who's boss, but in a funny way. She's a lot like you. And I'm hoping she's a good cook, although that's less important. We haven't had a dinner at home together, ever. But, I'm looking forward to that changing."

"Sounds like you've thought this out thoroughly enough. Is there anything else you need? Are you planning on living on base, or will you two buy a house?"

"She's been saving, and I've been too. There's really nothing to spend my pay on while overseas, and we get extra for being in less-than-desirable predicaments."

"James. No details. Please, honey."

"I think I'll have her come down to Georgia and look at houses while I'm training. Maybe you could help with that, since you just bought a house. It would be a big help to me if she had some support while I'm gone, since she's not officially in the army fold yet."

"I'd love a road trip with Tiny, son. I hope to love her the way I love you."

James began to speak quietly, "So, tomorrow night, can you take me to Tiny's, so you can meet her folks? She and I are leaving the next morning. She thinks we're going to visit Dad's parents in Michigan, but I'm taking her to the beach in Sarasota. I'll propose on the beach at Siesta Key at dusk, and then go for a nice dinner to celebrate."

"Sounds like a great plan. I hope she says yes quickly and doesn't make you sweat!" I whispered back.

"Me too. Geez, I'm nervous about that part. I mean, I shouldn't be, because I'm 99 percent sure she's gonna say yes, but it's definitely going to be a surprise. We've never actually talked about it, officially."

"Of course she will…but if she doesn't, then I'm not leaving her big tips anymore when she does my hair," I whispered. "So, tomorrow's our last day. Anything you want to do before you're a marked man?"

"Get some crabs! Where's that place you and Ellie go?"

"Mike's?"

"Yeah, let's go there for lunch tomorrow. Maybe we can eat outside on the deck."

"OK, but get some sleep first. Tomorrow's my last day to have you all to myself, ever."

"Uh, Mom, Tiny's not the stingy type. I can all but promise you that she'll be your favorite daughter-in-law!" James said, giving me a big squeeze.

"The fact that you're my only child makes that highly probably, no?"

"Yep. Love you, Mom. I'm going to bed." He kissed the top of my head then headed upstairs.

James left early the next morning to take the guys back to Andrews Air Force Base. Tiny said good-bye and headed home shortly after. James was back in time for a late breakfast on the patio. He and I ate and talked about John, vacations, and holidays. While he was taking the plates inside, I went downstairs to get the really special things I'd been saving for him. I had a cardboard box full of memories, including his papa's wooden cigar box full of precious things. Inside were photos that James had never seen. James saw me coming up the stairs and tried to help, "Let me get that, Mom".

"I'm good", I said. "Come see what I've got here. This stuff is all for you, Sweetie." He followed me to the living room, and watched as I carefully placed a large, seemingly plain brown cardboard box on the floor. That plain brown cardboard box had been my treasure chest.

I first handed James the photo of him on the Shovelhead with his dad's helmet on, grinning ear to ear. James rubbed the photo between his thumbs and index fingers. "Why haven't I seen this?" he asked, smiling, "Geez, Dad must have had one giant melon! That helmet looks like it's having me for lunch..."

Next was the picture of James in my belly, barely covered in that lime bikini. "Crap, Mom! Is that you? Somebody call Jenny Craig! Ha ha!"

"Very funny, son. You were enormous! Those extra curves were all your doing."

Lastly, I handed James the black-and-white photo of him on John's furry chest, only hours old. James stopped smiling. He sat down in John's chair but this time didn't speak. His face was troubled, his lips tight together and his jovial brow replaced by pained eyes. James took a deep breath then peered into the photo of him sleeping soundly on his father's chest, his own tiny hand curled around his father's finger. John had watched James sleep for hours that day and those following. John's inherent love for James was captured perfectly in that moment. And that little baby boy would soon emulate him unerringly.

I went to the kitchen to give James a moment with his dad, alone. I put the dishes in the dishwasher, as quietly as I could, then sipped on another cup of coffee before peeking in on James, trying to collect himself.

"There's one more thing," I said smiling and walking over to him. I sat beside him on the ottoman, gave him a squeeze, and then pulled a dusty black bottle from the cardboard box on the floor. "Daddy bought this when you were born, son. He put it on layaway; twenty bucks a month for a year at some snooty wine shop, just because Robert Parker gave it ninety-eight points! We couldn't afford it...But, you know your dad—he had to have the best! Anyhow, he wanted to give it to you on your twenty-fifth birthday. But, maybe you and Tiny could share it on the beach after you get engaged. I think your dad would have liked that idea..."

His eyes were red, but he didn't cry. I was wishing he were a little boy again, sitting on my lap, and putting his toys in my hair. To this day,

I don't understand why God took John instead of me. John was the fun parent. My eyes began to leak. James could never fathom my worry for him, my need to see his face and remember his papa.

James put his arms around me. "I miss him, too, Mom. Please don't cry."

I shook them off as happy tears, for him and Tiny. But I wasn't missing John as much as James at that moment, knowing that things would be different now. And Georgia is so far away...They'll be moving around like we did for years on end, so it's not like I can pack up and move down there to spend time with them. They'll probably be going somewhere else in two years.

* * *

We picked crabs on the deck at Mike's for an hour before heading up to Tiny's family. I spent the evening with James, Tiny, her folks, and her four sisters. It was a little strange, since I hardly know them, but they seemed just as nervous. I think they know what is coming.

I arrived home to find Calvin waiting anxiously for me behind the laundry room gate. He had peed all over the floor. I was gone awhile, so I wasn't really his fault. It took a full bottle of Febreeze to get rid of the smell.

I sat on the patio chaise wrapped in the gray blanket, while Calvin played in the yard. It was a night like any other solitary night, except for the fact that I had a new little buddy to sit on my lap. After some tea, I made it upstairs and got in bed. Around midnight, Calvin decided that he was not a crate kind of pooch. He chewed through the plastic part that holds the lock to his cage and (quietly) busted out. I woke up at 3:00 a.m. with Calvin sleeping on my face—not exactly conducive to sound sleep, but at least my nose wasn't cold for once. When I finally got back to sleep, I had hoped for a dream about John...

Instead I got an Iranian dictator, with a Russian ally who had something in common with John Travolta—A different kind of hustle...And a butt-chin.

The Iranian was plotting a new attack, with weapons purchased from Russia. He had a small group of men with him, one taller and colder looking than the others. He was called Popoff. The men had a map of Israel on a folding table in front of them. Popoff was holding a black briefcase. Calvin started licking my face at 7:00 a.m., so I woke up and let him out the back to pee. I tried to get back to sleep, but I was no longer tired. My new dream confused me. I wondered if it was related to the dreams I had about Barishmal, the Saudi king, the diplomat, or the Old City of Jerusalem attack.

I wanted to call Allen. But I didn't know where he was. I was curious to learn if the dream I shared with his colleagues at the Pentagon did any good. But, it's not like Allen would tell me either way. Is there rhyme or reason to my sleepy thoughts, or is it just my imagination? I'm hoping the latter.

I remember having very vivid, frightening dreams as a child. When I was four, I didn't sleep for almost a week. I would go into my parents' room and beg them to let me sleep with them. When Mom asked me why, I told her that "the man dressed in black that takes away dead people is in my room." I suppose any other mother would have been shocked. But, my creative mind came honestly. Mom, too, had memorable, morbid dreams as a child.

Later on, I had a dream that a family friend, an older man, who was in good physical health, was floating up into the clouds. The next morning, we got a phone call that he had died that night, peacefully and unexpectedly, in his sleep.

But the strangest coincidental dream was when John was overseas, somewhere in Asia. I was in Georgia, in our little base apartment, with

James. In my dream, there was an explosion. I saw John grabbing and holding his leg, which had been hit with a stray bullet. I prayed for him immediately and asked God to please protect him from harm.

John called the following day. During an exercise, the guy next to John was hit in the leg with a bullet from a gun that was not supposed to have had live ammo in it. John was OK, but his buddy was injured pretty badly. I never told John about any of my coincidental dreams. And, it had just been so long since I'd had any new ones, I guess I had forgotten ever having any.

I couldn't go back to sleep, so I got up and went through some mail. Now that my little row house was the home base for a philanthropic foundation, I got pleas from nearly every organization out there asking for donations. Some of them look interesting enough. It's just that I've already committed funds to a few organizations that I know John loved. I'd rather make a large impact on a few than send bits and pieces to the masses.

I checked my e-mail. There was a stock tip from Dad. I trust his judgment. The only person who spends more time in stocks is John's dad, but he doesn't let anyone in on his plunderous investment activity.

It's raining this morning. The temps have been climbing steadily since March arrived. My fig tree should be here today or tomorrow. I got a confirmation e-mail from UPS that it's on the way. Good thing the ground will be soft enough for planting.

7

Brown and a Hunky Seal

~

The following week was quiet except for one e-mail from Allen and a post-card from Jack. I wonder if they are on a trip together or at least on the same continent. I assume they are away, since I haven't seen either of them.

The second anniversary of John's death is nearly here. He was buried a week after his forty-fourth birthday, in the first week of spring. A metaphor. The cold wet of winter giving way to warm, color, and new growth. Perhaps spring will bring the same for me. I thought about my goals for my third year without John.

This past year was by far easier than the first. I'm finally building a life for myself, although not one I would have wished for. The vast part of me that is still mourning my loss remains. But, it's more like scar tissue now than an open wound. It no longer pains me to see his photos or recall time we spent together. I simply ache. He still appears in my dreams from time to time. But I no longer feel that he is trying to be in my life. It's me who's been trying to pull him back. He doesn't belong to me. And hasn't for quite some time.

Nana will be here in a couple weeks for a visit. She's never been this far north before. She wants to see Baltimore, Annapolis, and DC...And she loves Obama. Go figure. I'm going to try to get a White House tour for Nana and myself. Maybe Allen can pull some strings.

I can't wait to see her. She's a wise woman. I miss her freckles and dimples desperately. It feels as though she's known me all my life. She ruled the roost in that outdoor Kenyan kitchen, but I'm a worthy contender when there's a Whole Foods and a credit card available. I'm hoping to give her a run for her money, or at least spoil her a little bit in my own little kitchen.

The UPS guy arrived with a slender ten-foot-tall box. Tarzan's new upstairs neighbor. I ordered this Brown Turkey Fig because they are hardier than the French, Italian, or Spanish varieties. Another package was beside the fig, a smaller, square box from an APO address with no name. Inside were vacuum-sealed fresh green olives, plump, roasted pistachios, coffee beans, and candied chestnuts. There was a note:

"Red Rider, Details from your last dream did not come to fruition, because the plans were intercepted."

Interesting. I think it's from Allen, but I'm not sure. The postcard Jack sent looked like it could have been from Turkey. The candied chestnuts and olives were a strong hint. But the pistachios could have come from Israel or Jordan or anywhere around there, really. The coffee was maybe from Africa? Or, perhaps this is a joke, and they are all from California, less the coffee, which is probably from Starbucks. I would have thought the package was from James, but he doesn't know my super-secret agent code name. Doesn't matter. I opened the package and started plotting my menu.

Roper saw the tall package outside my door and couldn't resist stopping over to see the specimen fig. Good thing I went ahead and ordered one like I told him I did.

"Oh, it's perfect!" he cooed. "It's got buds on it but hasn't leafed out yet. That's a good sign. It won't experience transplant shock as badly this way," he added, running his fingers over the slim primary trunk.

"I love fresh figs! You should see the Pink Kadota that I have at my other home. She's really a shrub, since I cut her back every fall. But the leaves have a really interesting shape...not as rounded as these."

"Prudence, I didn't realize that you're a land baron. Where's your other home, dear?"

"Northern Baltimore County, horse country. There's a family from Connecticut renting it right now. I'm not ready to sell yet."

"I love that area! My grandmother had a farm up there off of Masemore Road. God only knows what's happened to it! My parents and uncle had no attachment to the property. That upset Gran. She had hoped to keep it in the family. They sold her farm just a few months after she died." Roper looked as if he would cry. He took a deep breath, fanned his eyes, and continued, "Gran was always sweet to me. When I was in school, I dreamed of taking care of her and the farm when she got old. But, she died before I was old enough to help. I can see why she didn't want to sell that farm. It had been in her family since the early 1800s. It had a large, deep stream meandering through it. Great for trout fishing...I loved it there. Unfortunately, my parents and uncle had that farm pegged as their retirement plans. Those three hundred acres were worth half a million, and that was twenty years ago!"

"That's awful. Families are something, aren't they?" I asked, my face sympathetic.

"Indeed." Roper sighed. Then his solemn face quickly perked up. "So, Prudence, I've seen a couple of good-looking men at your door. Anyone I should know?" I knew Roper would notice James, Allen, and Jack. Any girl would.

I responded casually, "Nope. Just buddies of mine. I've been a widow for two years. My late husband was an army officer."

"And the young, brawny one helping you in the yard. A bit of a cougar, are you?"

"Uh, no. That's my son, James. He's recently got engaged. He's an officer, too. I'm very proud of him when I'm not a nervous wreck over his safety."

"I can see why!" he commiserated. "I can hardly watch the news. It's all very upsetting. What an absolute mess!" It was nice to hear that I wasn't the only person upset with our nation's current state of international affairs.

"Yeah. It is a grand mess." I looked at my watch and tried to excuse myself without being rude. "I'm volunteering at the gallery on State Circle today. I'm supposed to be there in ten minutes, so I have to go. I'm sorry."

"Oh, you must know George, then?" he asked nosily.

"Yes, he's a bright spot in my life. I can always count on a good laugh when he's around. Do you know each other?"

"George and I have been friends for many years. We were more at one time, but you know George—he's quite the party girl! Too much fun for someone like me," Roper said, sarcastically, while rolling his eyes.

"Oh. I see. Speaking of George...He's gonna be cross with me if I'm late. I should go. But, please stop by again, OK?"

"Sure will, now that I know you aren't hording *all* the hunky officers in the area. Ha ha!"

I stepped into the house to grab my bag then was out the door. I was only a few minutes late, but that made George late for his cigarette date and quite tetchy.

A friend from church called while I was volunteering. They are short a gal in the nursery this Saturday night and asked if I could pinch hit. Of course I will! I rarely get to hold a baby these days. Besides, Saturdays are considerably less crowded. As a bonus, I will avoid Pepperhead Ed.

I drove by the Baltimore house on the way to church. Mrs. Connecticut has revived my boxed garden. Daffodils are blooming at the gate, and my Virginia creeper has wound herself around the front stone façade. The grass is a tidy green carpet, and the front porch has some lovely outdoor furniture adorning it. Very inviting. Much better than how I left it, brown and lifeless. I wish I hadn't driven by. Now I miss the house. But I can't live there without John...and I think I'm getting better at being alone. I pulled into church then headed to the nursery to get my baby fix.

I returned home to Annapolis a few minutes after nine. There was a note wedged in my front door.

1900 hours

Pea – Got back earlier in the week. Wanted to see how you're doing. If you're up for company, call my cell. I'll be around the corner with a few buddies for an hour or two.

JH

I quickly dialed his number and got his voicemail.

"Hi, Jack. It's Pea. Just got home from church, and it's 9:00 p.m. If you're still in the area, come on by...I'm about to put some late dinner on."

There was a knock at the door about twenty minutes later. It was Jack—although it didn't exactly look like Jack. He looked a little more refined. His hair had grown about an inch, and he was donning a tidy 'stache and beard. It seems that Jack's a brunette, with icy-blue eyes. I guess his trip didn't require a haircut or shave. I had a goofy smile on my face when I answered the door and found him there, looking so hunky.

"So, what do you think? A little less military?" he asked, flashing a full-on smile.

"Yes, and yes! You look less harsh."

"Well, in that case, I guess I need a haircut and shave!" he teased.

"No, I mean, I like it. Less harsh is good! A shiny shaved head can look a little meat-head-y..." I said, my nose scrunched up.

"Meat-head-y? You mean I look stupid with a shiny head?" he asked, playfully irritated.

"No! I know you're intelligent, but when you have that shaved head and the rest of you so trim, you resemble a gym rat, just a little." He could see that I was trying to compliment his physique in a roundabout manner and looked pleased.

Teasing Jack is fun. He seems to appreciate a little playful banter. He's less serious than he comes across. Although, he scared me a bit when I saw him at the Pentagon. He looked and talked like a machine that day.

"So, can I come in? It's raining a bit, and I can't use the squeegee on my head when I have hair," he said, shaking the wet from his jacket.

"Sorry, yeah, come in. I just wanted to make sure my gay neighbor gets a good look at you. He keeps tabs on my male company."

"Male company? Do you have a lot of that?" he asked, uneasily.

"Not lately," I sighed, as if disappointed.

"I guess that's good to hear. Mmm, what do I smell? We were over at Buddy's Bar for a beer. I didn't eat. Wanted to see if you were hungry first."

"I'm famished, actually. I got a surprise package full of goodies from an APO address. So, I made a menu to include its *very generous* contents!"

"A mystery package? Hmm. Now I'm curious..."

"You didn't send it?" I asked, surprised.

"No, but I wish it were my idea. What was in it?"

"Fresh olives, coffee beans, pistachios, candied chestnuts...I think that's it."

"An APO address, huh?"

"Yeah. The UPS guy brought it the same day as my fig tree."

"Pea, I don't think UPS delivers from APO addresses. The US Postal Service delivers all military mail from overseas."

"Well, maybe that's changed. They could have a contract with other carriers in certain areas, right?"

"Yeah, maybe. But I doubt it. Are you going to tell me what you did with the pistachios?"

"Homemade pistachio gelato."

"Pea, you have quickly become my favorite person. And the candied chestnuts?"

"Sautéed with bacon and Brussels sprouts?"

"Yes!"

"Hope you don't mind a vegetarian meal..."

"Bacon isn't vegetarian, Pea."

"Well, I know for a fact that the pig that is now this bacon was a vegetarian. Doesn't that count?"

"If it doesn't, then it should...Look, I'm feeling a little guilty here. I always get stuffed when I come to see you but forget to bring something. Well, I don't actually forget. I just have no idea what you like. I'm not cheap, I promise, it's just that, you don't seem like the typical flowers-and-chocolate type."

"Yep. I'm more of a live plant kind of gal. I love stuff like really fruity olive oil, coffee, fluffy slippers...But I get embarrassed when people get me stuff. I'd much rather just have some good company."

"Fair enough. But, I still feel guilty," he said, looking somewhat defeated.

"Fine, feel guilty!" I said, in a sassy tone. "You said you're Catholic, so I guess you're predisposed to guilt anyhow..."

"Ha. You're funny. And right...It seems you are right about a few things lately..."

"Are you going to fill me in or keep me up all night wondering? Were my dreams anything or just a bunch of nonsense?"

"No. I'm sorry. Trust me, you don't want to know that stuff anyhow. But I did want to thank you for your help. I don't suppose you've had anything else keeping you up at night? Something we might be interested in hearing?"

"Can we keep it light tonight? I feel like a freak already. Let's just eat and pretend that I'm normal."

"Pea, being normal is overrated. Minds are fascinating to me. There are things internally communicated to people by something we can't explain. I think I know where that stuff comes from." I was curious about Jack's faith and was hoping we could speak frankly about these things, as close friends do.

"So, Jack, do you go to church, or are you more of a theoretical type of Catholic? You know, the Christmas and Easter kind?"

"It's been awhile, but I go when I can. Or when the ministers come to us. You can't be picky about denomination in the military. You get what you get, and that's fine with me. My mom would turn over in her grave if she heard me say that, but I'll take whatever reasonable guidance I can get, when I can get it. We have a chapel at the Pentagon and a padre right now. I spend time with him when I can. However, a little redhead has been keeping us rather busy lately, investigating some pretty tyrannical characters..."

"Not fair, Jack. You can't tell me anything, but you're going to make vague comments that drive me nuts, huh? I suppose Allen won't tell me anything either!"

He laughed. "You're right about that one! Allen's even more tight-lipped than I am. I shouldn't have brought it up. I could get into trouble for even joking about that stuff. Seriously, I could get canned, or worse."

"Or worse? Then stop. But, since you're sitting there doing nothing, go get some wine from the basement, please."

"What do you like?"

"Everything that's in my basement is pretty good. I marked the ones that are peaking. They have a small white sticker on the bottle."

"Peaking?"

"Yes, you know, ready to drink?" I stated.

Jack got a funny smile on his face. "Shouldn't we let them finish peaking before we disturb them? It seems like the decent thing to do..."

"Jack, just get one with a sticker on the bottom!" I said sternly, trying not to blush. Jack was teasing me.

He looked confused but went down anyhow. He came back up five minutes later, empty-handed. "OK. Now I'm really feeling insignificant. The three hundred bottles all look exactly the same. And half of them have your little circle stickers on them. Could you be a little more specific?"

"You're exaggerating. There aren't three hundred...You're entirely useless, Commander Houchins!" I teased. I opened up my laptop. "Never mind, I'll see what's ripe....John put everything on a spreadsheet when we started collecting."

"A spreadsheet? For wine? No wonder John and Allen were so close! Allen has a spreadsheet for which panties to wear on which days." Jack chuckled then continued, "Allen doesn't loosen up much. Which is why he's the youngest general in US history, since, geez, I don't know, the Civil War."

"Are you serious?" I asked, thoroughly impressed with Allen.

"No. Custer was the youngest. But, Allen's got to be a close second. He's only a year older than me, but career wise, he's ahead eight or more years. He's the anointed one. I wouldn't be surprised if he ended up being the king of the FBI, or a senator."

"John always envied his career. He moved fast, even when they were junior officers together. But, there is more to him than that. I think he's a good guy, if he'd calm down a bit."

"Oh, you know about Allen's lady friends?"

"Yeah. John told me almost everything. Not that any of it was appropriate for the ears of a lady. Allen has a reputation for speed both on and off the field. I'll leave it at that."

Jack seems a little insecure when I bring up Allen. But, Allen's growing on me. I'm starting to have the same kind of respect for him that John did, though I still question his devotion to our current foreign policies...and his tendency to objectify the female species...

Jack and I ate and laughed for nearly three hours. And, although I (really, really) enjoyed his company, I felt a little funny having him in the house after midnight. Especially since I like his new look a little more than just a little. "Time to go, Chief," I said, clearing the dishes from the kitchen island.

He didn't respond (or give me a bear hug). Instead, he just quietly followed me to the sink with the glasses, set them down then stepped deep into my personal space. He looked down into my eyes and said softly, "I like spending time with you, redhead," then gently tucked my hair behind my ears. I shivered, feeling his fingers in my hair. I couldn't move.

Jack's not playing fair. I think he just officially tossed his hat in the ring, even though the ring was not yet open for business. Do men touch the hair of women they aren't interested in smooching? I don't know much about dating, but I think that was a strong hint on his part. I'm not sure what to do. I haven't been single since I was sixteen.

Calvin was happy to see Jack leave. He was anxious for my lap and attention. Tomorrow will be warm and sunny. I'm taking Calvin to the bay to chase seagulls and roll in seaweed. My folks will be at the cottage all weekend, and I haven't been there in a while. Tomorrow will be a day for solitude and some time with God. It is the two-year anniversary of John's death.

The phone rang early the next morning. It was the renters. They have a box full of mail (sympathy cards?) for me to pick up. Calvin and I went for a walk to the coffee shop then I packed up Booger for an overnight trip. Mom won't be super excited about a puppy at the cottage, but Calvin has gotten better about his bladder control indoors. Maybe he'll surprise us both. Besides, I need his happy smile to keep my spirits up.

We arrived at the cottage two hours later, with strong sun and 65 degrees. The cottage was as it's always been, rustic and cozy. It's on a tiny, private peninsula. There were very few people wading in the waters. The bay was calm, still frigid, but not enough to deter a purebred water dog.

As soon as I popped open the car door, Calvin took off for the beach. A flash squall had washed up all kinds of great driftwood and old brick, mangled remnants of antique crab pots, and some interesting-looking shells that Calvin was rolling on, perhaps to scratch his back. I found a log to sit a spell and spend time with God in his sanctuary. I thanked Him for easing my sorrow and asked for His guidance for the coming year. We didn't go in until the sun was setting.

Mom and Dad had some fragrant tea and hot cinnamon rolls for me when I got back. We sat by the windows and let our minds wander into the unending views. It was so calm and clear that one could almost see across the bay to Virginia.

Three of my uncles were fishing off the pier next door. I could hear Steven and Benjamin arguing over bait. Do rockfish prefer squid or bloodworms tonight? It seems there were strong arguments on both sides. Perhaps the beer was talking.

Uncle Ron later brought over a flounder that had found its way into his crab pot. Very unlucky flounder. He would be stuffed with crab imperial for dinner tomorrow.

The next morning, we had breakfast at Schiebel's, a greasy spoon that my grandpa and I had eaten at together shortly before he died. This part of Maryland was like no other—no fancy cars, hard bodies, or spray tans to be found. Things are simple here. My cousin is the local sheriff, and his wife, Audrey, owns the flower shop.

Some of the locals trace their roots to St. Mary's City, where the Ark and the Dove landed with some of the first freedom seekers from England. People here are friendly folks who like the slower pace that southern Maryland offers.

The area is different than when I was a young girl. Only fishing shacks dotted the shoreline for miles. Now there are downtown professionals buying old cottages and putting grand beach homes on top of them. Luckily, during the week, the townies are still in DC and Montgomery County, and the locals have the run of the place.

They can go to the one grocer, the one gas station, or the one hardware store, the one church, the one school, or the one liquor shop. My grandpa was once deemed mayor of this tiny colony of happily rundown everyman villages.

Dad and I did some fishing after breakfast, then Calvin, Mom, and I spent some time on the beach. Mom wanted us to stay another night, but I was starting to miss my house. It was beginning to feel like my home. My refuge. Calvin climbed into the open window and put his paws on the steering wheel. He was ready to head home, too. I packed up Booger, and we headed out.

I heard the answering machine beeping as I walked in the front door. Four people had called. I was overjoyed! I didn't think anyone actually noticed when I was away.

"Pea, honey, It's Nana. My son's gonna be at Howard University for a conference in a week, and I was wondering if I can change my visit, make it sooner, so I can see him, too. His wife isn't coming, and I would have him to myself. Hope that's OK. I already told him I could meet him in DC for a date. Love you, baby! See you soon!"

Message number two was Allen. "Pea, it's me. I'm back. Wanted to thank you for your help at work a few weeks ago. It was good that you came in. I was wondering if you had any new ideas for me. Gimme a ring."

Number three: "Mrs. Brandt, this is Laura Martin, from BB&T bank. I'm the financial manager assigned to your foundation. We need to schedule a meeting to discuss growing your foundation's assets. Please call me at your earliest convenience."

This is good. I need some help with investing. Teddy and Dad give me tips all the time. But, I don't know how to do it all online, and I'd rather have someone buying and selling for me who can send me navigable reports a couple times a year.

The last message was from James. "Mom, it's me. Just wanted to tell you that I love you. I'm proud of you. You've turned out to be quite a strong person, and I'm sure Dad is proud of you, too. I'm sorry I can't be home today. I love you. Bye."

I made a cup of tea, then sat down to think about what James had said in his message. Is that how he sees me? Strong? Seems odd, because I feel scared all the time. I said a quick prayer: "Dear Lord, thank you for the time I had with John. And thank you for giving us James. It's almost like I still have John when I see and hear our son. And, thank you for my life. Please guide me this coming year and help me heal further. Amen."

I smiled at all of the good in my life, the blessings the Father has sent in the form of friends and the foundation. He's helped me be independent, for the first time in my life.

While sipping my tea, I left Allen a message. "Allen, it's Pea. Just returning your call. I wanted to thank you for the goodies you sent and tell you that you can stop by to hear any *new news*, if you like. Hope your trip was bountiful."

He called back shortly after. "Hey, Pea, It's Allen. Can I come by? Is there a chance you might feed me?" he asked, in a desperate voice.

"There is always a chance. But, it's almost 8:00 p.m. on a Sunday night. Why haven't you eaten anything?"

"My stomach got seriously messed up. Something I ate on the plane. Ugh. I'm just starting to be able to hold down food, and I thought of you..."

"So you think of me when you don't want to vomit?" I teased.

"No, actually I think of you when I *do* want to vomit. Don't be silly, Pea. I think you know what I'm trying to say. You know, you're a good cook...I'm a good eater...I'm hungry...You're right down the street."

"Where are you?"

"In Arlington."

"How exactly is that right down the street?"

"Well, it's Sunday night, no traffic. I live right off of Route 50. I could be there in forty minutes. Please, Pea! I'm starving! I've been eating out for almost four weeks straight. I'm turning into a sausage!"

"Fine...How does stuffed flounder sound?"

"Pea, I owe you. Seriously, I'll dig holes whenever you want if you'll feed me every once in a while. Oh, and before I forget, what was with the weird message you left? What box of goodies?"

"Very funny, Allen. I know it's from you. It wasn't from Jack. And the note was addressed to Red Rider. The UPS guy dropped it off with my fig tree last week. It was from an APO address, so I assumed it was you, or Jack, sending it from overseas. Who else would address me as Red Rider?"

"UPS doesn't deliver from APO addresses. Was it your regular UPS guy or someone new? What did the note say? Wait. Never mind. Tell me when I get there." He hung up and was at my front door in thirty-two minutes, which is next to impossible. Allen looked weird.

"Where's the box, Pea?" His serious tone made me nervous.

"I told you it had goodies in it. But I ate most of them...*Really*, Allen, are you trying to be funny?"

"Where's the note?"

"Right here...Could that other guy, Joe, have sent it? He didn't seem the type to send a gift to someone he doesn't really know, and I can't think of..."

Allen interrupted me, "Pea, this is a bit alarming. Why don't you tell me what your latest dream was about?"

"Well, it wasn't very specific...An Iranian was plotting an attack on a folding table with a map of Israel in front of him. There were several other men, but one was very large and had a Russian accent. He was called Popoff."

"Did you watch the news at all while I was gone?" he asked intently.

"You told me not to, so I didn't, and quite frankly, I'm much more relaxed because of it..."

"So, the potential problems with Russia are twofold. The Russians are selling small arms to terrorist groups all over the world, but more specifically, they are trying to sell nukes to Iran. Have you seen the Iranian president on the news? Talking about wiping out Israel? Russia wants Iran to buy the nukes from them for that. Russia would make a fortune. Europe's preoccupied with the bankrupt countries in the EU, and the US is spread pretty thin already in Afghanistan and Iraq. Nobody else seems to care what happens to Israel. Even some of the Jews in the States don't seem to care about Iran having nukes that could be used on Israel. Crazy."

"Oh, I see. The Russians sell weapons to the jihadists and make a mint each time a big terrorist attack goes down...And even more if Iran levels Israel using Russian fireworks?"

"Yes, the Russians are the only ones selling weapons capable of defeating the Israelis. The US is aligned with Israel. Which means the US will essentially be fighting Russia, again. Not with bodies but with missiles. Sounds a lot like the 1980s in Afghanistan." Allen and I had the same alarmed look on our faces. Great. Another unwinnable war.

Allen did see a silver lining in all of this. He continued to explain. "If Iran is buying nukes from Russia, that must mean that their nuclear plants aren't yet capable of producing weapons. They must still be in the intermediate stages, which is good, I guess. The Iranians must be considering a major purchase from Russia rather than waiting a few more years to have their own nukes. Russia will make billions if a war is started now between Iran and Israel. Because there will be plenty of jihadists waiting to get in on the fun. They'll buy weapons from Russia, too. If Iran waits to attack Israel with their own nukes, then Russia won't make one *red* cent."

"One *red* cent? Aren't you funny! So Russia is pushing for Iran to attack now, so they'll make more money. Who do you think the Russian guy in my dream is? Would knowing his identity help at all?"

"Maybe...if he's a major player in the attack you warned us about. Look, Pea, this is all highly classified. You could really be in danger if someone knew you were predicting this stuff...If you knew too much..."

"Do I already know too much?" From the look on his face, the answer is yes. "Should I look at photos and try to figure it out? Are you telling me that the dream that I told you guys about...that there was an attack planned? Is that why you were gone?"

"Pea, if someone finds out you're involved, it wouldn't be good for you. The Russians...They're a whole different animal...I'd rather go one-on-one with a terrorist than a Russian any day. Just keep mum about all of this. It's dangerous."

"Is James over there?" I asked, barely audible.

"I can't tell you where he is, Pea. I'm sorry."

"Allen, I tried to talk him into leaving the army when he was home last week. He's engaged now. I could make a job for him, managing the foundation. He could be up here with his new wife. Maybe live a normal life, a safer life."

"Come on, Pea, you know that's not gonna happen. He was chosen for special ops over a year ago. John was chosen, too, but he turned us down. James is just like John, but better. I've seen him. He's focused on staying in. His wife will hopefully be supportive of that. I hope that you will be, too."

"You mean he'll go far if he isn't killed! Special ops? John would have told me! I know that's what he wanted. And James? This is the first I've heard of any of this, Allen. Are you sure?"

"Yep. John didn't want to put you through that. But James is determined. He'll be better than John and me put together. He's gonna go far, Pea."

"I'm going to have a little talk with my son. How is it you know all of this before I do? If special ops is so great, then why were you always complaining about the lifestyle, the travel, and the injuries? You could have had a family..."

"Maybe. Unfortunately, the stuff that made me a great commando also makes me lousy marriage material. I had a hard time turning that stuff off when I got back. There *are* reasons to stay in that are hard to explain..."

"Things such as?"

"We have the brotherhood, the understanding between those who served. The thrill and the physicality of it all. We love the idea of the modern warrior. Things haven't changed much since the beginning of recorded history. Even before fire and wheels, there were good fights!"

"I see nothing sexy about seeing your friends die, Allen. You have a screw loose. You're wired wrong or something, and I thought James was right in the head, but it seems that I don't know much." I was feeling frustrated, hopeless. I can't escape my fear. It won't leave me alone.

I looked over at the stove. I'd forgotten about dinner. I put on a fake smile and changed the subject. "So, Allen, are you going to eat something or not? Food's getting cold. And no more talk about secret stuff or Russians. Seriously, I've heard enough for one evening."

"Fine, no more heavy. Just think about what I said. I don't want you exposed to any of this. John would come back from the dead and club me if he knew that I'd put you in any kind of danger."

"It might be worth getting into danger to see that!" I said, laughing and picturing John pummeling Allen.

"Funny, Pea. Real funny."

I've decided that from now on, I'll be calling Allen when I need to empty the fridge. I don't understand why he's not heavy with the appetite he's got. I imagine the stress level he's under might have something to do with it...

Allen, Calvin, and I sat outside for a bit. Calvin likes Allen more than Jack. Allen is more aloof and therefore more of a challenge. But, as the evening wore on, Allen got quieter and quieter. It was nearly eleven when he stood up, said he had to go, and hurried out the door. I know that face. He was thinking very seriously about something and needed to be alone to do it.

The week went by rather quickly, as I was busy getting ready for Nana's visit. I made some progress with the wine cellar and cheese cave in the basement. There's a farmer in Talbot County who agreed to sell me raw milk for my cheese, but I would need to keep quiet secret since the FDA is cracking down on guys like him. Farmers with raw milk products have been demonized by the FDA. You'd think they were drug dealers or something.

Today is my birthday. Number forty-four of only God knows how many more. I've already called my folks to tell them that I'm not up for company today, just in case they decide to show up at my door and sing to me again. Teddy sent me some fluffy pink-and-green polka-dotted slippers, and James sent some pink peonies, roots intact—my favorite.

I was making Nana's room up when the doorbell rang. I went downstairs to find another UPS box, addressed to Red Rider with an APO return address. I immediately dialed Allen.

"Allen, hi. It's me."

"Hey, Pea, what can I do for you?"

"Another box came from UPS. From an APO."

"Did you open it yet?"

"No. It's sitting on my countertop."

"Go ahead and open it."

"OK, let me get the scissors...Oh...it's something in bubble wrap..."

"Well, what is it?"

"Hold on! I almost have it. Oh. It's vodka. That's odd. I don't drink vodka. There's no note." Allen went silent for almost a minute. I started to panic. I was nearly hyperventilating, waiting for him to say something, but he didn't. "Allen? Are you still there?"

"Pea, I don't know what to say. Did you tell anyone else about your dreams? I mean anyone?"

"No!" I insisted.

"Did anyone overhear you talk to Mac when he picked you up at the coffee shop last month?" he asked, his voice laced with anxiety.

"I don't know! I wasn't really paying attention. It was cold. I was in a hurry to get coffee and get in the car. What about that Joe guy who sat in on our little meeting?"

"No. Joe doesn't so much as fart without telling me first. Stay there. I'll call you back in an hour or so. I need to make another call."

"About?"

"About why someone would send you such a thing! Such an *obvious* thing! I'll call you back soon. Don't touch or unwrap the bottle of vodka. It may have prints..." He hung up.

Great. Nana is arriving tomorrow, and I'm being stalked by a Russian arms dealer. I made myself a stiff drink—not vodka—and sat on the patio.

I've never feared for my life before. Last year at this time, I would have happily been snuffed out if it meant that I could be where John is. I must be healing because now I'm thinking of all the reasons I want to live. I am living now. I guess that's a big change since last year.

Allen called me back an hour later. "Pea, I don't know if you're safe or not. I don't think anyone would try to hurt you, but I want to make sure you're not by yourself so much. Would you mind if someone stayed there with you for a while, so we can make sure you're not in any danger?"

"Someone? What, like a guy in an cheap black suit who wears sunglasses 24/7?"

"No. I was thinking someone like Joe. He's very good at guarding people."

"Forget it! Joe looks like a homeless guy!" I shouted.

"Pea, be serious. He's a professional."

"A professional what, exactly? How much would he be here?"

"A lot."

"Great...Like, I'd be under surveillance?"

"No, you *would* know someone is watching over you. It's not exactly the same thing, Pea."

"So I'd have a bodyguard? Good God! This is ridiculous! Nana is coming tomorrow to visit for a week. I can't have a homeless guy sleeping on my couch!"

"Who's Nana?"

"A friend from Africa."

"Does she know anything?"

"No! I told you—no one knows anything but you, Jack, and Sasquatch! And I don't want him following me around day and night!"

"Just tell your company that Joe's an officer friend of John's, teaching at the naval academy, his rental place isn't ready, and you offered him your couch for a couple weeks..."

"With that hair and beard? No one will believe that!"

"I'll have Joe clean up before heading over. Really, Pea, this is the only way I'm comfortable with you being out of my sight."

"I had no idea my personal safety was of such concern to you. I liked it better when you were making fun of my hair and irritating me."

"Sorry. I'll try and irritate you more. Joe will be over in two hours with some equipment so that he can work from your house. He'll show you photos of some Russians. I'm curious to see if you can identify this Popoff guy. I've never heard of him. I'll check in with you soon."

"Wait! What am I supposed to do with him? Do I feed him, or give him smoke breaks, or anything?"

"No. Just pretend he's not there. This'll be the cushiest detail he's ever had. Trust me."

"I hope John does come back and club you. You're scaring me half to death!"

"Bye, Pea." And he hung up.

Happy birthday to me. I'm forty-four today, and I have a crazed Russian sending me vodka. Well, I guess, on a positive note, the vodka could be considered a birthday present.

8
Homeless Hit Man
~

Joe arrived. He was clean-shaven, with a very short buzz cut, so he did look somewhat presentable. More like a high-end bouncer and less like a Yeti. Technically, though, I don't know what he is as far as the military is concerned.

He came in and asked quietly if there was a small corner he could set up in. I showed him to my great-grandpa's desk in the living room. There's Internet there and a small bookshelf for him to use. I set up the couch for him to sleep on and offered him some dinner, but he didn't eat.

Nana sent me an e-mail. Her plane is arriving at 3:00 p.m. tomorrow. So I'll have tomorrow morning to go through photos of Russians. After Nana arrives, I hope to lighten up a bit, not think about my new life as a super-secret informant—who is no longer a secret and therefore has a bodyguard living on her couch. Nana's no dummy. She's gonna have lots of questions for me that I can't answer. I'll just ask her not to ask. Besides, Allen got us a White House tour. Maybe I'll hint that Joe had something to do with that and Nana won't mind him hanging around.

The next morning, Joe was up and working on his computer when I came downstairs. I was surprised to see that he had a cup of Dunkin' Donuts coffee and a bagel sandwich on the desk already.

"Joe, did you leave?" I asked.

"No. I have someone bringing my meals," he quickly replied.

"You don't have to do that. You can eat here. God knows I always have food in the house. You can confirm that with Allen or Jack."

"No, thank you. It's better if you go about your regular schedule without interference."

"Well, I'm going to the airport this afternoon to pick up a friend who is staying with me for a week. Maybe you can rest a bit when I'm out."

"I'll be close by in another car, Ms. Brandt."

"Are you kidding? You have to follow me when I go out?"

"Yes, ma'am," Joe responded in a formal tone.

"Allen is just trying to irritate me with this, right? I mean, it's a bit much, don't you think?"

"Just following orders, Ms. Brandt."

"I'm sure you are. Would you like another cup of coffee?"

"Yes, please. I'll get it, thank you."

"And you ate already?"

"Yes, ma'am."

"Fine. I'm going to take the dog for a walk. Do you need to accompany me or not? I'm not sure how this is supposed to work."

"Just live as you normally would...I'll be nearby."

"You'll be following me?"

"More like watching from a distance, just in case there is a need for my assistance. You won't see me," he promised.

"Fine. I'm taking my dog for a walk and not seeing you."

"Yes, ma'am."

I took Calvin all over Annapolis this morning. I was a little weirded out by the fact that someone was watching everything I do. Was he telling Allen everything or just watching over me like I was some kind of high-profile person of interest?

Joe was right; I didn't see him once in the almost three hours that I was out. The weather was beautiful. I sat out at the docks for a bit, threw crackers to the ducks, then watched some sailboats bathing in the harbor after being shrink-wrapped for the winter.

By then it was lunchtime. I took a crab cake back to eat out on the patio and a new cookbook I picked up while I was out. After eating and flipping through the book for a few minutes, I unintentionally fell asleep in the chaise, with Calvin curled up next to me.

I thought my mind was replaying a dream I had last year. John was there with the three men who were brighter than he and who appeared to be angels...Until I saw their faces. It was Allen, Jack, and Joe. Were they brighter than John because they are still living? Is he telling me that they are my angels? There was the small woman in the corner, holding a picture and walking toward the men, just as she had been before. In my previous dreams, she had been crying. Now she was slowly walking toward the three bright men and John with the photo in her hand. The woman was me. The photo was of Popoff. I suddenly woke and went in the house to find Joe.

"Joe, I just saw Popoff in my dream. Allen said you have some head-shots for me to look at. His face was so clear..."

"Good. I'll pull up the headshots. Give me a minute...Here they are. You're sure he's Russian?"

"Yes, his accent is very heavy, unmistakable."

"OK. Well, I have about three hundred, give or take a dozen, pos-sible candidates here. Of course, the guy you saw may be someone we know nothing about. If that's the case, then you can help me by describ-ing his features, and we can enter him into the system."

I only had an hour before I needed to leave to pick up Nana, so Joe and I went through the files rather quickly. I narrowed the men down by eye color, build, hair color, possible height and weight, etc. Then there were about seventy-five to look at. They all looked so similar—higher, stronger cheekbones than an average European male. But Popoff had a huge, square, cleft chin, so I knew him immediately when I saw his photo on the screen.

He's smoking a cigar in the photo. The callous blue eyes could have belonged to any of the men in the photographs, but Popoff has larger, deeper-set eyes than the others. His dark-blond hair is shoulder length, thick, and unruly. The profile says that he was last seen, in 1988, with someone named Pavel Petrov. But there was no known photo for Petrov.

Joe seemed pleased with the identification, although he didn't say. But, as soon as we were through, he called Allen. There was no hint of enthusiasm in his voice. It was just as monotone as usual, but he spoke quickly, which led me to believe that the information I provided was at least helpful.

I left to get Nana. I had no idea where Joe's "mystery mobile" was or what it looked like, so I guess I wouldn't know if he was following me or not.

I parked the car and went into the arrivals area at BWI. I stood around for about ten minutes, looking for her. When Nana came up behind me and tapped my shoulder, I turned around and gasped. I couldn't believe it was her, in a wool poncho, fitted jeans, and some tall brown leather boots. Nana looked great. Last time I saw her, she had her ratty clothes and apron on, a bandanna on her head, and no makeup—not that she needs any. We gave each other a big, long squeeze. I had missed her company so much.

"Nana! I can't believe you're here! I've missed you!"

"I missed you, too, Sweet Pea! My mornings were so tedious after you left. I had gotten used to you keeping me company and helping me clean up after the children. I just got back a month ago. The weather was nice, so I stayed at the orphanage longer than I usually do. Ginger said you got your foundation set up pretty quickly. The graduates are chomping at the bit to leave for university!"

"I'm glad to help. Being there was the best experience I've ever had in humility. I miss those faces and the simplicity of village life."

"Baby, why don't you plan on going every year? I do. It's not like you're missing out on anything here. You could spend Christmas with thirty-three orphans who would be happy just to have a new pencil!"

"I'm still hoping to have Christmas with James one of these years. He just got engaged, so I guess I'll see less of him in the future than I even do now."

"Sugar, you need to be real with yourself. If your boy's getting married, he'll be home a whole lot less. I hardly ever see my baby boy, which is another reason I came up this week. I haven't had him to myself for an evening in years...His wife isn't really into him spending time with me. She's got some insecurities. She listens to our phone calls and everything. A little paranoid, I think, for someone so beautiful and educated. But, he doesn't seem to care or even notice. She's one of those society types, from a well-known black family in Atlanta. I'm a little lowbrow for her taste."

"She sounds like a real pill. Nana, I can't imagine anyone not absolutely adoring you. Teddy's wife was insecure like that. She had to be the center of attention all the time...Other women were kind of looked at as competition, which, of course, was ridiculous. Anyhow, are you hungry? I'd love to take you to my favorite dive for a stellar crab cake. The blue crab kind."

"Sounds good! Never had a blue one. Mississippi is more known for shrimp. But I've heard about Maryland crab cakes. I'll try anything with seafood in it, especially if it's fried. You could fry a tennis shoe, and I'd eat it!"

"Nana, I have to tell you. I have another guest this week, too. It was totally unplanned, but...It's a dude, and he's crashing on the couch. He's a nice guy, very quiet. He works with a friend of John's and is helping with a few things. Just ignore him, if possible. His name is Joe."

"Hmmm. A nice friend of John's is staying on your couch? Is he black?", she asked.

"No. He's a jumbo jar of mayo..."

"Too bad. Well, is he at least handsome?", she asked, raising one eyebrow. "Because there is not one good-looking, single man left in Jackson, Mississippi! And if there is, he's either lazy or crazy!"

"I wouldn't say Joe's handsome. But he's not unpleasant-looking either. Just kind of serious and intense. Not much of talker. I think he's about thirty-four or thirty-five, something like that, although it's hard to tell, because he's, like I said, intense."

"Too young for me! Too bad. However, if I could get a peek at Obama, I would be happy 'til I'm in the ground!"

"Nana, I don't get it, but I know you love the guy. My buddy, the same one who has Joe sleeping on my couch, got us the White House tickets, so I can't really tell him to get rid of Joe. The tickets are hard to get, especially in the spring. It's cherry blossom season in DC, and every Japanese tourist and otherwise is visiting this month."

"When can we go?"

"Tomorrow."

"Great! Can I take pictures?"

"Not sure. They'll tell us when we get there. Either way, it'll be a fun day. There's plenty to see downtown. We can go to Georgia Brown's for dinner."

"You want me to eat Southern food up here?"

"Well, I was thinking you'd like the scenery. We could catch the after work crowd. There are plenty of successful, single, and good looking brown boys in D.C.!"

"Pea, now you're speaking my language!" she joked.

Nana and I went to Koko's since we were so close to Baltimore already. I drove her around the Inner Harbor first, since she'd never been there. It's funny how well she seemed to blend into village life in Kenya, and yet now that she's here, she is so urbane and stylish. She's got this kind of kooky, funky bohemian thing going on, which suits her perfectly.

Her hair is a mound of wild, soft, caramel curls, the very same shade as her beautiful skin. It's all over the place and bounces a bit when she walks. Very cool. Hard to believe she's almost sixty.

Later, we arrived in Annapolis. Nana and Calvin got cozy immediately. She and I had some tea and caught up on what she's been doing the past month. She works part-time at a geriatric clinic nearby as a nurse. She is mostly retired, though, living in the home her mother left her when she died.

I didn't know that Nana has three brothers and a sister. She says she doesn't talk to them. They were conspiring to put their mother in a nursing home. There was no need for that. Herb left her a significant amount of money when he died to pay for whatever care she needed at home. When Nana's siblings tried to coerce their mom into signing over her house and bank accounts, Nana got the local ombudsman involved who threatened to prosecute them for elder abuse. Nana's mother died shortly after and left everything to Nana—because Nana was the only one who wasn't trying to take her money or stick her in a nursing home.

Joe came in about an hour after we arrived home. He was probably outside, down the street, watching the door. I wonder if Roper has noticed him yet. My life must seem all too interesting to those who don't know any better.

When Joe came in, Nana and I sat outside with the heaters on and sipped wine until the wee hours. Her company is so soothing to me. An elixir of sorts. I told her that there was a man, a really great guy, who was, I think, interested in me and who had touched my hair the last time he visited.

I must have sounded like a thirteen-year-old giggling over such a simple, innocent act as Jack touching my hair. I think Nana would have rather heard that he picked me up and sat me on the kitchen island so he could kiss me without me trying to get away. I have to admit that I thought about that the last time he left. Then I felt insanely guilty for thinking it. I give up.

The next day, I had Joe take us to Washington, since he'd know where to park and all that. He waited outside the White House for us, since it was probably safe for me to be in there without him. If it wasn't safe in the White House, I imagine it wasn't safe anywhere. Nana was so excited. Seriously, she had to pee three times in the hour we were there. She didn't get a glimpse of Obama, but she did get to see the royal doggie, and I guess that was at least something to tell her buddies back home. I'll try to get Allen to secure a signed photo from Obama sometime for her. She'd be over the moon.

We did end up at Georgia Brown's for dinner. I've always wanted to eat there, but John and I didn't go to dinner in DC much. Nana spotted some of the local professional athletes and the CEO of the BET television station. The food was outstanding, and there were lots of beautiful brown men there to tickle her eyes. Then there was pasty-white Joe, watching us from the bar. I'll have to tell Allen what a good job he's doing. I thought this would be harder, having a shadow of sorts.

Joe got us home safely in a government-issued car. It was really handy having him there today. We didn't have to worry about where to park or walking back to the car at night by ourselves. But, we were exhausted. Nana and I had one cup of tea then she retired to James's room, and I curled up on John's chair with Calvin. Joe had his headset on and looked to be sending some e-mails. I wondered if he had a family I was keeping him from.

Jack called the next morning and asked if it would be OK if he relieved Joe that afternoon. Joe needed to check in at home and get some fresh clothing. I agreed. That would mean that Nana would get to meet Jack, the guy who touched my hair.

After talking to Jack, I grabbed Nana, and we took a walk with Calvin. I showed her where all the best shops and galleries were in case she wanted to go out by herself and relax at all. The weather's been nice. Spring is here, and the chill of winter has nearly past.

Nana's never been on a boat before. I thought that a harbor tour up the river, then maybe some lunch, would be fun. So, we took Calvin back to the house and each grabbed a sweater. Joe accompanied us on the boat ride but kept his distance, as always. Nana was starting to think I was some kind of celebrity—or something.

"Pea, what's going on here with these 'friends' of yours? Why would you need a man looking after you day and night? Was your husband important?"

"No. I'm a big nobody, Nana. I wish I could explain it to you, but they are just a precaution."

"They?"

"Yes, Jack will be here later to relieve Joe."

"Jack, the one you like?'

"I don't know. I think he's great. I just can't picture myself with a man other than John. I feel so guilty! I'm not as opposed to the idea as I was, for instance, last year, but the concept is still very foreign to me. I've never kissed anyone but John! I don't know anything about this kind of stuff!"

"Good God, Pea! Are you serious? No wonder you're such a mess over John! You never had *anyone* else in your life?"

"No. I know. I'm a weirdo."

"No, honey, I think it's sweet," she said kindly.

"Sweet meaning pathetic, right?"

"No, sweet meaning, I wish I had somebody love me that way, and so does every other person I know. Did John date other people before you?"

"I don't know. He was eighteen when we met and had been out on dates. I know he kissed other girls before me. He must have! He was the best kisser ever!"

"That good, huh?"

"Oh, yeah. That good at *everything*! I'm afraid of dating...I know that at some point, people who like each other have some kind of physical thing, too. Not sex, necessarily, but intimacy, like a great kiss, holding each other, that sort of stuff. Nerve-wracking stuff."

"Oh, girl, I love that stuff!" she teased.

"Normal people do. Nana, I'm just terrified of it."

"Understood. And all this bodyguard business? Will you fill me in someday?"

"Yes, when we're old ladies, I promise. Wait 'til you see Jack. He's pretty cute. He'll be at the house around two." After we finished our boat ride, we headed to Middleton's for soup, salad, and a beer. Joe was outside Starbucks smoking a cigarette. As we finished up our food, I casually looked down the block again to see if Joe was still there. He wasn't.

I got a little nervous and started looking up the street and then across the street at the market. There was Jack, with his serious work face on, sunglasses, jeans, and a soft-looking blue chambray shirt. His top three buttons were undone, and his sleeves were rolled up. He had on a weathered brown leather belt with rivets in a western-style pattern and some chukka boots. He was chewing on a straw. Damn. He'd cut his hair and shaved off his face pet. I guess he'd sent Joe home for a bit.

I put some sweetener in my iced tea then looked up. Jack caught me looking at him and nodded hello. Nana saw me smile at him.

"Is that Jack? Good God! Honey! Where can I get me one of those?" She was talking too loudly, and he must have read her lips because he cracked a smile. My face was, I'm sure, red at this point. I didn't want Jack to know that I told Nana anything about him. Too embarrassing.

We finished our lunch with a piece of chocolate chip banana cake and coffee. Jack was sitting on a park bench now, talking on the phone while keeping his eyes on us. Nana and I headed back to my house so I could let Calvin run around the backyard a bit.

Nana wanted to do some shopping and get some exercise. She put her walking shoes and some sweats on and headed out.

Jack quietly knocked on the door twice then let himself in. I figured I should keep the door open, since I didn't have an extra key for Nana.

"Come on in. My life is an open book!" I shouted as Jack stepped into the entryway.

"Oh, come on, Pea. Is it that bad having people worry about you?" he teased before sitting down on the couch with me.

"No, Jack. I'm kidding. Joe's been great. I hardly notice him. Not nearly as intrusive as I thought he would be."

"Hey, would you mind if I keep watch 'til tomorrow? Joe's son has a T-ball game tonight. But he can come back, if you prefer."

"No, that's OK. I was wondering if he has a family. I don't know how any of you keep up *domestic relations* with your schedules."

"It's not easy."

"I can imagine! So are you going to talk to me or just sit at your laptop and mumble quietly into the headset like Joe does?"

"It's up to you. I've never actually watched someone I know before... and it's been awhile. This is different."

"Are you hungry?"

"No, I'm on the clock. So, no eating with the informant, getting cozy, etc."

"I saw you were chewing on a straw."

"Aren't you observant?"

"Are you a smoker? Because you don't smell like one."

"I started smoking during my separation from Steph...It helped..."

"Steph? That's the first time you've said her name."

"I stopped about six months ago. I hated what it was doing to my body. I need all my lung capacity for this job," he said, smiling.

"I imagine babysitting a hot chick must be absolutely exhausting. Am I rendering you short of breath?" I had a big smile on my face.

He smirked and fired back, "You're not feeling quite as awkward today, I see." Was he amused with the confident me? He went to the kitchen to get a drink.

I think Nana was trying to give us some space, because she was gone for almost three hours. I was starting to wonder if I should send Jack out to find her. Maybe she got lost. The streets here all look the same at first glance.

Just then, she bounced in the door, arms full of bags. "Pea, do you know there's a hat store down the street called Hats in the Belfry? I bought everything that fit over my big hair!" Jack peeked out of the kitchen and caught her off guard. She couldn't resist confirming what I had told her. He is very nice to look at.

"Hey there, handsome, do they rent you by the hour?" Nana said playfully, while playing with the rim on her new hat.

"Uh, no, ma'am. I'm not an escort," he mumbled.

"Well, you should be! I can't believe Pea lets you in the front door looking that delicious!"

Jack didn't know quite what to say. He wasn't sure what I'd told her about the brawny characters hanging around all day and night, so he just smiled—and, of course, she melted right there.

"Uh, Jack, this is Nana. She volunteers at the orphanage in Kenya for a few months each fall. I met her when I was there last year."

"You were in Africa? Pea, you are just chock-full of surprises," he said to me with a somewhat amused look on his face. I guess I hadn't told him about Africa or the land pirates we encountered there or my foundation for John. I'm sure he'll inquire at some point.

Jack's phone rang. He stepped outside to take the call. As soon as he was out of sight, Nana mouthed, "Yummy!" I nodded in agreement. Unfortunately, Jack is, indeed, yummy. If he weren't, his company would be easier for me.

I made a big dinner in honor of Nana's visit. Jack didn't intend on eating but gave in when he saw the three-pound filet of beef coming out of the oven, medium rare, with a charred crust of fresh herbs, apple-wood smoked salt, and smashed garlic. Needless to say, there were no leftovers. Even the juices were sopped up with crusty olive bread. Poor Calvin was devastated.

The three of us stayed up and chatted, then I put new bedding on the pullout couch for Jack and went upstairs. It was weird enough that a handsome man who possible finds me interesting, too, is under the same roof. I couldn't sleep at all. Having Jack here feels very different than when Allen was here, burying Calvin. Thank God Nana is here, or I might be tempted to go back downstairs and spend the night just look-ing at him. I need to keep this professional, after all; he was, as he said, on the clock (despite the fact that he had just stuffed his face).

Early the next morning, around 7:30, there was a quick knock at the door. Jack looked out the window and saw a guy dressed in regular clothes get in a double-parked car and drive away. Jack got a look at his plates. There was a package on the mat addressed to Red Rider.

The package had a UPS tracking number on it and looked official. Jack immediately got on the Internet and ran the tracking number. It was invalid. He asked me to grab the other boxes I'd received. All invalid.

"Pea, did you actually see the UPS guy drop the other packages off?"

"No, I never actually saw the brown truck or the person put the packages on my porch."

It could have been anyone. Jack carefully took the package into the kitchen and opened it. "Joe tried to get prints off the vodka bottle, but it was clean. Let's see what your secret admirer sent you this time."

It was a good thing that Nana was upstairs in the shower. Jack and I quickly looked inside the small, cold box. There was a small tin with Russian writing on it, surrounded by dry ice. There was a note:

"It seems the redhead wants to play with the big boys."

Jack opened the tin. Of course it was caviar. It doesn't get more obvious. Jack looked pissed. My lower lip began to quiver as a frightened tear fell from the inner corner of my left eye.

I tried to keep the waterworks at bay by holding my breath for a moment. I was scared to death. Jack could see it on my face. He started toward me then stopped, not sure what he should do. I suppose he's not allowed to touch someone he's guarding, unless he's grabbing them or falling on top of them to protect them from, say, a bullet or grenade.

His face was confused and angry, yet somehow empathetic. "Pea, I'm sorry. I'm not sure what to do here. It's against protocol, but...Can I hug you? I know you're scared."

I nodded and looked up at him as another tear found my cheek. I grabbed my lower lip between my teeth to keep it from trembling. If I wasn't so frightened, I would have been embarrassed for being so emotional in front of him. He took another step toward me and wrapped me entirely in his arms. I was shaking, but refused to come undone in front of Jack, someone who gauges weakness for a living...

Jack leaned down and murmured in my ear, "Pea, you don't need to worry. We'll protect you." He held me for a minute or two then, with a sincere voice, said, "If you're OK for a few minutes, I'm gonna make some calls. Usually guys lower on the totem pole do this kind of work. I'm outta practice. But, Joe will be here at 9:00 a.m. What I don't get is who would know anything about you in the first place, besides Allen, Joe, and me. Really, your safety aside, that's the biggest concern here."

There's an insider somewhere. A mole? Someone who knows about dreams that I've only told three people. I must be unknowingly interfering with something. But, how do I stop now?

Jack went outside for what seemed like an hour. Nana came downstairs in a new hat, patchwork jacket, and boots. She looked like a younger Chaka Khan but with freckles and funked out to the max. She looked like she was feeling good, until she saw me and my wet, red face.

"OK. What's going on here, Pea?" Nana demanded.

"Somebody sent me some hate mail, that's all," I said, sniffling.

"And who would do that?" she asked, with her head cocked to one side.

"Somebody who finds me irritating. It's not that hard to believe."

"Is that why Dick and Harry are hanging' around here, watching you?"

"Yes, but please keep it to yourself. We don't know who's sending the mail. But, Jack's outside looking into it. Can we just try and think about something else for a while? I need to calm down."

"Sure, baby. Let's go get some breakfast and coffee. But first, I'm gonna make you up. You look like somebody just drove in here and parked on your face!"

"That bad? Great. And Jack probably thinks I'm a ridiculous sissy."

"Pea, it's obvious to everybody here what Jack thinks about you. And, it ain't ridiculous! Come on, honey, let's get you lookin' better. You'll feel better, too. You and I are going to the salon. A black-girl salon. We'll spend the whole day there and get every treatment they have!"

"Do they know how to do white-girl hair?" I asked skeptically.

"Sure, baby, white-girl hair's easy! Let's just get you changed up and a cold rag for your face...maybe some moisturizer...We can get coffee and breakfast on the way. Where's your Yellow Pages?"

"In the cabinet under the kitchen sink."

"You get upstairs and put something pretty on. I'll take care of everything else."

"Thanks, Nana."

"Sure sugar, now get upstairs!" she ordered. Nana's so direct, so easy to get, and beautiful. I can't understand why there isn't a man who's snatched her up yet.

I came down looking better and feeling better. Nana was watching Jack out the window. He was still on the phone. It was nearly nine, and Joe was, of course, at the door ten minutes early.

Nana and I headed out to a salon on the other side of Annapolis, the side without the fancy restaurants, rare-book stores, microbreweries, or fifteen-thousand-dollar paintings in the window. It was my first time on this side of West Street.

We walked since it was nice out. I assume Joe was close behind, a little more careful today, since the third package came.

We passed from the wealthy side of the historic district to the West Street corridor where the neighborhood was being revitalized, then to the area where there were bars on the windows and lots of dressed-up brown folks socializing outside. After all, it was Sunday morning.

We walked past a church that had the windows and doors shut. But that didn't keep us from hearing the live music upstairs. The choir was turned up, and the hands were clapping in unison to godly praise. If we weren't so hungry, we would have gone in and joined them.

The salon opened at noon. We had almost two hours to eat, so we stepped into a greasy spoon with a line out the door. We ordered some coffee at the bar counter and took it outside to drink while we waited for a table. I took a quick look around for Joe. I felt safer when he was in view.

A half hour later, the hostess called for Nana. We went inside to a tiny table for two. It was loud in there—lots to talk about on a Sunday morning after church. The staff was friendly and the food, delicious. Nana and I took our time, chatting with the couple sitting next to us, who had roots in Mississippi. There was boisterous laughter, a few curse words, and smiles all around. I found myself feeling very at home there with Nana.

Off to the salon down the street...The ladies there rarely take appointments on Sundays, as they are generally closed. But Nana promised them we'd need lots of pampering, so they had two ladies on staff, ready to do our hair, nails, and skin treatments. I was really excited. My hair is so crazy half the time. Maybe this stylist had some tricks up her sleeve to share. I'd brought my own makeup for them to put on me. I doubted they had anything on hand for pasty white girls like me.

Being at the salon with Nana was the most fun I've had in months. We were both out five hundred dollars by the time we left, but I had forgotten all about the morning and was actually enjoying myself.

My hair was wild and sassy, my makeup, flawless, my hands and nails, like a lady of leisure, with a sexy, urban edge. I felt great. Nana looked like a million bucks, too, although it was tough for those girls to improve her, considering she looked so good to begin with.

We left looking like two Motown divas, or at least one diva with her frosty white girlfriend. As we made our way back down the street, I started to hum "Ebony and Ivory." Nana looked at me and just shook her head and said, "Sweat Pea, you are so messed up! God knows, I never thought I'd love a little white girl as much as I love you!"

I looked up and down the street for Joe and felt relieved when I finally saw him. Nana and I decided to do some shopping since we looked so pretty. We headed back to my side of town. I think we patronized every boutique on Main Street.

I haven't gotten that many looks since...ever. Nana was getting more than her share, too. One distinguished-looking man nearly tripped, he was looking so hard. I said, "See, we have a few brown boys on our side of town, too! That man's probably in the navy. He just has that look."

"That look is what I'm looking for!" she mumbled in my ear before she flashed him a big smile. Nana turned and looked again after we had passed him on the sidewalk. He had come to a complete stop to watch Nana walk away.

We ducked into the City Dock Café for coffee and scones. There are always plenty of local students there, debating whatever philosophies they picked up in class. We had to have been the oldest chicks in there by twenty years or more, but we felt young, and being around young people with so much intellectual energy swirling about can't be bad.

The distinguished man from the sidewalk came in. He ordered a coffee then made a beeline for Nana. "Excuse me, miss. I know this is a bit forward, but your smile brightened my day. I was wondering if I might see your smile later, for dinner."

Nana was as cool as a cuke. She replied, "I don't have dinner with strangers, even if they are handsome." The look on her face made her answer hard to read. I'm not sure if it was a yes or no, but the dude seemed to catch her drift just fine.

He grinned then politely asked Nana, "If we took a walk with our coffee, maybe sat at the dock for a while and talked a bit, would we still be strangers?"

Nana was still straight-faced. "No, I guess not. But, I'm here visiting my girlfriend this week. We haven't seen each other in a while. I wouldn't want to insult her hospitality," she said, then glanced at me.

I quickly horned in, "Nana, I'm tired, to tell you the truth, and would love a little catnap. What did you say your name was?" I asked, as I looked at Nana's admirer.

"Sergeant Williams, but I go by Serge."

"Your first name is Sergeant?"

"Yes, my father was in the army, and he named me. Unfortunately, he wasn't around much after that, so I decided to join the navy, just to needle him a bit. I'm a retired commander in the navy."

"Of course you are," I said as I smiled at Nana. "Commander Williams, would you be so kind as to keep Nana company while I go back to the house for a nap?" Nana was pleased although not willing to lose her cool façade entirely just yet.

I continued, "Nana knows where I live. Perhaps you could walk her home after dinner?" I winked at Serge.

"I'd love to. And your name, please?"

"Nana calls me Pea, so can you, too." I looked at Nana. "Call me if you need me." Then my eyes cut to Serge. "By the way, Commander Williams, there are two burly men and a ferocious dog at the ready if you offend my Nana in any way. Capiche?"

"Duly noted," he said, in his official voice. I slipped out of my seat, kissed Nana on the forehead, and waved good-bye. I was thrilled for her. He was just the type of guy I'd want her to have.

When I got back to the house, Jack was on the phone, out back. I interrupted him with a piece of lemon pie from the fridge and whispered, "Can you have a piece of pie with me? I promise I won't tell Allen." He smiled, put his index finger up, and whispered back, "Gimme one minute." I went back in and put some tea on.

He stepped in the back door and did a double take. "Geez, Pea! What did Nana do to you? You don't look like...Well, you don't look like you!" Jack had a befuddled look on his face. I couldn't tell if he liked it or not.

"Jack, I like not looking like me for a change. I feel saucy today, and I like it. Do I look silly?" I asked.

"No, not silly, just high maintenance, that's all. The blood-red nails are just a little vampy don't you think?" he asked, raising his eyebrows.

I snapped back, "Well, apparently, 'vampy' works for Nana, because she just went fishing and caught herself a squid!"

"Really? Anyone I know?"

"Commander Sergeant Williams?"

"I've heard of the guy."

"I think they're about the same age, but it's hard to tell. He obviously takes good care of himself. Very clean-cut. I didn't know Nana liked clean-cut guys."

"Pea, all women secretly love clean-cut guys. Is she out with him now?"

I nodded and smiled. "I think she'll be home sometime after dinner. I'm hoping, anyhow."

"Where's Joe?" he asked.

"I think he's still outside. There's a bench across the street that he's gotten quite familiar with." I took a deep breath, smiled, and asked, "Why don't you send him home for the night? You can handle security detail until morning, I assume?" I was trying to ask him to spend the evening with me without sounding like an infatuated dingus.

"No, I gotta go. I have an appointment this evening."

"Oh. OK, well, it's just more fun to talk to you than Joe, since he doesn't make a peep."

"I'm not really supposed to either, Pea."

"Then you wouldn't want some pie before you go?"

"Sure. Then I need to scoot."

I opened the back door so Calvin could run around a bit. He'd been in the laundry room all morning long. I sat outside and watched him chase his docked tail, which he will never actually catch. Jack took one sip of tea and finished his pie quickly. He was all about work now.

"Pea, UPS hasn't been delivering the packages. The guy that brought today's little gift owns a courier service nearby. He must have been hired to deliver the packages. He has no idea what they are or who from. It will be interesting to know who's been having him drop them off at your house." I wasn't paying any attention to what he was saying. I was fixated on the fact that he'd turned down my offer for an informal date.

I smiled and said coolly, "It's just as well that you don't stay. My mom's sent five hundred e-mails asking about you, just this week. She and Dad want to come by later, anyhow."

"Does she like me?" he asked, anxiously.

"I hope not, because if she does, then she will irritate me to death with questions anytime I mention I've seen you."

"In that case, maybe I *should* keep watch tonight..."

I cut him off. "Too late. You already said no. I'm going up for a nap. Thanks for coming by so that Joe could go home for a bit."

"Pea, I came by to see you. Joe just had a good excuse for me to do that." His face was soft, apologetic.

"I'm tired, Jack. I'll see you later." I went up the stairs and shut my bedroom door, feeling more rejected than was tolerable. I felt like crying again. I wasn't really tired, just humiliated.

* * *

I had asked Joe to stay outside and down the street so that my parents didn't suspect anything. I stashed his computer and bedding in the coat closet before they arrived.

Mom and Dad brought me some coffee beans, which I appreciated. Mom was very anxious to meet Nana. Luckily, her new friend, Serge, had her home at a decent hour. Dad was so happy to see her. Of course, Mom was feeling left out, because we talked about Africa the whole time.

We had a late dinner. Nana wasn't hungry but ate some pie anyway. Mom and Dad ended up leaving around eleven. Mom wanted to stay over until I told her that Nana was staying in James's room. Mom doesn't like the pullout sofa because it's only a double. She prefers a queen. Very appropriate and convenient, as Joe would be sleeping on the pullout tonight...and tomorrow night, etc.

I thought about Jack, more than I'd like to. Why was he so interesting to me? Would I think about him if he weren't so much like John? It's good that he left. I shouldn't want to be alone with Jack anyhow. Especially if he finds me repulsive. Maybe Jack's just toying with me.

Nana said something that stuck with me, "You can go on a date without having to marry somebody. Some company couldn't hurt. You may even find yourself having fun and enjoying yourself. You deserve it; you've suffered enough, honey." But, I don't think I can just 'have fun' and date anyone. I've had the best. It's like going from the Grand Prix to driver's ed...or Pepperhead. I drifted off to sleep and began to dream about Popoff...

He was showing a group of terrorists a new-generation rocket launcher. Instead of being heat seeking, it uses magnetic force. Once the target is locked in, the magnet-tipped rocket seeks metal on the target, not heat. It wouldn't allow the last-minute movements of an aircraft, for instance, inhibit impact. Target impact would be nearly guaranteed.

There were nearly thirty terrorists there with Popoff, about fifty miles from the Israeli border. There was a clear map of where they were. I wondered how much money Popoff would make from the sale of such a weapon...That is, if there is a Popoff, and a rocket launcher, and a sale.

The rest of the night, I slept surprisingly soundly. I must have been exhausted from the long day prior. Nana was downstairs with Calvin when I came down for some breakfast in the morning.

"So, Nana, are you going to fill me in on your date last night? That was some kind of confident man! Did you have dinner?"

Nana teased, "I can keep a secret, too, baby. But, since you did threaten his life if he got fresh with me, then I'll tell you. We did just like he said. Sat out by the sailboats, made some small talk, then had dinner a couple hours later...on his sailboat!" She flashed into a big smile and did her happy dance.

"Nana, what were you thinking? Getting on a stranger's boat, 'for dinner'? Was your chicken breast on the menu? Ha ha!"

"You know me better than that!" she countered.

"Do I? I can't believe you are so trusting! What if he took you out to sea, never to be seen again? It happened to Natalie Wood!"

"Who's Natalie Wood?"

"Oh, forget it. It's dangerous! That guy could have been a serious jerk, Nana. He could have hurt you!"

"Sugar, who do you think you're talking to? I can take care of myself. I would have sent that man straight to Jesus if he woulda so much as looked as me sideways!"

"So, he was a gentleman?" I asked innocently.

"Yes, and a bitchin' cook, girl!"

"No kidding?"

"He moors his boat in the harbor from late March 'til September, then heads south...Sounds like he's looking for a shipmate."

"Are you gonna see him again?"

"Yes, today, I think."

"Great! But aren't you going to see your son today and stay in DC tonight?"

"Yes, I think I'm having lunch with Serge, and then I'll catch the metro downtown to meet my boy."

"I really have very little to do today if you're gonna be out with Serge. Actually, I need to make a phone call. Maybe I'll take you down-town myself, Nana."

I dialed Allen. He'd probably want to hear about my dream.

"Good morning, Pea. You want to tell me about your weekend? I haven't had a chance to talk to Jack yet. Did it go well?"

"Yes, everything is fine, except that I got another package."

"You did? I'm surprised Jack didn't call me about that right away."

"Maybe it wasn't that big of a deal. I got a little emotional. The note was threatening, and I got scared, so..."

"Is there anything else?"

"Yeah. I had a very *suggestive* dream last night that maybe I should tell you about."

"Suggestive, huh? I get it. Can you come in later this morning? I can send Mac."

"OK, but I have Nana this week. Can she come along as long as we drop her off downtown before heading to the Pentagon?"

"Mac's not a taxi, Pea. Nobody's supposed to know anything about this. It's potentially dangerous for you."

"I think we're past that potentially part, Allen. Wait 'til you see the note."

"What time, Pea?"

"Noon, Cornhill Street, at the circle."

"Fine," he huffed.

I had one more little request. "Allen, is it possible that we talk alone this time? I feel more comfortable telling you these things. Having three people involved is just more confusing to me. You can pass on whatever you feel is notable. You're the boss anyhow, right?"

He seemed surprised. "I thought you and Jack were friendly?"

"I'd rather just tell you. I've known you longer, and you know me better. I don't feel as weird."

"Whatever you say." And he hung up.

I told Nana we'd have a limo driver picking us up and taking us to DC at noon. I asked if she could see Serge earlier, maybe for breakfast. She texted him, and he was happy to get to see her sooner. She headed out to have breakfast with him at Chick and Ruth's Diner.

Joe was sitting at his little office area near the kitchen, typing away on his laptop. I told him that I'd be going to see Allen today for the afternoon, but, of course, he already knew that. Later, he followed us to Cornhill Street and passed us off to Mac.

We dropped Nana off on the National Mall, where she could see the Hirshhorn Museum and the Smithsonian buildings. We would see the National Gallery of Art together tomorrow. She was beyond thrilled to have an afternoon and dinner with her son. I assume she'll stay at his hotel, although I forgot to confirm that with her.

Mac and I arrived at the Pentagon and snailed our way through security. Allen was waiting for me by the elevator, like last time. He had my cup of tea in hand and ordered lunch for us in his office.

I gave him the note that came with the caviar on Sunday morning. Funny, I didn't think about the fact that UPS doesn't deliver on Sunday, much less from an APO address. It shouldn't have been a surprise that the packages were coming from a courier down the street. Allen asked about the dream, so I filled him in, with as much detail as I could remember. Some things were clearer than others, like the missile and the map where the terrorists were training inside the Iranian border. As usual, he looked at me as if somehow I'd pulled the dream straight out of my ass, but he listened anyway, trying not to discourage me, despite the fact that what I was telling him was probably nonsense.

"Pea, I don't know if it's possible to have a rocket with a remote magnetic trigger. This is interesting. Well, I guess if your little sewing gig doesn't work out, you can always apply for a job as weapons developer at Raytheon!" he chuckled.

"Allen, I know this all sounds silly, and I hope you understand how stupid I feel even being here right now. But, I am happy to amuse you, sir," I sneered.

"I'm going to pull up a map here. Do you think you could pinpoint the area you saw in your dream? The place where you think these guys are training with this Popoff?"

"Sure. Right here, in Iran. About fifty miles from the Israeli border. Is that possible?"

"I can't say. I'll have to look into this. Don't feel stupid, Pea. I appreciate you sharing this stuff with me, whether it turns into anything or not. But, I am a little concerned that your note this time was more specific than the other. I'm just wondering who could have known about all of this. I'm certain it wasn't anyone on this end. But, it's improbable that some random person heard you talking to me. Are you *positive* that you didn't say anything about your dreams to *anyone*?"

"Allen, I've told you. You're it. The guys you brought in to listen, well, I did know Jack, but you saw the look on his face. He didn't know anything about my silly dreams until that first meeting here in your office."

"OK. I know. I'm just not sure where to look for this person who is sending you undesirable mail."

"The olives and candied chestnuts were entirely desirable, and the pistachios! I was in heaven for an entire week before I found out they weren't from you!"

"Pea, why would I send you food from overseas?"

"I dunno, maybe you were trying to be nice? Or thoughtful?"

"Yeah, thoughtful. Not me. Sorry."

"So, onto the next topic...What do I do now? Joe's been at my house for several days. Can he go home, or is he going to be a permanent fixture? I have to tell you that I feel safer now, having someone around for security since Tarzan died, but how long are the taxpayers going to pay for me to have a guardian, if my dreams are all meaningless?"

"I think you know that the information you gave us has been beneficial."

"Worth all of this?"

"Yep. Truly impressive, considering you came up with all of it on your own. You were right on the money with several things. I hope that what you told me today will be useful, too, and I think it will be, considering your record."

"Allen, are you going to bomb the area I told you about in Iran?"

"Look, Pea, I'm not going to entertain your questions if they could get me fired! You need to understand how serious all of this is! It's not a joke or a game. People die. If I send in a team to take out a terrorist camp and only half of my guys come back, who do you think has to call their families? Stop asking me stuff like that!"

"Are you going to tell Jack and Joe?"

"No sure yet. I think since we have someone in the loop that shouldn't be, maybe I'll keep this conversation to myself for now. I'll have the guys downstairs look at the map you showed me with the satellite and see if there's any activity."

"Please don't tell anyone where the location came from," I pleaded.

"I know. Look, if anyone asks why you were here today, tell them that we were having lunch because we're dating or something, OK?"

"I don't look like your type. Nobody would believe me."

"Pea, all guys like cute redheads. And it's pretty safe to say that most guys also like a woman who is unpredictable, which you, my dear, are entirely!"

"Yes, but redheads who are twenty-two, not forty-four, Allen."

"Whatever, Pea. You have unfounded self-esteem issues. You were a catch back then and a catch now. There, are you happy?" I couldn't tell if he was amused or irritated.

"Yes, mostly. I just love how you change the subject when I ask you a question that you don't want to answer," I said, with a furrowed brow.

"It's called redirecting, and it works. Right now you're thinking about keeping your hair red and whether Jean thinks we are dating or not. Two minutes ago, you were asking me if I was going to bomb a bunch of thugs in Iran. Am I right?"

"You're irritating, Allen."

"Yes, but so are you, Pea. Eat your lunch so it looks like we were eating lunch, please."

"I'm not hungry. I'm feeling nauseated since you said I'm your type. Ha ha!"

"Very cute. I'm gonna have Mac meet you at the elevator in fifteen minutes and take you home."

"It would look more like we're dating if you took me home..."

"It would look even more like we're dating if I had lipstick on my collar and my shirttail hanging out," he said, with one eyebrow cocked and a slick smile.

"I can't believe you just said that!"

Allen winked. "Pea, I gotta go. I'll call you later, OK?"

"Don't expect me to answer after the shirttail comment, Allen."

"Bye, Pea." He grabbed his laptop and slipped out the door with a big smile on his face. I was smiling, too. I couldn't believe he admitted that he thinks me attractive and a catch! I suppose I shouldn't feel flattered considering the girls he's associated with. Not exactly top-shelf stuff. However, at my age, I'll take any compliment from anybody and be grateful.

Jean stuck her head in and asked if I'd be staying awhile. I said no and thanked her for ordering such a nice lunch for us. She smiled and offered me more tea. "No, thank you, Jean, I'm leaving now." I got up and headed for the elevator, where Mac was waiting for me. I was getting used to being driven around in an official-looking government vehicle. The windows are tinted, and I can watch people peep through the window and wonder who I am. If only I could remain anonymous to the person tormenting me with nondescript packages and threatening notes.

9

Between a Rock and a Hard Chest

$\sim$

I haven't seen Ellie for a while, so I called her on the way back, with Mac driving. She and the hubby had been in Italy, visiting family, for three weeks and just returned. Getting out of the country sounded like a good idea to me, too, but then I wouldn't have Joe to follow me around, which I am also growing accustomed to. Having a person in the house is a nice change, even if he doesn't talk to me or eat my food.

Ellie and I decided to take a sunset boat ride this evening. I asked her if I could bring a friend along, someone who was crashing on my couch for a few days. She said sure and didn't think anything of it. Another reason I adore Ellie is that she's just like a guy—doesn't ask a bunch of questions or try to read into things that I don't care to discuss. She must be the least nosy female in the continental United States.

When I got home, Joe was there, as usual, quiet as a church mouse, with his Dunkin' Donuts coffee.

"Joe, did you get a break while I was out with Mac?"

"Yes, ma'am, thank you. I snuck home to see my wife and little guy for a couple hours."

"Is he in school?"

"Yeah, kindergarten."

"And your wife?"

"She's home. He needs to have one of us around before and after school. I travel with the general a lot too, so, it all works out."

"Joe, do you mind the water? I guess I should have asked before I planned a boat ride for Nana and myself earlier this week. Anyhow, my buddy and I wanted to take a ride in her boat tonight, and I told her a friend—you—would be coming along."

"I don't mind the water at all. Actually, I love it."

"So, Joe, are you technically in the army or navy?"

"Technically, no."

"OK, I get it. No more questions. We need to head over to Ellie's boat around six. Hey, did anything happen while I was out?"

"The phone rang a bunch," Joe said.

"Oh. Anyone with a Russian accent?"

"No. Just someone from your bank, your mom, Jack, and someone named Janie."

"Wow. Nobody ever calls me. I guess I need to leave the house more often. You must feel like a secretary."

"It's good that you use a landline. Much easier to trace calls."

I went in the kitchen and put some coffee on. Of course, my first thought was to call Jack back and see what he wanted. I was overly sensitive last evening. He must have had something very important to do, and the traffic out here is a nightmare in the morning. I can't believe I was so petty. I made an absolute ninny of myself. I left a message for him.

"Hi, Jack. It's me. Joe said you called. I'll be out this evening. If you want to call me back, I should be home around nine."

I called Mom back, and she was out, too. Then the bank gal. I sent up an appointment for tomorrow morning. She has a promising financial plan for the foundation. Lastly, I called Janie, my buddy from Minnesota. I hadn't talked to her in ages.

"Hey, Prudie Pie! I haven't heard from you in months! Is everything OK?"

"Yeah, fine, I've just been busy. I went to Africa for several weeks late in the fall. When I got back, I set up a foundation in John's honor. Then the holidays were here, then James came home and got engaged, then a friend I met in Africa came to see me...I've been sewing more and volunteering. I guess I'm trying to get a life, Janie."

"Geez, that's more stuff than most people do in a decade," she snickered.

"I wanted to be busy when the anniversary came around. It was easier this year. I feel better. Much better. It's still hard, but I'm piecing a life together for myself here, in Annapolis."

"Annapolis? You moved? You forgot to mention that."

"Oh, and I moved. That house was just too much to handle and too expensive. I sold the car, too. Tell you the truth, I feel a lot freer, out from under those monthly payments, mortgage, etc."

"You sold the car?" she gasped.

"Yes. James wasn't happy, either. It was nice. Now I drive a little hatchback that goes by the name of Booger. It's ugly and small, but I hardly go anywhere, and I don't care if it gets abused. James was horrified when he saw what I downgraded to."

"So when can I visit? I love Annapolis. Where did you take me for mussels last time I visited?"

"Middleton's?"

"Yeah. I want some more of those. Soon. I love Maryland. It's like heaven for a veggie like me. In Minnesota all the restaurants serve meat with a side meat! Annapolis is all about the seafood! Perfect!" she gushed.

"Janie, how about an early summer visit?" I asked, hoping to avoid more visitors until normalcy returns.

"How about sooner? I hate the heat you all get there in the summer. Can I come late April? We can celebrate my birthday together like we used to!"

"Let me see when James will be home next. He's getting married on his next leave, and then I'm taking a trip to Georgia to help his wife buy a house. I have tons to do before I'll be ready for a visit, Janie."

"I can help with all that. Please? And I'd love to see James and go to the wedding!"

"Things are just kind of up in the air right now, and I really need to spend some time with my soon-to-be daughter-in-law, just the two of us. She's going to have lots to do, and I want to be available to help her."

"Please? I won't get in the way, I promise!" she pleaded.

"Janie, I love you, and you're a big help, but I want to do this with Tiny. She's going to be overwhelmed as it is."

"Her name is Tiny?" she queried.

"No. Her real name is Roberta."

"I like Roberta. She could go by Bobbie...That's cute, don't you think?"

"Tiny's been her nickname since she and James were in high school together. She likes it, and it suits her. It's a bit of a joke that her track coach started, and it stuck. She's almost six feet tall! Perfect for James. You'll meet her, just maybe not in April."

I hated to turn away a visit from a friend, but Janie's husband, Jim, is still in the army reserves and is on a SWAT team, a full-time police officer. He would have all kinds of questions and would not want her here if there were a potential problem. He would also not want his wife hanging around someone who has dreams about terrorists and Russian arms dealers. Whether the dreams are true or not would not matter. Jim would think I'm weird, and he's too straight-laced for his wife to have a weird friend—even if he and John *were* close. Jim's very cautious. I'm starting to be a big fan of cautious myself.

By the time I got off the phone, it was time to quickly eat something then meet Ellie at the boat, which is actually a fifty-foot yacht and has more square footage than my little abode.

"Joe, will you please eat a sandwich? We'll be out most of the evening, and they already ate, so we'll just be having beverages..."

"Uh, I guess. Thank you."

I tossed Joe a sandwich wrapped in plastic and grabbed one for myself along with a bottle of Syrah for Ellie. We headed out to the harbor docks.

As we walked, my mind started to wander. It's early April now. Easter is around the corner. I'll probably end up at Mom and Dad's for that. Ugh! My immediate family is dwindling. Why couldn't God just have given me ten kids? I get so irritated when Mom talks about how great her life used to be when Teddy and I were little. I'm starting to understand why those memories seem better than her current reality. Mothering was the best season of her life. I'm starting to feel the same way. I'd do anything to have James back on my hip and John in my arms again.

We finally got to the dock. I have to say that it is pretty stinkin' cool to be picked up on a yacht by your favorite buddy. Ellie popped open the wine as we headed out. A boat ride is always a nice distraction. Ellie's hubby is a good motor boater. We only *almost* hit two sailboats while leaving the harbor.

Annapolis is America's sailing capital. There is an unwritten rule that sailors always have the right-of-way, even if they have no idea how to operate their vessels or, more likely, if the skippers are too intoxicated to sail in a straight line. Doesn't matter. Rules are rules. For Ellie's husband, this unwritten rule is infuriating. For everyone else, it's just how things are around here.

We docked around eight then went to McGarvey's for some hot crab dip. Ellie's hubby was stressed out from driving the boat and needed a beer. Joe hardly opened his mouth the whole time, as predicted. But, he did have a beer, since I told him that Jack had had a piece of pie with me earlier and wasn't fired over it.

Joe followed me back to my place. I wasn't tired yet. I was craving sweets and felt like baking, so I put some cookies in the oven. I had started some tea then headed out back and waited for the oven timer to go off, when the phone rang. It was Jack.

"Hey, redhead. How was your boat ride?"

"Jack, it would be nice if I had just a smidge of privacy. How did you know where I was?"

"Joe told me. Sounds like a fun evening."

"Yeah, it was."

"I'm gonna send Joe home for a bit. He's been at your place almost five days now, minus the T-ball game. Someone will need to relieve him."

"Who?"

"Another guy, just like him, but taller and better looking," he said, chuckling.

"I like taller and better looking. But, I also like the fact that Joe doesn't horn in on my business, where I'm going, who I'm talking to, etc. Do you think the taller, better-looking guy could be as unintrusive?"

"Probably not. But the taller, better-looking guy's got a new motorcycle. That was his appointment last night. My order came in. She's black and turquoise. Gorgeous. Would the little informant like a ride to the Eastern Shore for dinner?"

"Is that allowed?" I asked.

"If the van followed us, it'd probably be OK..."

"What van?"

"Yes or no to dinner, Pea?"

"Jack, you don't need to do this. I was being silly yesterday. I guess I felt a little rejected, which is silly, but whatever, it was a weird day. Maybe it's better if you just do your job and not have some friendly relationship with a person who is evidently not right in the head."

"Is that what you want?" he casually asked.

"Yes." Actually no, but I'm obviously too ridiculous to date a man who can dismember my ego in half a second.

"You're sure?"

"Yes, Jack." I tried to sound as unemotional as I could. Play it cool. I wasn't going to sweat him out loud.

"OK...But I do need to relieve Joe."

"Fine, but no date, OK?" Maybe he'll argue.

"OK. Then I'll see you tomorrow morning around nine." He sounded a little disappointed but not as much as I was hoping.

"Oh, Jack, I have a meeting at ten, then need to pick Nana up downtown around noon," I said.

"I'll need to go with you for that stuff," said Jack.

"That's fine. See you tomorrow." I hung up the phone. Crap! I forgot about the cookies. I ran back into the kitchen, smelling the barely burned cookies. I suppose Joe was on his headset and didn't hear the timer. I grabbed the pot holders.

As I was bending over to get the cookies out of the oven, a large rock crashed through my front window, right by Joe, sitting at the desk. He jumped up and grabbed his gun then turned the lights off. Joe carefully looked out what was left of my historic blown-glass window. Poor Calvin hid under the table and started to whimper.

"Stay in the kitchen and get down!" Joe commanded, then he opened the front door to try to get a look at who was running down the street. He got on his phone and ordered another person to chase him down, "He's headed north on Market Street, on foot...Gray hoodie sweatshirt, dark pants, about five-eight, Caucasian, I think."

I was shaking. I had no idea there were others here in Annapolis watching me, too. That must be "the van" Jack had referred to. An unmarked van, perhaps? I was under surveillance, or at least whatever a protected person was called.

Joe stayed with me at the house. There was a knock at the door. It was Roper. Joe signaled for me to open the door. Roper can't know about all this!

I thought for a second, then quickly messed my hair, pinched my cheeks, and unbuttoned the front of my blouse, trying to look interrupted.

"Just a minute!" I shouted through the broken window.

Roper shouted back, "Prudence, are you OK? I heard a crash! Your window is shattered! What's happened?" I opened the door and stepped outside. Roper looked at my disheveled hair and blouse. He was bewildered.

Joe was hiding behind the open door, listening. I put on a casual, amused face and said to Roper, "I think it was probably just some rogue lacrosse fans. Did you hear that Navy beat Clemson today? It's nothing short of a miracle. I went to the game...Pretty rowdy at the end. My girlfriend and I were at Armadillo's afterward. There was some trouble brewing between their team members and our local boys. You know how that goes..."

I tried to convince him that it was a prank and I wasn't at all bothered. "I'm not going to report it. That old window had a crack and wasn't insulated. Now the Historic District Association can't turn down my request to replace it! It's a blessing in disguise!"

"Prudence, are you kidding? You need to call the police. This could be something more. The neighborhood deserves to know if vandals are in the area!" Roper demanded.

I smiled and started into an impish laugh. "You're just jealous that you missed the entire Clemson lacrosse team, drunk, at the bar. Seriously yummy! They can throw their rocks my way any night this week!" I said suggestively then slowly licked my lower lip.

Roper let out a shocked snicker, his mouth gaping, as I continued, "Really, I'm fine, better than fine...Um, I actually have a 'friend' over this evening, so if you don't mind, we're going to clean this up, then get back to our 'cookie baking,'" I said, then winked.

Roper cocked one eyebrow then smiled and replied, "Prudence, you are much more mischievous and interesting than I could have possibly imagined. And I'm very good at imagining!"

"I'm sure you are..." I smiled again, a naughty smile that I haven't used in years. I waved him off and shut the door.

As soon as the coast was clear, Joe stepped out from the nook. He was trying really hard not to laugh. I imagined Jack and Allen were going to hear about this in great detail.

"Uh, Ms. Brandt, I got ahold of Jack. He's on his way. The hoodie that 'threw his rocks your way' is down the street, in the van, with my guy. When Jack gets here, I'm going to see if he wants to cooperate or not. He may have a connection to the packages you've been getting."

I smirked. I'm never going to live this down. Who knew my mind was so deep in the gutter? I sure didn't.

Joe called Allen as well, to fill him in. Allen asked to speak with me. "Pea, are you OK? I can come over if you need me."

"I'm fine. Just a little rattled. Please tell me that Joe didn't tell you everything."

"Sorry, Pea, but this is something you're gonna hear about for a long time! I would have paid big money to see that!" I'm glad Allen couldn't see how red my face was. He just wouldn't drop it and continued, "Joe says you should get an Oscar for that impromptu acting. Good thing you're on our side!"

Allen couldn't resist laughing at me. And, after all the crap I've given him about his past, his job, and everything else, I guess I owed him a good laugh. At least he was looking out for me. I told him that Jack was on his way over and that I was fine. He asked again to come over, but he sounded like he was at work, so I told him to get back to the task of finding "the vodka and caviar." He agreed and said he'd call again tomorrow.

Jack arrived an hour later. He surveyed the damage to the window and put a tarp up to cover the broken panes. We could still see out the window on the front door.

Joe had told Jack everything. I could see it on his face. Jack began his assault. "So...Pea, it seems you have even more talents than we were made privy to!"

He took one look at my embarrassed, bright-red face and started laughing hysterically. Joe chuckled, too. He was on his way out the door to go introduce himself to the hoodie. I was starting to feel sorry for the guy. Joe doesn't even have to open his mouth to be scary. I made a suggestion, "Joe, you should take a diaper for the hoodie guy. I keep a few upstairs under the sink." He snorted then darted out the doors and down the street for an impromptu interrogation.

Jack was considerably amused. "Pea, I am *really* impressed with you. Joe gave me a play-by-play. You are truly a force to be reckoned with! I can't believe you came up with that blouse-and-lacrosse bit in a matter of three seconds! Poor Roper! He's probably at the bar now, trying to find himself some company after hearing you talk that way!"

"Jack! For your information, there was a game today, and Navy came back from the dead to win it. I saw it on the local news. And enough about Roper already! I don't want to even go there. Nauseating!"

"OK, well, Joe won't be back tonight. Are you tired, or frightened, or anything? Really, Pea, you are something."

"Will you tell me who the 'hoodie guy' is? I'd sleep a lot better."

"I'll tell you what I can, when I can, but don't expect anything any-time soon. If Hoodie does talk, then we'll have plenty of follow-up to do before having some concrete answers. He's likely a nobody who got paid by a somebody to scare you, which apparently didn't work! I've never heard of anyone getting aroused after having their home vandalized. Ha ha!"

"You're a jerk, Jack. I'm going to sit on my patio and have some burned cookies and milk. Are you coming?"

"Am I invited? I was under the impression that you wanted a taller, better-looking, uninvolved guy. *Not* a date." He said while following me into the kitchen.

"I changed my mind. Maybe it was all the excitement, but now I'm thinking that I could be persuaded to have some company tonight, under the circumstances. I can't believe I said that stuff to Roper! He's gonna think I'm a tramp!" Jack leaned against the island while I plated the cookies. Then I took out the milk and set it on the counter. When I turned back around, he was right there behind me. He had moved without a sound. I avoided eye contact, and tried to get around him, but he kept getting in my way. My face was turning red, I could feel it. Jack smiled as he stepped closer to me and I counteractively stepped backward(retreated)until my back hit the refrigerator. Checkmate.

Jack playfully trapped me between himself and the fridge then got a funny, frisky grin on his face. "Joe says your little parody was enough to make Roper go straight..." He said laughing, while he took my right hand, held it out, and inspected my so-called vampy nail color. It was the first time he had hold of my hand. I was more than a little nervous. Then he said in a less teasing, more tender, manner, "Maybe I was wrong about the color. It's not that bad. But, it's not you, either. You seem like a softer, more natural gal to me. Pretty without trying to be. And witty. And, of course, *very* funny when she's trying to be naughty!" He was quiet for a moment then stopped smiling. I looked at my hand in his palm. My hand looked so small and insignificant next to his. His was scarred. Obviously abused, doing only God knows what.

Jack was genuinely serious now. Looking straight into my eyes, he murmured, "I think you're pretty close to being perfect, Pea."

He took my other hand, too, then placed them both high on his chest, as high as they would reach. I was petrified. I nearly lost my breath when he put his hands over mine and gently pressed my palms into his chest.

I peered up, clearly unglued. He watched for a reaction as he slowly leaned in and gently kissed my cheek. I closed my eyes for a moment to register what was happening. My cheek was tingling, and I shivered. When my eyes opened, he smiled and asked, "Was that OK?"

"Yes," I said, in a still, small voice.

It was better than OK. I hadn't been kissed in over two years. I let the little fire inside me breathe, just a little. I looked at our hands, still together. I leaned into him a little for support since I could barely feel my legs. Is it possible that such an innocent act could incapacitate my lower limbs? I'd forgotten how it felt to be held, to feel so warm.

In a quiet voice, I made a request, "The other cheek would like one, too, please."

He leaned down again, slowly, and kissed my other cheek. His lips lingered for a moment, then kissed my eyelids, then the tip of my nose. I smiled and looked up at him. He smelled like peppermint. I tried to move my hands to his shoulders, but he wouldn't let them budge. I smiled at the idea of being held hostage while his tender blue eyes flirted with mine. If he'd had hair, my fingers would have been happy to be lost in it. I sighed.

"What's wrong?" he asked.

"I miss your hair," I said in a pout.

He smiled and whispered in my ear, "You could convince me to grow it out...a bit."

"A bit? What, like an eighth of an inch? I wouldn't even attempt to convince you for less than two inches! Besides, any feeble attempts on my part would just make you laugh." I knew this for sure, especially after he guffawed at my little skit with Roper.

Jack and I were standing so close together. I couldn't contain my curiosity any longer. I decided to just stop being an absurd little sissy and take full advantage of the fact that his mouth was only inches from mine. I looked him in the eyes while lifting my chin, the tiniest bit, so that our mouths were touching. Jack countered me with two little pecks on the lips. He took a breath then began to kiss me the way I needed to be kissed—deliberately.

It was intoxicating, euphoric...He released my hands and curled his fingers around my face so gently that I couldn't be sure that he was even touching me. His lips were so soft, comfortable. There was no space between us, but I couldn't get close enough to him. He was so warm. And so was I. I hadn't felt desire or desirable in much too long.

I should have known such an intense man could have innate passion yet be entirely in control of himself, and it's a good thing he was. Lucky for me, Jack was a gentleman and didn't want to make me too uncomfortable. He kept himself completely composed—all but the hungry look in his eyes. His hands never left my face except to once run his fingers up and down my spine. The small exposed area of my neck, between the top of my shirt and my hairline, stood at attention after feeling his tender touch. I guess this was my first kiss as an adult. Much different than my first-ever first kiss, when I didn't know what to do with my mouth. Jack and I were in sync with little effort. Astonishing after only a matter of minutes. My anxiety was gone, replaced with the anticipation of what could be.

This was all so new, like starting over. But I needed to calm down. I pulled away enough to signal a time-out then put my forehead against his and smiled. He smiled back, contented. "How about some burned cookies?" I quietly asked. He nodded, kissed my nose, and took the plate of cookies to the patio.

I followed him, which was difficult considering my legs felt about as steady as a wet noodle. My mind was debating whether I had done something wrong or not. I didn't intend on ever having a man in my life again. I'm a widow, not the chippy in the skit with Roper tonight.

I thought again about what Nana had said, and James, and everyone else. John had been gone for over two years. I wasn't rushing into anything or trying to forget my feelings for John. He just wasn't coming back to me, period.

I decided not to allow guilt to steal my happiness tonight. I have been robbed of so much already. I will enjoy myself, while still being me—a quirky, neurotic, forty-four-year-old girl who's only ever kissed two boys.

I sat down next to him on the chaise and handed him a glass of milk, while replaying the last few minutes in my head. Jack looked at me with his head cocked to one side, and asked, "What's going on in that head of yours, Pea?"

"I was just thinking." I said as I nibbled on a cookie.

"About?"

I quietly told him, "You're only the second boy I've ever kissed." I took a sip from my glass. My cheeks were still burning, bright pink. If they weren't already overstimulated, I'd be blushing.

"Really?" He chuckled. "If I didn't know better, I wouldn't believe you. Honestly, I don't ever recall being so wrapped around a little finger after one kiss." I nearly passed out from that one kiss.

"Jack, I wouldn't consider that *one* kiss. Do you ever come up for air?" I asked, still dazed.

"There are definite advantages to being able to hold my breath for five minutes and twenty-three seconds." He smiled and put his glass down, then took my hands, kissed my palms, and put them on either side of his neck while he leaned in and whispered in my ear.

"Second boy you've kissed, huh? It's a good thing, because you're downright lethal. You could render a man absolutely useless in a matter of minutes, young lady." He kissed my ear. I think he was teasing me, but I don't care. I was enjoying his attention more than I could have imagined. I can't believe this man finds me even remotely interesting. The rock, the hoodie, the van, the diaper, everything, had fallen off my radar. I was content to feel what I was feeling. Safe, wanted, and completely happy to be me, for the first time ever since losing John.

Jack was still a little hungry, so I rummaged through the fridge and put together a few more things to munch on while we sat rather quietly on the chaise together. It's a good thing I'd bought the double chaise. There was plenty of room to sit side by side. Maybe too much room for a chilly spring night.

"Are you cold?" he asked. He must have felt me shiver.

"Habitually. I'll go grab a sweater."

He had a better idea. He put his arm around my waist, pulled me closer, and curled me up into his side with my head on his chest. Much better. I didn't dare move. I felt perfect. Jack was in Calvin's spot, so

Calvin jumped up and got cozy between Jack's feet. Maybe Jack was growing on him.

"So did you end up getting a Lowrider?" I asked.

"Yeah, it's pretty sweet. Has a sissy bar and a cushy seat for a passenger. Do you think you might be up for a ride sometime soon?"

"Yes, but not tonight. I'm quite comfortable right now," I stated, then closed my eyes and started to let my mind wander a bit. I was so warm.

I must have fallen asleep. I awoke feeling Jack ease out from under me. "I think someone's out front. It might be Joe. I'll be back in a minute." He kissed my forehead and slipped into the back door, very quietly. I got up and cracked the door, so that I could listen. I was hoping it was Joe but wanted to be sure it wasn't another unwelcomed guest. But it was...

"I'm Officer Tesh, and this is Officer Harrison. A neighbor called to report some vandalism here. I see that the window here has been destroyed. Mind if we take a look and ask some questions?"

Jack used the same story I did about a student or someone trying to be cute after losing the lacrosse game today against Navy. I came in to meet the officers and explained that I didn't feel the need to file a report because my homeowner's insurance didn't cover vandalism. I added that the window was cracked beforehand and needed replacing anyhow.

The officers were unconvinced. But, since I didn't intend on filing a report, there wasn't much they could do. I told the cops that I invited a male friend over to keep me company in case anyone was tempted to take advantage of the broken window. The tarp wasn't much of a deterrent if someone really wanted to get in. Luckily, I had no problem with Jack staying tonight to watch me...watch him.

It was almost eleven when we finished up with the local police. About the same time, Joe phoned Jack. Jack stepped out back to take the call. I assumed it wasn't for me to overhear. When he came back in, he was in a jovial mood. Jack said that Joe was successful in extracting information from Hoodie. I would have been more pleased with Joe's progress, but Jack's presence was enough to keep my mind and eyes occupied. I could think of nothing else but his general splendor.

I didn't want to be tired, but the day was so long and full of surprises, I was just emotionally beat. We lounged on the couch a bit before I went up to bed.

"Jack, how long were you and Steph married?" I hoped that he would tell me a little bit about her without me probing too much. I'm wishing she wasn't the trophy wife I picture her to be.

"Aren't you curious about anything else?" he seemed puzzled.

"Yes, but I thought I could ask you about that, then go back and ask what you used to do to kill time before you were married...Was she younger than you?"

"Yeah. I'm forty-seven, which makes her forty-one now. We married when I was forty and she was thirty-four. We've been apart for a little over three years. Like I said, she was hell-bent on having babies, and by the time we figured out that I was the problem, things were already strained."

He seemed like he was trying to be upbeat, but I could see he felt that he had failed her. He was going to take all the blame for their divorce...

"I was never home. It really wasn't her fault. A child would have helped. She was lonely without me, and she didn't feel like the two of us would be complete unless we had the 2.5 kids, the dog, the picket fence, etc., etc."

"Do you ever think about what would have happened if you had some help, I mean with the fertility stuff?"

"Sure, I think about it. I've seen her since the divorce, just to settle up on a few things. She's happy. Actually, beaming. It was hard to take at first. I mentioned that she found someone else rather quickly. No kidding, I think she put out a want ad for a guy with a high sperm count the day she left." Jack shook his head, paused, then continued, "She was on a mission, and she got what she was looking for. We had only been separated for seven months when she announced she was pregnant. I was pretty pissed. She could have at least waited until the divorce was final. I mean, the guy seems OK. That was just kind of a sucker punch as far as I was concerned. What about you and John? Why didn't you have any more kids?"

"John and I were engaged when we got pregnant with James. Well, let me back up. I mentioned John was Catholic, super Catholic, actually. He had every intention on waiting until our wedding night, and I did, too, although I didn't think it was quite as naughty if we were getting married in a few months." Jack cracked a smile, as I continued our story. "I was so afraid of the whole 'mating' thing. Everyone made such a big deal about it, teased me about it, joked about how naïve I was. I just kind of got sick of the comments and wanted to get it over with, so we could enjoy our honeymoon without some ridiculous, unattainable expectations of..."

Jack started laughing. "Ridiculous, unattainable expectations? Geez, Pea, didn't anyone bother to tell you that the mating thing's supposed to be fun?"

"Just fun? I could hardly think straight! And the fact that it was all so new to us both made it even better. It was a little tense at first. But, we were best friends and ended up laughing a lot. It wasn't awkward at all after we finally relaxed and just enjoyed each other. Ummm, I'm talking too much...I suppose I don't need to go into details. Sorry." I was blushing yet again. The strange thing is that Jack looked a tiny bit envious, or something. Perhaps he'd wanted some meaningful first time but settled for a crazy-hot girl in the backseat of her fast car...

Jack took my hands and warmed them in his. He looked as if he were trying to remember something, or perhaps trying to forget. I wondered if Stephanie was to him what John was to me.

He spoke softly, intently, "I imagine if I would have met someone like you when I was in school that I would have wanted the same thing. But, I didn't, so I just threw myself into work. I liked the excitement and danger. You know when you're that young...Well, I should say that we were trained to think ourselves invincible, immortal. We were pretty intense. It wouldn't have been fair to have a wife and kids back then anyhow. My job was similar to what Allen did, but we were gone longer, more like 70 percent of the time, versus every couple of years for a full year. I wanted a family but was really married to my job. Things were different back then. Family came second. No exceptions and no explanations..."

I knew what he meant. Things *were* different back then. John and I struggled with that, too. John wasn't a Special Forces guy, but I remember him gearing up for invading Haiti and not being able to tell me exactly what they'd be doing there. The ladies didn't know where their husbands were or when they'd be back from missions. It was dangerous, and it was terrifying for those of us at home waiting for a phone call to hear the outcome.

"So, why'd you guys stop after James?" Jack asked again.

"I tried desperately to get pregnant again, but it just wasn't in the cards for us. I always thought it was some kind of reparation for my initial impatience. I practically forced myself on John that first time."

"So you overpowered a guy my size, huh? I find that hard to believe!" Jack was laughing now. I must seem weak and fragile to Jack. I guess me physically forcing John to do anything was highly improbable. I never considered that maybe he wanted to give in all along and was just waiting on me.

I continued, "I guess I was *moderately* convincing. Later on, when traditional procreation methods weren't working, I suggested we see someone. But John was against it. He didn't believe in it. He thought that we should be grateful for what we already had—our son. Of course, I argued for fifteen years with him about that. But, he wouldn't budge. I don't know why it was so easy that first time, then never worked after that. Beginner's luck, I guess. So what did you do with yourself before Steph?"

"Uh, I wasn't as bad as Allen, but I had my moments, which I am not proud of. You get lonely sometimes. Dating was hard to do because of my schedule...So, I improvised. Are you disappointed?"

"No. I'm not surprised. I thought you were a little *too* smooth the first time I met you. You've obviously had *plenty* of conversations with strange females..." I was feeling more than a little insecure at this point. He was obviously accustomed to more fruitful fishing expeditions.

"Not 'plenty'! I wasn't *that* bad. And there's no comparison. You are the most intriguing female I have ever met. Really, Pea, you are so different than anyone else: bright and witty but shy and innocent at the same time. Quite a combo. I knew you were different after our first conversation."

"I didn't think I'd see you again," I confessed.

"Yeah, right! I'm sure you were surprised that I didn't show up at your door an hour later, pledging my eternal devotion!"

"It's a good thing you didn't, because my dog died that night, and I would have thought you were coming over for...you know..."

"Ha! I can't imagine any guy being so bold with you unless he *likes* getting shot down."

"I know people do that stuff; Ellie told me so."

"I don't blame people who do. I've seen all kinds of unscrupulous behavior from good people. You've handled yourself quite well. You're stronger than you look."

"That's what my son says. Of course, he looks like the Hulk. I find it funny that he would call anyone else strong. He's a beast. Probably a lot like you in your twenties."

"Am I so deflated now? I think I'm hanging on pretty tight for someone pushing fifty!" Jack snapped.

"Jack, he's twenty-four. But he has better sense than his age. He's getting married. The girl goes to my church and does my hair. It was her idea to go red..."

"You're not really a redhead?" He made an overly shocked face then started laughing. "Even I coulda guessed that!"

"Oh, and I'm sure your Stephanie resembled Rapunzel! Perfect, honeyed blonde with natural highlights from the sun..."

"Uh. No. She got her Barbie blond at the salon, although she tried to pass it off as natural when people asked."

"Well, Jack, now you know everything about me...How I scare myself silly when I dream, how I wrestled my fiancé to the ground and got knocked up, and now, the fact that my God-given hair is a mousy dishwater blond. Geez, I never intended on getting this personal with you. But, for the record, I think I was supposed to be a redhead. I feel more like me now than I did before. James likes it..."

"And Allen likes it..." he said.

"He did admit that to me when I saw him earlier in the week. As a joke, I think."

"I think not. He's very protective of you. In the five years I've known him, I've never seen him like hover over a woman the way he does you."

It was odd that Jack sees Allen as somehow protective of me. Allen seems so detached from people in general, now. He didn't used to be that way. I remember him being so affectionate with John and me. He was always hugging John and flirting and joking with me. James was always on Allen's lap or shoulders when he was little. I guess no one else saw that part of Allen but us. It made me sad to think that Allen didn't love us the way that we loved him. I still didn't know why he ignored John's funeral.

"Allen and John were close, even after John retired. Allen was his XO when he was in the Eighty-second. They lived vicariously through each other. Allen wanted a family, and John wanted to be a badass Special Forces guy. Allen was always over. He was just like a flirtatious older brother who likes to eat. Really, I don't think he'd have anything to do with me now if I weren't a decent cook!"

"Neither would I!" Jack laughed.

I gave him a hard look then said, "Jack, you and Allen can have each other. It's no wonder you're both single with nothing to do but pick on me. I don't know why I put up with either of you!"

"I think you like being teased, Pea. And don't forget that you dish out quite a bit yourself." He was right. And seeing him smile at me made me want to kiss him some more.

"I don't suppose you'd want to give me another reason to put up with you before I go up to bed?" I suggested, trying not to blush.

He leaned over, gently kissed my forehead, and smiled. I was waiting for more. I frowned.

He looked at my disappointed face and muttered, "I didn't think there were any girls like you left. So, I'm not giving away the farm on our first date. Good night, you stingy little redhead. Sweet dreams. If they aren't, you can debrief me in the morning..."

I headed upstairs, slipped into my jammies, and got into bed. He was right. I was feeling stingy. But he had given me plenty to think about already—like how it felt to be entirely enveloped by him. His lengthy arms nearly wrapped around me twice. And, hearing his breath in my ear when he whispered nearly scrambled my brain and launched my dormant hormones into a drunken stupor. I had no idea that a forty-four-year-old woman could have such astonishingly raw urges. I remember feeling this way for John but never thought it could happen twice. I don't know what to think of all of this. I'm simultaneously happy and confused. For two hours, my conscience debated both sides of the coin. I concluded that being alone with Jack scares me (in a good way?).

The next morning, I brushed my hair and my teeth and took my time putting makeup on before heading downstairs. I never gave much thought to how I looked or what I was wearing when Joe was downstairs. But, Joe isn't downstairs; Jack is. I slipped into my softest long-sleeved T-shirt, a fitted pair of jeans, and my fluffy pink-and-green polka-dot slippers.

When I got downstairs, Jack had already let Calvin out for his morning pee and little Jimmy Dean sausage poops. Sure beats cleaning up after Tarzan's morning routine. I'll scoop the poop later, when Jack isn't looking.

Jack was in the kitchen on the phone with Allen discussing the Hoodie intel. That, coupled with what I told Allen in his office, seemed to be plenty to keep the three of them busy for a bit.

Why was I feeling shy all of a sudden? I wondered if Jack was thinking about last night as much as I was. Then again, that's impossible. I quietly made my way to the kitchen and put some coffee on.

When Jack finished his call, I leaned against the kitchen island, an arm's length from where he was standing. I wasn't sure how to greet him. The best I could come up with was hi.

"Hi, yourself. Did you sleep well?"

"Umm-hmm."

"Good. No scary Russians?"

I shook my head.

"Regrets?"

"No. Actually, I was feeling guilty for not feeling entirely guilty." I bit my lower lip to keep from smiling. I was trying to make sense but too embarrassed to speak coherently.

"Are you sure you're not a closet Catholic?" he teased.

"Yes, I'm sure. Too many rules for me." This amused him.

"Pea, you seem to have more rules than any non-Catholic I've ever met."

"Self-inflicted rules don't count because they aren't coming from a guy in a white hat living in a castle somewhere in Italy."

"Mmm...Even if they're the same rules that your church has...that consequently originated in my church?"

He had a point. I decided to change the subject. But, I was not going to debate our religions this morning, not after telling him about my first experience with John last night. Next thing, we'll be tackling the topic of politics and then there will be nothing left to speak of tomorrow.

Men are all the same, easily distracted by food. You can always rely on their stomachs for support when you want to talk about something else. "Are you hungry?" I asked, spying possible breakfast eats in the fridge.

"Actually, starving. I've been up since five; that internal clock thing is irritating."

"Omelet?"

"Please."

I made a nice breakfast, and we ate outside. I had so many questions for him.

"So where are you from, Jack?"

"San Diego, of course. When I was a little boy, I wanted to be a SEAL. They train in San Diego, you know, so I'd see new recruits all over the place. My dad was in the navy, too, which is why we lived there in the first place. He was stationed at North Island Naval Air Station. He wanted to fly. There's an awful lot of pilot worship in the navy. But he had bad eyes. Back then, they didn't have Lasik. Dad was one of the many surface warfare officers with unrealized flying aspirations."

"I think you mentioned your mom rolling over in her grave. Is your dad still living?"

"He is. He's eighty-five. Still in pretty good shape. But I was closer to my mom. I miss her a lot. She's been gone awhile now, maybe fifteen years. Had cancer. I suppose if she were still around, she'd be happy that I finally met a gal who can cook! She was really something. Great sense of humor. My sister's a lot like her. My dad is the opposite, a bit stiff. Mom would make fun of him all the time. It was hysterical! I mean, she loved him, but man, could she bust his...uh...chops."

"Your dad's a bit stiff? That's shocking!" I laughed as he flashed a dour look my way.

"Very funny, Pea. Am I so severe?"

"Yes, but just when you're working. That austere work face is a little intimidating."

"But all I do is smile around you! I try to leave my work face at work," he insisted.

"Do you live in Allen's office? Or do you have a home?"

"I have my own office, thank you very much. It's not a nice as Allen's, but I have my dad's desk, even if it is in the basement at the Pentagon where the nobodies are. Lots of florescent lights and no windows, but whatever. If I want a view of the Potomac, I just camp out on Allen's couch and work."

"And your home, Jack?"

"I don't spend much time at home since the divorce. Steph kept the house we bought together. It was really hers anyhow. I didn't get much of a say regarding the location or decor. I don't miss the stark-white ruffled couch and the Louis-the-whatever French furniture anyhow. I rent a little house in Del Ray, near Old Town Alexandria. I have a room-mate, another squid. It's not much, but it's close to work."

"And Stephanie, she's pretty? And tall?" He nodded.

"She's turned a few heads. But that didn't matter much, when it came down to it. We had little in common. I was closing in on forty. She was accomplished and looking to get settled. It was good timing more than anything. We didn't have the background that you and John had—the friendship, I mean. I think it would have made a difference."

I was finding myself jealous of this Stephanie person. Perhaps a Greek goddess with the sex appeal of a pinup...and the intellect of a Gillian Anderson type. He caught me comparing myself to her in my absurd little mind.

"Pea, I can hear your gears turning. Don't discount yourself. The way you've come into your own is remarkable, considering how lost you were. And I like spending time with you. It's easy, natural. You have so many layers. And you make me laugh. That's the stuff that lasts!"

Is it even possible that I'm dialoguing with the hunk on my couch? I was trying to be cool. He couldn't know the true depths of my inse-curity. I'll bet he's been everywhere and seen everything. He's so much more interesting than the former housewife sitting here. I had plenty more to ask him.

"Next question. What's the most beautiful thing you've seen on your travels?"

"The girl who shivered after I kissed her cheek last night..." He tried to look serious, then started to laugh, realizing exactly how corny he sounded.

"That is not funny, Jack! I know I'm ridiculous. I'm not exactly cool like you are, with all that 'giving away the farm, stingy redhead' crap! I was shivering because I was cold!"

"You were anything but cold, young lady. I was about to put you outside to cool off."

"Jack, if you ever try to kiss me again, I'll send you straight to Jesus!" By now, he was laughing so hard that he nearly choked on his food.

"Where'd you get that 'send you to Jesus' line? Really Pea, the madder you get, the funnier you are."

"Nana gave me that line. I guess it's not as threatening when I say it. I'll remember that next time you infuriate me, which I imagine will be about two seconds from now." Jack put his arm around my shoulders and pulled me into his side. I tried to push him away, maintain my false irritation, but my efforts were pointless. I wanted to be closer to him. And I loved being tucked into his side. He put his hand under my hair and gently caressed my neck. At once, I was covered in goose bumps.

Jack had some questions for me, too. "Speaking of Nana...In all seriousness, why did you go to Africa last year? How long were you there? Did you go by yourself?"

"That's more than one question."

"Yeah, but it's all related. If Steph would have pulled something like that, I wouldn't have let her go, even if we were divorced."

"Well, it just so happens that John wasn't here to deter me, and at the time, my personal safety just wasn't a priority. I was broken. I needed to find a reason to go on. Seriously, I'd lie in bed every night, just hoping to go to John. I felt dead inside. I didn't think there could be a 'me' without him."

"So...you went because you had a death wish of some sort? You know, there's nothing glorious about getting yourself killed for no good reason."

I shushed him then continued, "I went to see a friend in Kenya. She started an orphanage after she retired. I needed a reality check—to see how fortunate I am, how blessed I am, and how silly I was being. I have so much compared to those little ones. That trip changed my outlook on so many things. And, I met Nana there. When I got back, I set up a foundation. I wanted to do something that mattered, in John's honor. Actually, the reason I was at that Wounded Warriors event was because I made a donation, and someone called to thank me and invite me to the event. It was just coincidence that Ellie, my best buddy, was in charge of planning the whole thing. She practically forced me to go. Then I met Maggie, then you, etc., etc., and now we are having breakfast on my patio..."

"Wait, back up—were you safe the whole time you were in Kenya?"

"Not really. We could have easily been killed. There were young men with machine guns on the countryside, waiting for us to pass through, so they could rob us."

"Who's us?"

"My dad went with me to Kenya. Our driver and Ginger, my friend who started the orphanage, were all in the car when it happened."

"Did they hurt you?"

"No. Just scared us half to death. But I'd do it again in a heartbeat. I needed some sense scared into me. Allen told me that would happen, and he was pretty against me going. James wasn't thrilled with the idea, either, but he wasn't around to protest, so...I went."

"Allen let you go?" Jack looked pissed all of a sudden.

"Allen has zero say in what I do, Jack. He actually took me to the airport, after a three-hour-long verbal spanking."

He was shaking his head, his breathing louder. "I would have talked some sense into you! I can't believe anything worse didn't happen. A hundred-pound female and her geriatric father! Who did you pay off to get around safely?" I decided not to tell Jack about the teens with machine guns.

"I was in good hands. I prayed a lot. And it was part of His plan for me. The trip, the children I met, John's foundation, Nana, all of it..."

"You forgot the part about meeting me..." Jack added, gently running his finger down my spine.

"Is that part of the plan? I'm unsure at this point. I sat up last night, so confused. I don't know what to do about this you-and-me thing. I'd been so decided on being a martyr before I met you. You've ruined everything!" Jack was smiling, getting a kick out of his modest conquest.

I smirked then continued, "I didn't give you my phone number that night at the Kennedy Center, because I knew I would like you. I didn't want any man in my life but John, even if I didn't actually, physically have him anymore. I was just content with memories of us. And I don't know how things work these days. I never even dated anyone but John. You can't imagine how strange this is to me!"

I was getting myself even more confused. I wish I could keep my mouth shut and maintain some composure, but for some reason I felt the need to confess these things to Jack.

"Easy, Pea. You don't have to have everything figured out. Nobody does. I didn't plan on meeting you, either, but I did, and I'm glad. You don't owe me an explanation for how you feel, then or now. You're being careful. That's a good thing. But so am I. I'm not in a rush either, OK? My last experience wasn't exactly ideal, and I'm not running down the aisle again with blinders on."

"I talk too much." I said quietly, looking up at him.

"Yes, sometimes. But I happen to like listening, as long as you aren't beating yourself up for being happy."

"Is that what I'm doing, exactly?"

"Yes," he said sternly.

"Have I ruined everything? You probably wouldn't touch me again with a ten-foot pole now." I started to nibble on my lower lip.

"I'll do better than touch you with a ten-foot pole...I'm going inside... putting your apron on...then doing the dishes. And that will be something I've never done for any woman but you." I followed him in the back door to the kitchen.

"Maybe if you would have done housework then Steph would have kept you longer!" I teased, laughing.

"Ouch, be nice, or I'll change my mind!" He smacked my tush then grabbed my apron.

I asked in my best Betty Davis voice, "Do you like wearing women's aprons?"

"I'm serious. Stop it, Pea!"

"Actually, you look like an after-hours entertainer with my apron on..."

"Really?"

"Should I call Roper to come over and take a look at you dressed up in my clothes?"

"Pea, you're pushing your luck..."

"You do look nice in pink paisley."

"Last chance, redhead."

"Can I tie the back for you, Jack?"

"As long as you make a nice-looking bow," he chuckled.

"Fine, turn around," I ordered. Jack faced the sink, his back to me. I marveled at the way his T-shirt followed shape of his back. Just looking at it made me giggle like a silly teenage girl. At least his back couldn't see me fawning over him.

I smoothed his shirt out over his shoulders, then down his back. He was very still. I reached around to get the apron strings, an excuse to put my arms around his waist. I pulled the strings together then started to tie the bow...

"Pea, I was kidding about the bow. I think a knot would suit me better." He turned around, looked at me, and smiled. "Is my shirt wrinkled, or are you trying to flirt with me?" he asked, as he gently pinched my cheeks.

I was embarrassed. "I told you I'm no good at this stuff! I was smoothing out the wrinkles, but then figured it was a good excuse to touch your back." I looked up at him with big eyes and a shy smile.

"Should I get you some mittens? I could feel your ice-cold hands through my shirt!" He took my hands and wrapped them around his waist, this time facing me. I pulled the back of his shirt out a little so I could put my hands on his back and warm up. He flinched, so I quickly pulled them out.

"Pea, you need to warn me if you're gonna do that."

"Very funny. I make you cold, and you flinch when I touch you. Perfect. Well, at least you do dishes." I smiled.

"You just surprised me, that's all. I like your cold little hands on my back."

"You're not a very good liar," I said, tightening his apron strings.

"I'm actually a great liar. But only while being held captive, and not by some little redhead and her pink-paisley apron!" I tried to smirk, but a laugh came out. I was about to help him with the dishes when I saw the clock.

"Oh, it's almost ten! I have a meeting with my banker in twenty minutes. Then I have to pick Nana up at noon, downtown. I need to get cleaned up. Jack, don't forget to dry the dishes. I'm going to check for spots later," I ordered.

"Pea, I'm going to break the back window, too, if you don't knock it off!"

"Oh, shoot! I forgot to order a new front window! What if someone breaks in while we're out?"

"I'll have Joe's guy pull the van around and watch the house."

"Great. Can you figure out what size window I should order? I don't suppose you've ever done any construction work?"

"No, Pea."

"I wonder if Allen knows how to install a window?" I asked, batting my eyelashes.

"If you want Allen, then get Allen. You can't have us both!" He was getting a little irritated. At least now I know how to get a rise out of him.

"Do I have you?" I asked, innocently.

"Am I doing dishes in your frilly apron?" he responded with a bored look.

"Is that a yes?"

"Go get ready before your china here starts hitting the floor, woman! Is this stuff replaceable?"

"No! It's postwar Wedgewood. It was my grandma's."

"Kidding, Pea. I have very capable hands. You'll see…"

"Don't hold your breath, chief!"

I couldn't stop smiling as I scurried upstairs and tried to put something decent on. Of course, I ended up in the same thing as always: long-sleeved T, jeans, boots, sweater. At least I'm *consistently* boring. I touched up my makeup and brushed my teeth again, pulled my bedcovers up, and threw the pillows on.

Jack was finished and ready to head out the door. "We have to take your car today, since I brought my bike last night. I was in a hurry and didn't really think I'd need the official car brought over for today. Is that all right?"

"Sure, but no comments about my car. Please understand that I used to drive a hundred-thousand-dollar car, and now I drive a green go-cart named Booger."

"*Really*, what did you drive?"

"Well, it was more John's car, but we took it everywhere. He liked to go fast. An E63 AMG Mercedes."

"I think I would have liked John very much."

"You're actually a lot like him...I hope that doesn't make you feel a little uneasy."

"Hey, I'd rather compete with a dead guy than my boss! I'm happy to be like John. It seems he had very good taste in almost everything." I was glad he wasn't offended that I probably liked him, at least initially, because he reminds me of John.

We got to the car, and Jack's eyes just about popped out. "You got rid of an AMG and bought this?" Now he knows for sure that I'm not sane.

"No comments, Jack. Period. I've heard it all, and it's no longer funny."

"Not funny? More like hilarious! Seriously!" He leaned on the car and started laughing.

"Jack, you can either get in and shut up or wait for me to get back later this afternoon."

"I'm getting in...but I think we'll have to open the sunroof so my head can breathe! This is the funniest car I've ever been in! I didn't even see a car this small and ugly in Mexico!"

"JACK! Enough already!" I shouted.

Now that I was mad, he was laughing even harder. I couldn't help it and started to laugh, too. Jack's face was red, and his deep laugh echoed a gulping walrus! It was the most hysterical man-laugh I'd ever heard.

We finally settled down and headed to the bank. "My meeting will be about an hour, so make yourself comfy." I started to chuckle after seeing the look on his face. Of course, he wasn't comfortable at all in my car. He got out and stood by the bank entrance.

Laura and I went through all the paperwork she needed to have signed, and we talked about my hopes for John's foundation. Do I want to grow it? How do I want to solicit donations? Will I be paying myself a salary for managing the foundation? Do I want to invest the capital in a mixed portfolio or stay safe with all CDs and other interest-earning, protected investment products?

It was good to get everything down on paper finally and project how much money I'll be able to donate next year.

I thanked Laura and came bouncing out of the bank with a huge grin on my face. I was so pleased. The foundation should be growing at least 5 percent per year, which will be more than enough to donate about twenty-eight thousand dollars this year, and more the following years, if we allow the principle to grow at a steady rate. Very exciting.

Jack was outside waiting for me. He could see how excited I was, and it was contagious.

"That good, huh?" he asked.

"Yes! John would be so proud of me. I know you think this car is ridiculous, but I'm going to be able to put twenty-two Kenyan students through college with the money I made on the sale of the AMG. I can't wait to tell Ginger. We'll have a scholarship in John's name in addition to an annual gift to Wounded Warriors, Archdiocese of the Armed Forces, and Catholic Outreach International. If I'm frugal, then the principal will double in about eighteen years, and I can ensure the foundation will go on indefinitely. I'm really pleased. Really, really pleased."

I was so happy. I was thinking of all the people we would be able to help. At least, if I can't have John back, I can keep his memory alive to more than just myself. It would make me so happy to see his name synonymous with generosity.

"Pea, I'm sorry I made fun of your car. I didn't know. I think you're great for living with less so that you can be generous," he said, as he looked at me with admiration.

"It's not about me. It's about John. I want others to know how much he still matters."

Jack was quiet, maybe registering what I said about John in his mind. We walked back to the car in silence then Jack unlocked the passenger side door and opened it for me.

"So, Pea, can I drive?"

"Can you drive a stick? I'm gonna guess no."

"Ha! I was driving a stick when you were still in middle school."

"Oh, I forgot how old you are."

"Your comments are starting to hurt a little."

"Maybe it's your joints that are aching. Perhaps you should switch to Centrum Silver."

"Perhaps I should pick up the little redhead and toss her in the harbor."

"Yes, but then the little redhead would be even colder than she is now."

He put my hands in his shirt and held them there, then leaned over and kissed me, much less carefully than before. There was an eager edge to his breathing, and his mouth, unyielding. I might have passed out last night if I had gotten this kiss first.

I pulled away a tiny bit so I could whisper, "Can I have my hands back so I can touch your face while you kiss me?" He let go then leaned in again to finish what he'd started. My hands moved gently over his chest, then shoulders, and up his neck. I stroked his jawline while he moved from my lower lip to my upper lip, my left and right cheeks, and then, of course, he kissed the tip of my nose. I asked him, with my eyes still closed, "Why do you always kiss my nose?"

He whispered in my ear, "Can't help myself. It's so cute, and I don't want it to feel left out. Besides, it's time to go get Nana." Jack's degree of punctuality is borderline irksome.

I had told Nana to meet me in the west wing of the National Gallery of Art at noon, in the solarium. When Jack and I arrived, Nana and I had a light lunch there in the cafe. Jack was close by, nursing a coffee.

"So, Nana, how is your son? What did you two do?"

"Girl, I had the best time! He and I carried on like when he was little and it was just us two. I was so happy that I cried when he dropped me off here and drove away. It was perfect. He wasn't as reserved as when his wife's around, keeping tabs on everybody. We had dinner, went to Georgetown for some shopping...He even surprised me with tickets to see *Wicked*! We got in late, then stayed up and talked. My little baby boy has meetings all day today and tomorrow. He'll be so tired."

"I'm so glad you had a good time. I'd like to meet him next time you two rendezvous in DC." I thought about someday meeting James like that, just the two of us.

"So, sugar, how did things go with you? I see that Joe is off today?" Nana said, after scanning the room and finding Jack.

I tried to sound as casual as I could, "Nana, don't be alarmed, but someone vandalized my house a bit...Threw a rock through my front window, and it's shattered."

"WHAT? Honey, you need to tell Nana what the H-E-L-L is going on! I'm worried and not sure you should stay there if someone is trying to hurt you. Who is it?"

"Nana, I don't know who it is. There are several people trying to figure that out. But I feel pretty safe with Joe and Jack around. They got the guy who actually threw the rock, but he was put up to it by somebody else. If you want to stay somewhere else, I understand. I'll get you a room at a B&B nearby, so you won't have to worry about some goofball thug trying to wreck my nerves."

"No, sweetie. I'm not leaving you, at least not for two more days. So, besides the flying rock, what else happened when I was downtown?"

I knew exactly what she was fishing for. I started to smile. A big one. Nana looked at me, sat up straight in her chair, and nearly shouted, "Did that hunky Jack lay one on you?" I was glad she guessed, so I didn't have to say it—too embarrassing with him nearby.

I whispered back, "Nana! I can't explain it...how it felt...just...the best thing...*in a while*."

Nana was shaking her head back and forth and doing a little dance in her chair. "Oooh, I am so glad you got that over with! And to think that's what you were avoiding! Crazy girl!" she said, slapping my knee.

"I know! I was just so scared. It was like being sixteen all over again. But it was mind-blowing! I can't stop thinking about it! I'm terrified, but I think I'm going to just try and see what happens," I said, beaming. I glanced over to the other side of the café, where Jack was sitting, mumbling into his headset. He caught me smiling in his direction.

"That's wonderful, Sweet Pea! Just what you need! And he's a cutie pie. Almost as tasty as my Serge. Speaking of which, Commander Cocoa sent me flowers to my hotel room, twice! He wants to see me today. Would that be OK? I know I'm leaving soon, and we still have lots of fun to do, but that man! He just does it for me, you know? We don't have men like him back home. Trust me, I've kissed every frog in old Miss!" Nana said, beaming.

"Nana, I think it's wonderful! Maybe you two have something. You may as well try and find out while you're here. You can come see me whenever you want. You don't have to leave in two days, or you could come back next week. Really, I just want you to have a good time."

"Well, enough about our beautiful men. Since we're here, I want to get some culture in. Do you know anything about any of these artists?"

"Yeah, actually, art history was my major before I got knocked up. Let's start with the Impressionists. They're my favorite, and I'll bet you recognize a few..."

We spent a couple hours browsing the gallery then headed home. I drove, and Jack sat in the back. Nana couldn't stop laughing at poor Jack squished up in the backseat of Booger.

When we got home, Nana called Serge. They went out for an evening boat ride on his rather large sailboat named *Beatrice* after his beloved mother. Jack and I took Calvin for a walk and to pick up some groceries. We walked almost three miles to Whole Foods.

I wanted to impress Jack, so I decided to use the most effective weapon in my arsenal. My cooking. Stuffed raspberry duck breast and duck legs confit. Wild rice with chanterelles and pecans. Swiss chard from my garden. Rustic olive bread with pesto butter. Pearberry pie and ice cream. My mind was plotting the evening, what I needed to cook first, second, etc. I will show no mercy tonight.

We held hands as we walked. I had been quiet for more than twenty minutes (a record?). Jack finally interrupted my scheming.

"Pea, what are you thinking about? Are you up to something?"

"I'm making you dinner tonight."

"You always make me dinner," he said, gently squeezing my hand.

"Tonight, I'm bringing out the big guns."

"Big guns? You mean all that other stuff was just a warm-up?"

"Um-hmm." I gave him a quick glance then started humming to myself. He was getting excited, and so was I. This was going to be an easy kill. I couldn't wait to see his face when he smelled all of the savory goodness coming together in my little kitchen.

"So you're gonna put the last nail in my coffin tonight, huh?" he chuckled at my straight face.

"Yep."

"Should I be afraid?" From the sound of his voice, he thought I was bluffing.

"You mentioned being rendered useless last night? Tonight you will be rendered speechless."

I liked being confident for once and knowing that I'm not putting on airs. The one thing I know I'm good at is food. He thought I was kidding until he stopped walking, faced me, and saw that I was entirely serious. He grabbed my other hand, which, of course, was a Popsicle.

"What are we gonna do with these little refrigerators, huh?" He blew his warm breath into my hands, curled up in his.

"I usually wear gloves, but then you can't see my vampy nails, and I think you secretly like them..."

"I can neither confirm nor deny the said comment," he said in a staid voice.

"I knew you liked them," I sassed.

"Get over yourself, redhead," Jack said as he patted me on the head in a patronizing fashion.

"I'm not the arrogant one here, Jack. But you, sir, *are* going down tonight!" I had a wicked smile on, and he seemed to like it.

It was around 6:00 p.m. when we finally got to the store. I put my jacket in a cart and laid Calvin in it, pulled out ten dollars, and handed it to the security guard. "Would you please keep an eye on my puppy for a bit?" Of course, he agreed; few people can resist Calvin. He is the most beautiful puppy anyone has ever seen.

I got a basket and started picking through mushrooms, then moved to the raspberries, and so on. Jack just followed me around the store, mentally logging each new addition to my cart, trying to figure out what I was making. Jack's never actually seen me cook. I may even put him to work. I'd love to see him in my apron again, elbow deep in bread dough. And I have the perfect wine for tonight...a French Cab Franc, or maybe a Meritage from Howell Mountain? One for the dinner prep, and one for dinnertime. I imagine dinner won't even be ready until midnight. Jack's just gonna have to go to work tired tomorrow. I looked at Jack, smiled, then told the butcher that I need a freshly dressed Muscovy duck between six and seven pounds.

The butcher responded, "Yes, miss, we just got some in from Canter Hill Farm this afternoon, and they're real beauties."

Jack looked at me, clearly delighted. "Duck? You're making me a whole duck?"

"Yes, and I doubt there will be anything left to nibble on tomorrow."

"In that case, I may have to nibble on you," he whispered into my ear. My face immediately went bright red. He was trying to embarrass me, and I suddenly couldn't remember what else I wanted at the butcher's counter.

"Jack! You're going to work tomorrow, which means that you will be in the cafeteria, nibbling on mystery meat and potato chips! And stop with that naughty talk. Someone might hear you! If I'm not safe in the house with you, then I'll call Allen for a replacement watchdog." Jack didn't like that comment, but he couldn't stop laughing at my mortified face...

"Pea, I was kidding. I was going to nibble on your nose, so don't get overheated here."

"Fine, but I'm trying to concentrate, and you're making it difficult." I tried to seem mad, but being angry with him was becoming increasingly difficult.

"What did you think I was going to nibble on, redhead?" he murmured softly as he leaned over and his lips grazed my neck. Ugh! Is he trying to kill me? I'm not ready to even consider entertaining those thoughts. I could just see John in my mind, disappointed in me. I was starting to feel guilty. Maybe I was giving Jack the wrong signals or something. I liked being playful with Jack. But I didn't know if he was gauging my interest in being horizontal with him or just teasing me.

My eyes pleaded with him. "Jack, I can't think about that stuff now. I can't. Please, stop."

He could see that I was truly upset and apologized. "I'm really sorry, Pea. I wasn't trying to push you. Just trying to make you blush. I love it when your cheeks match your hair. But it won't happen again." He took my free hand and kissed it, then put his other arm around my shoulders, gently pulling me in to kiss my forehead. He kept his arm around me until we got to the checkout.

I handed the check to the cashier then asked Jack to call a cab so we could get the bags home. I'd bought too much stuff to walk home. "I'll get Calvin. Be back in a sec."

It was almost dark now. Tuesday night, so there were only a few cars in the parking lot. I walked outside the sliding doors and started over to the security guard to get Calvin.

It was then I heard a loud engine and saw a van heading right into the front of the store. I thought it was going to hit me until the wheels squealed to a stop a foot from where I was standing.

Two men jumped out of the back and came at me. I breathed in deeply so that I could come up with a decent scream, but one man grabbed my head and covered my mouth and nose with a strange-smelling rag. The other man grabbed my legs. I kicked and threw my arms, trying to break free.

My mind started to race. I knew what was happening, but I felt dizzy. My blurry eyes saw the security guard yelling into his headset while running toward me and the two men in hats and sunglasses, who now had me on the ground. I heard Calvin barking. Everything went black, but I could hear mumbling and the rumble of the van as I made a last-ditch effort to free myself from the hands holding me down. It was then I realized that I was already on the floor of the rumbling van.

10

Jack

~

I slid into the security vehicle and headed out after the silver van. First, I called Joe to get his guys over here then dialed Allen as quickly as I could, my hands shaking.

The van was weaving in and out of traffic. I was about to blow through a red light at a four-way intersection, intent on following the van through the red light, when an eighteen-wheeler crossed the intersection right between me and the van, fifty feet ahead of me. I hit the breaks. The truck driver saw me coming at him and slammed on his breaks in the middle of the intersection. I honked my horn and shouted for him to move. He was too stunned to respond. I attempted to hop the median strip and drive on the other side of the road, but the cars there had a red light as well and all were at a complete standstill. Cars filled the lanes, leaving me no exit from my current point. This security car is a joke! It's just a rental car painted black with the security company's info on the side. And no lights! It's utterly useless to anyone who actually needs security! I finally got ahold of Allen after three tries.

"Allen, it's Jack. They got Pea! They're in a silver GMC van heading north on Riva Road. I have our guys on the way, but it's too late to catch them by car..."

The fury of hell was in Allen's voice. "Who was on watch?" he asked.

"I was, Allen. It's my fault. I did a shit job of protecting her," I confessed, like a dog with his tail between his legs. "There were three total, two tall and one stocky Caucasian driver, in hats and sunglasses. We were at Whole Foods on Riva Road. The security guard got a good look at them."

"What! Did you just stand there with your head in your ass?"

"No, sir. I was carrying the groceries. She stepped outside about ten seconds ahead of me, and they grabbed her."

"Get her back, Commander Houchins!" The niceties had ceased. Allen spoke to me like a master sergeant at boot camp.

"Sir, I tried to follow them, but a truck cut me off, and I lost them at an intersection. I have no idea where they are headed. Send whoever—whatever—you can!"

"Get Marty on the horn. Tell him to give you whatever you need. I'm on my way."

"Yes, sir," I replied, completely humiliated, and for good reason. I'd lost them. I needed to know where they were taking her. I followed Allen's orders and dialed the NSA, only twenty minutes away.

"Marty, it's Jack Houchins from the Pentagon. We lost a Tier I informant about ten minutes ago, goes by Red Rider. She was kidnapped out front of the Whole Foods on Riva Road in Annapolis. I have a witness and description of the vehicle: late-nineties' GMC Safari van, silver, dark windows. Inside, three Caucasian males with sunglasses and baseball caps. I followed them to Route 50 then lost them there. They're headed west. Can you pull up a satellite visual? They have to be near 301 by now, if they didn't exit and go north on 97."

"Sir, do you know where they'd be headed?" asked Marty, calmly.

"Not sure. Listen, this informant, she's very, very valuable. If we lose her in the next half hour, we won't get her back. Do you understand?"

"Yes, sir. I've got Ruben Winfield here with me. You know him. He's pulling up the satellite now. Give me thirty seconds. You think he's around the 50/301 interchange?"

"Yeah, I have no idea where they'd take her except downtown or to BWI. We suspect a Russian arms dealer is behind this. Does the NSA have anything on a Pavel Petrov? Without going into hows and whats, Red Rider's identified him in some suspicious stuff with Iran in the past weeks. Do you have anything on that?"

"One moment, sir...Yes, I see that a terrorist training camp was taken out early this week about fifty miles from the Israeli border. We swept the camp afterward and found remains of two Russians, but no Petrov. The two men were Alexi Volkov and Basil Popov."

"Popov? The guy with the chin?"

"Yes, sir, sounds like Popoff."

"He's dead?"

"Yes, sir."

"Do we know anything about the other guy, Petrov? Was he was at the camp before it was taken out?"

"Not sure, sir, but I can pull up calls made from the camp before the bombing took place."

"Is it possible that Petrov and Popov are the same guy?"

"No, sir. They are not the same guy. Popov has the cleft chin. You can't miss it. The other guy, Petrov, is possibly a lean build with dark hair. We can't identify him fully because we haven't been able to get a head shot or full-body shot...It's like the guy's a ghost."

"OK. Could you please scan the area for cell phone activity? See if you hear anything—Red Rider, redhead, anything in Russian."

"Yes, sir...OK, sir, we have a visual on the van. A traffic camera caught him flying through a red light at 93 miles per hour on Riva. Looks like he's headed toward the airport on 97 North now."

"Do you have guys nearby? Get them on this. Red Rider is a pet project of General Gravenstein's. We *cannot* lose her. Is that clear? Put Winfield on."

"I see. Right on that, sir. I'll get him."

"Yes, sir, this is Winfield speaking."

"Shut down 97. I want helos in the air and cruisers on the pavement. Call BWI with code-red security. No aircraft in or out. Period. This is a serious national security issue here. Shut down all of Northwest Anne Arundel County if you need to. General Gravenstein is in a bird on his way over from the Pentagon. Get him on his cell, and tell him that I'm on 97N to BWI. I'm in a security guard car. Maryland tags. 452SFP. Get a decent cruiser ready for me at the airport exit to 195. I'll be there in less than ten minutes."

"Yes, sir, copy that. We're watching the van via satellite now, sir. Our guys are headed out to close down 97 North and South. Glen Burnie police are getting it started, as they are closer, sir. They have their entire staff on it, and it should be complete in approximately seven minutes, sir. Should we relieve them when we arrive?"

"Keep them there to watch the traffic and exits. I don't want any chance of the suspects getting away with Red Rider. I want your teams on the ground, ready to take out the van without harming her. Is that understood, Winfield? One more thing, I need surveillance of 24½ Market Street, Annapolis, 21401. It's Red Rider's home, and the front window's been taken out."

"Yes, sir. I'll have a van ready for Annapolis in five. I'll relay barricade info to teams four and nine, who are six miles from the said shutdown zone, sir. And your car is on its way."

Oh God, I forgot about Nana. "Winfield, get me the cell phone number for retired commander Sergeant Williams, please."

"One minute, sir...Here it is. I'll connect you."

"This is Serge," answered a deep voice.

"Commander Williams, this is Commander Jack Houchins. I'm a friend of Pea's. Is Nana there with you?"

"Um, yes. What seems to be the problem, Houchins?"

"Sir, did Nana mention Pea having a friend staying with her, watching over her?"

"Yes, she did. Is Pea in trouble?"

"Sir, can I ask what your security clearance was before you retired?"

"Look, son, I retired ten years ago. Does it really matter?"

"Could you keep Nana there with you? I don't know if it's safe for her to return to the house. Pea's been taken. This is highly sensitive information, and I can't go into details other than she's in serious danger."

"I see. Is Nana aware of any of this?"

"No, sir. Everything was civil until this week—actually, until the day Nana arrived."

"Nana wasn't stirring up trouble, was she?" Serge asked under his breath.

"No. Coincidence. Just keep Nana until you hear from me. Don't tell her anything. It could be dangerous for her."

"Copy that," replied Serge, quietly. I could hear Nana in the background, in near hysterics, asking what had happened to her Sweet Pea. Then I heard Serge, trying to calm her, "Nana, Jack's gonna call us back as soon as he knows anything...Sit down. Try and breath, Butterbean, Pea's gonna be fine..."

"Thank you, Commander Williams. I've got Specialist Winfield at the NSA here on the line as well. If you need to reach me, he'll connect us. I'll pass you to him now. Thank you. Marty—are you still on the line? Status on the 97 shutdown please? And the van?"

"Yes, sir, I'm here. Glen Burnie Police Department has officers on both sides of the highway, sir. Traffic is stopped, north and south. All exits are closed between Severna Park and Ellicott City, with state and county police at the ready. Sir, the van has now passed the Severna Park exit, still headed northwest toward BWI. Runways are down and awaiting further direction."

"Do you see me on the satellite? How long 'til I catch the van?" I asked anxiously.

"Sir, you are six minutes from the van. But we have two helos approaching the van in three minutes." Six minutes is not good enough. I pushed my foot to the accelerator until the car started to shake. I held steady at 105 miles per hour.

I was trying to be calm and use my work voice, but all I could picture in my head was Pea being hauled off somewhere and tortured. She's not one of us. They would happily break her into pieces. They'd keep her alive just to hurt her more. I wondered how her dreams worked. Would she dream the same types of things or see anything worth telling them anyhow? I remembered hearing about a program the Soviets had in the Cold War era, some psych hospital in the middle of nowhere, full of people with talents like Pea, only less honed. They did tests on them and gave them all kinds of drugs to enhance their premonitions...Only God knows what else they did to those people. I wonder if that program is still secretly running, under the radar...with Pea to be the crown jewel of the psych ward...against her will. I could feel my pulse hammering. I took a deep breath and tried to slow my breathing.

My voice was as calm as I could get it. "Marty, how long 'til the van stops in the barricade?"

"About two minutes, sir."

"So, they're going to have a minute to get out and run before the helos get there? Is that what you're telling me? Where are your teams now? ARE THEY AT LEAST CLOSE?"

"Yes, sir, that's what it looks like. We have them driving on the shoulders. A total of sixteen cars—twenty-four agents. We should have men on the ground nearby when the suspects exit the van with her, sir. All agents and police have been told to keep the life of the informant out of danger, as much as possible."

"We need the suspects alive, too. There's something big going on here, Marty. They aren't the top guys, but we need to see what they know. I'll get Joe on that as soon as you get them into custody."

"Yes, sir. Stay on the line. A call is coming in...It's the general, sir..."

11

Big Boots

~

I'm trying to recall what John used to tell me about being captured—what to do, what to say, what not to say. So far, I'm feeling fortunate as I only have sore arms and legs from where they grabbed me and shoved me in the van. I can't see anything. Most of my face is covered. I was asleep, and now I am pretending to be. I wonder when I am supposed to be waking up.

Ugh! One of the men just put his boot in my ribs. He's probably checking to see if I'm awake...but I won't make a sound. I'll be limp.

I wonder if Jack saw them take me. He must be a wreck, if that's even possible. I should have waited for him to follow me out. It just felt like we were two people out together. That would be why they aren't supposed to talk to or eat with the person they are watching. I guess one can get comfortable and let his guard down.

I don't know how fast we are going or why someone is holding my head to the cold metal floor of this van. I didn't see who took me, and now I'm wishing I hadn't seen any faces, ever, in my dreams or otherwise. I don't know where we're headed. Perhaps a dark, hot room somewhere underground. I wonder if Allen knows where I am?

What will they do to me? I'm sure it'll be worse than just having someone put me down quickly. I imagine they could have done that at the grocery store, if they wanted to. The unknown is definitely the worst I can imagine. I wonder if John can see me here, alone in the dark. Perhaps I will see him soon. It's just the time in between that I fear. No matter what, my fate couldn't be worse than watching John die in that hospital bed. Nothing will ever hurt me like that again. Physical pain couldn't touch losing John. If I pray silently, I wonder if John could maybe hear me too...

"Heavenly Father, as with all of creation, my fate is in Your hands. You have provided me with more life and more love than anyone I know. You have always looked after my family, and even after You took John home, You gave me friends to show me the way back into the living. Thank You for my family, especially James. Please protect him after I am gone. Please grant him and Tiny enough love to overcome any problems they may face together. Please give them children to fill their hearts. Please also protect my parents, Teddy, John's family, and my dear friends, especially Ellie and Nana. I accept Your will entirely. If I am to see you soon, I hope that You count me a worthy follower and are pleased with me. Please forgive anything I have done and forgotten to ask forgiveness for. Please also provide someone to love Allen. Even though I'm still mad at him for ignoring John's death, he's been good to me this year, and I can now see why John loved him so much. Soften his heart toward You. Make Your presence known in his life. And, I want to thank You for Jack. He's made me feel alive again, and I thank You for his company. Please send him a worthy sparring partner as well. I guess that's it. Thank You. In Your Son's name, I pray. Amen."

The van started to slow down. I continued to play dead as the two men poked at me again, to track my lethargy. They were speaking Russian. Of course, I had no idea what they were saying, except that they are very, very irritated, in their yelling back and forth. I wonder if they know who I am or if they are just doing someone else's dirty work. I imagine the latter.

The van came to a stop, and then I suppose the driver changed his mind and stepped on the gas. We're on a bumpy road now, maybe the shoulder? I hear something overhead. Helicopters or airplanes...Are they taking me to Russia? We're going faster now, and they've let go of my head, but I still can't move my arms or legs. They're bound pretty tight.

"Get up! I know you're not asleep!" someone shouted—in perfect English. One of our own. He must work for Popoff.

"UGH!" He kicked my gut. He must have a boot the size of Brazil.

"Why all this fuss over you? I should have asked for more money! We have a bit of a problem here, Red Rider. It seems the Russian finds you of interest. He wants you either at your next destination or dead. You choose."

I thought for a second. "What would you choose if you were me?" I asked in a calm voice.

"I'd rather be dead!" He started into a bellowing sort of laugh that would have sounded grandfatherly, had I been in another situation.

"Is there any way you could tell me what I did that was so irritating to whomever I may or may not be going to see next?" I asked politely.

"I wish I knew. You look harmless enough. I can't imagine how such a small person has caused such a big problem!"

"I don't know what problem you're referring to. Could you fill me in, please?"

"You'll be filled in plenty, soon enough. Now shut up. We may have to run, so get ready. If you fight me, I'll kill you on the spot. Got it?"

"Yes. But, would it be better for me if you killed me now...rather than who I'm going to meet next?"

"Are you asking me seriously, or are you trying to be funny?" he asked, muffling his laughter.

"I'm not really in a position to amuse you, here, tied up on the floor of your van. I'm just weighing my options."

"Your options are getting slimmer by the second. If I don't get outta here, then I don't get paid! Which means you will most certainly be dead." He wasn't laughing anymore.

I heard him yell up to the driver, "I'm taking her, and we're going to make a run for it. There's a car down the street waiting for us on the other side of the trees. Switch out the van at the train station..."

I could hear a helicopter overhead and the van driver shouting, "GO! NOW!"

At once, the back doors flew open, while the van was still driving down what I think was the shoulder. One of the men grabbed me and pushed me out of the moving van, then jumped out behind me. I heard the doors slam shut two seconds later. I was rolling from a rocky area to smoother one, but I hit the ground so hard that I had no control over where my still-bound body was headed.

My head smashed into something hard and pointed, maybe a tree or a rock? I finally came to a stop on a patch of grass. I could feel wet warmth soaking my hair. I started to feel light-headed again...Maybe this was better...to be dead before I made it to wherever they were taking me.

I had pain all over my body. I was starting to feel cold. I wished the sun was still out...Maybe someone would see me.

This was better than what I imagined would happen five minutes ago. Dying of a head injury had to be better than meeting that Russian who detests me—not nearly as scary.

The man who followed me out of the van was shouting on his radio, "She's dead! She hit her head. I'm headed to the other car!" I heard the big boots running away.

The helicopters were very close now. They shook the ground under me. I could hear them, but just barely, because there was someone talking. A familiar voice in my ear. It was John. "I'm here, my wife." His voice, calm and tender.

"John? Are you here?" I felt his touch. It was different than before, restful and feathery.

"I'm sorry you are hurting, sweetie, but it won't be long. You'll like where we're going. Everyone's waiting for you." He's here to take me home.

Then seven gunshots. Then silence.

12
Reproof

~

"Allen, it's Jack. I'm here. She's out of the van, on the ground. We're about two hundred yards away. I got the one who was running. He's dead. The other two from the van made it to the train station."

"You're in deep shit, Jack! Do you know what this looks like? Only three of us knew about her, and she was swiped on YOUR watch! I'm having them take you in."

"Please, Allen, let me see if she's OK first! I need to see if she's going to make it! The paramedics will be here in less than a minute. It's all my fault! Please. Please let me stay with her until you get here."

"Fine. But you are not to be alone with her! Got it? Keep an agent with you. You can watch her until I get there. THEN YOUR ASS WILL BE ESCORTED TO MY OFFICE! I'll be there in a minute."

13

In Stitches

~

Something touched my cheek. It was warm. "John?"

"No, honey, it's Jack. Can you hear me?" His voice was quiet, affectionate.

"Am I dead? I heard John. He's here with me. He's come to take me."

"Sweet Pea, it's Jack. You aren't dead. Are you disappointed?" Jack asked calmly.

"I'm not sure yet. If I have to be afraid all the time, then I'd rather be dead." Speaking was difficult. There was a stabbing pain inside my chest. I winced as I took another breath.

"Baby, I got the guy who was running. Sweetie, I'm going to take this thing off your eyes, OK? Don't move your head. Don't move anything. Please, just stay still." I felt pressure on the back of my head.

He very gently pushed the covering up over my eyes, onto my forehead, and into my wet, bloodied hair. He kissed my cheeks and then my nose. His salty tears burned my battered cheeks. I tried to smile, but my face hurt so much.

"Jack, it hurts. I can't move anything. My arms, legs..."

"I know. Just please stay still. I've got my shirt on your head to try and stop the bleeding. Am I hurting you?" he asked, his voice cracking.

Overhead, helicopters were circling the area, looking for the empty van that had held me captive. There were lights flashing, more brilliant as the minutes past and the sun descended. Faint sounds of ambulances were in the distance, perhaps a medical team for me, and a black bag for big boots.

Two police units and a SWAT team arrived and set up shop nearby to deter any curious onlookers (rubberneckers), and to figure out a detour for the eight lanes on route 97. Muffled voices were barking orders into radios and orange cones were going up. The larger, heavily armored cops with automatic rifles surrounded Jack and I until the medical help approached. I could hear the sirens getting ever closer, until they abruptly stopped and several EMTs threw open the back of the ambulance.

Jack leaned over me, with one hand behind my head and the other cupping my face, ever so gently. My eyes wandered down to peek at his chest. I softly muttered, "Jack, do you know that your chest is bald, too?" He kissed my nose and smiled. He seemed relieved that I was joking, until I grimaced at the unrelenting pain on my right side. I tried to curl up, but even insignificant movements were excruciating.

"Pea, I wish you couldn't feel any of this....Just hang on one more minute. The paramedics are here getting ready for you. And Whole Foods gave you a refund. They felt guilty for having such incompetent security."

I whispered, "Yes, he was impotent...He didn't even try to shoot blanks at the guys who snatched me..." I giggled, but it hurt my ribs.

"You're in serious trouble with me for that comment, young lady! I said incompetent, not impotent! The swimmers are dead in the water, but the delivery system works great, thank you very much!"

I could tell he was trying hard to keep a straight face.

"Jack, will you go with me to the hospital? I hate hospitals. I haven't been in one since James was born."

"I can't, honey. I have to go in to work. I'll come see you as soon as I can. Allen's coming to keep you company, OK? I wish I could go. I want to go. I just really made a mess of this. I can't tell you how sorry I am." His tears fell to my face, meeting my own tears. I tried not to cry but had no control. I needed Jack with me.

"Please stay!" I pleaded. "Allen doesn't kiss my nose...and he's going to tell me how bad I look...and I'm so cold...Will you put my hands in your shirt?"

"Please don't move, Pea. Listen, I have to go. I'm so sorry. This is all my fault. I wasn't paying attention. I was thinking about my stomach, as usual. Dinner, I mean."

The pain was increasingly more intense. I shut my eyes. Tried to concentrate and keep quiet. Tears were streaming out. "I'm so cold, Jack."

He tried to keep me lucid and positive. "They'll have you bundled up in a minute or two. You'll be perfect, Sweet Pea. You'll be fine. But your nails did get a little messed up. Nana may be upset with you." said Jack, trying to redirect me from my pain.

"Jack, please call her, and my folks, and James and Ellie...Where's Calvin? What are we going to say happened?"

"Not sure yet. But, Allen's got plenty of experience with cover-ups. Now try and rest. I have to go. Allen's here. See you soon, OK?"

"OK, Jack." He kissed my nose and gently removed his hand from the back of my head. I watched him walk away, bloody shirt in hand, looking down at the ground, until he disappeared into the dark.

Someone else was holding something to my head. Allen. He looked me over and moved my hair around, trying to estimate my blood loss. He asked the EMTs a few things that I didn't understand then began giving them orders.

"Pea, it's me, Allen. They're gonna pick you up and put you on the bed here, OK? It's going to be uncomfortable." He gently cut my bindings off so they could move me. Every touch hurt something. I think it felt better before he freed my limbs.

The EMTs began cutting my clothing off. I was embarrassed that Allen was present, although less so than if it were Jack seeing me in all of my pasty-white glory. But, I didn't want to be alone. I reached out for him, and he held my good hand. He looked intently at my face the whole time, never once wavering.

I said in a whimper, "Allen, if you make fun of how I look, I will never, ever make you dinner again."

He shook his head, while taking a deep breath, "Pea, I gotta be honest. Having my best friend's wife here naked and nearly dead is not my idea of a good time. You're a mess. But your sense of humor seems intact. That's a good thing. Can you feel all of this? How bad from one to ten?

"Ten."

"OK, we'll get you something to take the edge off. You're going to feel a pinch, OK?

"Is that supposed to be funny, Allen? A pinch after all of this is a bit of a joke, no?"

"Just stay still. And stop trying to be funny." He began to barely whisper, "Seeing you like this is killing me, Pea..." He pinched the bridge of his nose and paused for a minute, then continued in a grieved voice, "You're the closest thing I have to family. I feel awful that this has happened to you. It's my fault."

"Allen, John was here with me. I felt his touch...He was talking to me..."

He cracked a smile, and his tone lightened a little, "Did John mention he's gonna kick my ass for all of this? Because he has the advantage of invisibility, and quite honestly, he was much better at the hand-to-hand stuff."

"I'll tell him you said that." Finally some pain relief—it was as if my arms and legs had somehow disappeared...

"Look, Pea, in all seriousness, I'm not sure what to do here. Someone knows about what you can do. I can't put you in danger anymore. I just don't know what to do with you at this point. We need to figure out who is behind all of this. No more secrets, OK? I'll tell you when whoever is responsible is dead." His voice was angry but controlled. He was still holding my hand, looking into my now-glassy eyes.

"Allen, I'm not as sympathetic to bad guys as I was before. I promise I won't call you a government stooge anymore."

"Uh, thanks, Pea. There are three other people here, and they can hear you..." Allen wasn't used to being teased with all his medals on.

"Do they know that you're a one-star dork?" I giggled. Everything seemed so funny all of a sudden.

"No. But now they know that the little naked redhead lying here likes to pick fights with generals." Allen looked irked...which made me laugh even harder...

"I still can't believe you even made it out of Ranger School! John was always tougher than you. And all those women! I'm surprised they didn't kick you out of the army just for being such a whore! Ha ha! Did you ever catch anything?" I tried to stop smiling but couldn't control my face.

"Pea, I think they gave you too much painkiller. I can't believe you said 'whore'! That might be the worst thing I've ever heard out of your mouth!"

"Geez, Allen, I used to say absolutely filthy things to John all the time," I declared in a slightly slurred voice.

"I'm sure you did. That would explain his twenty-plus-year, non-stop fascination with you. The way he loved you, it was hard to watch sometimes. Enough to make a guy jealous, even. I'm glad you're back in my life now, even though John can't be with us. God, I miss him."

I then remembered why I had been angry with him for almost two years. "Allen, where were you? You didn't answer my calls or respond to my e-mails."

Allen looked guilty; his face sank. He spoke in a soft whimper. "He was at my place that afternoon, before he died. I didn't want to believe that he was gone. I just couldn't see him like that. I couldn't bear it. I'm so sorry. Can you forgive me?"

"I needed you! You were part of us, our family..." I said as I squeezed his hand. Getting upset with Allen just made breathing harder, and I could see the pain on his face when he talked about John. I didn't want him to hurt anymore. "Allen, I'm glad you told me...I thought you just didn't care about us." I lost my train of thought when I felt a tingling sensation rush over me. "I can't feel anything now. Just...cold..."

"Pea, you're gonna be fine, OK?" he reassured me.

"Will you go with me in the paddy wagon, Allen?"

"No, but I'll go with you in the ambulance. A paddy wagon is for convicts, Pea."

"Oh, sorry."

"Allen, why can't Jack be here, too?"

"You and Jack have a little something, huh?"

"I think so. He's a lot like John, don't you think?"

"I don't know, Pea. I guess so. Look, I don't want to upset you, but he did a lousy job today. It doesn't look good for him. I doubt he had anything to do with any of this, but he let his guard down, and that's the opposite of what I expected from him. He was my top guy."

"It's my fault, Allen. I forced him to eat at my house and stay up late talking to me and drive me all over the place! Don't let this ruin him, please, Allen!" I started to cry again. The thought of Jack personally paying for all of this was too much.

As Allen wiped my tears away with his hand, I felt someone tug-
ging at my scalp. "Pea, stop talking so much. You need to calm down so
you'll stop bleeding. They're trying to stitch you up here. Look, I'll think
about what you said. But there's no wiggle room in my job. My hands
may be tied. Now, be quiet, and try to rest."

I couldn't argue anymore. It was hard just keeping my eyes open.
"Len, my jus fleezing...I neeb a blankeps..." I felt his hand stroking my
forehead...It felt nice...

"Go to sleep, Pea," he ordered.

"Lub nu, Len."

"Close your eyes, please, Pea." I was afraid to go to sleep, but I
couldn't stop my head from floating off.

"K." His eyes were red. He pulled another blanket over me, and I
was out.

14

Prognosis

⌒

I woke up at Walter Reed Hospital with no clue what time it was. Nor could I feel my body. It was a rather nice change from the last time I was lucid. My thoughts were a little jumbled, so I asked my nurse for some tea, and tried to remember how I ended up here. I recalled glimpses of the worst, I guess. Getting kicked while I was in the van, being airborne then hitting something hard, Jack's salty tears, and how I wanted him to stay with me. Lastly, I remember Allen staring into my face, full of apologies and looking so broken. Quite an evening.

James called as soon as I was coherent. His voice was wretched, desolate.

"Mom, Allen called and told me what happened. I'm so sorry!"

"Sweetie, don't worry. All my parts are accounted for and I'm going to be back to normal in a few weeks."

"We're doing work-ups for a training trip next month, but my XO said I can take two days leave to come up. Uncle Teddy called and offered me a ticket."

"No need, Sweetie. I've got a few breaks here and there, but I'm going to be fine. I don't want you coming all the way up here just to watch me sleep all day. James, you wouldn't believe all the good drugs they have me on! If I didn't know better, I'd think I was floating! Really sweetie, please save your leave for when I'm better, then come up." I wanted James to calm down. I'd never heard him sound so fearful. "What else did your Uncle Teddy have to say?" I asked, hoping to change the subject.

"Just that he's called seventy times and none of the nurses will tell him anything. He's really irritated! He's been calling from Amsterdam. He's there this week for some airline contract negotiations. But, I think he's trying to get home so he can see you."

"Tell him that I'd prefer some good chocolate over a visit! Good chocolate is absolutely imperative to my recovery! Besides, I don't want him to see me like this. I'd never hear the end of it. He's a meanie! No, seriously James, tell him I need chocolate. Pronto."

"I will mom. Hey, are you sure you're gonna be ok? Allen was pretty upset when he called. I mean, he tried to sound all tough and everything, but I could tell he was crazy worried about you." Then James became very quiet, his words almost childlike. "Mom, promise me that you're ok...because...I didn't get to see dad before he..." James took a jagged breath, then choked up.

"James, honey, this is entirely different. Daddy's injuries could not be fixed. He couldn't have made it, son. There was nothing anyone could have done to save him. Sweetie, seeing him like that was excruciating. I can't forget how he looked that day, no matter how hard I try. James, I promise, I'll be fine. You just get back to what you were doing. There's nothing to worry about here."

"Mom, are you sure, positive?" he asked insecurely.

"Yes, my boy. Positive. I love you. Now, get back to work before you're buddies think you've gone soft..."

"OK. I love you, Mom." James whispered in somber tone.

"I love you too, sweetie. I'll call you tomorrow, ok?"

"Yeah. Ok. Tomorrow. Get better. I love you. Bye."

As much as I wanted to see James, I didn't want him to know about what's happened with me since Christmas time. I wanted to keep him away until all of this secret stuff was behind me. I was about to drift off again, when I heard Allen's voice. He got an update on my company from Joe, stationed outside my door, then stepped into my room.

The look on Allen's face confirmed the fact that I resemble road kill. He tried to make light of my injuries and be funny , which unfortunately is not his forte. "Well, hello, Sleeping Beauty!" Allen said in a really awful John Wayne impersonation.

"Allen! What time is it?" I was so happy to see him.

"Let's see, it's almost 10:00 p.m., the day after all of the festivities. You've been asleep for about twenty-two hours."

"Do I look as awful as I think I do? Honestly, how scary do I look?" I asked, cringing.

"Let's just say, you won't need to dye your hair red for a while! It's the deepest shade of crimson I've ever seen. Almost looks natural," he chuckled. I smirked. If I could reach him, I'd yank out a few arm hairs.

He continued, "You broke a few bones, here and there, but they got your head stitched up pretty quick, which was the main concern. You'll have some scars when all is said and done. Not as cool as my scars, but pretty tuff, nonetheless...I should have taken a Polaroid. You looked like someone put you through a giant cheese grater!"

"Allen! Why can't you just be nice and tell me I look fine?"

"Fine. You look fine...one fine step up from a rotting corpse..."

"That's even harsh for you, Allen. Someone with zero tolerance for humility in general, General..."

"Pea, I have a bone to pick with you regarding your little rant in front of the EMTs...If you hadn't been bleeding to death, I would have put you across my knee!"

"What did I say?" I asked defensively.

"I'm not repeating any of it. Let's just say that I really know what you think about me now."

I reached for his hand, and pulled him in to hug me. I put my good arm around his neck and told him, very quietly, in his ear, "Allen, please, don't be mad...You know I adore you..." I couldn't help but giggle. Talking to Allen was so much easier with all the pain medication. Besides, it's hard being mad when I feel this good.

He looked at me strangely, a little uncomfortable, possibly embarrassed. He's not big on the mushy stuff, so he changed the subject and asked if he could sign my cast. I nodded. He grabbed a Sharpie from the desk and wrote on my cast:

"Prudence-You are a serious pain in the ass!!! A.g."

"Nice, Allen. Thanks a lot." I frowned.

He started to chuckle, then put his hand on my forehead while he told me what had happened since I arrived at Walter Reed. Just as he was wrapping up, his cell started vibrating. He glanced down at the screen. "Two guys from my old platoon were just admitted. Road side bomb. I gotta go, Pea. I'll be back tomorrow, OK?" I nodded and then watched Allen hurry down the hall before I drifted back to sleep.

* * *

The story is, according to Allen, that I got hit by a drunk (not myself, another drunk) in the Whole Foods parking lot. NSA agents talked to the security guard and the manager there. They agreed to go along with the story if it meant they got to take credit for helping catch the dude who was drunk driving in their parking lot.

Nana stayed with Serge on his boat. Close quarters = trouble (the smoochy smoochy kind). She was here to visit after Allen left then went down to Jackson to swap out her stuff. She'll be back in a couple weeks.

The following day Ellie called and wanted to know how I got hit by a car at a grocery store with an empty parking lot. I told her I was paying attention to a cute guy instead of watching where I was walking. When she finally saw Jack, she believed me.

Mom and Dad have been here each day to see me. It's nice to finally be awake for their visit. They got a hotel room in Chevy Chase—very convenient for Mom to feed her shopping addiction and eat some great food. The restaurants there are stellar. They brought me breakfast this morning, then left to do some more shopping (poor Dad!).

Teddy finally got a call through to my room. He felt terribly guilty for not being able to visit so he sent me three-dozen 'Fragrant Cloud' roses in an antique vase. My room smells like my British grandmother's midsummer garden. Winnie lacked resources but had a superb way with tantric roses.

Mom said someone was kind enough to install a historically accurate new front window at my house. I suspect it was George and Roper. Roper must think I have the worst luck in the world. He'll want the full scoop when I get home.

It was a full two days before I saw Jack. I was starting to worry about him. I was sleeping when he arrived.

I felt a tickle on my nose and smiled when I heard his voice.

"Hey, pipsqueak, are you awake? I'm growing my hair and my 'face pet' again. Open your eyes and take a peek..."

"Your whiskers tickle my nose." I giggled and opened my eyes. "Jack!" I started to tear up. I tried not to, but I was just too happy to see him to care.

He nuzzled my cheeks and brushed the hair back off my forehead. "How are you feeling? Are you in any pain? I can barely see you in that mummy suit!"

"I'm fine, really more than fine. I can't feel my body at all. They keep me high here round the clock. I'm starting to sympathize with crack addicts...I've missed you, Jack. Where have you been?"

"Uh, getting reprimanded. You don't want all the gory details. However, I was told that you were pleading my case, quite convincingly. I don't deserve your trust. I should've gotten canned, right then and there. Oh! And another thing...Good God, woman! You're even funny when you're half-dead! I heard you got cheeky with Allen in front of the paramedics!"

"What? What did Allen do to you? What happened?"

"Let's just say that I probably won't be making captain this year, or next year, etc. etc."

"Jack, I'm so sorry. Are you ruined?"

"No. Not ruined. Just stunted indefinitely. Really, Pea, I deserved worse than what I got. I should have been seriously demoted. Allen was very generous. You must rub off on people that way. I was due to retire in October, if I want. My thirty-year mark and all...Besides, the navy isn't the only thing I have to keep my mind occupied anymore..."

"It's not?"

"No. I have something better..."

"What's that?"

"A saucy little redhead with supernatural powers..."

I giggled then asked, "You have her, huh?"

"I'd like to," he shyly replied.

"Really? Even though she's kind of a mess?"

"Like I told her, she's pretty close to perfect. So easy to be with. I'm hoping she'll want to spend time with me, too. Even if I'm lousy at keeping her safe," Jack said, looking vanquished.

"She thinks you're good at lots of stuff..."

"Such as...?"

"Doing dishes...Looking great in a pink-paisley apron...Making her cheeks blush..."

"Anything else?"

"You make her feel pretty, which is hard to do," I stated matter-of-factly.

"Well, I guess it is hard to feel simply pretty when you're beyond beautiful," Jack said, tucking stray hairs behind my ears. I closed my eyes. It's been almost forty-eight hours since he last touched me. Too long. I felt his warm, tender lips move over my face...all over my awful-looking, scraped-up, makeup-free face. I must look hideous.

Jack makes me feel like a young girl again. I can't tell him that while lying here in this hospital bed, covered in bandages, looking like an invalid. But, the fact that I'd rather be alive right now, instead of being dead with John, is significant.

When I was nearly bleeding to death on the side of the highway, and I heard John's voice, I didn't let go and follow him home...because I heard Jack. I wanted to live. I hung on for what we could be. Jack thinks he's failed me, when in reality he's been nothing short of a milestone in my life. I can't believe that two years ago, I was living in such a very small box. My life is certainly different now. I would do anything and everything to have John back. But, that's not possible.

I looked up. Jack was sitting there, curious. But he didn't pry too much.

"I suppose you've had lots to think about the past couple days, huh?" he murmured, stroking my cheeks.

"Yeah." I smiled and took his hand. "Come closer, please..." He smiled and carefully leaned over me. I wanted to hold him, but I only had the one functional arm. I kissed his ear, then whispered, "Jack, please take me home."

"You need a bit more time here to make sure everything is healing up well, and....Joe will need to stay with you...until this is all figured out..."

"I'd rather you do it..."

"Forget it! I'm a horrible watchdog! Joe's better at this stuff. He'll do a better job. Besides, Allen would take my head off if I even asked! I'm on his shit list, Pea."

Then I remembered my roadside skin show... "UGH! Allen saw me naked! I wish I *was* dead!"

"Allen mentioned nothing about that. Maybe he's more a gentleman than you thought."

"Or having a momentary lapse in his standard unscrupulous character," I suggested.

"Pea, I should have been there with you, and I'm sorry. But I'm glad he was there since I couldn't be—even if he got to see the goods! Ha! But I don't wanna picture him seeing you, so let's talk about something else, OK? Everything for your return home is covered. Nana's coming back to take care of you. Nana insisted, and she's a nurse, so that works out well. And I took some leave so I can help Nana get you up and down the stairs for a while."

"You're gonna be around the house?" I asked, excitedly.

"Yep, that's the plan...if it's OK with you. I don't think Nana can put you on the chaise outside, and I know that's your favorite spot. It's warm out. You'll need some sun after being in here. And George has Calvin. He'll bring him home after you're discharged."

He gave me the scoop on everything else that I'd missed.

"Your mom's been a mess. However, I commented on her new hairdo, and she seemed to forget how upset she was for almost an hour! She's quite cross with Nana for taking over your care, but honestly,

Nana's actually skilled and seems better at keeping things quiet, so that'll be best. Your dad's pretty confused about all of this...He knows something's up, but he's too busy consoling your mom, aka shopping therapy, right now to investigate. Oh, and Allen told your folks that Joe is the patient advocate assigned to your case to explain why he's been hanging around your room."

"So, will Joe be 'hanging around' when we're together now?"

"Are we together? Could you consider seeing a man who nearly lost your life? I thought you had better sense than that." He looked down at the worn tile floor. His confident façade was exposed, but that made him even more endearing to me.

"I've felt more alive this week than I have in two years," I whispered, lifting his chin. I let my hand wander down his neck. He had my favorite blue chambray shirt on. I played with the unbuttoned collar, put a shy smile on, and continued, "However, I can neither confirm nor deny that you've had any part in that, Commander Houchins." I kissed his nose and smiled. He must know how I feel about him. His eyes were intense, like when he first kissed me. Tears fell from his face, mingling with the salty wet of my own. They didn't sting now. My body was healing. Jack put his cheek to mine, and we were quiet together for what seemed like hours, until my nurse shimmied in with a syringe.

"Time for your pain meds, Miss Brandt," ordered Karen, my plump afternoon nurse, with a wide smile. "Here comes your happy nap!" Karen motioned to Jack and told him to leave. "Commander, she needs some rest. These are gonna knock her out pretty good, so let's wrap it up here, OK?" Then Karen started to sing under her breath, "I get by with a little help from my friends...Oooh, I get high with a little help from my friends..." while inserting the syringe into my drip.

Karen was used to friendly people on her floor, and Joe's seemingly grouchy disposition does intimidate people rather easily. "That crabby man outside the door looks like he could use a happy nap, too," she teased.

Karen smiled at Jack and me then stepped out, after again reminding Jack to split when I started snoring. Soon after, the waves of warm started... warm everywhere but my hands... "Jack, my hands are cold," I murmured.

"Of course they are," he said, pulling the blankets up over my shoulders. He gently placed my free hand on his face and held his hand over mine. "I thought I'd lost you, redhead," he whispered, kissing behind my ear.

Another tear fell to my cheek, and he carefully wiped it away with his thumb.

I was so tired, but I didn't want Jack to go. "When am I going to see you again?" I asked, a little unsure.

"How about next time you open your eyes?" he suggested. "If it's OK, I'll ask Karen to call me when you're stirring. I'll bring you some dinner."

"I'm not hungry. But I'd love some good coffee..."

"How about a chocolate mocha shake? A big one. You need some calories, woman!"

"OK, Jack," I conceded. "But I wish I was home, making you dinner instead..."

"Me, too. And we will, Pea. We'll have lots of dinners *at home*," he said, winking.

If I hadn't been so sleepy, I would have asked what he meant by that. But I suspect I already know.

His hands found my face again and made a soft, circular motion over my temples—so relaxing.

My eyes were dilated from the meds. I tried to focus on Jack, but something bright and a little blurry walked in behind him. Something familiar. Someone I hadn't seen like this before. The physical presence of John's spirit. He was breathtaking.

John stood there, very still, watching Jack's hands hold my head so gently while lulling me to sleep with easy fingertips. I thought I was hallucinating from the pain pills. But, my arm hairs were standing on end, as they always do when John is near.

John looked strong, healthy, and vibrant. No wrinkles, no gray in his hair—as if the accident never happened. His scars were gone. He was new again.

I stared at John curiously, wanting to touch him, hug him, and tell him how much I missed him...to tell him about James and Tiny...to see what he's been doing without me...to ask what his eternal life is like... to know if he was sending me those dreams from the heavens. But I couldn't find the words, because I was ashamed. Jack was here, touching my face. And John could see that.

I was overcome with anxiety, unsure how to feel. My blood pressure monitor began to beep.

"Pea? Baby, are you OK?" asked Jack. He looked at my sullen face, concerned. "Are you hurting or cold?" Jack took my good hand in his hands and warmed it with his breath. "Sweetie, you're an ice cube! You need an incubator! I'll bet they have one in the NICU that's your size!" Then Jack kissed my lips and whispered, "Keeping you warm is a full-time job. It's a good thing I'm retiring soon..."

John watched intently as Jack fussed over me. John's face was soft. He wasn't angry, jealous, or hurt. He began to smile. I suddenly realized that John wasn't here to make me feel guilty. He looked relieved but forlorn, like a doting father giving away a treasured daughter to someone exceedingly worthy.

I smiled back at John, as tears fell uncontrollably. Was this good-bye?

Jack finally stopped looking at me and turned his head to the foot of the bed. When he saw nothing, he asked tenderly, quietly, with an eyebrow raised, "Pea, is *he* here?"

"Yes," I mumbled. I tried to say more, to sound lucid, but crying while my head was floating off was rather difficult.

Jack promptly removed his hands from my face and rested them on his lap, out of respect for John. "Should I leave?" he asked, eyes saddened.

"No. Jack, I don't want you to go..." I whispered, barely audible. I couldn't hold my head up anymore and reclined fully into the pillow behind me. I took in one long, last drag of Jack's face before shutting my eyes.

I felt a kiss on my nose then heard Jack's rugged boots tiptoe across the linoleum floor. Jack stopped outside my door to ask Joe who'd be relieving him tonight.

"Terrence," Joe replied.

My arms tingled, hairs still at attention because John hadn't left. I peeked through my eyelashes. John stood over my bed, unmoving, like a statue. His look was unchanged.

"John?" I whispered, "Are you leaving me? Protecting me?"

He didn't respond. Perhaps it's not over. He must know someone's coming for me. Someone that Joe, Jack, and even Allen can't protect me from. I trembled in my sleep, fearing the worst.

* * *

That evening, when I opened my groggy eyes, Jack was here in my room, sitting on the side of my bed, stroking my hair.

"Jack, did you see someone in my room before you left earlier?" I asked, still a little weirded out by the presence of both my former husband and my current boyfriend in the same room.

"No, but you were talking in your sleep."

"When?" I asked.

"When you fell asleep, after your pain cocktail."

"I wasn't asleep. I just nodded off for a minute or two. I heard you leave..."

"No, babe, I stayed with you the whole time. Your dad picked up this shake. I was going to do it, but he wanted to get out of the hospital for a bit. He just got back a few moments ago."

"But John was here in my room, and you were, too. You asked if you should leave...I said no...Remember?"

"Sweetie, Karen asked me to leave. I stayed because Joe had to go home, and I don't know the guy that was taking his place, so I stayed..."

"You mean Terrence?"

"Yes. Did Joe tell you about him?"

"No. I heard you ask Joe who had the night shift."

"You couldn't have heard that. You were asleep—out cold! But you certainly are chatty while you sleep...Something about John being 'breathtaking,' his body being beautiful, young, and perfect, and all of that...I don't know what you were dreaming about, but it sounded like you were having fun!" Jack teased. "If you hadn't lost him two years ago, I would be seriously jealous."

"Oh. I'm sorry about that. I thought you were here, too..."

"You mean *with* you and John and his beautiful body? That's not my kind of thing, Pea," Jack said, chuckling.

"Jack! Don't be gross! But please *do* ask Karen to come by my room. I want her to tone down my meds. I thought I saw John watching you touch my face and warm my hands. He just stood there, smiling the whole time..."

"So, John's OK with the you-and-me thing? That's good, right?" he asked.

"Just get my nurse, Jack. And don't bother to stick around for my outer dialogue next time I sleep!"

"Fine, but I'd just like to know how long 'til you drop John and start dreaming about me?" he asked with a great deal of sarcasm.

"Don't hold your breath, chief," I teased, laughing.

Jack leaned over my bed, held my face, and gently kissed my lips. "I think it's gonna be sooner rather than later, redhead...Although, competing with a dead guy is something I *haven't* done."

"I think he's glad I have you, Jack. That's what my dream was about."

"Good. Then he won't mind if I kiss you some more. But, first, you are going to eat something." Jack took my good hand in his then shivered. "Geez, Pea! You're an ice cube! You need an incubator! I'll bet they have one in the NICU that's your size! Keeping you warm is a full-time job. It's a good thing I'm retiring soon..."

I looked up, and John was at the foot of my bed, watching Jack fuss over me, just as he had in my dream a few hours ago. John and I exchanged glances. I didn't understand why Jack said the same thing about the incubator twice or why John left my room and came back to watch Jack touch my face again. I sat there, baffled, looking at John for direction.

John's face was discouraged, like I wasn't trying hard enough. I was thoroughly confused by his goading expression. He cocked his head and looked at me, frustrated, like he was saying, "Sweetheart, please pay attention!"

I was trying to think, but I had too many programs running. And having narcotics awash in my veins wasn't exactly helping my analytical skills. I gaped at the foot of my bed, dazed and stoned, for nearly a minute before I realized that what Jack said was right. I hadn't been awake earlier. I was dreaming out loud. And what I saw in that dream was in real-time now. My very own *Groundhog Day* (ah-ha!) moment.

I let out a triumphant giggle. After two long years, I finally get it. John had to spell it out for me. The dreams *were* from him. He's been giving me little slices of the future all along of events either in the works or yet to come. The assassination of Barishmel, the death of a Saudi king, the jogger in DC, the terrorist camp near the Israeli border, and Popov, all foretold in my dreams, became reality. Not because I had conjured them up myself, but because those events had previously been set into motion. Perhaps the laughing monks in Red Square and the three angelic men will make better sense, too, as time passes. Maybe, with John's help, I will even identify Pavel Petrov.

John must have known that I would confide in Allen to save whom-ever I can, especially if that whomever is James. But, maybe John's intentions went beyond that. To show Allen that death is just a passage-way to a new life. That we are intentional beings with purpose, both here and beyond. I hope that I have done well with the information that John provided. That my interference has helped, not hindered, a future with a positive outcome.

What Allen said about the 1980s in Afghanistan resonated with me. Its aftershocks are still being felt, some thirty years later. Is it possible that something similar but significantly worse is at hand? If a powerful Russian is mobilizing the jihadists to begin war with Israel, just to sell weapons, then there will be no end to the human suffering. It will eradi-cate millions in the Middle East, and our young ones in uniform will be further at risk. Our political alignments will dictate our involvement, and James will be one of the first to go. I can't help but think that John knows all of this and his purpose in communicating the future to me involves stopping whatever storm is brewing.

As I began to get myself worked up (again) over things I cannot control, I looked up at John standing there like the rock he's always been to me. And that rock was wholly relieved when he saw my light bulb finally go on. His aggravated look was replaced with a warm, wide smile, the same smile that soothed me for half a lifetime. Being mar-ried to an anxious knucklehead like me must have been exasperating for him.

Jack watched me steadily giggle and gaze at seemingly nothing. He had that puzzled, insecure look on his face. "Pea, is *he* here?" he asked, moving his hands from my face to his lap, just as I saw him do before.

"Yes," I sighed.

"Should I leave?" he asked, eyes saddened.

"No. Jack, I don't want you to go..." I whispered, reassuring him with a fond gaze. His eyes were burning with ardent devotion. Why a man like that would look at me that way is a great mystery. He carefully cradled my cheek with his hand and delicately stroked my lips with his thumb.

I peered over at John one last time. His soft gray eyes seemed a little down when Jack touched me. John bore the same forlorn, fatherly grin as in my dream just hours ago.

To experience this degree of fervor from two men, at the same time, in the same room, is certainly peculiar. I have been blessed indeed. The fact that only one is technically alive is of no consequence. I closed my eyes and took a deep breath, floored by how fortunate I've been in the past and how I am even more fortunate at this moment, despite my last few hapless days. Any girl would be pleased to be me, even in my current state of mangled mummy. I have three fine men in my life now: my John, our son, James, and now Jack, a tough guy in his own right, whose tears washed over my face at the roadside.

I pressed Jack's hand into my cheek and smiled as his thumb traced my lips so gently. Feeling his tender touch was enough to spark a warm blush.

Seeing Jack and I look at each other that way must have felt a little awkward for John, like being a third wheel. His brilliant light went dim. Always the consummate gentleman, John lovingly smiled at me and then vanished, allowing my new suitor and me some time to catch up. In private.

Bonus excerpt from The Mole by Audie Cockings, coming spring 2015

THE MOLE: LITTLE RED RIDER
BOOK II

The sky was losing its sherbet hues to a restful indigo. Thin, light lines of cotton batting stretched across our slice of the canvas, offering a glimpse of a modestly marbled parchment moon. It was late evening, nearly eight o'clock. The air outside was just chilly enough to warrant the down comforter, and the trees swayed in unison to the late spring breeze.

From my back patio, Jack and I had the best view in town, the illuminated dome of the Naval Academy chapel, its weathered green copper roof and cupola, the shining star of this pre-Revolutionary town. I imagined couples cuddling under this same backdrop in 1908 when the chapel was commissioned, cadets wooing young women in long dresses and ladylike updos, who would vote for the first time eleven years later. The men, much like Jack, chivalrous, attentive, manly men, who knew how to use a sword, a gun, and change a spare tire (or carriage wheel).

Jack laid me down on the chaise, tucking pillows under my right arm and leg casts to elevate them, then sat down beside me and leaned in. My red hair was rather untidy, but Jack seemed to like it. I was enveloped in pillows, like a lit match stuck in a marshmallow. We were forehead to forehead, finally enjoying quiet moments that had escaped us during the two-week stay at Walter Reed after my accident.

Jack's malleable side is less honed than John's was. But, Jack has a tenderness about him that's familiar. No comic charm or clever lines, but he certainly knows how to make me smile. Jack's still not entirely sure of himself, but that's comforting to someone like me. It's like we're both afraid to mess this up, whatever *this* is.

When I met Jack, I was still broken, and he knew it—not like I was with John, who was instantly smitten with my sassy remarks and confidence. Lucky for me, Jack didn't take my brokenness for weakness. He was still reeling from his divorce, wanting to try again but afraid of failing.

His thumbs were at my temples, hands deep in my hair, gently moving over my scalp, carefully enough to merely graze my stitches (and corresponding bald spots). He lifted my chin to kiss me, but first he released a deep sigh of relief and a contagious smile that made us both relax a little. I brought my hand to his lips, tracing his smile with my fingertips. I felt nothing but a comfortable peace that had been missing since John left me.

I closed my eyes as Jack gently took my good hand, kissing my palm then pressing it into his cheek. When his lips finally touched mine, I tried to kiss him back, but I found myself smiling again instead, feeling full, blessed, as if Jack were a latent gift, a consolation for the pain I've endured (however poorly). Because, after seeing his face so grieved, so afraid for me when I was dying, I can no longer question the fact that he cares for me deeply, and I'm finding myself less anxious in his company.

Things are as they should be between us. I could almost forget that I'm a widow.

I sighed and opened my eyes to read his face. His eyes were open, just a few inches from mine. He was watching me enjoy our exchange. I smiled then quickly shut my eyes. Seeing him look at me that way makes me giggle. I felt his lips flutter over mine again then he tucked me into his side and put his arm around me. It's so good just to be still with him. Being home, with Jack here, is enormously restful.

* * *

All was well until around 3:00 a.m. I woke up to my own scream and Jack nearly shaking my marbles loose. "Pea, wake up! Calm down, baby. Open your eyes!"

Terrence burst through the patio door, gun in hand and pointed at Jack. I was still half asleep, shaking, and in hysterics. Jack had his hands on my face. I know what it must have looked like to Terrence.

"Hands up! Step away from her, Commander Houchins!" Terrence said in a hushed but firm voice.

I tried to intervene, "Terrence! It's OK! I'm fine! He's just trying to wake me. Please put the gun down, Terrence. Please!" I was already confused, but the gun pointed at Jack scared me to death. Terrence didn't stand down until Jack got up and stepped away from me with his hands up. It was as if I hadn't said anything at all.

"Terrence! Please, I was having a nightmare. Please!" By now, I was nearly hyperventilating. "Terrence, I need to see Allen. Please call him." Terrence spoke quietly into his headset then put his gun back in his vest. Jack was still until Terrence stepped back into the house. Jack studied my face, his eyes empathetic.

My face was soaked. I struggled to catch my breath. I couldn't verbalize the things I had seen to Jack. Allen would be livid.

I had seen James in my dream. He was lying naked and still on a table in a stark white room. His midsection was covered in the tattered baby-blue wool blanket I'd knit for him when he was born. A bright, white light shone down on him. There was a man on a cell phone in the room with James. As he spoke into the phone, James's blanket began to turn red.

I could only see the man from behind. He had very short, dark hair under an officer's cap. He was wearing dress blues. His voice was no doubt the one I'd heard in my other dreams. There was no Russian language, but the voice was distinct. It had a clever, almost whimsical sound to it, while at the same time being autocratic, dictatorial. He had seemed tall in my previous dreams, but next to James, he was less than average height.

I couldn't hear his words, just his strange tone. He was laughing as James bled. The red soaked the blanket then began pouring off of the table and onto the floor. The sight of my James bleeding, dying, set off waves of fear that I've never experienced, such concentrated hurt at my core that I couldn't find the words. A fluttering sensation entered in my chest. I felt dizzy, nauseated. My face, neck, and T-shirt were wet through with tears. My backside was covered in sweat. I trembled as I mentally recalled my dream. I reached for Jack to steady myself.

"Baby, how can I help?" Jack asked sympathetically. He was trying to stay calm, intently focused on my bereaved face. My staggering breath attempted to tell him my son was in danger.

"James," I whispered, still crying. Jack's soft expression left his face, replaced by a furrowed brow and a tight jaw. I looked at his arm. I could see his pulse in his forearm. He was boiling inside.

"Tell me what to do, Pea. What do you need right now?" He was confused, frustrated. Angry but contained. Fearful for me. But, he can't protect me, not really. Petrov is going to hunt me down and take whatever he chooses as collateral in the meantime. Collateral as in my son. I may just be prolonging the inevitable. Petrov must be set on acquiring me, one way or another.

I no longer wanted to be outdoors in the dark. I looked at the back door. Jack nodded. He took me in his arms and carried me inside to the couch. He held me on his lap, my head on his shoulder. He stroked my muddled waves with the back of his hand, trying to calm me. "Baby, I'm sorry," he whispered in my ear. "Are your dreams ever just random? I mean, maybe you're afraid of something happening to James and your worry is fueling your dreams tonight."

I forced out a timid reply. "Jack, I've never dreamed about James before, not like tonight. My dreams of him are always pleasant. I'll think about him playing in the willow tree behind our old house. I've dreamed about giving birth to him, and his first haircut. But, never him dying."

I wanted to relax, but I couldn't. I was sorry to ruin our perfect night beneath the stars, but I needed Allen. Allen knows me, knows James. He knows that I would give myself to Petrov if that meant keeping James safe. I don't want to be a Mary. I would rather have my son alive, even if that means giving in to a twisted Russian terrorist. Jack couldn't understand that. He wouldn't allow it.

www.ingramcontent.com/pod-product-compliance
Lightning Source LLC
Chambersburg PA
CBHW051943240626
47153CB00005B/1605